SHADOW
HIGHLANDER

DONNA GRANT

St. Martin's Paperbacks

This is a work of fiction. All of the characters, organizations, and events portrayed in this novel are either products of the author's imagination or are used fictitiously.

SHADOW HIGHLANDER

Copyright © 2011 by Donna Grant.
Excerpt from *Darkest Highlander* copyright © 2011 by Donna Grant.

For information address St. Martin's Press, 175 Fifth Avenue, New York, NY 10010.

ISBN: 978-0-312-53348-9

Printed in the United States of America

St. Martin's Paperbacks edition / September 2011

St. Martin's Paperbacks are published by St. Martin's Press, 175 Fifth Avenue, New York, NY 10010.

10 9 8 7 6 5 4 3 2 1

To my readers.
This is for you!

ACKNOWLEDGMENTS

So much more goes into getting a book ready than just the writing. I'd like to thank my fabulous editor, Monique Patterson, for her brilliance and utter awesomeness. To the best assistant editor I know—Holly Blanck. Thanks for always answering my most mundane questions and never getting irritated. (At least not that I know of. lol.) My thanks to everyone at St. Martin's who helped get this book ready.

A special thank you to Tricia Schmitt for the gorgeous cover. And to my agent, Irene Goodman.

Also, a note to Melissa Bradley, who does the most marvelous job on the Danger: Women Writing reader loop. You give so much of your time for us, and I can't thank you enough.

Last, but not least, my family. To my husband for listening endlessly to plots, worries, and frustrations, and still having the perfect answer every time. To my kids, who get as excited as I do about my books, and who are always willing to tell everyone (even the drive-thru workers) that I'm an author. Love y'all!

ONE

Loch Awe, Southwestern Scotland
Summer 1603

If there was one thing Galen Shaw knew, it was magic. And there was only one reason for that magic.

Druids.

He grinned and glanced at his companion, Logan Hamilton, as Galen realized they were close to the Druids. Very close.

Right now, he and Logan appeared to be nothing more than travelers, when in fact they were Warriors, immortals with primeval gods locked inside them.

It all began centuries earlier when Rome invaded Britain. The Celts, unable to defeat the Romans, had turned to the Druids for help. In answer, the Druids called up ancient gods locked deep in the pits of Hell—gods so vicious, so depraved, the Devil himself imprisoned them.

Once loose, those gods chose the strongest warrior from each clan and became one with that warrior. Melded with the gods, the warriors, now immortal, had powers that made them unstoppable. Ruthless. Bloodthirsty.

The Romans knew they were defeated. But after Rome was gone, the Druids had been incapable of coaxing the gods from the men no matter how much magic they utilized. All the Druids could do was bind the gods, preventing them from ruling the warriors.

The gods, however, weren't deterred. Their infinite power allowed them to pass from generation to generation, always choosing the strongest, the bravest of warriors. Waiting for a time they could once more roam the earth as conquerors.

So it remained until an evil Druid, a *drough,* named Deirdre began to unbind the gods, turning men into Warriors. Now Galen and Logan, as well as other Warriors, were waging war against Deirdre and her bid to rule the world.

The Warriors of MacLeod Castle had been lucky so far. They had executed Deirdre, or at least they thought that they had killed her. Her black magic had been stronger than any of them realized, however. She lived, and because of that, Galen now searched for a cluster of Druids who might hold the key to uncovering an ancient relic that could be used against Deirdre.

"The magic grows stronger," Logan said as he jogged ahead of Galen to crest the top of a hill.

Galen scrubbed a hand down his face and sighed. They had been traveling for days, and thanks to their unnatural speed, they had covered twice as much distance as a mortal man. Yet it didn't deter the unease that pricked at Galen's soul.

He couldn't help but think something significant, something crucial was about to happen. Whether it was to him or Logan or to their effort to impede Deirdre, Galen didn't know.

And that's what bothered him the most.

Logan paused as he reached the top and whistled long and low, the sound filled with delight and wonder.

Galen lengthened his stride and hurried to Logan's

side. He halted beside Logan and stared at the rugged, untamed beauty before him.

"It's no wonder they call it Loch Awe," he murmured.

He had seen many places in Scotland, but Galen had never viewed the spectacular vista of Loch Awe until now. Its grandeur made him feel . . . inconsequential.

His gaze took in the mountainsides with their vivid green mixing with the brown of the earth. Bright green grass blended beautifully with the dark green treetops that covered the steep slopes leading down to the long, narrow sapphire waters of the loch.

Galen sighed, his eyes soaking up the dramatic splendor. The water was smooth as glass in places and rippled with the breeze in others. From their vantage point, they could see the loch in its entirety as it stretched out before them.

The woods along the slopes were thick, perfect hiding places for Druids trying to stay alive and out of Deirdre's clutches. Dotting the smooth water were various small islands, even one with a castle.

As much as Galen knew they needed to find the Druids, he couldn't seem to move. The majesty of the loch left him spellbound, captivated. Fascinated.

"It's breathtaking," Logan murmured. "Everything is so still, so serene. Completely opposite of the cliffs and crashing waves of MacLeod Castle."

Galen pulled his gaze away from the loch and turned his head to Logan. Logan was always smiling, always jesting, so it was unusual to see him so serious. Galen could only nod in response.

"Galen," Logan whispered, his voice deepening in caution.

At once Galen stiffened. "Aye, I feel it. Again."

It had been several days after they'd departed MacLeod

Castle that Galen and Logan experienced the tingling awareness that they were being watched. But it wasn't just any feeling. Magic was involved.

And they were feeling it yet again. It was different magic than that of the Druids they sought, but magic just the same.

"Deirdre, do you think?" A muscle in Logan's jaw jumped as he said the hated name.

Galen turned and looked behind them. He took in every detail, searching for anything or anyone that might involve magic. There was nothing but empty land, with only a peregrine falcon flying above them.

He watched the bird of prey for a moment with its distinctive slate and white-barred belly before he turned back to the loch. "I still cannot find the source, but if there is a chance it's Deirdre, we need to be careful."

"We're near the Druids. Their magic is everywhere. I would hate to be the ones responsible for leading Deirdre to more of them."

As part of their power, Warriors were able to feel the magic of Druids. The stronger the magic, the stronger the Druid.

The group Galen and Logan searched for had been hiding for decades, if not longer. Deirdre, though a Druid herself, took little care to worry about continuing the magic of the land. She much preferred to find and kill other Druids. After she took their magic, of course.

"If we go by what Isla told us, Deirdre is alive but without a form. She will be working on discovering a way to restore her body and her magic."

Logan absently scratched his jaw, his lips twisted with frustration. "Which means she'll be looking for a Druid. I understand. We cannot tarry. It's just that I hate being watched, especially by something I cannot discern or fight."

Galen understood all too well. It was in their core to want to fight, to yearn to see the blood of their enemy, thanks to the god inside them. Some Warriors controlled their bloodthirsty nature better than others.

As far as he knew, Galen was the only Warrior who wanted to suppress his god and forget he had any power. No Warrior would understand, but then again, none of them had their god's power give them as much pain as his did.

Never being able to touch someone without seeing their thoughts was a miserable fate. He didn't want to know what was in the mind of his friends.

Yet his power went beyond even that. He had controlled someone's mind before. And it had cost him part of his soul in doing it.

He pushed aside the frustration over his power and focused on his mission. Galen pulled out the map drawn by Ramsey, another Warrior, and compared it to the loch. Galen looked to the spot where Isla had told them they would find the Druids.

Logan glanced at the map. "Do you think we'll discover the Druids where Isla said?"

Galen shrugged. Isla was a Druid who had been used by Deirdre and forced to become a *drough* to save her family. Isla was now being sheltered at MacLeod Castle and had, in fact, told them about the artifact. Because she had become a *drough* against her will, the evil hadn't been able to take control of her, making Isla the most powerful *mie,* or pure Druid, they knew.

"I think the Druids will be close to where Isla told us. Actually finding them, however, will be the tricky part." Galen rolled up the map and used it to point to the far side of the water. "The place is over there. We'll have to walk around the loch."

A strand of Logan's golden brown hair fell into his

eyes. He brushed it out of his face and shrugged, his hazel eyes dancing with excitement and mischievousness. "Sure you doona want to go for a swim?"

Galen chuckled and shook his head as he tucked the map in the waist of his kilt. He had known Logan for years, and in those years, they had done much together.

"Come on, old man," Logan teased. "I doona think the current will be too swift for you. You're only two hundred and fifty. You can make it across."

Logan was the youngest of the Warriors at one hundred and fifteen. The only one younger than Logan was the lone female Warrior, Larena, who happened to be the wife of Fallon MacLeod, their leader.

"Keep it up, *lad,* and I'll make you regret your words," Galen said with a grin.

Logan had been a Godsend to the Warriors. It was easy to become despondent and dreary when you had lost everything and eternity stretched out before you, but Logan always knew how to lighten people's moods with a jest, a tease, or a grin. His smiles were infectious, and his banter notorious.

Galen was pleased Logan was with him on this trip. Logan pretended he was lighthearted and indifferent about his past, but Galen knew firsthand Logan was not a Warrior you wanted against you. Because deep down, Logan hid a streak of hostility and bitterness that burned within him.

Logan's mouth tilted in a lopsided smile as he glanced back at the loch. "I tell you, Galen, I could use a hot meal. Eating at the castle has spoiled me."

"You?" Galen shook his head sadly. He missed not just the delicious meals, but the companionship he had found at MacLeod Castle. "I was getting my own loaf of bread that I didn't have to share with any of you. I've had none for days. I'm eager to return."

"Then let's find those Druids."

Once again Galen felt the tickle on the back of his neck, as though they were being spied upon. "Time to get moving."

"Aye," Logan said, and fell into step beside him as they began their trek around the outer edge of the mountains rimming the loch. "We'd get there faster if we swam."

"Maybe."

"I could move the water for you so you wouldna have to get wet."

Galen looked at Logan and saw his cocky grin. Because of their gods, each of them had a unique power. Logan could command oceans. Any body of liquid, big or small, was his to control.

Enhanced strength, speed, and senses completed the package for all Warriors.

In some ways it was a heady experience to be a Warrior, but knowing the evil that resided inside them, knowing how easily they could kill while surviving forever, made life hell.

"Nay," Galen said. "We'd cause too much of a distraction if you moved the water. Besides, we run faster than horses. We'll be on the other side of the loch in no time."

Logan grunted and rubbed the back of his neck. "I want to know who is watching us."

"I suspect we'll find out soon enough. With the Druids nearby, it could be them."

"Nearly all the way from MacLeod Castle? I doubt it."

Galen's gaze traced the hilly landscape, selecting the best route to take. "Whoever it is, they cannot hide from us forever. We'll find who's been spying, and then we'll discover why."

"I want that privilege," Logan said between clenched teeth.

A tingle of worry began in Galen's mind. Logan didn't become heated unless Deirdre attacked them. To see the anger sizzle around him like a thick cloud was unusual. And disturbing.

There was no point in asking Logan about it, though. There was only one other person he could talk to about Logan and that was Hayden. Hayden and Logan had bonded as soon as they'd met, forging a friendship that went as deep as brotherhood.

Maybe Hayden knew something Galen didn't. After all, Galen had assumed Hayden would be the one accompanying him since he had a hatred for *droughs*. And with Isla being a *drough,* although against her will, it would keep Isla alive that much longer if Hayden wasn't around waiting to kill her.

Thinking about the black-headed Druid made Galen wonder what had happened since they had departed MacLeod Castle.

It seemed Logan's mind was also on Hayden because he asked, "What you saw in Isla's mind when you touched her, was it as bad as Hayden said?"

"Worse." So much worse than anyone could have imagined. It had shocked even Galen, and he had seen many things since his god had been unleashed. "I saw horrors while in Deirdre's dungeons, but what Deirdre did to Isla was unthinkable."

Logan fell silent for several moments. "You haven't asked why I came instead of Hayden."

"I expected Hayden to accompany me, but I am happy to have you with me on this journey."

Logan continued to face forward so that Galen could see only his profile. "Hayden would have run from Isla. I forced him to confront her."

"Why? You know how much he hates *droughs*. He's as likely to kill her as look at her."

"You saw him when he brought her broken body into the castle. You saw how protective he was."

"And then we discovered she was *drough*."

Logan leaped over a fallen tree and shrugged. "From the moment Isla asked him to kill her and he didn't, I knew that he had to stay at the castle. Isla needs him. And he needs her."

Galen couldn't fault Logan's thinking, and Logan knew Hayden better than anyone. "Then maybe you should have remained behind to remind him of those things."

There was a pregnant pause before Logan said, "I needed to get away."

Galen was so taken aback by Logan's words that for a moment he could only stare at his friend. Questions swam in Galen's mind, but one look at Logan's closed, hard expression and Galen knew he would get nothing more out of him for the moment.

As much as Galen wanted to know what motivated Logan, he knew better than to ask. If he did, Logan would feel free to pry into his own secrets. And Galen had many.

One of which could isolate him from other Warriors forever.

He had spent most of his life as a Warrior apart from others. There was much he had given up once he had realized the full extent of his powers to read other's minds.

Without even intending to do so, he had found a home—and a family—at MacLeod Castle. He didn't want *anything* to jeopardize that.

TWO

Tomorrow Reaghan planned to leave the only home she had ever known.

The small village went about its daily life, unaware, and uncaring, of the turmoil that ripped through one of their own. Reaghan didn't want to leave. She was a part of the land, the village, and its people.

Yet how could she ignore the insistence of her own feelings?

It was true the Druids who had left the village over the years were never seen from again, but there was an exciting world out there. She yearned to see the world for herself and to experience it—all of it—but she also feared leaving.

She didn't know what was out there. Though she did knew *who* was out there—Deirdre.

Not to mention that the only men left in their dwindling group just tottered about, barely able to stand on their own. Neither of them would be fit choices for a husband. Besides, they were already married.

Reaghan wanted . . . more of a life, more *in* her life than what she had. It wasn't that she was unhappy with the Druids. In fact, she was very content. But the part of her that wanted and needed more wouldn't be denied.

The ache, the need, to see and experience more had grown in the past six months to the point that she could no longer push it aside. It was as if her future were right in front of her and she had only to reach out and grab it.

Every time she had tried to talk to Mairi about it, however, the elder was quick to point out why the village needed Reaghan.

Mairi and the other elders meant well, but Reaghan had to make this decision on her own. It would likely tear her in two, but she had to leave. There was something out there for her to do; she just didn't know what it was yet.

Then there was the parchment Reaghan had come upon in Mairi's chest by accident. It had been so old the edges had crumbled when her fingers touched them. The words, though faded, had been in Gaelic—a language Reaghan had never read before, but somehow she had recognized the words. Had understood them.

That surprise faded to nothing when she read her name and discovered she wasn't from Loch Awe but instead came from a group of Druids of Foinaven Mountain.

There was no mention of her parents. Nothing about why she had been sent to Loch Awe or what had happened to make her parents send her away. Had her parents died? Did she have other family?

Just those few sentences, so very few words in the parchment, but they created more questions.

There had been so many questions running through her mind. Her head had swum with suspicion and supposition. Mairi had been like a mother to her. She wanted to give the elder a chance to explain things.

As usual, Mairi had given evasive answers to her initial questions, and Reaghan sensed if she mentioned the parchment Mairi would lie. And Reaghan couldn't handle that. For some reason Mairi and the other elders thought they had to lie to her about her past. But why? What was so awful?

Regardless of what it was, Reaghan wanted the truth.

But Mairi wouldn't give her the truth. Not even a glimmer of it. No matter how many times Reaghan asked about her parents, Mairi would give the same response she had given for years—that they had found her and saved her from a fever.

That's when she began to question everything the elders told her. They had been lying to her for years about where she came from. What else were they lying about?

Reaghan had put the parchment with her own things and begun to plan to find the Druids and the home where she belonged. It was as good a place as any to begin, and maybe it would halt the persistent feeling inside her that told her there was something for her to do.

On the morrow Reaghan would depart the safe haven she had known for ten years and strike out on her own into a world she didn't know.

Tomorrow, everything would change. For better or worse. She was fearful but eager. Nervous but exhilarated. It was the start of a new life, one she intended to seize with both hands and make the most of. Whatever the outcome.

She had dreams she wanted to fulfill, like anyone else. But she didn't want much. She wanted to be happy, to find a man with whom she could share her life and start a family. She wanted children to fill her days with laughter and memories.

Reaghan was brought out of her thoughts when someone bumped into her. She blinked and focused on the faces around her as they stood in the middle of their small village. Mairi shook her head in frustration as she began to speak of their need to hunt for food.

The pounding began at the base of Reaghan's neck and worked its way up to her temples, increasing with each beat of her heart. She didn't know why her head had begun to ache the past month as it had, and she feared there was no cure for it.

She put a hand to her forehead. The coolness against her skin gave some relief, but not nearly enough. Reaghan tried to hide her grimace of pain as she turned away, but Mairi's brown eyes were sharp, despite her age.

"You're hurting again, child. You need to rest."

The soft, comforting hands that had helped heal Reaghan from the fever so long ago took hold of her arms now and guided her to her cottage.

Not that the structure could be called a cottage. The Druids had moved around Loch Awe for years until the young ones began to go away, leaving only the older Druids and a few others who didn't want to abandon the beauty and safety of the loch. That's when, hundreds of years ago, the Druids had decided to make a permanent village hidden away from the world by magic and blending into the surroundings.

Reaghan leaned her hand against the trunk of the giant oak that stood in the middle of her home. She looked up to see the branches of the noble tree as supports for the roof, which was covered with leaves and vines to shield them from the elements. Large, cut limbs were bound together with vines and used for the walls. The skillful use of the trees blended with the magic created an illusion that one could mistake the cottages for nothing more than the forest.

All the Druids used what nature supplied them with to craft their homes. Many travelers walked past their village and never saw it.

"Sit," Mairi ordered, her voice brooking no argument.

Reaghan allowed the old woman to push her down into a chair. The throbbing of her head always began slowly, building with intensity. And each day when it came, it grew worse, lasted longer. Reaghan would be weak for hours afterward, her body not her own.

Something wasn't right. Reaghan knew it in the marrow of her bones. But no matter who she asked or what she asked, no one had any answers. Maybe the headaches were connected to the long-ago fever Mairi had saved her from and no one wanted to tell her.

"I'll be fine," Reaghan said, and took the cool, wet cloth Mairi handed her. She put it to her forehead and sighed. Just speaking made her head pound worse. The ache was so terrible she couldn't clamp her teeth together.

Years could have passed as Reaghan endured the pain, concentrating on keeping her stomach from souring. Just as suddenly as the ache had come on, it disappeared. For long moments Reaghan didn't move, afraid her head would begin to hammer again. Her body was weak, and all she wanted to do was lie down and sleep.

Finally, she dropped the cloth and raised her head. "It is gone."

"For now," Mairi murmured. Her eyes, filled with concern, dropped to the table as she tapped the wood with a fingernail. "How bad was this one?"

"I was able to handle the pain."

Mairi smiled sadly and cupped Reaghan's cheek. "My darling girl, that is not what I asked."

"It was worse than the one from yesterday."

Mairi lowered her hand and looked away, but not before Reaghan saw the resignation in her old brown eyes.

"You know what is happening to me, don't you?" Reaghan asked.

Mairi released a long breath. "Reaghan, sometimes it is best if you don't know the answers to all your questions."

It was too much. Reaghan stood and moved around Mairi, needing to be alone. Her body was weak, but she couldn't stay with the elder a moment longer. She needed some time alone. "I'm going to go for a walk."

"You do understand we need you, don't you, Reaghan? Our numbers decline more each year. I fear that one day I will be the only one left."

Reaghan's heart clenched in her chest as Mairi's words made her pause near the door. She understood the panic that ran through the village as their numbers declined. "What will be, will be," she said without turning around.

She didn't slow once she left her cottage and walked out of what the remaining twenty-three Druids called a village. Reaghan didn't stop, not even when the only child, Braden, called to her to pick berries with him.

Reaghan felt as if she were slowly going daft. There was much more going on than just the aches of her head. Her dreams had also been filled with images she couldn't explain but felt she had seen with her own eyes. People. Places. Events. All of which she knew she hadn't experienced, yet she knew she had. Somehow.

It was illogical. She had never left Loch Awe, so how could she have seen a magnificent castle on the cliffs or the mountain peak where she somehow knew evil was bred?

Reaghan paused beside a pine, her hand upon the rough bark, and took a deep breath. The sunlight filtered through the overhanging branches and leaves, making the vivid, interesting designs on the ground that Reaghan had always found so fascinating. But not today. The smell of pine, of decaying leaves, and a hint of some sweet flower did not calm her as it usually did.

The anxiety inside her only grew with each day, filling her so that she could barely close her eyes at night. There was a part of her that screamed for her to leave posthaste before . . . before what, she didn't know. She only sensed that something was going to happen.

She knew she was safe with the Druids. They might not answer her questions, but they had shown her only love and friendship since she had awoken from the fever.

There was safety in the village. Reaghan knew of Deirdre, knew how the *drough* hunted other Druids. Yet

Reaghan wanted to know where she had come from. There might be family still on Foinaven Mountain.

Reaghan shook her head and swallowed past the painful lump in her throat at the thought of leaving Loch Awe and the Druids.

Her thoughts ground to a halt when she heard the keening call of the falcon. It was as if the bird of prey called to her, *for* her.

There was magic with the bird, of that Reaghan was certain. She didn't know how or why, only that it was so.

Reaghan watched the magnificent bird fly over the loch before swooping into the trees. Falcons were majestic birds, and the peregrine was the fastest of them all. It moved with artistry and grace, precision and deadly intent.

The bird landed on a thick branch high in a tree not far from Reaghan, folding its wings against its sleek body. She could have sworn the bird's sharp eyes turned to her as its blackish-colored head cocked to the side.

Reaghan was disappointed. She would have preferred to watch the bird fly. She could have pretended she was the falcon, and the vast expanse of sky her only prison.

With a sigh she lowered her gaze and stilled. Two men stood below her at the shore of the loch. Her fingers dug into the bark of the pine tree as her heart raced frantically and her stomach dropped to her feet like a stone.

Their gazes moved slowly, as if they searched for something—or someone. She stood inside the magical confines of the village. As long as she stayed within the border, the men would never see her. Why that filled her with regret, she wasn't sure.

"We've been searching for four hours," one mumbled.

The blond nodded. "I well know. I'm no' about to give up, though."

A glance at their two different kilts told her they weren't from the same clan. Travelers maybe? What were such handsome men doing at Loch Awe unless they were on their way to MacIntosh Castle? And what could they be looking for?

Many times she had watched such travelers and yearned to speak to them. What could it hurt? She was leaving on the morrow, once she gathered the rest of her items. What better way to test what awaited her than speaking to strangers near the safety of the village?

And if they are from Deirdre?

She would step back into the magic barrier and watch as the men, confused, looked for her.

Her decision made, Reaghan took the step that put her outside the magic. The men, as one, turned their heads to her. They stared at her, silent and intent.

She didn't worry about the men seeing the village. Yet. For the moment, they seemed satisfied to observe her. The men looked affable enough, but Reaghan knew better than to trust on appearances alone. Everyone hid something.

"Hello," the one closest to her said, and she felt her breath catch in her chest.

His voice was rich and smooth, friendly. The sound of it made her blood quicken, causing her to want to hear more. He had thick, dark blond hair that was tied in a loose queue at the back of his neck.

Even from a distance of twenty or so paces, she could see the vibrant cobalt blue of his eyes. The way he watched her, studied her, made gooseflesh rise on her skin as awareness skidded around her, through her.

He stood with his arms to his sides, seemingly at ease despite the corded muscles she glimpsed in his arms and chest. There was a predatory elegance about him that told Reaghan he could—and would—defend what was his. To the death.

Unable to help herself, Reaghan let her gaze run over his chiseled face. His forehead was high, his brows thin and golden. His cheeks were hollowed, his chin hard, and his jaw squared. That jaw was shadowed with a beard, making him appear more interesting, more dangerous.

More enticing.

Reaghan tried to swallow, tried to think of anything but the very male, very appealing man before her. She knew she was being rude in not answering him as she looked her fill, but how could she not? He was everything a Highland warrior should be.

His lips tilted ever so slightly in a smile, as if he knew what went through her mind. Reaghan wanted to move closer to him, to touch his skin and run her hands through his hair.

She yearned to feel the strength of him, to have his muscles move beneath her hand. She longed to run her fingertip over his wide lips, to look deeper into his stunning blue eyes.

Her blood pounded in her ears like a drum the more she thought about touching him, of learning him.

It was as if for the first time in her life she was truly alive. Sounds she hadn't paid attention to before filled her ears, scents she hadn't noticed before swirled around her, and the colors of the forest and loch seemed more brilliant, more effervescent than usual.

All because of one man.

She inhaled a shaky breath and pulled her scattered longings back inside her. She would look at her reaction to the man later in the privacy of her own cottage when his cobalt gaze wasn't on her, reading her every emotion.

"Hello," she finally replied. She knew the elders wouldn't approve, but it had been so long since she had seen anyone other than those in her village, especially men of marriageable age.

"Do you live around here?" the other man asked.

Reaghan regretfully shifted her gaze from the first man

to the second. His wavy brown hair hung freely about his shoulders. His smile was wider, more teasing, but she saw darkness lurked in his hazel eyes, a darkness he tried valiantly to hide. He was the same height as the first, with the same build, though he was leaner.

She licked her lips, wariness stealing over her for the first time, crushing her newfound excitement. She didn't know these men, didn't know where they had come from or what they wanted. Was this fear what she would experience once she left the village? "Many live on Loch Awe."

"My name is Galen Shaw," the first man said. His words were unhurried, casual. "My friend is Logan Hamilton."

Just knowing their names eased some of Reaghan's trepidation. She was just a step away from safety and Druids who would come running, their magic—inadequate though it was—at the ready. It gave her the courage to ask, "And what brings you to our loch, Galen Shaw?"

He grinned, sending ripples of perception through her as the corners of his eyes crinkled. "We're looking for Druids."

"Druids?" Reaghan's heart fluttered like a butterfly caught in a net. So that's what they had meant when they said they had been searching for hours.

Gazing at Galen's handsome body made it difficult to breathe, to think, but the mention of Druids nearly choked her. No one spoke of Druids. "You realize there are no more Druids? Those who claimed the old ways were burned as pagans."

Logan moved until he was even with Galen and gave her a teasing wink. "Aye, my lady, but we know the truth. Druids are most certainly around, and it's verra important we speak to one."

She wondered what they would do if she told them she was a Druid. It was the truth, though she held no magic of her own. Such was the way when Druid blood was diluted with those that had no magic. It was what was slowly becoming of her people, one reason they fought so hard to keep her among them.

"I'm afraid you gentlemen are wrong. There haven't been Druids around here in centuries."

"We have proof," Galen said.

This was getting interesting. Maybe too interesting. Reaghan knew she ought to send the men away, but she was having too much fun. Besides, she liked the way her body and senses came alive with Galen. It was peculiar and terrifying, but breathtaking at the same time. "What proof?"

"Another Druid sent us."

Galen pulled out a rolled parchment from his kilt and spread it out for her to see. Reaghan recognized it as a drawing of the loch. She raised her gaze to his and found him watching her closely.

"That only proves someone has been to the loch and can draw."

"True enough. Except it was a Druid who told us we could find the village of Druids here," he said, and pointed to the spot on the map where her village sat.

Reaghan didn't know what to say. Her fellow Druids had long thought there were no more of them out in the world, that they were the last. The parchment Reaghan had found the other day proved there had been other Druids, but there was no evidence those Druids still existed.

She wanted to know. She had to know. If there were more Druids, she was going to find them.

"Reaghan."

Startled, she turned her head to find Odara, one of three elders, to her left. Odara stood like a bent soldier with her stooped shoulders pulled back and her graying red head held high. She was only able to look down at the men with her green eyes because of her vantage on the slope.

"These men claim to be searching for a Druid village," Reaghan told her.

Galen nodded and again pointed to the location on the map. "A Druid sent us. Isla promised we would find a Druid village here."

For long moments Odara silently measured the men, her green gaze moving first to Galen then to Logan.

It was Logan who finally spoke. "We can feel your magic. We know we've found the Druids."

Reaghan's blood drummed deafeningly in her ears as his words sank in. They could feel the magic of the Druids? Who were these men? And what did they want with Druids? She suddenly began to doubt her wisdom in talking to them. Had she just put everyone in terrible danger?

"Please," Galen said. "We would like to talk to the elders. It's extremely important."

Odara sighed and clasped her hands in front of her. "Do you expect me to take your word for it, young man? That you can feel magic?"

Logan coughed to cover his laughter as Galen sent him a warning glare. Reaghan couldn't take her eyes off them. It was fascinating to watch how they interacted with each other. The young men of her village had long ago departed, so this was all new to her.

"Young man?" she heard Logan say on a choked whisper.

She had no idea why Logan would find that amusing, but obviously he did.

"I doona lie," Galen told Odara. "We're here in an effort to fight Deirdre."

At the mention of the name, Odara sucked in a breath, and her hands began to shake. Her gaze darted around, as if at any moment, Deirdre would jump from behind a tree. "What do you know of her?"

"Too much," Logan muttered angrily.

Those two words, laced with such revulsion along with

a hint of anxiety, was enough to make Reaghan believe them. It wasn't just the words, though. She had always had the ability to tell when someone was lying to her if she could look them in the eye. Galen and Logan weren't lying. About any of it.

Reaghan was more intrigued than ever. She had heard stories of Deirdre before, the *drough* who wanted to rule the world. It was one of the reasons her village was hidden, why they were wary of strangers.

"Odara, I think we should listen to them," Reaghan whispered.

Odara, who knew of Reaghan's ability, let out a deep breath and nodded her head as she looked to Galen and Logan. "Stay with Reaghan. I will return."

Once Odara walked away, Reaghan opened her mouth to begin asking the men many and varied questions. She wanted to know as much as she could before the elders returned and seized the men's attention.

"It was your magic we felt."

Galen's words halted any questions Reaghan had thought to ask. The skill to sense lies or truth wasn't magic. Reaghan had tried magic. She had none. "You're mistaken. I have no magic."

The falcon gave a loud cry above them, its shrill call echoing around the forest and loch. Reaghan paid the bird little heed. She was too shaken by Galen's words. She wished it were her magic he had sensed, but she knew firsthand there was no magic to speak of inside her. She was a Druid with no power.

A pity, that. She would have liked to be a part of whatever Galen and Logan had come to her village for. To be a part of something meaningful, something that changed the world, appealed to her in ways she never expected.

It wouldn't matter anyway. As much as the men capti-vated her, once the remaining women spotted the new arrivals, Reaghan would be forgotten. And that was for the best, especially since she was about to leave on her own adventure.

It was all working out perfectly. Mairi and the other elders would be occupied with Galen and Logan, leaving Reaghan free to depart without any fuss. Reaghan didn't like the prospect of a long farewell.

"We're never mistaken," Logan said, his voice breaking into her thoughts.

Galen's brilliant blue eyes held hers. She was caught, trapped in his gaze, and she found she didn't mind at all. "Your magic is very strong. You just don't know it yet."

THREE

Galen couldn't take his eyes off Reaghan. The last thing he had expected to see while hunting the Druids was a woman so striking, so breathtaking he doubted his own sanity for a moment.

As soon as he had seen her, as soon as her remarkable deep gray eyes locked with his, the attraction had been instantaneous. Urgent. All-consuming.

In all his years, Galen had never felt something that seemed so . . . right.

It wasn't until she spoke in a soft, sensual voice that he knew she was real. That and the fact Logan seemed as taken aback as he.

The first thing Galen noticed was her eye-catching auburn hair, which fell around her shoulders and back in unruly curls. Then his gaze had clashed with her deep gray eyes, and he'd been lost.

The way her gaze moved over his body left him scorched, the flames of desire licking him. His balls tightened in expectation. He couldn't breathe, couldn't think. He could only look his fill at the most beautiful woman he had ever seen.

It wasn't just her exotic looks. It was the way she held herself with regal bearing and elegant poise. She should be sitting on a throne somewhere, not living among the trees, was his first thought. Yet the forest welcomed her, as if it had opened itself to be her home.

Even from a distance he could tell she was tall for a woman. Her simple gown of soft cream did nothing to hide her slim, shapely form from—her breasts to her small waist to the swell of her hips.

It was her face, however, that struck him breathless. Her eyes were large and expressive in a heart-shaped face. Brows slightly darker than her hair arched over her eyes, adding to their allure. She had high cheekbones and full, luscious lips ripe for kissing.

He imagined himself stroking her creamy skin, pulling her against him so he could feel her warmth, her softness.

Galen inwardly cursed himself and his god. He couldn't touch Reaghan, no matter how much he hungered to do just that. He knew what would happen when he did, and he couldn't put himself—or her—through that. He was at the village to further their cause, and he needed to remind himself of that. Despite the fact that Reaghan was the loveliest thing he had ever seen, or likely ever would.

However, he was surprised she denied her magic. He had known as soon as he saw her that the magic he'd felt since reaching the loch had been hers. And it was unbelievably potent. It pulsed around her, shielding her. So much so that Galen wondered whether hers or Isla's was more powerful.

"How can she think she does no' have any magic?" Logan whispered.

Galen shrugged, but he wanted to find out. He took a step toward Reaghan, and though she raised a brow in question, she didn't retreat. "Why do you say you have no magic?"

"Because I don't. I've tried countless times to do magic as the others have, but nothing happens. It is the way when Druids marry others. The magic is diluted until there is nothing."

Before Galen could answer her, the elder Druid returned

with two others. It had taken them hours to find the village, and if Reaghan hadn't appeared to them, Galen knew they'd still be looking. There must be shielding magic cloaking the village. It would explain how they could feel the magic, but not see the village or Druids.

Galen bowed his head in acknowledgment to the elders, and though he was anxious to return to MacLeod Castle, he would have liked to have a few moments alone with the beautiful Reaghan.

"As I have told Reaghan, I am Galen Shaw. This," he said, motioning to Logan, "is Logan Hamilton. We've come in search of Druids."

"So I'm told," said the middle Druid with dark hair liberally shot with gray.

Galen imagined she had been quite pretty when she was younger, but time and the stress of hiding from Deirdre had taken its toll.

She took a deep breath. "I am Mairi, one of the elders, as I'm sure you've surmised."

Logan stepped forward and smiled. "Thank you for seeing us."

Mairi motioned to her right. "This is Odara, and on my left is Nessa. What makes you think you have found Druids?"

Galen pulled out the map and unrolled it. "We have come from MacLeod Castle."

"MacLeod?" Nessa murmured, her face suddenly pale.

"Aye," Logan answered.

Galen lifted the map so all three, as well as Reaghan, could see. "We have Druids at the castle, and one used her magic to tell us we could find a group of you here."

Odara raised her chin and looked at them with green eyes full of distrust. "How do we know Deirdre didn't send you?"

"For one thing, we would have wyrran with us if she

had sent us," Logan said. "For another, Deirdre is no' one for diplomacy."

Galen nodded. "She is searching for Druids now, and could very well send wyrran here. Time is of the essence."

"We didna come to harm you," Logan said, meeting each elder's gaze. "We came for information, and to help you if you will allow us."

"What can two men do?" Mairi scoffed. "You do not even carry swords."

Galen exchanged a look with Logan. Isla had cautioned them not to let the Druids know they were Warriors. They were skeptical enough without adding that to the mix.

"We can hold our own," Galen answered. "None of you will come to harm while we are here. There is no need to pretend you are no' Druids. We know you are."

Nessa laughed, the sound humorless and dry. "You think we will allow you inside our village? You must be addled."

Galen glanced at Reaghan to see her brow furrowed, and her gaze on him. "We came in search of information about an artifact, a relic that has been passed down through the generations. This artifact could be used against Deirdre. Do you know of what I speak?"

Mairi folded her hands at her waist. "If we did, why would we tell you?"

Logan muttered a curse beneath his breath and raked a hand through his hair.

Galen wasn't about to give up so easily. "We are fighting a war with the most powerful *drough* of all time. Deirdre has very potent magic, but there has to be a way to be rid of her and her evil. Your kind is suffering and slowly being wiped into extinction. Help us fight Deirdre. Help us to win," he urged.

"We do not allow strangers into our village," Nessa said with a sniff.

Mairi exhaled slowly. "Your words are difficult to hear, and though I would like to believe you, I cannot."

"What do you need for proof?" Logan asked.

Nessa snorted. "Anything."

Galen fought for patience. He knew gaining access to the village would be difficult. "Is it no' proof enough that we have a Druid who told us where to find you?"

"I wish it was," Mairi murmured. "Reaghan? What do you sense?"

Reaghan turned her head to the elders. "They speak the truth, Mairi."

Mairi and the other two drew closer, their heads bowed together as they whispered. With Galen's advanced hearing he could hear them discussing whether to allow them in. They didn't trust him or Logan, so they would be careful. Yet, somehow, it was Reaghan's statement that helped them.

The women broke apart and Mairi stepped forward. "Though it goes against our determination to keep the village secret, we will allow you inside because we want Deirdre gone. Reaghan has seen into your eyes and observed the truth."

"You will be allowed inside," Odara said, her wrinkled face pinched with anger, "through tomorrow. After that, you must leave."

Galen nodded in agreement. One night wouldn't be enough time, but it was better than nothing. "Thank you."

As much as Galen wanted to celebrate the small victory, in truth, he hadn't won anything. The Druids still didn't trust him or Logan, nor had they admitted to knowing of the artifact.

"How much can we learn in so short a time?" Logan asked as they followed the three elders.

Reaghan suddenly appeared beside Galen. "Not much,

I'm afraid. You must earn their trust to learn anything or to stay longer."

"How?" Galen asked.

"That I cannot tell you."

Logan shook his head as his lips compressed into a tight line.

Galen shortened his strides so he put distance between the elders and himself. "What did Mairi mean when she said you looked into our eyes and saw the truth?"

"It's something I do," Reaghan said with a slight shrug. "If I look into a person's eyes when they are speaking, I can tell if they are lying or not."

"That's convenient," Logan said.

Galen agreed. "When was the last time your elders allowed anyone into the village?"

"Not once that I can remember, but that has just been ten years," Reaghan answered.

"Just ten years?" Logan repeated with a frown. "What happened ten years ago?"

Reaghan lifted a slim shoulder in a shrug. A small frown appeared on her brow and her body stiffened. "I contracted a fever that killed many Druids. Mairi stayed by my side the entire time until I was healed."

"And your family?" Galen asked. "Are they here?"

"I don't remember my family. In fact, I recall nothing of my life before I awoke from the fever. Mairi said it's better that I don't remember." Reaghan's lips were pinched as she cut off her words.

"Maybe she believes the past is better left buried," Galen said.

Her eyes met his for a moment before she turned her face away. "These people are my family. I will not see them harmed. You've been allowed inside. If you want more information, as I said, you will need to earn their trust."

Galen kept scanning the forest with his gaze. It wouldn't surprise him if the Druids had someone watching. "We appreciate your elders' allowing us inside your village. It is most fortunate we found you."

Reaghan stared at him, her silver gaze intense, as if she were searching his soul for the truth. For the briefest of moments Galen wanted to reach out and touch her, to pull her against him and hold her.

But he couldn't—and wouldn't. He had no desire to see her thoughts, and touching her would ensure that he did. While other Warriors fought to learn to use their powers when not in their Warrior form, Galen fought to keep his power from intruding on his life.

He'd failed so far.

The simplest, smallest touch would give Galen a glance into anyone's mind. And he didn't want that kind of knowledge. People's minds were meant to be private.

The longing, the heartache, the anger, the grief he saw could be so relentless, so intense it brought him to his knees. To not be able to touch someone, to hold someone, to feel the comfort of a hand or the passion of a kiss without his power intruding, had sent Galen away from everyone.

He went through life trying his damnedest not to touch anyone except when he had to. Even when he battled the wyrran he saw into their wicked minds, saw the evil they yearned to swathe the world in.

It left him disgusted and sick to his stomach, but he would endure it if it meant more wyrran were killed.

Galen paused when he saw the stone pillars so similar to the structures that dotted many of the isles around Scotland.

"Beautiful, isn't it?" Reaghan said. "I'm always taken aback when I look at them."

The pillars stood half the size of an oak with a thick

slab of stone laid atop them. They were covered in the ancient text of the Celts. Mixed with the language was intricate knotwork that wound around the stones in a lavish and spectacular display of craftsmanship.

"Incredible," Logan murmured.

Reaghan smiled and let out a contented sigh.

"Who crafted these?" Galen asked.

She shrugged. "As far as I know, they've been around for centuries."

"Can anyone in your village read the language?"

"Can you?"

Galen looked at Logan and chanced telling Reaghan half the truth despite his curiosity at her not answering him. If they wanted to find the artifact they were searching for, they would need someone from the village on their side. "Some of it."

"What does it say?"

Logan moved to the stone nearest him and pointed to the top. "It says Loch Awe and the surrounding area are protected by the magic of the Druids, and to do evil is to provoke that magic."

Reaghan's silver eyes were ablaze with excitement. "And the rest?"

"We'll need more time to decipher it," Galen said.

"Interesting." Reaghan's smile was bright, lighting up her face with a warm glow.

Galen felt as if someone had punched him in the stomach.

"Come," Reaghan said. "It's time you saw the village."

Galen watched her walk through the pillars and knew that somehow the stones were responsible for hiding the Druids.

"Are you all right?" Logan asked Galen.

"Aye. Why do you ask?"

Logan snorted and gave him a wry smile. "Because I

saw your face when Reaghan smiled. If you find her attractive there's no reason you cannot take your pleasure with her if she's willing."

"If only it were that easy, my friend. If only it were that easy."

FOUR

Galen took a deep, calming breath and followed Reaghan through the pillars. Once through, he was able to see the village. It wasn't hidden by the same shielding magic Isla used at MacLeod Castle, but it was similar.

Logan halted beside him as they surveyed the small settlement. Dotted along the slope of the mountain were cottages built around trees or between clusters of trees.

"This wasn't what I expected," Logan said under his breath.

"If their magic is waning, as Reaghan said, this is probably the best they could do, but it also means it willna keep the wyrran from finding them eventually."

"We doona have much time. Deirdre knows there are Druids here."

Galen clenched his jaw and nodded. "If she was coming to take the artifact, then it means she will most likely send wyrran here in the hopes of finding Druids."

"We need to convince the Druids to leave with us."

"You know that willna happen."

Logan turned hazel eyes to him. "Even if we get the artifact, I cannot leave Druids here to await their death by Deirdre's hand."

Galen agreed with Logan, but he could tell by the way the Druids lived that they were entrenched in the land.

Galen didn't even want to entertain the thought of forcing them to leave.

Reaghan turned and waved for them to follow. Galen tried to tamp down his growing desire and started toward Reaghan and the elders. He, like Logan, had anticipated something different. For one, he had envisioned more Druids.

He counted just over a score. And many of the twenty-three were old and frail. The only younger ones were women who didn't stand a chance against wyrran.

"We have guests," Mairi's voice rang out when Galen and Logan came to stand behind her. "They've come from MacLeod Castle and are looking for ways to destroy Deirdre."

At the mention of the MacLeods the people began to talk, no longer paying attention to Mairi. Galen couldn't fault them. He'd felt much the same way when he'd learned the MacLeods had been found and were taking a stand against Deirdre.

The MacLeods were the eldest of the Warriors, the initial ones to have their gods unbound. And they were the first to escape Deirdre.

"How did you find us?" someone shouted.

"A Druid told us where to locate you," Logan answered. "There are four Druids at MacLeod Castle."

At their obvious skepticism Galen said, "There are still groups of Druids in Scotland. They are hiding, just as you are, but they are out there."

"We feared Deirdre had captured everyone except us," Odara said.

Galen couldn't believe they thought their magic was strong enough to outlast Deirdre, but it was clear they did. What did they have that gave them that kind of protection? Even as Galen stood near the elders, he felt little magic coming from them.

With such insignificant magic, they had to have something they felt could keep them safe. Something like the artifact. And if they had it, there was no way they would willingly give it to him or Logan if it left them vulnerable.

The only choice Galen would then have would be to convince the Druids to return with him and Logan to the castle.

"I'm afraid we don't have an extra cottage for your use," Nessa said.

Logan smiled charmingly. "Doona fash yourself. Galen and I enjoy sleeping under the stars."

Nessa humphed and turned on her heel to walk away.

"She is wary of strangers," Odara said.

Galen looked at Nessa's retreating back, her white hair showing a few dark strands, and her plump figure. Her lips were constantly puckered, as if she had bitten into something sour and never got the taste out of her mouth. "It's understandable. In these times, you have to keep yourself safe."

"We may look weak and frail, but we can defend ourselves," Mairi stated.

Logan leaned a shoulder against a giant oak and winked at the women. "We've encountered the magic of Druids before. We know better than to anger you."

"If what you say is true and you have Druids at MacLeod Castle, what kind of magic do they have?" Odara asked.

Of the three, she was the most curious. Her bright red hair had faded, but he could still see the color through the silver that now colored her hair. Her green eyes regarded him steadily, as if waiting to see if he lied.

"We have a healer who is also able to communicate with trees. Another was raised in a nunnery and had no idea of her magic until she came to the castle. She's learning, and quickly. We also have a Druid who can use her magic to take people's emotions from them unto herself," Logan said.

Galen nodded. "Then there is Isla, who led us here. She and her sister were captured by Deirdre five hundred years ago. Deirdre forced her to the *drough* ceremony, but she did it unwillingly so the evil never took hold of her. Her magic is the strongest I've ever seen."

Mairi twisted her lips in revulsion. "And you trust this *drough*?"

"The MacLeods trust her, so aye. We trust her."

Galen could sense magic, luminous and intoxicating. Reaghan's magic. She was near, just behind him to the left. She hadn't gone far once she had taken them to the elders. She stayed close enough to hear their conversation, and he wondered if she had anything else to add to the elder's comments.

"These MacLeods," Odara said. "Are they men? Or are they . . . something else?"

"You mean are they Warriors?" Logan asked.

Galen sighed heavily and ground his teeth together. Logan gave him a small nod to let Galen know he thought they should tell the elders the truth. There was no reason not to, Galen supposed.

"The MacLeods—Fallon, Lucan, and Quinn—were the brothers Deirdre captured three hundred years ago. She unbound the god inside them and turned them into Warriors. They escaped and have been fighting her ever since," Galen answered.

Mairi fisted her hands before smoothing her palms down the front of her gown. "You cannot trust Warriors. They are pure evil."

Logan pushed off the tree and folded his arms across his chest. Gone was his easy smile. His hazel eyes were dangerously hard, his nostrils flaring. "Just like with people, some are evil and some are good. The MacLeods had their entire clan and family destroyed. Why would they align themselves with Deirdre?"

"The gods inside them are evil. Everyone knows what happened with the first Warriors," Odara said.

"The gods are no' in control of the MacLeods," Galen answered. "The spell Deirdre found only freed the gods partially."

Odara snorted. "Surely you've seen what they change into?"

"Aye," Galen said. "We have. Every time Deirdre has attacked the castle it's the MacLeods in Warrior form who have beaten her back and protected the Druids."

Mairi softly touched Odara's arm before she could say more. Mairi then turned her brown gaze to Galen and Logan. "We need to think over all that you've told us."

Galen watched them stride away. He scrubbed a hand down his face, unsure if they had done the right thing by admitting the MacLeods were Warriors. It didn't matter now. What was done was done.

"I knew it was going to be difficult, but not like this," Logan muttered testily.

Galen nodded in agreement. He surveyed the village but all the Druids looked away from him when he caught their eye.

Reaghan's magic seemed to envelop him, and he turned to her, careful not to touch her. His gaze discovered her hiding behind a tree. He could tell by the set of her mouth she wanted to ask questions, and he was willing to answer, especially if she could tell him something about the artifact.

She moved from behind the tree and started toward them when Mairi shouted her name. With one last look at him, Reaghan turned and disappeared behind a cottage.

"Shite," Galen grumbled as he leaned an arm against a pine trunk.

Logan, his feet braced apart and his arms at his side, said, "What now?"

"I doona know. I've no' wish to frighten them, but we cannot just sit around waiting for them to tell us anything."

"We doona wait. We start to ask questions."

Reaghan grudgingly went to Mairi. She had wanted to speak to Galen more, but she couldn't ignore a summons by Mairi. Reaghan would talk to Galen and learn more about the MacLeods, these Warriors they spoke of, and more importantly the Druids they said were there.

What the two men had told her had reinforced Reaghan's belief that she could find more Druids. She wasn't fool enough to think she wouldn't have to keep a watchful eye out for Deirdre and her wyrran, but she could do it.

She would do it.

Maybe she could go to MacLeod Castle. Whoever these MacLeods were, they put their lives on the line to protect Druids from Deirdre. Maybe she could help them in some small way. Someone certainly had to.

Reaghan entered Mairi's cottage and quietly shut the door behind her. It was one of the roomiest cottages in their village and had a gorgeous view of the loch. Mairi stood looking at that view now, her back to Reaghan.

"What do you think of the newcomers?"

Reaghan clasped her hands behind her back. "Why do you wish to know my opinion?"

"You found them. You spoke with them first."

Reaghan licked her lips and thought of Galen, of his striking features and blue, blue eyes. She thought of how her body had come alive, how an awareness of him had stolen over her. "I believe they were sent by a Druid. I saw the truth of it in their eyes. I also believe they are fighting to keep Deirdre from winning."

Mairi turned to face Reaghan, her wrinkled brow furrowed deeply and her hands fisted in her skirts. "There is much you do not know."

"You mean about the Warriors? I've heard the tales. If there can be good and evil Druids, why couldn't there be good and evil Warriors?"

"Because Druids are born with nothing but good in them. The gods inside the Warriors are the purest form of evil, Reaghan. They were so malicious, so destructive, that they were locked away in Hell by their own kind. What does that say?"

"That the gods are very powerful."

"And the Warriors cannot be trusted."

"I don't believe that," Reaghan argued. "Aye, we were born with pure magic, but inside every man and woman there is both good and evil. The choice a man or woman makes decides whether they will live a life of good or evil. A *drough* makes a choice to become evil. The Warriors didn't have a choice when the gods were put inside them. I don't see why some couldn't fight on the side of good."

Mairi let out a long, frustrated breath. "Mayhap you're right, but regardless, you cannot trust these men."

"They spoke of an artifact. You acted as though you knew exactly what they sought. Why have I never heard of it before?"

Reaghan didn't bother to tell the elder she had known of this "artifact" for some time, after reading the markings on the pillars just as she hadn't told Galen she could read the markings. Again, she wasn't sure how she understood what the markings said, only that she did. She was excited that someone else could read them as well.

Mairi turned her back to Reaghan once more to look at the serene loch. Her knuckles had turned white as they gripped her skirts. "There are many things only we elders know. And it must stay that way."

Reaghan knew she had been dismissed. If she didn't know better she would think Mairi had turned around so Reaghan couldn't look in her eyes and see if she was lying.

Reaghan left the cottage and paused. Mairi hadn't forbade her from interacting with their guests, but she knew that's what Mairi wanted. But it wasn't what she wanted.

She had only to follow the stares of the women to find Galen and Logan. To her surprise she found Braden hiding behind a tree as he watched their visitors. The men sat facing each other, both lounging against a tree. They spoke in hushed tones, but their gazes missed nothing.

"Would you like to meet them?" she asked Braden.

He spun around and looked at her with wide, brown eyes. "I was told to stay away from them. Are they bad?"

"I don't believe so, but you must listen to your mother, Braden. She is doing what she thinks is best for you."

"You've talked to the men, haven't you? I heard you were the one who found them."

She smiled down into his upturned face, so full of life and innocence. It was curiosity that made him ask that question, not ulterior motives as she would suspect of others. "Aye, I did. They are rather imposing, aren't they? But they are just men."

He glanced over his shoulder at them and frowned. "They doona have weapons."

"Because they knew we wouldn't allow them into our village with them. Weapons or not, they are Highlanders, Braden, and I've no doubt they have stood in many battles."

His face brightened then. "Oh, aye. I bet they have."

He ran off, leaving Reaghan smiling. Braden had a way of brightening her days. She was sure having men around would help the lad, and she regretted that his first real look at a Highlander, a warrior, kept him from interacting with them.

Someone needed to teach Braden to use a sword, and it wouldn't be any of the women. He would need someone like Galen.

As soon as the thought went through her mind she knew it could never be. Braden's mother was very protective. At the forefront of every Druid's mind was hiding from Deirdre and surviving one more day. The magic of their village kept them safe.

Reaghan tucked her hair behind her ear and wished she had taken the time to braid the unruly mess before she saw Galen again.

She wasn't the only one who found the men appealing. The younger women, the ones still of childbearing age, had gotten up the courage to approach Galen and Logan.

Reaghan hesitated. Logan was smiling, and whatever he said had the others laughing as well. The five women were hanging on his every word and practically rubbing against him.

Her gaze shifted and clashed with a cobalt-blue one. Her stomach fluttered as if birds were trapped inside. She was nervous and restless to be near Galen. A heady combination for a woman who knew nothing of men.

Galen's lips tilted in a grin. He motioned her over with a wave of his hand. His gaze was warm, welcoming and beckoning her closer.

Reaghan was about to go to him until she remembered the other women. She didn't want them to overhear her questions. Maybe it was better as Mairi said to leave Galen alone. She dropped her gaze and hurried to her cottage before she changed her mind and went to the tempting Highlander.

Galen frowned as Reaghan disappeared from view once again. She had been about to come to him, he was sure of it. What could have kept her away?

She had seemed concerned about the other women, but surely that wouldn't have kept her from asking the questions he knew burned inside her.

Reaghan was like a caged bird. She longed for freedom, could see it, taste it, but was afraid of it just the same. These Druids were the only thing she knew, and with most of her memories gone, she was afraid to trust anyone but them.

He could understand her reluctance, but eventually, he knew she would break free of her restraints, she would shake away the fear that kept her rooted in the village. And she would sprout her wings and fly.

Strange that he wanted to be there when she did it. He imagined she would be magnificent when she became the woman who answered to no one and bravely went out into a world filled with cruelty and evil.

But she would shine, and she would live.

FIVE

Galen stood at the pillars looking over the designs and markings left by the ancient Celts, the morning sun giving off just enough light to bathe everything in a golden glow.

"You could no' sleep either, I take it," Logan said as he came to stand beside him.

Galen shook his head. "These Druids trust their magic, but I doona trust Deirdre. She's going to come here, and it could be any day. I kept watch most of the night."

"Did you see anything?"

"Nothing. It's quiet."

Logan grunted and folded his arms across his chest. He jerked his chin to the stone columns. "Did you learn anything else from the markings?"

"I did." Galen glanced around them to make sure there weren't any Druids near enough to hear them. "The stones, along with the area used by the Druids, are protected by Druid magic, a magic used to hide something of significance."

"The artifact."

Galen nodded. "That is my reckoning. Where it's at is another matter."

Logan moved nearer to one of the pillars and ran his hand over more markings. "It says here the object must stay in the confines of the stones lest it be found by Deirdre."

"Does it say how Deirdre would discover it?"

"Nay. Wait." Logan moved around the pillar and squatted. "It says the object is sacred and must be kept safe from everyone but the Druids."

Galen blew out a perturbed breath. "How do we convince these Druids we are the only ones who can keep the artifact secure?"

"I doona know that we can." Logan straightened and continued his perusal of the stones. "Reaghan didna know how to read the Celtic markings."

"I'm no' so sure. She never answered me, and there was something in her eyes. I think she can read it. We also have to consider that at least the elders can."

Logan rubbed the back of his neck and yawned. "Why can Reaghan read it and others cannot?"

"I have no answer."

"There are four men in this village. Three are halfway in the grave, and the other is barely old enough to pick up a sword. They are prime candidates for an attack by wyrran."

"You are no' telling me anything I have no' already considered. I doona know how long they will welcome us, but I doubt it will be for very much longer. While we're here, we need to gain as much of their trust as we can."

Logan's smile was wide as he faced the village. "I have an idea."

"What might that be?" He knew that smile of Logan's. It was full of mischief and meant Logan had a plan that required the use of his well-known charm.

"You doona trust me?"

It was said with such false innocence that Galen rolled his eyes. "I think it would be better if I knew this idea beforehand."

"The women are starved for male attention. I plan to

spend a wee bit of time with them. Mayhap make them laugh and put them at ease so they will give me the information we need."

"More like starved for children. Need I remind you it is possible for us to get a woman with child? Look at Quinn and Marcail."

"Aye, I know," Logan said. "I've no desire to have one of the women attached to me. I might flirt, but I'm staying out of their beds."

At that moment Galen caught sight of auburn curls and creamy skin, eyes of silver mist and curves that made his mouth water.

"I see someone has caught your attention," Logan said. "Not that I blame you. She's verra pretty."

"Don't you find it more than odd that she doesna realize her magic is strong?"

"Maybe it was no' hers we felt." Logan shrugged. "Maybe it was the magic of the ancient Druids."

Galen shook his head. "Nay. It was hers. I feel the magic of the ancients. It is sturdy, but old. Reaghan's feels different. Stronger. Steadier. Brighter."

"Hmm," Logan said. "Tell me, how long has it been since you've allowed yourself a woman?"

Galen pulled his gaze away from Reaghan and looked at Logan. "How is that any of your business?"

"In all the years I have known you, in all the times we have met up, I've never seen you with a woman."

"It's no' for lack of wanting. I have my reasons."

"I gather those reasons have to do with your power."

Galen knew Logan wouldn't leave the subject alone until he was satisfied with the answers, though Galen was loath to give those answers. "I have to touch someone to see into their minds."

"Aye. I ken."

"What you doona know is that unlike most of the Warriors who must allow their god loose to be able to use their power, mine is constant."

Logan's hazel eyes narrowed in a frown. "So that is why you doona willingly touch anyone."

"That is why."

"I'm sorry, Galen. I had no idea."

Galen shrugged away his words. He didn't want anyone pitying him. He had come to terms with his life as best he could. He was destined to face it alone, even though it grew more and more difficult with every Warrior who found a woman to love.

He knew he was destined to watch others find love and happiness, to hold their lover's hand, to be able to comfort them without releasing their power. That's when it ate at him the most.

How he envied them. He didn't begrudge their contentment, but he longed to have a woman of his own.

"Maybe there is a way around it," Logan offered.

"I've tried, Logan. For two hundred and fifty years I've sought anything and everything to stop it. Do you think I like reaching for a lover, even just to kiss her, and seeing into her mind? Do you think I like the grief, the misery, the resentment, or the disdain I see? Do you think I enjoy knowing their deepest fears or their greatest regrets?"

Logan's answer was a whispered, "Nay."

Galen turned away from his friend. He shouldn't have let his emotions get away from him. It wasn't Logan's fault. He had just been trying to help, but help wasn't something Galen would ever receive.

"Galen—"

He held up a hand to stop Logan. "I'm the one who should apologize. Sometimes it gets to be too much."

Like when he saw a woman who stirred his blood and made him want to take her into his arms and kiss her. To touch her body and learn her curves. To reach for an auburn curl and wrap it around his finger.

He walked away before Logan could say more. He needed time alone, time to study the village more. And get his discontent under control.

Reaghan knew something was wrong by the way Galen held his body, rigid and angry. The regret on Logan's face was enough to reveal something personal had transpired.

Her curiosity always got the better of her, and she couldn't help but wonder what had gotten Galen so upset. He seemed the type who was always composed, always in control. The type of man who wouldn't let his anger get the better of him.

She had spent the majority of the night dreaming of Galen. His cobalt eyes, his long, dark blond hair, and his beautifully muscled body.

It had never occurred to Reaghan that a man could look so good, be so tempting. She had seen her share of men—and women—who traveled by the village on the way to MacIntosh Castle. But none of them could compare to Galen's rugged perfection.

She decided to follow Galen instead of doing her morning chores. Reaghan had no sooner taken a step than Mairi blocked her path.

"Off somewhere?"

Reaghan wasn't fooled. The elder knew exactly what she was about, but if Mairi wouldn't come out and ask then she wouldn't give the elder the answer she sought. "I thought I would go for a walk."

"I've seen you watching him."

"Him who?"

Mairi's brown eyes narrowed, disappointment in every line of her face. "Don't play coy with me, Reaghan. You know I speak of Galen."

Reaghan raised her brows in question. "What about him? He's a man, something we haven't had in our village in quite some time. I would think you would want every woman of childbearing age to try and catch his eye."

"It is true I would like to see more children in our village, but not at your expense."

Reaghan was taken aback by the elder's words. "Me? What do I have to do with anything?"

Mairi sighed loudly and took a step closer, shrinking the space between them. "I'm not your mother, but I only want the best for you, as any mother would for her child. That is all."

"Of course," Reaghan said and turned toward her cottage. The truth was there in Mairi's eyes, but it wasn't the entire truth. "I have herbs to tend to."

Reaghan shut the door behind her once she was inside her home and leaned back against it. The ache in her chest was so profound, so fierce, she couldn't catch her breath. What was Mairi keeping from her?

They had always been so close, sharing everything. Or at least Reaghan had assumed they shared everything. How could she have been so wrong?

With a small cry she buried her face in her hands and let the tears come. For long moments her body was racked by sobs, her soul withering more with each tear.

Eventually Reaghan wiped away her tears with the back of her arm and sniffed. She tried to recall anything, any small piece of information or fragment of a memory from the time before she awoke from the fever, but it was as if a wall had been erected in her mind, a wall she couldn't penetrate, knock down, or climb over.

She should have left as she had intended that morning. She should have kept to her original plan. Instead, she had stayed because of deep blue eyes and a sensual smile that made her stomach flip each time she thought about it.

Reaghan took a deep, quivering breath. It would do her no good to let Mairi know she was upset. Mairi would only ask questions, and Reaghan didn't want to lie to her, but neither could she tell her the truth. So as soon as she could, Reaghan was leaving.

She had to. Her dreams the night before had been filled with Galen, but also of castles, people, and places that fascinated her. In her dreams she knew these people, intimately knew the castle surrounded by a moat.

Once she awoke, the details of the people and places faded, but they remained in her mind. It only spurred her to find where all this was leading her. She knew in the depths of her soul that the places she dreamed about were real.

Mairi and the other elders knew more about her past, but they wouldn't tell her. Reaghan knew they thought they were doing that for her own good, and maybe they were. But she needed answers. Answers to the weird images she saw in her dreams, the faces she recognized, and places she saw.

She needed answers to why she was in Loch Awe instead of Foinaven Mountain.

Reaghan sniffed again and started for the table when the pain slammed into her. She doubled over, her head hammering. Nausea rolled viciously in her stomach. She shut her eyes when the room began to spin.

Her knees trembled, and she knew if she didn't lie down soon, she would fall. Reaghan reached out her arm and tried to feel for the table. Her body tipped forward, but it was empty air, not the edge of the table, her fingers grasped.

Reaghan let out a strangled cry as she landed hard on the floor. Her head, already throbbing, felt as if it were cracking open from the intense and constant pain.

She curled onto her side and knew she had to stay still to quiet her stomach and ease her headache. The pain was blinding. The slightest sound was amplified until her ears rang and it echoed inside her head a hundred times over.

The sunlight that fell through the open shutters and onto her face made her feel as if her eyes were being burned. She used her arm to cover her eyes, but the damage had already been done.

This headache was the worst yet, and she feared they would steadily increase until it killed her.

SIX

Galen would have preferred to keep to himself the rest of the day, but the need for them to earn the Druids' trust so they could find the artifact and get the Druids to safety had him smiling and talking to all who would venture near him.

He also expected at any moment that one of the elders would make them leave. He wasn't sure why they hadn't, but he wasn't going to question it.

He also wanted to read more of the markings on the stones at the entrance, but he didn't want anyone seeing him doing it. But everyone continued to be most curious about him and Logan, so much so that he couldn't take a step without someone watching him.

To his disappointment he never caught another glimpse of Reaghan. He couldn't help but wonder what she was doing and where she had gone off to. The village wasn't large, but the thick forest made it simple for a person to hide and remain unseen.

Galen hadn't learned much through his questioning of the Druids. None knew how to read the markings on the columns, and though they were curious, they were guarded, even silent at times.

They feared for their very lives, which he understood. He wished he could tell them what he was, but if they didn't trust him now, they surely wouldn't after that.

He had caught sight of Logan throughout the day. Each

time Logan was with a different woman, making her smile, making her laugh. Logan had the women lowering their guard in a way Galen never could. It was Logan's specialty, and he was a master.

Galen looked at the sky through the thick foliage of the forest, surprised to find the setting sun had turned the sky purple and orange and the deepest red. Despite having to keep his true self from the Druids, he found he enjoyed being around them.

Their magic was soothing and helped to ease the troubles which hounded him relentlessly. Although Galen considered that it could have been the pure majesty of the loch and the forest that eased him.

He couldn't say which he enjoyed more. He could stare at the loch all day and watch the way the wind played upon the water. The peregrine they had seen the day before must have a nest nearby because it flew over the village several times.

Galen paused to lean against a pine on the edge of the village, the loch visible between two trees. He could just make out the sun glittering on the water, and he found he wanted to see more of it.

He made his way to the water down the steep slope. He halted several paces from the water's edge and stared, but his gaze wasn't on the magnificent sunset. It was on Reaghan.

Her beautiful auburn locks were unbound and glowed fiery red in the sunset. The bottom of her gown was soaked as she played in the water with the boy, Braden. Her laughter was pure and musical.

He couldn't help but smile when she chased after Braden and caught him up in her arms, making him squeal and laugh. She gave Braden a kiss on the cheek and set him down to play again. Before she ran after him a second time, she paused and turned her head to look at Galen.

A slow, sweet smile pulled at her lips, making his blood

heat and his body yearn to touch what he could not dare have.

"She's beautiful, isn't she?"

Galen turned to his left to find Mairi navigating the slope to stand beside him. "Aye, she is."

"She is destined for great things."

He would rather continue to watch Reaghan and Braden, but Mairi made sure she had his full attention. Galen clenched his jaw before he asked, "Why do you tell me this?"

"Because it's important. You will leave soon. Do not give Reaghan false hope."

"I would never do that."

"You don't think I see the smiles she sends you or the way you watch her? It's evident you want her."

Galen faced the elder and looked into her eyes. "Just because I want something does no' mean I'll take it."

"We know nothing of you or Logan."

"You allowed us inside your village."

Mairi smiled slightly. "You have no weapons, and though we are women, it would take some doing for two men to gather all of us."

Galen blew out a sharp breath. If only Mairi knew the truth . . . "What is the real reason you doona want me near Reaghan?"

"I've told you the truth, Galen. She is destined for great things."

And Galen knew he was far from great. He would only harm her, and somehow Mairi saw that. He couldn't blame the elder for wanting to keep Reaghan safe. Galen would do the same in Mairi's situation.

"Please. I'm begging you. Keep your distance from Reaghan."

"I will no' ignore her."

Mairi bowed her head. "Thank you."

His enjoyment gone, Galen turned and walked away. He needed to find Logan anyway and see if he had learned anything new.

It was no surprise when he found Logan with another woman. This one had flaxen hair and voluptuous breasts she kept jutting toward Logan's face.

Logan spotted Galen and nodded in greeting. He said something to the woman, gave her a quick kiss, and made his way to Galen.

"I didna mean to interrupt."

Logan winked and smiled knowingly. "No harm done."

Galen could only shake his head. "I'm glad one of us is making headway."

"Come," Logan said. "Let us walk."

They strode side by side deeper into the forest, away from the village. Once they knew no one was near, Logan turned to him. "Did you discover anything?"

"It seems the Druids were curious enough about me to want a closer look. They spoke, and a few answered some questions. No one I talked to knew how to read the pillars," Galen answered.

"I learned the same. I was able to get a bit more out of a couple of women. These women could do with more Warriors around. They are in desperate need."

Galen bit back a laugh. "Just tell me what information you gleaned."

"They are hiding something here. I gather it's the artifact, but they doona call it by a name. They rarely speak of it, but occasionally they would mention something about the Druids protecting the object."

"Just what the column stated."

Logan nodded. "My thoughts exactly. I pressed for more, but the woman quickly stopped talking when she realized she had let that wee bit of information slip."

"What else?"

"Druids have been leaving the village for some years. What you see is all that's left. The young men were either killed by wyrran that came sniffing around, were taken by the wyrran, or left on their own accord."

Galen leaned a shoulder against a tree. "With everyone thinking they are so safe, it will be easy for Deirdre to invade."

"Aye. I've had the same thoughts. The magic here is old, but the Druids themselves have little magic. They will be no match for the wyrran."

Galen growled at the mention of wyrran. "Unless Deirdre comes herself. She could have found another Druid and already used magic to return her form. In which case she'll be coming here herself."

"Shite."

"I'd hate to return empty-handed to the castle, but unless we make some headway soon, I imagine we'll be asked to leave."

Logan quirked an eyebrow. "I'm surprised they have no' already asked."

"I expect it will come with the dawn. Mairi warned me away from Reaghan."

Logan grunted and rolled his eyes. "I've noticed Mairi doesna allow Reaghan out of sight for long. I'm no' sure what Reaghan has done to have that kind of attention, but it would make me daft."

"Interesting. I didna realize Mairi watched her so. There is a deep bond between them that's evident." Galen scratched his jaw and frowned. "But when we came upon Reaghan yesterday she was alone."

"True enough. It didna take the elders long to locate her, though."

Galen shifted and put his entire back against the tree. "Do you think the artifact could be on Reaghan? Maybe a pendant or something?"

"I doona think so. For some reason it appears as though they treat Reaghan as if she's the most precious thing in the world."

"I wonder if it has anything to do with the fever they helped heal her from."

"Could be," Logan said. "If we doona know what the artifact is, we cannot just take it."

Galen grimaced. "I doona think we should steal it even if we know what it is."

"It's Deirdre we're talking about, Galen. If this could end it all, wouldn't you take that chance?"

"Aye," Galen said with a sigh. He knew Logan was right, though he hoped it didn't come to them pilfering anything. "I hate to do that to these Druids, but they are no' leaving us much choice."

"Once we have the artifact, then you can have Reaghan. I have a feeling she'll come with us if you ask her."

As tempting as that was, Galen couldn't chance it. "You know I cannot."

"Then I will. She needs to get out of here and meet other Druids. To have a life. Even you should be able to see she needs that."

"She seems happy. I've no' seen them mistreat her. In fact, their attention proves how much they care for her."

But the thought of journeying back to MacLeod Castle with her for several days left Galen burning bright with need, a hunger he feared would only grow the more he was around her.

Logan rubbed his hands together and grinned wickedly. "If I find it, I'm going to take the artifact."

"Without asking first?"

Logan flattened his lips. "You read the pillars, Galen. It said it cannot leave. The Druids willna part with it."

"Do these Druids know that? They cannot read the text."

"The story could have been passed down to them. Do no' underestimate the Druids."

"Exactly. Take your own advice," Galen countered. "You doona know what these Druids might try to do."

Logan scoffed at Galen's words. "The only one with any amount of magic is Reaghan, and I doona believe she'd do anything to you. I hear you, Galen, I do. But I'm thinking of Deirdre and the threat she poses. I'll chance these Druids' ire in order to do whatever it takes to end Deirdre."

Galen nodded slowly. "Aye, my friend. I feel the same. I was just as angry as you when we learned Deirdre wasn't dead, as we'd thought."

"Angry doesn't being to describe how I feel."

Galen paused, unused to the vehemence in Logan's voice. The Logan before him now was one Galen saw only in battle, and it just proved how deep Logan's hatred for Deirdre went.

"We will find the artifact," Galen promised his friend. "Everyone is counting on us, and I doona want to return without it. I willna return without it."

"Agreed. The ones we need to focus on next are the elders. They'll know where the artifact is."

"That willna be easy," Galen said. "Let me see what I can do with them first. You keep questioning the women who continue to fall into your lap. You may discover more than we could hope for."

Logan nodded and ran his fingers through his hair. "Someone besides the elders has to know something. We just need to determine who that is."

"I say we doona waste any more time. I'll see if I can find Odara. She seemed the most agreeable of the three elders."

"Good luck," Logan said with his customary smile in place. "We'll need it."

Galen grinned after Logan, but stayed long after his

friend had returned to the village. Something didn't seem quite right. What disturbed him more was the warning that the artifact couldn't be removed from the village lest Deirdre discover it. With Deirdre occupied with gaining a form once more, it was the perfect time to get the artifact out of the village and to MacLeod Castle.

Galen decided it was time to see what he could learn from Odara. He had learned which cottage was hers earlier in the day. To his delight, when he knocked, she opened the door.

"Galen? Is there something you need?"

He decided to use some of the charm Logan found so successful and smiled. "Aye. I wondered if I could have a moment of your time."

She hesitated before inviting him inside. "Of course. Please come in. Have you eaten supper?"

"Not as of yet."

"Then please dine with me. I do hate to eat alone."

Galen inclined his head and took the seat she showed him. "I gather the village once had a significant number?"

"Oh, aye," she said, and bobbed her graying head as she spooned soup into a bowl. "I do recall hearing that our group of Druids had been one of the largest in Scotland. It breaks my heart to see so few of us left now."

"I can imagine." He smiled when she set the bowl in front of him. Galen stirred the delicious-smelling soup as he waited for her to join him. "Have you thought about leaving and joining another group of Druids to help your numbers grow?"

She smiled forlornly as she slowly lowered herself into her chair and patted his hand. "If only it were that easy. We have been in this area since long before the Romans came to Britain."

"Sometimes change is for the best. You have no men to

protect you or to marry the women to give this clan the children it needs to continue. You are dying."

"I know." She sighed and put a spoonful of soup in her mouth. "Believe me, it is something on the minds of every person in this village save for little Braden."

Galen took several bites of the soup before he said, "Have you thought of inviting men no' of the Druid heritage into the village?"

"Our magic is already diminished to the point that if we mix again, there may be no magic to the offspring."

"Then I think I can understand why so many have left."

"Aye," Odara replied softly. "If I were younger, I might contemplate it myself. I longed for children, and the daughter I was finally blessed with was taken by the wyrran many moons ago."

Galen set down his spoon. This time he was the one to cover her hand with his own. "I'm verra sorry."

"Deirdre has made it so that it is the way of life. You either die at her hands, or die alone."

"I wasn't lying when I said the MacLeods would welcome all of you. We could protect you much better than even your magic here."

She cocked her head and studied him a long moment. "There is something you aren't telling me. Something about yourself you think you need to keep secret?"

"I am here to help you as well as to seek the artifact that could help end Deirdre."

"Galen, what is it you are hiding from us?"

"Nothing you need to fear. Of that I give you my word."

SEVEN

Galen knew Odara wasn't entirely convinced, but she didn't push the issue. They ate in silence for several moments before Galen decided he would just come out and ask her what he needed to know.

"The columns we passed through on entering your village. They are verra old."

"Ancient," she said with a pleased grin. "When I was younger I used to sit and just stare at them. I've always longed to know how they came here and who erected them."

"Can you read the writing?"

Odara shook her head. "Nay. No one can. Somewhere in our history the elders stopped teaching how to read the markings."

It was just what he had hoped to hear. "You know what we seek?"

"An artifact," she said without looking up from her bowl.

"Can you tell me more about it? Is it here?" Galen decided to see if she would lie to him. They might not understand the Celtic writing on the stones, but he was sure they knew not to take the object outside of the magic.

Odara sighed and set down her spoon. Her brow furrowed as she leaned back and raised her gaze to him. "I wish I could tell you what you want to know, but you know I cannot."

"Even if it could end Deirdre's reign?"

"As tempting as that is, I cannot make that decision alone. The elders, as one, must agree, and that won't happen. I'm sorry."

He held in the ire that rose inside him. He and the other Warriors were doing everything they could to win against Deirdre. Why couldn't the Druids recognize that and join forces with them?

"We were told by our Druids that there were several groups with similar artifacts. These artifacts were created in an effort to one day fight Deirdre."

Odara folded her hands on top of the table. "We've been isolated here for many generations, Galen. I cannot tell you what other Druids may hold."

"Just as I thought." He wasn't gaining any information.

"However," she continued, "I do remember when I was just a lass overhearing one of the elders speak of an object. He didn't say so, but it was obvious he meant another band of Druids."

Galen tried to hide his excitement at this new revelation. "Did he say where these Druids were or what the artifact was?"

"I'm afraid not," she said with a sad smile. "I'm sorry I cannot be more help."

Galen leaned back in his chair and rubbed his jaw. "I'm afraid verra soon Deirdre will find this village, Odara. We hurt her. Badly. At one point we thought we had killed her, but it seems her black magic is more powerful than we anticipated."

"You attacked her?" Odara asked with surprise and a wee bit of fear. "You are but a man, Galen."

He smiled then, wishing he could tell her the truth. "We were with the MacLeods. Deirdre had captured the youngest brother, and we went to Cairn Toul to free him. In the process, we cornered Deirdre and proceeded to kill her. We then released the Druids and others being held in the mountain."

"So the Druids have returned to their homes? Could the ones taken from us be on their way back?"

He glanced down, hating to tell her the truth. "I'm afraid no'. They didna make it off the mountain. We found only one alive, Isla. She is the Druid who told us Deirdre wasna dead, that Deirdre had put spells in place to ensure she would never die."

"Then how do we defeat Deirdre?" Odara cried. She shook her head and rose from the table to pace her small home.

Galen turned to watch her, one arm resting on the back of the chair. "I believe she can be killed. She knows of the artifact here. She was planning on coming to take it when we attacked her. She's floating around now without a body, and her magic has been depleted. But it will be restored, as will her body. When that happens, she'll come for this village and the artifact."

Odara paused and took a deep breath. "She'll never find it."

"Doona be so sure. I've seen her skill with torture, experienced it myself. Few can withstand it."

"What do you suggest we do?"

He stood and faced her. "Allow me and Logan to escort the village and the artifact to MacLeod Castle. There you can be protected. Deirdre has attacked the castle several times, and has lost each time. She willna be eager to do it again."

"Many fear the Warriors."

"More so than Deirdre?

Odara bit her lip. "Aye."

"I doona understand."

"Evil is evil, Galen. The men who hold the god inside them may not be evil, but the gods themselves are."

Galen took a deep breath. "Have you seen any Warriors? Have any harmed you or this village?"

"Nay."

"There are Druids at MacLeod Castle. They wouldna put their lives in the hands of those who couldn't protect them," Galen said.

After a moment Odara sighed. "I need to speak to the other elders. But know this, Galen, they may well not believe your words."

"Then all of you will die, and with you, our chance to destroy Deirdre."

Reaghan stayed at the edge of the loch long after the sun set in the hopes of seeing Galen again. She didn't know what Mairi had told him, but whatever it was, it had made him walk away.

Though it had never bothered her much before, Reaghan shuddered at the thought of another meal alone, or even one she shared with Mairi. She would much rather share a table with a large group of people where the conversation never ended and the laughter was loud and boisterous.

She had never eaten a meal like that, but in her dreams, in the flashes she saw of another life she was sure she had lived, she'd had such meals.

Reaghan walked aimlessly through the forest. She kept as far from the village as she dared, but always within the safety of the magic. She might want to leave soon, but she knew the dangers of wyrran and Deirdre, especially at night. It had been years since a wyrran had been seen, although she wasn't fool enough to think they would never return.

In fact, she couldn't shake the feeling they would return. And soon.

Reaghan stopped and leaned back against a tree, her

heart in her throat. She didn't know where that feeling had come from, but she knew it was true, just as she knew she needed to seek out the Druids in Foinaven Mountain.

She couldn't explain it, and it frightened her. The headaches, the dreams, and now this feeling of impending doom. Something was going on, something she wasn't sure she wanted to understand.

But she knew she was involved whether she wanted to be or not.

In the past she would have gone to Mairi and confided her fears. Now, the only person she found herself wanting to talk to was Galen.

He had seen the outside world, knew what awaited her. And he knew of other Druids, Druids who might be able to answer some of her questions. It crossed her mind then that maybe she should travel with them when they returned to MacLeod Castle.

She would be safer with them. Alone, she was an easy target for those who would prey on her.

It was a risk. She didn't know much about Galen or Logan, and if she considered leaving with them, she needed to know them better.

It was too bad she didn't know anything about this artifact Galen sought. She would be willing to help him find it in exchange for being guided to either MacLeod Castle or even Foinaven Mountain.

A smile pulled at Reaghan's lips. The elders might not tell Galen or Logan anything about this artifact, but they might tell her.

Reaghan pushed away from the tree and started for Nessa's cottage. She didn't stop until she stood in front of her door. The door opened almost as soon as Reaghan knocked.

"Reaghan," Nessa said, shock in her voice. "Is everything all right?"

"Aye. I wondered if you could spare a few moments?"

The elder motioned Reaghan inside. "Of course. Is it the pain of your head which troubles you?"

"Nay," Reaghan lied. "I find myself curious about Galen and Logan. I always thought we were the last of the Druids. Yet they say more are out there. I wonder how many."

Nessa shrugged and sat at her table, an empty trencher in front of her. "It's hard to speculate."

"But you have to wonder." It was a chance she was taking in making Nessa admit her thoughts, but Reaghan had to do it so Nessa would know she couldn't lie to her.

Nessa frowned. "Trying to determine just how many Druids are still left in Scotland isn't something anyone can do except maybe Deirdre."

Reaghan seized the opportunity and sank into the chair opposite Nessa. "This artifact Galen seeks that they say is in our village, why have I never heard of it?"

"It is something we keep private and divulge to only a few."

"There are only twenty-three of us left. How few do you need?"

The elder shook her head and looked away. "Why do you want to know about this artifact?"

"Because I'm curious. Because I've been living here for ten years and knew nothing of it. How is that? Do you not trust me?"

Nessa laid a hand atop Reaghan's. "We do trust you, Reaghan. You are one of us."

"If you trusted me then I would know of this artifact. It has to do with my memories being gone, doesn't it?"

Nessa looked away again, which was answer enough.

"You won't tell me, will you?"

"I'm afraid not," Nessa replied.

Reaghan pulled her hand out from under Nessa's and stood. She hadn't expected to come away with all the answers to her questions, but she hadn't thought to leave without some kernel of information.

"I will leave you then," Reaghan said.

She left before she said something she would regret. For so long she had considered these people her family, the ones who would always be there for her.

What had happened in her past and the memories that were closed to her? Had she done something terrible? Her mind raced, imagining scenario after scenario. She thought of the worst and tried to picture herself taking someone's life.

There was no way she could have done such a thing. But then again, she didn't know the person she had been before the fever.

Before her memories were taken from her.

Reaghan's mind was in a whirl of chaos. For an instant, she felt as if she might break into a million pieces, her heart wrenched from her body.

And then she heard it, the sweet, lilting melody.

Oftentimes they were able to hear the music coming from MacIntosh Castle. The sounds carried swiftly over the loch, making Reaghan almost feel as if she were in the castle herself.

She let herself drown in the music, let it quiet her battered soul. The melody from the flute was one of her favorites, and it never failed to seep deep into her bones.

Reaghan forgot her agitation, forgot her anger, and walked toward the loch. What better way to ease her soul than listening to such splendor?

EIGHT

After leaving Odara's, Galen wandered aimlessly before he found himself once more at the loch. He told himself it was because he loved the quiet beauty of it, not because he was searching for Reaghan.

But he knew it for the lie it was.

He didn't want to fight the attraction, the deep yearning that tugged at him. If he didn't battle it, he would end up touching Reaghan, and then everything would shatter when he saw into her mind.

Reaghan deserved better. Her mind shouldn't be violated, her secrets shared, her innermost feelings exposed for him to see. She was too pure, too exquisite to be marred by what he was.

He had already destroyed one woman before he had realized just how potent his powers were. Galen couldn't—and wouldn't—do that to Reaghan.

All the same, his body screamed for release, for Reaghan. His cock ached to bury deep inside her slick heat. His body cried out to feel Reaghan's skin, to breathe in the scent of her hair, to taste her essence. Just to hold her.

Galen had never felt such yearning, had never known such hunger for a woman. Her smile. Her gray eyes. Her radiant, auburn locks. It took but the barest of thoughts to conjure her in his mind.

How he wanted to be able to draw her into his arms, to press her against him and feel the crush of her breasts.

How he longed to sweep aside her hair to expose her neck so he could kiss the delicate, sensitive skin at his leisure.

How he craved to cover her lips with his and explore her mouth until he was drowning in her.

How he desired to thrust into her wet heat, to see and feel her climax beneath him.

All without ever knowing what was inside her mind.

Galen lowered himself between the roots of an oak and leaned against the massive trunk with a resigned sigh of what could never be. The gentle, constant lapping of the water against shore lulled him. He hadn't slept the night before, and he could feel the weariness creep over him.

His gaze lifted to the heavens, to the millions of stars that winked down at him and the crescent moon that shed its light over the loch.

Then the music began. The sound of the flute was as lovely and special as Loch Awe, but it wasn't until the bag-pipes joined in the haunting melody that Galen truly enjoyed it.

He leaned his head back and breathed the magical air of Loch Awe. He might be leaving the village without the artifact, but he had found a special beauty in the loch, one that resonated with his soul.

It wouldn't defeat Deirdre, but if he was ever captured by her again he knew what memories he would call up to help him through the lengthy, bleak hours of eternity.

Loch Awe. And Reaghan.

As if his thoughts summoned her, she moved out of the shadows, as graceful as a feline, as ethereal as an angel. She stood at the loch's edge, the water touching the hem of her gown as she swayed with the music coming across the water.

The melody began soft and sweet, but grew in tempo until the sound echoed evocatively around the loch. When it came to a crashing end, Galen wanted to call out for more.

He never uttered a sound, but Reaghan turned her head and looked at him. He didn't move, afraid he would scare her off.

"Galen."

Her velvety, gentle voice whispering his name left him struggling to pull a breath into his lungs. It was the way she said it, breathily, sensuously, with a hint of surprise, that had his blood burning and the passion he struggled with roaring to life once again.

"I often come to listen to the music," she said when he didn't speak. "Have you ever felt so isolated from the world that you wanted to scream?"

Galen knew exactly how she felt, had experienced that emotion many times in his two hundred and fifty years of immortality. "Aye."

"What do you do about it?" She turned to him, her gaze searching his.

"Pray that I can make it through."

Her brow furrowed and the tip of her tongue peeked out to lick her lips, sending a jolt of longing shooting straight to Galen's cock.

He bit back a moan, thankful he was sitting down because he feared his legs wouldn't have held him. His fingers bit into the bark, and he felt the tips of his claws sink into the tree.

"I fear I will succumb to this feeling," Reaghan said. "My past is blocked to me. I know nothing of my family or why I'm here. Mairi knows. Yet she will not tell me."

Galen tamped down his passion and focused on anything but the lovely beauty standing with the moonlight shining upon her auburn curls. "Mairi must have a good reason for keeping your past secret."

"I found a parchment with ancient writing on it, writing that I can read."

Galen raised a brow. "I doona understand."

"The writing is in Gaelic. I've never learned it, yet I can read the parchment as well as the pillars."

"What did the parchment say?" he asked.

"My family is in Foinaven Mountain. I want to find them." She walked to the tree and squatted down beside him. "I was to leave today while everyone was occupied with you and Logan."

Even though he knew he shouldn't ask, the words were out of his mouth before he could stop them. "What made you stay?"

Her hand reached out and touched his cheek. "I'm not sure."

Galen bounded to his feet and stepped away from her, praying her small touch wouldn't give him entry into her mind. Thankfully there was nothing, but he needed distance. She was too close, too alluring. Too damned beautiful.

If he didn't get away from her he wouldn't be able to hold back the tide of yearning that gripped him.

"Galen? Did I do something wrong?"

He fisted his hands. They itched to reach out and stroke her face, to smell her hair and feel the heat of her skin. He shook with need, a burning that threatened to set him ablaze if he didn't taste her soon.

"Nay," he finally managed. "You did nothing wrong."

He groaned when the first sounds of music reached them again. The melody was slow, the beat rhythmic, seductive. Erotic.

It mixed with Reaghan's strong magic and swirled around him, enticing him to give in to the yearnings of his body, urging him to heed the passion that Reaghan stirred to life.

He burned. He desired. He needed.

"Do you feel it?" Reaghan asked as she rose to her feet, her face tilted to the moon. "The music. It always makes me feel as though it is calling to me."

Galen couldn't take his eyes off her. She was swaying again, her arms held away from her body. Her eyes were closed and she tilted her head to the side, exposing her graceful neck and skin that begged for his touch.

He tried to keep his feet rooted, but his body had other ideas. He was powerless to fight against the lure of Reaghan's magic. It was the music that called forth her magic.

And Galen couldn't fight her magic. He didn't want to. It felt too good as it caressed his skin, heating his blood and making his heart pound in his chest.

He stopped in front of her, awed by the pure joy on her face. Then she opened her silver eyes and looked at him. The smile faded and desire sparked in her gaze.

"Reaghan, I cannot fight this."

Her head cocked to the side, auburn curls spilling over her shoulder to dance about her arm. "Cannot fight what?"

"This attraction I feel for you."

"You want . . . me?"

She said it with such confusion that Galen almost laughed. "Aye, but I shouldn't. Mairi warned me to stay away."

"Forget Mairi. What do you want?"

"God's blood. I want all of you. I want to kiss you, to have you against me so I can feel every inch of you. I want to lay you down and sink my rod inside you."

He knew he was being crude, but he did it in the hopes she would run away since obviously he couldn't. When she stayed her ground, her breath quickening and her pupils dilating, Galen knew he had made a dreadful mistake, but it was a mistake he couldn't regret.

This craving, this hunger was too strong to walk away from, and whatever might happen, Galen would endure it. He would endure it because he had to know what she tasted like, had to know what it felt like to stroke her creamy skin and hold her.

It had been so long since he'd had contact with a woman that he was almost afraid to touch her. But he had come this far. There was no turning back now.

He moved closer until he had her backed against the tree. The sensual melody only added to his desire, exciting him, imploring him. Teasing him.

Reaghan was his for the taking. He could see it in the way she watched him with wide eyes, her lips parted and her pulse beating rapidly at her throat.

Galen leaned toward her, but before he could allow his hands to touch her, he slammed them onto the tree. The bark bit into his flesh, but he felt nothing through the haze of his desire.

He let himself sink into Reaghan's silver gaze and allowed her magic to encircle him, stroke him. It was as beautiful and fascinating as she was, and it proved to him that he would never encounter another woman like her for the rest of his days.

When he was breaths away from kissing her, he paused, steeling himself against the images and feelings that would assail his mind as soon as he touched her.

His body shook with the need to taste her. His breathing was ragged, harsh. Every part of his body was attuned to Reaghan. Her gaze dropped to his mouth, and that's all it took to send him past the point of no return.

He placed his lips on hers in a quick, hard kiss and waited for the inevitable deluge of images and feelings. Only there was nothing. No visions, no voices, no emotions.

Shaken to his core and too afraid to rejoice, Galen kissed her again, this time longer, softer, his tongue sliding past her lips to delve into her mouth.

She sucked in a startled breath. Her tongue hesitantly touched his before she moaned and returned his kiss. It left him reeling, his body ablaze with need.

Galen was sinking. Spinning. Reeling.

He deepened the kiss as a low, satisfied moan rumbled within him. He needed more of her sweet lips, more of her exciting, fascinating taste. It had been so long since he'd felt something besides another's emotions or thoughts when he touched them that he never wanted to let her go.

His hands sank into her curls, awed at the cool, soft texture of her hair. Her arms wound around his neck, bringing her body closer so that her breasts rubbed against his chest.

Galen moaned, his balls tightening in response. He ached to pull her against him, to grind his arousal into her softness. Pleasure swam through his veins, begging for more. Demanding more.

He couldn't deny it, didn't want to. He let his hands wander down her back to her trim waist and the swell of her buttocks. He tried to be gentle, but his hunger was too great. She was his at that moment, and he would take all she had.

His arms tightened around her, jerking her body against him. Their kiss was wild, reckless . . . exhilarating. She offered all of herself, holding nothing back. She was everything that was innocent, but a profound, enduring passion smoldered within her.

When her body rubbed against his throbbing cock in time with the music, Galen could think of nothing else but having Reaghan. He wanted to lick every inch of her, touch every part until she trembled with need. Burned with it.

He kissed down her neck, bending her back over his arm. Her breasts thrust forward, her nipples straining against the material of her gown. Galen scrapped his teeth over a hard nub and smiled when she sank her nails into his neck.

"Galen," she whispered, her eyes closed and her lips swollen from his kisses.

She looked more stunning than ever. He never stopped to wonder why he couldn't see or hear her thoughts, he was just delighted for once that he had control over his power.

He put his hand beneath her knee and pulled her leg up against his side. He tugged at her skirts until his hand touched the bare skin of her thigh. He marveled at the feel of her warm, smooth flesh. When her skirts were bunched around her thighs, Galen sank to his knees and then leaned back on his calves. Her legs instinctively wrapped around his waist.

Galen groaned and licked the side of her neck. She fit snugly against him, her hot sex pressed against his cock. He shifted his hips so that his arousal rubbed against her sensitive flesh. A soft cry fell from her lips as her eyes widened.

"Don't stop," she begged. "Please, don't stop."

"Never," he promised.

How could he when his hunger demanded so much more and there was also her magic and the music? It was all too heady to resist. And he certainly didn't want to resist Reaghan. Not now. Not ever again.

He cupped a breast and pinched her nipple while he continued to grind against her. She whispered his name, the sound as amazing as the siren in his arms.

No one had ever made him feel so alive, so desired, until now. Until Reaghan.

There were no thoughts of tomorrow, no worries about the artifact or Deirdre. Only Reaghan and the passion that held both of them enthralled in its flames.

NINE

Reaghan's body was on fire. Every place Galen touched, kissed, caressed set her ablaze. She was excited, and eager to discover more of the thrilling passion Galen created.

She threw caution to the wind and pressed herself against him. Her mind spun as the wondrous feel of his rigid arousal teased and stimulated her sex. Each time his rod stroked against her, an astonishing new sensation stirred within her, centering low in her stomach and tightening, making her limbs heavy and her breathing ragged.

No man had ever touched her like this, but she knew the release, when it came, would be glorious. How she understood what to expect she didn't know. And at the moment she didn't care.

She wanted more of Galen, more of his hands, his mouth, his hard, muscular body against hers.

His fingers fondled her breasts, tweaking her nipples until her hips were moving against him in a rhythm that was as old as time itself.

The music drummed in her ears, the cadence enchanting. Just like Galen. Arousing. Exhilarating. Stimulating.

She never wanted this night to end.

His large hand splayed against her bottom and held her still as he ground against her. She moaned, and his lopsided grin was all pleased male.

It made her heart skip a beat. She lifted her face and kissed him. She loved the taste of him, his scent of pine, of the forest.

"God's teeth, you feel so good," Galen whispered in her ear just before he nipped her earlobe.

Reaghan shivered against him. "I've never felt anything like this."

"There's so much more."

"Show me."

His stunning cobalt eyes caught and held hers. He gazed deep into her eyes, as if he searched for something. "I should no' be touching you at all."

"Maybe not, but tell me if this doesn't feel right to you. Tell me you don't want me, and I'll leave."

His fingers dug into her skin as he clutched her tighter. "I'm afraid I willna ever be able to let you go."

"Then kiss me. My body is on fire, and I need more of you."

His mouth slanted over hers, his tongue mating with hers in a frenzied, passionate kiss while his hands roamed over her body, learning her.

All Reaghan could do was hold on to him. She learned the feel of his thick shoulders, the way his muscles moved and bunched in his back beneath her palms.

She was breathless, her body flooded with passion. The tightening inside her continued, until she didn't think she could stand another moment.

Then, his hand cupped her sex.

Reaghan gasped at the pressure he applied to her swollen sex. His fingers tangled in her curls, pushing them aside so he could fondle her.

She held still, afraid he would stop. And afraid he wouldn't.

When his finger dipped inside her, she sighed, the

pleasure so intense she couldn't breathe. But then he pulled his finger out of her and began to slowly, gently, rub against her clitoris.

Reaghan's eyes rolled back in her head as she savored the sheer delight that slowed her blood and sped up her heart. Each stroke of his finger was like lightning through her body.

Her hips moved of their own accord, seeking more of the pleasure that was building, steadily growing, swelling inside her. Small cries fell from her parted lips as his strokes grew faster, sending her spiraling down a path of potent pleasure.

Until the climax claimed her, dragging her into an abyss of never-ending ecstasy.

She cried out, Galen's name on her lips, but he took her cries into his mouth with a scorching kiss. He held her against him as she slowly came down from the exquisite orgasm.

Reaghan could feel his heart beating as rapidly as her own, could hear his harsh breaths. When the kiss ended she opened her eyes to find him watching her.

"That was glorious," she whispered into the silence. She didn't know when the music had stopped, only that it had.

He smiled and tugged at one of her curls.

"Galen," she said, and rubbed against his hard cock.

His eyes closed as he groaned. "Doona do that. I want you too desperately as it is."

"And if I want to feel you inside me?"

Galen's eyes snapped open. "You doona know what you are saying."

"I do. I want all of you."

She saw his need warring with what he somehow thought he should do. For too long Reaghan had watched as others experienced life. She wanted this, and she wasn't about to let Galen go without a fight.

"Please," she whispered, and kissed him.

He reacted instantly, the kiss deep, hot, and frantic. All of his passion, all of his longing, was poured into that kiss. And it left her breathless.

She reached and unfastened the brooch that pinned his kilt over his heart. Her hands eagerly lifted his saffron shirt and met warm skin and solid muscle.

He broke the kiss long enough to tug off his shirt, and then he took her mouth again. Reaghan's sex throbbed, eager to have him touch her once more, to take her on that incredible journey over and over.

"I want you naked," he said between kisses.

Reaghan pulled off her gown, her hands tangling with Galen's as they each tried to rid her of her clothes. They shared a laugh, their eyes locking.

In the next moment he shifted them so that she was on her back. She felt something soft beneath her and realized it was his kilt.

While he removed his boots, Reaghan quickly shed her shoes and woollen hose. And then he stood staring down at her. She gazed up into his face now cast in shadow. The moonlight bathed his skin and hair in a bluish glow.

She was able to see the magnificent muscles of his chest and abdomen in all their defined glory. She marveled at the corded muscles in his arms and neck and legs. His wide chest tapered into a vee leading to his trim waist and hips.

And jutting out, hard and thick, was his arousal, the very thing she yearned to feel inside her.

Galen had never been so entranced. The woman lying on his kilt, the woman who now offered herself to him, was the most stunning creature he had ever encountered.

She had thin shoulders, delicate wrists, and long, slim fingers. Her breasts were small and firm, the nipples pink. Her waist was narrow, her hips gently flared. Her legs were long and lean, and Galen hungered to feel them wrapped around him again.

But it was the auburn curls that hid the most precious part of her that held his attention.

He knelt between her legs and ran his fingers from her ankles to her hips. Her breath hitched and shivers raced over her skin.

Galen still couldn't believe he wasn't seeing into her mind. He had touched her repeatedly and yet it revealed nothing. He didn't understand it, but he wasn't about to turn away from this precious gift. After being without human contact for so long, he couldn't get enough.

Now, as he slid his hands up to her small waist, all he thought about was filling Reaghan, stretching her until he was deep inside her.

He cupped her breasts and held her gaze as he bent and took a tiny bud in his mouth. She groaned low in her throat. Her hands stroked up and down his back, spurring his desire with every beat of his heart.

When he reached between them, she was still wet. Galen wanted to take it slow, to savor every moment with her, but it had been too long since he'd had a woman, too long since he'd been able to make love without reading another's mind.

He guided himself to her entrance and pushed inside her. She was incredibly tight and startlingly hot. He leaned over her, his hands on either side of her head, as he thrust inside her slowly.

She gripped his hips, her back arching, as he filled her. Her lips were parted, her breathing erratic. Galen couldn't take his eyes off her, watching every fascinating emotion that crossed her face.

When she bent her knees and wrapped her legs around him, Galen gave a final push that seated him to the hilt. She felt so good that for a heartbeat he stayed as he was, reveling in the exquisite feel of her.

His tempo was slow, steady as he began to move within her. His yearning, his hunger wouldn't be denied though, and soon he was plunging hard, deep, and fast inside her. She matched his thrusts, her glorious curls spread around her.

Galen could feel his climax building, knew he was on the edge. Reaghan's body began to stiffen beneath him, and a moment later she peaked a second time.

The feel of her walls clutching him sent Galen tumbling to his own climax. He threw back his head as he thrust once more, burying him deep, as his seed filled her body.

When he was able to open his eyes again, he rested his forehead on Reaghan's and smiled. Not yet willing to let her go, he pulled out of her and rolled to his back, tugging her against his side.

Silence stretched between them. Galen was content, his body sated, but in the back of his mind he knew he would have to face the fact that Reaghan hadn't been a virgin. She said she hadn't been with a man, but maybe it was before the fever and she couldn't remember.

It didn't make him want her less. Reaghan had no reason to lie to him, and he knew the men of her village. Still, he found himself curious.

"I don't want this night to ever end," Reaghan said.

Galen rubbed his hand over her back. "I know, but it must."

"Will you take me with you when you leave for Mac-Leod Castle?"

He hadn't expected her to ask, though somehow he wasn't shocked. "You would leave your people, your home to come to a place you know nothing about? You doona even know me."

"Ah, but I do know you." He felt her smile against him. "And aye, to answer your question, I would leave it all behind. It will be difficult, but I feel that not only must I learn who I really am but I also want to help in your fight against Deirdre."

"I willna lie. Deirdre is hunting us. Until we are at MacLeod Castle anything could happen. Everyone here thinks the village's magic will keep Deirdre out."

"You don't, do you?"

Galen bent his other arm and put it beneath his head. "I know Deirdre was on her way here when we attacked her. Her black magic prevented her death, but as soon as her full magic has returned, she will come here looking for the artifact we seek."

"Have you told the elders?"

"I've spoken to Odara. She plans to speak to the others."

Reaghan let out a soft sigh. "We've always been safe here."

"And the wyrran attacks?"

"The wyrran have been unable to penetrate our magic. They've taken those of us who haven't been inside the shield."

Galen looked down at her and marveled yet again at how good it felt to touch her, hold her without his power intruding. "I've asked to take the entire village to MacLeod Castle."

"This is our home. They will not leave."

"Yet, you want to."

She shrugged and burrowed more tightly against him. "I love it here. I am a part of this village. For too long the Druids have hidden from Deirdre. We need to take a stand. Now is a good time."

"I need to find the artifact. It is important to our cause, and to the safety of every Druid in Scotland."

"Then I will help," she promised. "I questioned Nessa tonight. She said only a few knew of it. When I asked why I didn't know of it, she said only a handful needed to know and I wasn't one of them."

He kissed the top of her head. "We'll find it."

"I hope so. If the elders do not begin to trust you and Logan, then it will be only a matter of time before Deirdre comes to claim the artifact."

"Aye," he murmured. The thought of Deirdre invading the beauty of Loch Awe left him with seething anger.

Galen thought over all Reaghan had said. She wanted answers, answers she might find with the Druids at MacLeod Castle.

Just thinking about the castle made him recall how he had wandered Scotland for many decades searching for someplace he felt connected to, a place he could be a part of something.

That hadn't happened until he found the MacLeods. He'd found a home and a family at MacLeod Castle. Maybe Reaghan would as well.

TEN

The next morning Reaghan expected everyone to know she and Galen had been lovers the night before, but no one looked at her differently as she walked through the small village.

That is, no one except Logan.

He smiled at her, his hazel eyes knowing. "Galen tells me you want to return with us."

Reaghan hastily looked around her to make sure no one else heard him. "Aye."

"Good. I think you will enjoy it at the castle."

"I'm pleased you are welcoming me."

He cocked a brow. "You worried I wouldn't?"

"You and Galen are friends. He trusts your judgment."

Logan chuckled, a long stick in his hand that he repeatedly stabbed into the earth. "Galen has been around longer than I. He doesna need my permission for anything."

"Regardless, I think it important both of you agree."

"Galen wants to bring the entire village with us. Did you know he spoke with Odara about it?"

Reaghan nodded and tucked a strand of hair behind her ear. "He told me last night."

"Be careful in your questioning about the artifact," Logan cautioned in a low voice, his gaze wandering around them. "Whatever it is, everyone here reveres it and willna part with it easily."

"I cannot understand their need to keep it when it could help against Deirdre."

Logan's hazel eyes came to rest on her. "It comes down to trust and what they have believed for many generations. It will take a significant event for them to hand it over."

"Or we just take it."

He grinned. "You surprise me. These are your people."

"Aye, they are. However, Deirdre's threat is of great importance. We have been sheltered from the world here, but for how much longer? Galen said it will only be a matter of time before Deirdre comes looking for the artifact herself. I say we strike before she does."

"I like the way you think," Logan said, grinning again. "I wish you could convince the elders."

She sighed and found herself searching for Galen. "I as well."

"You think you will find the answers to your past at Foinaven Mountain?"

"I don't know, but I must try. I want to know where I come from and why I'm no longer with my family."

"Sometimes the past is better left alone."

"You can say that because you know who your family is."

"Was. I know who my family was, and I'd like nothing more than to forget," he ground out before he turned on his heel and walked away.

Reaghan was stunned by the fury in his tone. Was it better to have the memories and long to forget them? Or to never know and yearn to remember?

She walked to the loch to bathe and think about who she could speak with next about the artifact. What was it about this object that made the village keep it so secret?

If only she knew where it was. She could take it, and help Galen and Logan in their fight against Deirdre. Then she, Galen, and Logan could set out for MacLeod Castle.

A smile tugged at her lips as she thought of the

adventure that awaited her. Stealing from the very people she called her own wouldn't be easy, but she would be doing it to help save them all. Surely they would understand that in the end.

She removed her clothes and grabbed the soap she had brought before she stepped into the cool waters of the loch. The water rippled around her as she walked out into the blue depths until it reached her shoulders. She tilted her head back to wet her hair and began to lather the thick strands with the soap. After a long scrub, she dunked her head under the water to help rinse away the suds.

It was while she washed her body that she felt someone's gaze. Heat sizzled through her veins, causing her heart to beat unsteadily. She knew without looking it was Galen. When she turned toward shore, she saw him standing in the trees, his cobalt gaze filled with desire as he watched her.

She wanted him to join her, and nearly motioned for him to do so when she caught sight of Braden walking toward Galen. Reaghan smiled and shrugged. Maybe later they could go for a swim. She wondered what it would be like to feel the cool liquid lap at her skin while they made love.

Galen couldn't take his eyes off Reaghan with her skin wet and glistening in the morning sun, her auburn locks darkened by the water and slick against her head.

He recalled the taste of her skin, knew how it felt to hold her soft body against him. He grew hard just thinking about taking her again, of filling her and thrusting deep inside her.

When she looked at him, her smile welcoming, her gaze inviting, Galen had been about to throw caution to the wind and join her. He knew it was best if they kept their affair from the rest of the village, but when it came to Reaghan, he lost all sense of reason.

He reached to unpin his brooch when his enhanced

hearing caught the sound of quick, light footsteps coming toward him. Galen frowned, knowing he would have to wait to join Reaghan.

The footsteps halted, sliding in the pine needles on the ground. Galen looked over his shoulder to find Braden. "Good morn."

"Good morn," the lad said, his large brown eyes watching Galen carefully.

"I willna harm you, lad. You can come closer."

It took a few moments, but the boy drew up enough courage to stand beside Galen. "You're watching Reaghan?"

"It appears that I am."

"Reaghan is to be protected."

Galen's mind considered possible reasons. He squatted beside the boy and gave him a friendly smile. "True, but everyone must be protected."

Braden shook his head vigorously. "Nay. Reaghan is sheltered above all."

"Why?"

The boy looked down at his feet and shrugged as he kicked at the leaves with the toe of his boot. "I'm not sure."

Galen knew he lied, but he couldn't force the truth out of the lad. "Do you think we're here to harm Reaghan?"

"Oh, nay," Braden said, and raised his face to Galen. His brown eyes shone with honesty and youth. "I've seen how she smiles at you, and how you watch her when you doona think others are looking."

"Has anyone else seen me watch her?"

Braden grimaced. "Aye. Mairi."

"Ah," Galen said. "She's already told me as much. She does no' want me near Reaghan."

"I doona know why. You make Reaghan happy."

"I make her happy, do I?" Galen looked at the loch to find Reaghan swimming leisurely, her slim arms propelling her through the water.

Braden smiled, showing a missing front tooth. "She always plays with me, and never tells me I'm in her way. I like Reaghan. I want her to be happy."

"And you trust that I will make her happy?"

"My mum is always telling me I'll be the man of the village one day, and that I'll have to make important decisions. The elders tell me I have to learn to listen and trust myself, so that's what I did. I trust you to keep Reaghan safe and happy."

Galen rubbed his jaw and regarded the boy. Braden was astute for one so young. He could see it in the lad's eyes and the way Braden observed what went on around him.

"Braden, what your mother and elders told you is the truth. I'm glad you trust me with Reaghan, but I have to know, lad, why does she need to be kept safe? I cannot fully protect her unless I know."

Before Braden could answer, an unholy shriek filled the air. Galen stiffened, unsure if he'd heard a wyrran or not. But the second time the shrill screech came, Galen knew.

"What was that?" Braden asked in a small, terrified voice.

Galen grabbed Braden by his narrow shoulders. "Listen to me closely, lad, you need to get to the village and tell everyone to gather together and hide. Can you do that?"

Braden nodded woodenly. "What is it? What's come?"

"Wyrran," Galen said as he rose to his feet. "Tell everyone that Logan and I will make sure the wyrran doona get inside the village, but everyone must stay inside the magic."

"Aye," Braden said, and he took off up the hill as if Deirdre herself were after him.

And in a sense, she was.

Galen turned to go find Logan when his gaze snagged on Reaghan. She was closer to shore, her eyes wide with fear. There wasn't time for her to get out of the water. The magic of the village extended to the loch, but not the water itself.

That's when he realized the wyrran must have seen Reaghan and sensed her magic.

"Galen!" Logan shouted as he ran down the slope. He slid to a stop next to Galen and groaned as he saw Reaghan. "Shite. What do we do now?"

"Keep the wyrran from her."

"She'll see," Logan cautioned.

Galen turned his back to the loch and took a deep breath. "I hate secrets. She needs to know anyway."

"Why? So she'll push you away? Is that what you hope?"

Was it? Was Galen so used to being alone that he feared having someone close to him? Not that he had time to think on it now. "We need to keep the wyrran from finding the entrance to the village."

"Can they get through the magic?"

"I'd rather no' find out."

Logan nodded. "Then let's bring them to us."

"Aye." Galen glanced over his shoulder and met Reaghan's eyes. He wondered what he'd see in them after she witnessed his transformation. He doubted she would welcome him into her arms as she'd done the night before.

Galen refused to think about it. He held up his hand to tell her to stay put. When she nodded her understanding and moved deeper into the loch, he stepped into the forest so she couldn't see him.

He unfastened his kilt from over his heart and wrapped the length around his waist and then removed his saffron shirt. With the barest of thoughts he unleashed his god. His skin turned deep green, claws extended from his fingers, and fangs filled his mouth. He was what the Druids feared. A Warrior.

But he was also the one thing that could keep them from being taken to Deirdre.

Slight movement to his right alerted Galen that Logan

was ready. He nodded to his friend. Logan's silver skin did not disguise him in the forest as Galen's green skin did.

Logan smiled at him, showing his fangs, and moved off to find the wyrran. It wouldn't be difficult. Galen could hear them from where he stood. They were close. Too damn close.

An angry scream from a wyrran told Galen that Logan had been spotted. Galen stayed in the forest and waited for the yellow-skinned beasts to find him.

The first one burst through the trees not five paces in front of Galen. Its large yellow eyes glared with malice. It hissed through its mouthful of sharp teeth, its thin lips unable to close over all the teeth.

Galen hated the beings that had been made by Deirdre with her black magic. Despite being no taller than a small child, the wyrran had long claws on both their hands and their feet. And they used them effectively.

When the wyrran launched itself at Galen, he easily stepped to the side and swung his arm down, his claws slicing the wyrran's head off.

He didn't have long to wait for the others. Off to his left he heard Logan battling his own wyrran. The three wyrran who next came at Galen were smarter. They circled him, saliva dripping from their thin lips.

Galen stayed still, his eyes moving to watch the beasts he could see. His hearing alerted him to the wyrran behind him as it readied to jump.

He smiled, eager to feed his god with battle and blood. His god, Ycewold, liked nothing better than a lengthy, vicious battle.

A wyrran jumped on his back, its claws from its feet embedding deep in Galen's muscles while its hands shredded Galen's skin over and over.

Galen clenched his jaw as images of death and evil

filled his mind from the wyrran's touch. He fought against the tide of malice and let out a roar.

The other two wyrran on each side of Galen attacked at that moment. One sliced his leg while the other raked its claws across Galen's abdomen.

The pain from the wounds was brutal, but nothing compared to the horror of their minds. Galen had to get them off him, to give himself a moment without their malevolent feelings in his head.

Galen kicked the wyrran attacking his leg, sending the vile creature slamming into a nearby tree. He slashed his arm down and across the wyrran in front of him, cutting its throat with five long, brutal slices. With another roar, Galen reached behind him and grabbed hold of the wyrran on his back.

Blood spilled from Galen's wounds, but they would heal soon enough. The beast on his back bit his hand, the numerous sharp teeth cutting through Galen's flesh and bone.

Galen took two steps backward and slammed the wyrran against the tree. The creature's claws sank deeper into his back, but when Galen stepped away, it fell unconscious to the ground.

Galen wasted no time in cutting off its head with his claws, but when he turned to the one he had kicked against a tree, he glimpsed it running toward the loch.

Toward Reaghan.

Galen didn't think, just reacted. He chased after the wyrran, getting to it just as the creature stepped into the water.

The wyrran turned and raked its claws diagonally across Galen's chest with first one hand and then the other, making an X. Galen growled, his anger burning bright inside him, dampening the images from the wyrran's mind.

He kicked the wyrran's feet out from beneath it and used his boot on its neck to keep it down. The wyrran continued to slice at his legs and any other part of Galen it could reach.

Galen stared down at the despicable beast. "It's time you die." He plunged his hand into the wyrran's chest and pulled out its heart.

He tossed the heart away, and only when he knew the wyrran was dead did he realize he was at the loch. He blinked, his chest tightening.

Slowly, tentatively, he turned his head and found Reaghan watching him with her mouth open and horror in her beautiful gray eyes.

ELEVEN

Reaghan could only stare in wonder—and more than a bit of fright—at the creature in front of her. She knew it was Galen by his kilt and the blond hair that flowed freely about his shoulders.

She swallowed as she took in the sight of skin the darkest green. And those claws!

Her heart raced, her blood ran like ice as she looked at him. She shivered from the time she'd spent in the cool loch, but also because of the wyrran attack. Those skinny, diminutive creatures made her stomach turn.

Despite her fear she realized Galen was killing the wee beasts. He was brutal, fierce in his slaying, but the blood and wounds over his body proved the wyrran had done their own damage.

And then Galen turned his head toward her.

Reaghan's heart jumped in her throat as she stared into eyes she didn't recognize. Gone were his beautiful cobalt eyes, and in their place were eyes as green as his skin. And the color bled through the entire eye.

She wanted to run. But she also wanted to go to him and see if he was all right. She didn't know what to do, so she stood still, waiting for Galen to speak, to tell her everything would be all right.

He didn't say anything. For long, heart-wrenching

moments he just stared at her. There was something in his unusual eyes, something that made her yearn to take him in her arms and comfort him.

Reaghan licked her lips. "Galen?"

She heard the deep growl that came from him and flinched as he spun away. With her heart pounding, she started toward him.

From the stories she had heard she knew he was a Warrior, but she also knew he was not on Deirdre's side. She had seen the truth of it in his eyes.

Though she had felt Galen's kisses, knew the way his body moved over hers, she was apprehensive about getting near him in his Warrior form. The sheer power that radiated from him now was beyond belief, breathtaking, and more than a little daunting.

Movement out of the corner of her eye caught her attention. Reaghan swiveled her head to the right and saw a man atop a horse. His brown hair was streaked with gray at the temples, but it was the sneer on his face that made her gasp. There was so much hatred in that one look it made her take a step back.

She could feel his loathing, sense his need to capture her and take her . . . somewhere evil.

Wherever it was, it wasn't good.

"Get to the village, Reaghan!" Galen yelled.

She glanced at him to see Galen's gaze locked on the man. Reaghan hesitated, afraid to move, afraid the man might reach her before she could get away.

"He willna touch you."

Galen's promise, the deep, calming resonance of his voice, propelled her out of the water and behind him. Galen never took his eyes off the man.

She grabbed her gown, and with one last glance at Galen, she ran up the hill toward the village. She could hear the Druids and their frightened voices, the soft crying of some of the women.

Reaghan jerked her gown over her head and stumbled into the middle of the village where everyone stood huddled against each other.

"Reaghan!" Mairi shouted and jerked her into the group. "Are you hurt?"

"Nay, I was at the loch when the wyrran came. Galen and Logan are fighting them off."

Mairi's hand shook as she wrapped cold fingers around Reaghan's wrist. "What makes those two men think they can defeat the wyrran?"

"I saw them fight the wyrran when one tried to get me. We will be safe," Reaghan promised.

Mairi's brown eyes regarded her silently for a moment. "What did you see?"

"I saw the wyrran die." She wasn't about to tell the elder the truth. They would cast Galen and Logan out of the village, even though they had defeated the wyrran.

The thought of never seeing Galen again, of never tasting his kisses again, of never feeling his arms around her, left Reagan distraught.

Despite what she had seen at the loch she couldn't stop thinking of him. Galen was a good man, that she knew with certainty. He might have evil inside him, but he was a man of principle, a man who would fight evil until the end of his days.

Fury bubbled inside Galen when he caught sight of the man. The fact that the man was staring at Reaghan as if he'd found his salvation only made Galen's rage burn brighter, hotter.

The only thing that would cleanse him of it was the man's death. By Galen's hand.

Once Reaghan was out of the loch and running to safety, the rider jerked his mount around and kicked him into a run. Galen wanted to see Reaghan to the village, but he had to go after the man and try to end this now.

Whoever he was, he was Deirdre's. He might not have been created by black magic, but he had given himself to Deirdre in all ways. Now that he had seen Reaghan, he would chase her until he captured her.

Nay!

Galen hesitated a moment more, listening to make sure no wyrran ambushed Reaghan. Only then did he smile, his god eager for more blood and death. It would take no time for Galen to catch the man, not with the speed his god gave him.

Just as Galen started after him, a wyrran jumped in his path. In two quick swipes of Galen's claws the creature lay dead at his feet.

He could have sworn he had killed them all. Yet there had been another. What if there were more? What if the beasts were just waiting for someone to venture from the village? What if that someone was Reaghan?

Galen's blood ran cold with that thought. He looked after the man, silently promising the bastard he would find and kill him very soon. Then Galen pivoted and started toward the village. He pushed his god down, waiting until his claws and fangs were gone and his skin had returned to normal before he showed himself to the villagers.

His gaze found Reaghan almost immediately. She stared at him, fear and worry mixing in the stunning gray depths of her eyes. He wanted to reassure her, but he couldn't do so yet. Mayhap not ever again.

"Galen," a small voice whispered.

He shifted his gaze to find Braden watching him, his mother clutching the small lad to her. "Doona move," Galen cautioned everyone. "There may be a few more wyrran."

"Where is Logan?" a woman asked.

Galen wanted to know the same thing. He turned and faced the ancient stones. He knew better than to think the wyrran had somehow killed Logan. The wyrran were more pests than anything, though they could overwhelm with sheer numbers.

Still, Logan, like any Warrior, thrived on the thrill of battle, the smell of blood, and the scent of death.

Galen wished he had brought another Warrior with them. He wanted to look for Logan, but he couldn't leave the Druids. The forest became eerily quiet, the calm only broken by the long, shrill call of the falcon as it soared high above them.

There was something in the air, something that told Galen evil was near. He could feel his claws growing, and silently prayed his skin wouldn't turn, not yet, not until the threat arrived.

There was a rustle in the leaves, so soft only a Warrior with his enhanced hearing could have heard it. It was another wyrran, Galen was sure of it.

He turned his head and looked at Reaghan, silently telling her to be ready. She gave a small nod of her head, understanding and determination in her eyes.

Galen's blood began to burn, his god eager for more death, more bloodshed. More was coming, and his god knew it. Galen's gaze moved from tree to tree as he waited for the attack.

It came swiftly.

Wyrran moved to surround the villagers, their hungry yellow eyes looking over the Druids while they licked their lips in anticipation.

Galen unleashed his god and attacked the wyrran closest to him. There was a loud roar as Logan jumped from a tree above them, landing on the other side of the group of Druids.

Galen didn't hold back. He quickly made his way from wyrran to wyrran. And when one got too close to the Druids, Galen was swift to kill it.

His head was full of their wickedness and disgusting thoughts, but he refused to give in to the vastness of it. Too many people's lives were at stake.

It wasn't until he heard the scream of a small child and the wail of a mother that Galen forgot the wyrran and turned. One of the creatures had managed to get close enough to grab Braden.

Galen roared and leaped, arms back and claws at the ready. He grabbed Braden with one arm, wrenching him away from the wyrran. The boy's thoughts of death, of his mother being taken from him filled Galen's mind.

Braden's fear sliced through Galen like a blade. Galen didn't have time to tell Braden all would be well. Instead, he decapitated the wyrran with one swipe of his claws.

Braden was holding on to him with all his might, his small body shaking as his head was buried in Galen's neck. "I've got you," Galen whispered and patted Braden's back. "I willna let the wyrran take you, lad."

"I know," Braden said confidently, even though his voice cracked.

Galen made his way back to the Druids and handed the boy to his mother. He was amazed when Braden's thoughts went from something so dire to happiness in a blink.

It had been a long time since Galen had experienced anything but dark thoughts and he almost didn't want to let Braden go. The boy's innocence helped to wash away the depraved thoughts of the wyrran.

"Put him in the middle. They'll grab for the weakest first," Galen cautioned.

Before the words were out of Galen's mouth a wyrran

landed on his back, and the creature's jumbled thoughts of death, blood, gore filled his mind. Galen peeled back his lips and growled. But through his need to kill the wyrran he saw the revulsion and terror on the faces of the Druids before him.

Galen spun away and grabbed for the wyrran around the neck. Without much force at all, he snapped the creature's neck and threw it off his body.

When Galen looked up, Logan was smiling in satisfaction and dead wyrran littered the ground. "Are there more?"

Logan shook his head. "I found these as I was on my way here. I kept to the tops of the trees and followed them. Did any get away?"

"A man on horseback who I believe was with the wyrran."

Logan cursed and picked up a couple of the dead wyrran at his feet. He began to toss them into a pile.

Galen pushed his god down and faced the Druids. "The wyrran know where to find you now."

"You led them to us!" someone accused.

Logan growled as he stalked away, but Galen wasn't surprised the Druids assumed that. "Nay, we did no'. They are searching for a Druid, any Druid, to take to Deirdre. We battled her. We killed her, or at least her body. Her spirit is still here, and it will take the death of a Druid to give her the magic she needs to regenerate her body."

"What if you're lying to us?" Nessa asked.

"You could have asked any of the wyrran, or the man if you'd have liked. In case any of you missed it, those wyrran were trying to kill me and Logan as well. If we were with Deirdre, would they do that? Would we have stood between you and them?"

Odara stepped forward. "What do you suggest we do?"

"You need to leave. All of you."

Mairi shook her head, her grip on Reaghan firm, unyielding. "You ask the impossible, Galen. How can we trust you when you weren't honest with us from the beginning?"

"Would you have listened to us had we told you what we were?"

"Nay."

"And we would have gone off, leaving you defenseless against those wyrran," Logan said through clenched teeth. His god no longer showed, but he didn't hide his anger. "You would be on your way to Deirdre right now, all of you, if it wasn't for me and Galen."

"Thank you," Reaghan said. "Thank you both for saving us."

Galen let out a breath. "We will always protect you. It is what we have vowed to do. I realize none of you want to leave your home, the only place you've ever known, but believe me when I say the wyrran will return."

"They willna ever stop," Logan said as he tossed more wyrran onto the pile. "Deirdre has demanded a Druid, and they will continue to hunt until they find one."

Galen glanced down at the blood that covered his body and kilt. "Logan is right. They willna stop."

"And you think leaving is our only option?" Odara asked.

Galen flexed his back as his wounds healed. He was glad none of them could see it from where they stood. "Aye. Let us take you to MacLeod Castle."

"It's too far!" someone said.

"We'd never make it!" said another.

"Deirdre will claim us today or tomorrow. Why fight it?" said yet another.

"I'm not going anywhere with Warriors!"

Galen fisted his hands and yelled, "Fight back! Why are you all so willing to give up?"

"Not all of us are," Reaghan said. She removed Mairi's hand from hers and moved to stand beside him. "I will go with you and Logan to MacLeod Castle. I want to live, and I will fight Deirdre."

TWELVE

Galen was amazed at Reaghan's courage. He knew she was frightened of him and didn't understand everything that had happened. Yet, she was willing to trust him to keep her away from Deirdre.

"We will as well," said Braden's mother, Fiona, who broke from the group. Alongside her was Braden, who gave Galen a huge smile.

Slowly, others joined the growing group of Druids behind him and Reaghan. Then, to his surprise, Odara walked away from the elders and to his other side.

Eventually, all that remained of the original group was the two elders, the two remaining men and their wives.

"Please," Galen begged. "Doona stay here. Come with us."

Nessa shook her head. "You ask the impossible, Warrior. You have evil inside you. I would sooner take my own life than give it to you to protect."

Galen was more hurt by her words than he let the others know. He bowed his head to Nessa and turned to face the group behind him. It wasn't even midday yet. They could cover some ground.

"We leave in an hour. Take only what you can carry and as much food as you can find. We will be traveling fast."

The Druids scattered to carry out his orders. Beside him Reagan paused. He saw the questions in her eyes, knew he would have to answer them soon. But she was coming with him. She trusted him enough to get her to the castle, to the MacLeods.

Once she had walked away, Logan came to stand in front of him. "Are we just going to leave the remaining six?"

"We cannot force them. Do you have another suggestion?"

Logan shook his wet head. He had cleaned his kilt and washed the blood from his body. "Deirdre will have her Druid if we leave them behind."

"I know."

"You did well. I couldn't have spoken to them as calmly. It's why I had to leave."

"Nay, my friend, you could have."

Logan snorted wryly. "My way is with my claws and the need for battle. I doona have the time to talk stubborn Druids into doing what is the only option left to them if they want to live." He sighed, and then motioned toward the loch. "Clean yourself. I will guard the Druids."

"I'll make it quick." Galen turned and jogged down to the water.

The wyrran he had killed was gone, most likely picked up by Logan and now on the pile waiting to be burned. The Warriors did not wish to leave any sign behind that those creatures had even been there. It was enough the lone man knew.

Galen stripped off his kilt and boots before he walked into the loch with long strides. When he was far enough out, he dove beneath the water. His wounds were healed, yet his body was coated with a mix of his blood and the wyrran's.

He didn't have soap to use, so he scooped sand from the bottom of the loch and scrubbed away the remains of the battle. When he was finished he retrieved his kilt and did the same.

Once he was done, he put on the wet kilt, raked his fingers through his hair, and returned to the village. Most were already gathered together awaiting him and Logan.

He nodded to them and continued through the village. Galen wanted to have another talk with Nessa and Mairi. He had to convince them to leave with him.

Galen knocked on Mairi's door, and when the elder opened it she didn't seem surprised to see him.

"You've come to change my mind?" she asked. She left the door ajar and walked away.

Galen ducked under the low door and stepped into the cottage. "We should have told you we were Warriors, but we knew how much Druids doubt us. We wanted your trust before you knew the truth. I would have kept it from you longer if I could have."

"Would you, now?" she mumbled as she stirred a pot over the fire in the hearth. "I imagine you would have. Reaghan will not change her mind. I don't know what you said to her, but whatever it is, it worked."

"You heard what I said to all the Druids. Reaghan wants to live. Would you rather she stay and await the next wave of wyrran?"

Mairi sighed and set aside the spoon. "What I want is of no consequence, Galen. I do not have confidence in you, as Odara does, but neither do I think you to be as evil as Nessa does. This is the only home I've ever known. We've always been safe. Until you came."

"What do you know of the Warriors? Do you know we are immortal? Do you know Deirdre kills most of the families so the Warriors have no reason to return?"

Mairi's brown eyes caught his. "Is that what she did to your family?"

"What I'm trying to say is that change is a part of life whether we want the change or not. You need to decide if you want to take the chance of being brought to Deirdre or come with us. I know Reaghan would feel better if you were with her."

"I'll kill myself before I allow Deirdre to have me."

Galen rubbed his eyes with his thumb and forefinger. He could use the part of his power he had dared to utilize only once before. He could get inside Mairi's mind and command her to come with him. He didn't want to do that, but if she didn't change her mind before they departed, he would have no other choice.

"Help us fight Deirdre, Mairi. We have a common enemy. We should band together."

"There is so much doubt in my mind. I no longer know what to believe."

"Trust me," Galen urged. "I will see you to safety. I give you my vow."

He left then, knowing it was futile to speak more of it. Mairi would make up her mind, and whatever she decided, nothing could change it.

And as much as he didn't want to, he knew he needed to speak to Nessa as well. He was on his way there when he heard the scream.

By the time Galen reached Nessa's cottage, Logan was there and Druids were gathered around the doorway. Galen took hold of Odara's frail shoulders and pulled her away from the door to peer inside.

"Why?" Odara wailed and covered her hands with her face.

Galen took one look at Nessa and the two elderly couples slumped on the floor and sighed.

"What happened?" Mairi demanded as she pushed through the crowd.

"They killed themselves," Odara answered.

Mairi pulled Odara into her arms, their tears mingling. Mairi's gaze lifted to Galen's, and she gave him a nod.

Galen closed the door to the cottage and walked away.

He couldn't believe Nessa and the two couples had despised him so much that they would rather take their own lives than trust him.

"I gather Mairi is coming with us," Logan said as he caught up with Galen.

"It appears so."

Logan halted and blew out a breath. "They must have hated and feared us tremendously to take their own lives."

"Doona think on it. Soon we will be on our way back to the castle."

"Without the artifact." Logan crossed his arms over his chest and raised a brow.

Galen nodded. "There's nothing we can do about it. I'm hoping that since Mairi is now coming with us, she will bring it, and once at MacLeod Castle the others can talk her into handing it over."

"Our travel is going to be slow. Too slow. It willna take that rider you saw long to return to Deirdre and gather more wyrran."

"Let's hope he has to return to Cairn Toul to do that. We will be with the MacLeods by the time he finds us." He cursed and ground his teeth together. "I should have gone after him."

"Nay. You did the right thing," Logan said. "As it was, the wyrran nearly got away with Braden. I should have known they'd go after the lad first."

Galen rubbed his hand over the whiskers on his cheek. "I'd have chased them all the way to Cairn Toul if I'd had to. I willna allow them to take any Druid, much less a child."

They turned as one to the small group of Druids. The group was down to eighteen, but still a large enough crew that another Warrior would have been helpful.

"Do you think when the wyrran return they will bring Warriors?" Logan whispered.

Galen hid his scowl. "Pray they don't. We'll have our hands full if they do."

"Then we need to get moving."

Galen couldn't agree more. He walked to the Druids and looked at their expectant, fearful faces. "The pace we set is going to be swift. We'll rest as often as we can, but understand that we need to get as far away from this area as possible before nightfall."

"We will do the best we can," Odara promised. Her eyes were red, and tears still coursed down her wrinkled face.

He gave her a nod. "Either Logan or I will be in the lead and the other behind you. We need to stay in a tight group. The wyrran move fast, so if there's another attack, Logan and I need to be able to fight around you."

"Like this morn," Braden called out.

Galen smiled at the eager lad. "Aye, like this morn. If you become too tired and begin to lag behind, let us know so we can take a break."

"How long is the journey?" Mairi asked.

Logan shrugged and looked helplessly at Galen. Galen also shrugged. "As Warriors, we are able to run fast. That is how we came here, so I have no idea how long it will take to walk."

"Do any of you talk to trees?" Logan questioned. "We have a Druid who can hear and speak to them. We could send her a message so other Warriors from MacLeod Castle could meet us along the way."

Odara looked around and shook her head. "None of us have such a gift."

Galen glanced at Reaghan, wondering if with all her magic she could somehow do it. "Then let's be on our way."

He led the small group beneath the ancient stones, his senses alert for any out-of-the-ordinary movement, anything that might be wyrran or someone sent by Deirdre.

How he wished Fallon were with them. Fallon could

have used his power and had them all back at the castle in less than a blink. Instead, they were going to have to make the long, treacherous journey themselves.

He paused beside a steep drop. The Druids would have a difficult time descending it without help. If he called Logan to him, they would think he didn't want to touch them. How could he tell them he could read their minds with the barest of contact? They were half afraid of him now, and if they knew that, they would never go with them to MacLeod Castle.

Galen took a deep breath and approached the drop. He held out his hand to the first Druid. "Keep going. Follow the loch," he told them, trying his best—and failing miserably—to block their thoughts.

Even the brief time they touched him he saw their anxiety, their panic, their hopes, their dreams, and the terror which filled each and every one of them.

Each emotion filled him as if it were his own. It suffocated him until the touch was gone. He barely had time for a breath before someone else reached for his hand.

A few hesitated to touch him, but in the end they accepted his assistance. Reaghan was the last, and Galen almost sighed when he saw her. His head ached from all the thoughts he'd intercepted from the Druids.

Reaghan looked into his eyes and took his hand. There were so many questions swimming in her gray eyes, questions he couldn't run away from.

But no thoughts filled his head. He wanted to hold on to her forever and never let her go. He didn't know what was different about her, why he couldn't see into her mind. He was just grateful for the relief.

"Galen," she whispered.

"I know," he said. "Later."

"Promise?"

Her demand surprised him. He held her hand long after she was down the slope. "Aye."

A small smile pulled at her lips. "I will hold you to that, Warrior."

For the first time since his god had been loosened inside him, he liked the sound of being called a Warrior.

THIRTEEN

Reaghan's entire body ached as she crumbled to the ground after the many hours they had traveled. Galen and Logan hadn't been jesting when they said the pace would be quick. She was amazed at the distance they had covered since leaving the loch, taking only short breaks. Their noon meal had been eaten so quickly Reaghan hadn't tasted it.

But that's what happened when you ran from evil.

She looked over her shoulder, and in the distance she could make out the mountains which surrounded the loch. Her home was slowly fading into the distance. Sadness filled her. When she had been leaving, it was fear that propelled her forward.

Now, as she looked back, she thought of the years she had spent in the safety of the beautiful loch. She hoped one day she could return, but if she couldn't, she would keep her memories close.

Their respite was nearly finished. She could see Galen and Logan as they spoke quietly to one another, their heads close together. They kept away from the group unless they were walking. It was as if the Warriors knew how ill at ease they made the Druids.

It angered Reaghan that so many still doubted Logan and Galen's motives. The Warriors had saved them, but if it wasn't for the fear of losing their lives, Reaghan was sure many of the Druids would have ignored the men's urging to leave.

Reaghan thought of the man who had seen her at the loch, the man who had made her skin crawl. Galen had said he was from Deirdre. She didn't doubt Galen. There had been evil in the man's eyes.

Her thoughts then turned to Galen. She had been surprised to see he was a Warrior, but thinking back to what he had said, she should have known. There had always been something that set Galen apart from other men. Now she knew it was because of the god inside him.

Galen had said he would answer her questions, but Reaghan didn't want to wait any longer. As if he felt her gaze on him, he turned his head and looked at her.

Even from a distance, the connection that held them, wrapped them in its grip, tugged at her. She wanted to go to Galen, to have his arms envelop her and hold her tight against his hard body. She wanted to hear him say everything was going to be all right.

Even when she knew it probably wouldn't be.

All she had to do was observe how Galen and Logan studied the terrain, and how they kept the Druids in a tight group, to know they expected another attack.

Reaghan shivered as she recalled how easily Galen had killed the wyrran. Despite her fear, or maybe because of it, she hadn't been able to take her eyes off him as he had battled the wyrran in the village.

He had been magnificent, utterly lethal with his claws and body. She had glimpsed the fangs in his mouth when he had roared, and she had been spellbound. Everything about Galen in his Warrior form intrigued her, entranced her.

With him, she knew she was secure. When he had snatched Braden from the wyrran, Reaghan had known

Galen would've done anything to keep the boy away from the creatures.

How could anyone ever think Galen or Logan was evil? They had proven themselves without a doubt. The others, however, wouldn't be so easy to convince.

"Time to go," Logan called as he took the lead.

Reaghan bit back her groan as she rose to her feet. The rolling landscape was beautiful to behold, but becoming more and more difficult for them to cross because of their fatigue.

The sun was steadily sinking in the sky. It wouldn't be long before they stopped for the night, but it wouldn't come quickly enough for her. Reaghan looked forward to a decent meal and somewhere she could sleep.

A smile pulled at her lips when she saw Logan lift a weary Braden in his arms. Logan said something to Fiona, and then he lifted Braden over his head and settled the lad atop his shoulders.

"You seem surprised."

Reaghan jumped and turned her head to find Galen behind her. "I'm surprised Fiona allowed Logan to take Braden."

"Who better to protect the lad than a Warrior?" he asked, his cobalt gaze holding hers.

"Exactly. None of us could have carried Braden for long. I'm glad Logan has him."

"How are you holding up?"

She shrugged and fell into step as they continued. Their pace had slowed but still it was quicker than she would have liked. She couldn't feel her feet anymore, and her legs felt as heavy as tree trunks. "I'm doing better than most. It's the older ones I worry about."

"Odara," Galen murmured.

Reaghan nodded. "None of us are used to this."

"I wish we could slow the pace, but I fear we willna reach MacLeod Castle before the wyrran attack again."

"Are all the men at MacLeod Castle Warriors?"

"All but one," he answered. "His name is Malcolm Monroe. He helped one of us, and in return, Deirdre sent Warriors to kill him. Broc found them and rescued Malcolm, but the damage had already been done."

Intrigued, she asked, "What happened?"

"Sonya used her healing magic, but she couldn't mend his arm. He lost the use of his right arm. Malcolm was to be laird of his clan."

"So he stays at the castle?"

"Aye. Fallon, our leader, made him welcome."

She lifted her skirts as they started up another hill. "Why would Malcolm help you if he knew the danger?"

"His cousin Larena. She's the only female Warrior we know of, and she's helping us. Deirdre tried to take her, but Larena is Fallon's, and he wasn't about to give up the woman he loves."

Reaghan smiled and took a deep breath. "I cannot wait to meet Fallon and especially Larena. A female Warrior. Amazing."

"Aye. We all thought the same thing." Galen chuckled. "Woman or not, Larena can hold her own in battle."

"The stories of the ancient Celts and Romans are ones we hear continuously. The idea that the *mies* would align with the *droughs* is almost impossible to believe."

"Yet they did it for Britain. For all of us."

"Ah," she said with a grin. "The tales say the gods, though bound, passed through the bloodline."

Galen let out a long breath. "They did. To the strongest warrior of each generation."

"Which you were. Some say the men who hope to become Warriors find Deirdre."

"Maybe. I didna."

His voice was low, rage laced in every syllable. "I'm sorry, Galen. I didn't mean to imply you had gone to Deirdre."

"I know," he said before she could trip over more of her words.

Reaghan looked at the ground and bit her lip. She hadn't meant to make him angry. Whatever had happened to turn him into a Warrior wasn't pleasant. And if he hadn't gone to Deirdre, then how had he become a Warrior?

She was thankful he stayed beside her. He didn't speak again, but at least he hadn't moved away. On they walked, the clouds building above them and the loch fading behind them. Galen made sure no one followed, but always he was at her side.

It comforted Reaghan in ways she couldn't begin to explain. She felt as if she belonged with Galen, as if she had been waiting her entire life for him.

As soon as Galen spotted the grove of trees nestled in the valley, he knew it was the perfect place to stop for the night. The hills would hide their fire, and the night would consume the smoke.

Galen hesitated to build a fire, but the Druids needed to eat to sustain their strength. Just a little over half a day's travel and they were so exhausted they could barely stand.

Logan had stayed to guard the camp while Galen tracked and killed a deer. Each Druid carried a satchel of food, but Galen feared it wouldn't be enough to get them to the castle. Which meant they would have to stop more often to hunt.

The women quickly skinned the animal and began to cook it. The delicious aroma of meat roasting over the fire made Galen's mouth water. He hadn't taken food from the

Druids during the noon meal, but he would take it now. He and Logan's strength would not be compromised by missing a few meals, but they couldn't miss many.

As soon as the meat was declared cooked, Galen and Logan distributed the portions.

Logan turned his back to the Druids and the fire and faced his companion. "We're no' going to make it, Galen."

"We have to. Any one of them could hold the artifact. We cannot allow any of them to be taken."

"We need more Warriors."

"Which we doona have," Galen stated. He clenched his jaw, determined to see every Druid arrive at MacLeod Castle. "We can do this."

Logan turned his head, his hazel eyes meeting Galen's. "It's no' you I doubt."

Before Galen could ask what he meant, Logan faded into the shadows. Galen knew he wouldn't go far. Logan would scout the area and make sure they wouldn't be surprised by visitors.

Galen's gaze was constantly drawn to Reaghan. In spite of her own fatigue, she moved from Druid to Druid offering water and making sure they had all they needed. She spent extra time with Braden, making the lad smile as he ate.

Soon he would have to give Reaghan the answers she sought and speak of things he would rather forget. He could lie to her, but the attraction between them was too great to even consider lying.

He would give her the truth, regardless of how much it pained him. He had gotten angry earlier, but the thought of any man going to Deirdre willingly made his stomach sour.

Galen sat and leaned against a tree while they finished eating. To his surprise, Reaghan sat beside him. She offered him a smile then turned her gaze to the fire.

He took two bites of his dinner before he got up the courage to begin. He kept his voice low so others wouldn't hear. "I was out hunting when the wyrran came. They surrounded me before I could blink. And then I saw the Warrior. His skin was the darkest shade of purple, and he struck me unconscious with one blow to my head."

"You don't have to tell me," she said.

"Aye, Reaghan, I do." Galen swallowed his food. "I awoke in Deirdre's mountain, locked in a prison. I could hear others. Their screams of agony, their cries of misery. I knew I would die there."

"Except you didn't, did you?"

"I did, in a way. The Galen I was before died. Once Deirdre unbound my god, I became who you see now. I knew there was nothing Deirdre could do that would make me align with her. Others cautioned me that she had used their families against them. She asked countless times about my family, insulting my mother so she could get a response."

Reaghan took a bite of her meal and asked, "Did you? Respond as she wanted?"

"Nay. I told her my family meant nothing to me, and I proved it by ignoring everything she said and threatened to do to them. All the while I prayed they were safe. I was in Cairn Toul for twenty years. She never broke me, though she tried many times."

"How did you get out?"

Galen finished his portion of food and leaned his head against the tree. "Others had escaped. I knew there was a way. I just had to find it. When she summoned me to her chambers to entice me to her bed, I knew my chance had come. She thought I was content, so she didn't use another Warrior to escort me. Instead, she used her servants. It was nothing to get past them and away to freedom."

Reagan's eyes were huge with wonder. "Didn't she chase you?"

"Deirdre doesn't leave her mountain. She sent others, but I managed to get away."

"And your family?"

"I let them think me dead." He swallowed past the painful lump those words evoked. "I looked in on them when I was free. It was a chance I shouldn't have taken. Deirdre could have gone there first and killed them just to spite me. Fortunately, she didna."

"Did you talk to them? Your family, I mean?"

Galen shook his head. "I didna dare. They would have had questions, questions I couldna answer."

"I'm so sorry, Galen. I had no idea."

He shrugged. "It was a long time ago."

Long ago, but it still haunted his memories.

FOURTEEN

Reaghan was aghast at Galen's story. Her heart ached for him and the family he'd lost. The thought that someone like Deirdre could take a person and unleash an ancient god within that person left her with ice in her veins.

She glanced sideways at Galen. He sat still, his eyes the only thing moving as they scanned the area. "Tell me of the Warriors? I don't know if the stories I've heard are true or not. I saw your wounds earlier down by the loch, but they're gone now."

"Aye. Our wounds heal quickly. We're immortal, Reaghan."

She chewed and swallowed her last bit of venison before she reached for a water skin. "So you cannot die?"

"I can die, but only if my head is taken from my body."

Reaghan couldn't imagine anyone being able to do that to a Warrior. They were too powerful, too quick. Too deadly. "No one will ever get near you to do that then."

One side of his lips lifted in a smile as he turned his head to look at her. "I wish I could say you are right, but our battle with Deirdre continues. As long as it does, Warriors will fight Warriors."

"Is it true you have powers?"

He glanced at his hands before he fisted them. "Aye. Each Warrior has his god's power. We also change the color our god favored."

"Which is why you were green and Logan silver?"

"Aye. My god is Ycewold, a trickster god. All Warriors will change color. We have fangs, claws, and enhanced senses. Each of us has a special power as well."

She licked her lips as she tried to take it all in. Every answer he gave her led to new questions. "Like what?"

"Fallon can be standing before you, and in a blink, he's somewhere else. They call it *leum,* jumping. Lucan, the middle MacLeod, can command the shadows and darkness. Then there is Quinn, the youngest MacLeod, who can speak to animals."

Reaghan was speechless. "This goes beyond anything I could ever imagine. What about you and Logan? What powers does each of you possess?"

"Logan's god grants him the power to command liquid, any liquid. He could part a loch with just a thought."

"And you?" she asked when he said no more.

"Some Warriors have powers that are . . ."—he shrugged—"beneficial."

"Galen, what is your power?"

He sighed deeply, heavily. "I can read people's minds."

She blinked, unsure if she heard him correctly. "You mean you can hear my thoughts? Now?"

"Nay," he said quickly, and shook his head. "I have to be touching someone. It's only when others touch me, or I touch them, that I see into their minds. Other Warriors aren't able to use their power unless their god is released. Mine . . . mine occurs all the time."

Reaghan shifted to face him. "Are you telling me when we kissed, when we . . . You were reading my mind?"

His dark blue gaze bored into hers, his brow furrowed. "Reaghan, you're the only one I've ever touched that I doona see into your mind."

"But the others you can?"

"Aye."

That one word held a wealth of meaning. She could see how it distressed him by the hard line of his jaw, his compressed lips. "So every Druid you handed down the slope today, you saw into their minds."

He gave a single, simple nod.

"And the wyrran?"

Another small nod.

"By the saints," she murmured. She couldn't imagine how it must feel, to have that kind of power and not be able to control it. "How is it you cannot see into my mind?"

"I doona know. When I first touched you I was too stunned to do anything but want more contact. Then, later, it didn't matter. I found someone I could touch and not worry about seeing and hearing their thoughts. You cannot know what that means to me."

Her heart ached for him, but most especially because in his words she heard the despair he wouldn't admit. "Has there never been someone you could touch without seeing their thoughts?"

"Never. I've had to keep my distance from people for that very reason."

There was something in his words, something that told her there was more to it. "You left someone because of your power?"

He visibly swallowed and clenched his hands. "After I escaped Deirdre's I found a widow in need of someone to help around her cottage. In exchange, she fed me. I thought I just needed to learn to control my powers."

"What happened?" Reaghan whispered.

"I thought she wanted my touch, but every time I held her, she would think of her dead husband. I confronted her with it." He closed his eyes and shook his head. "The idea of someone in her mind was too much for her. Whatever kind thoughts she might have had for me turned vicious over the following weeks. Until she tried to plunge a dagger in my chest."

Reaghan covered her mouth with her hand. As a Druid she had been around magic her entire life. She understood there were things that couldn't be explained. But there were others who did not understand.

She scooted closer and lifted his hand into hers. "Try to see into my mind."

He leaned away from her, his face a mask of distaste. "Why would you want that?"

"Don't you want to know if you are gaining control over your power, or if it's just me?"

"Why would you think this had anything to do with you?"

How could she tell him about the dreams of people and places she had never seen before, but knew? Was it the fever that had caused her memory loss, or was it something more? "I have no recollections of my past, Galen. Maybe whatever is blocking those memories prevents you from seeing into my mind."

He gazed at her for several long moments before he closed his eyes. One heartbeat, two. Reaghan waited anxiously for Galen to tell her something, anything.

Finally, he opened his eyes. Relief blazed in his cobalt gaze. "I see nothing."

She released his hand and looked into the fire. Galen might be happy, but Reaghan felt disappointment. It just confirmed to her that there was something wrong with her mind. "As I suspected."

"I'm sorry."

Reaghan waved away his words. Her hope of him helping her to find her past faded into the night sky. "There's no need. You will never fear touching me and seeing into my mind."

"I know it upsets you, but it pleases me greatly."

Unable to help herself, she smiled at him. "And I'm glad. You saved all of us this morn. You and Logan both. Without you, I wouldn't be here now."

"Many still doona trust us."

"They probably never will. It is their way to distrust anything they don't know, and since they never leave the village, they know nothing. It doesn't help that we've always been told the Warriors are evil."

He chuckled and stretched his legs out in front of him before he crossed his ankles.

"How long have you been a Warrior?" She knew she shouldn't ask, but she was curious as to how long he'd been immortal.

"Are you sure you want to know?"

"I'm sure."

He rose to his feet in one fluid motion of power and agility. "Two hundred and fifty years. Now get some rest. Tomorrow will be longer than today."

Reaghan followed him with her eyes until he was lost in the darkness. It wasn't until she was on her side, her arm tucked beneath her head, that she realized an entire day had gone by without the ache in her head.

Galen found Logan leaning against a tree outside the camp. "I'll take first watch."

Logan shrugged. "All right. How did Reaghan react to your answers?"

"How do you think?"

"She seemed to take it fairly well from what I could see. And hear."

Galen grunted. "Mind your own business."

"So you really couldna see into her mind?"

"Nay." Galen took a deep breath. He looked out into the cold, lonely darkness. "She thinks it might be something from her past that is blocking me from her mind."

"And what do you think?"

"I think there is much more to Reaghan than meets the eye. There is no one I have touched in my years as a Warrior whose mind I haven't seen into."

Logan shrugged and pushed off the tree. "It should prove an interesting journey then."

Galen watched as his friend went to the fire and cut off another piece of meat with his claws before he moved far away from the fire and settled to eat.

As Galen walked the perimeter of their camp, his thoughts turned again and again to Reaghan. He hadn't wanted to try to see into her mind, but like her, he was interested as to why he couldn't.

He had assumed he was gaining control over his power, when in fact that wasn't the circumstance. And it probably never would be the case.

Galen was on his second pass around the camp when Mairi stepped into his path. He paused and considered the elder. "I gather you wish to speak to me?"

"I do. Can you spare a moment?"

He nodded and waited for her to come to him. She didn't fully trust him. If she wanted to talk, she would have to take those few steps to close the distance.

"I saw you speaking to Reaghan," Mairi said.

"I've spoken to many Druids today."

Her lips flattened briefly. "You know what I mean. Reaghan isn't meant for you, Galen."

"Who is she meant for?"

Mairi dropped her gaze, refusing to meet his eyes. "That is not your concern. You need to let Reaghan know you aren't interested in her other than as a friend."

"But I am interested. Very. Why should I lie to her and myself?"

Mairi's eyes snapped fire as she met his gaze. "Because I am asking it."

"Nay, you are demanding it. I will no' do as you ask. No' without an explanation." He crossed his arms over his chest and waited for her to speak.

His god demanded he touch her and see into her mind. He could find out all he needed to know with that one touch. But Galen had told himself he wouldn't abuse his power in such a way. Unless Mairi left him no choice.

Mairi rolled her eyes. She shifted from one foot to the other before she relented. "I will answer what I can. What do you want to know?"

"Who is Reaghan meant for?"

"That I cannot tell you."

Just as Galen suspected. "Was it a fever that robbed Reaghan of her memories?"

Mairi was silent so long Galen thought she might not respond. "In a manner," she finally answered.

"And before the fever? What happened?"

Mairi twisted her fingers, her anxiety vibrating off her. "Reaghan lived a full life. She was happy."

"There is something you aren't telling me. What is so important about her that it must be kept secret?"

She shrugged. "There is much I cannot tell you."

"Until you give me the answers I need, I willna stay away from Reaghan. I enjoy her company, and she enjoys mine. Why should we deny ourselves?"

Mairi gaze silently beseeched him before she turned on her heel and stomped away.

Galen shook his head after the elder. He suspected she wanted Reaghan kept away from him because he was a Warrior. And before she discovered that, it was most likely because Mairi hadn't known him, didn't trust him.

But the way it felt to hold Reaghan in his arms, to taste her sweet lips, was like paradise. Galen still recalled the women he had made love to before his god had been unbound. After his god was released, he had given in to his needs on occasion, though he regretted every one since he couldn't stop seeing into their minds.

Despite all of that, none of those women had felt half as good as Reaghan. Reaghan was special, and not just because he couldn't read her mind. It went much deeper.

He wanted her against him again, to caress and lick her silken skin, to plunge his fingers in her wild cascade of curls. He wanted her soft body atop him, to cup her breasts as she slid down his cock. He wanted to thrust inside her, to drive into her hard and fast and hear her scream her pleasure.

Galen cursed himself and the arousal that wouldn't go away, not with Reaghan just paces from him.

He looked at the stars through the tree branches, but the clouds blocked even the moon from his view. A storm was brewing, he could tell by the rising wind. Rain was coming, and he feared it would only slow them more.

FIFTEEN

It was the pain, the excruciating, stomach-rolling, body-twisting pain, that pulled Reaghan out of her sleep. She wanted to curl into herself, to let out the cry that built inside her.

Instead, she lay as still as she could, her eyes squeezed tightly closed as the agony took over. Her brain burned, and every beat of her heart made the throbbing even worse.

Reaghan tried to think of something pleasant, something which would help to ease her. Her mind immediately thought of Galen, but not even the memories of him holding and kissing her could help with the pain in her head.

The only thing she could rejoice in was that it happened while everyone was still asleep and she was already lying down. She didn't want Galen to see her like this and think her weak. He was a Warrior, an immortal with the power to read minds. What would he think of a woman who was brought to her knees by an ache in her head?

A tear spilled from between her lids and rolled across her cheek to her nose. Why were the headaches plaguing her? And why were they getting worse?

Every sound, however minuscule, echoed like a drum inside Reaghan's head. She winced at the call of a bird nearby that made her head feel as though it were cracking open. The soft crunch of a footstep nearly made her heart stop from the anguish.

She knew it was either Logan or Galen, and she prayed it wasn't Galen. Another tear joined the first, and soon the pain became too much to bear. Reaghan fell into the blackness that surrounded her, the pain beating at her from all sides, drowning her in an abyss of misery and grief.

Galen studied Reaghan. Her body was too stiff as she lay on her side, her back to him. She was curled into herself, her legs drawn up close to her chest. If he didn't know better, he would think she was in pain.

"What is it?" Logan whispered.

Galen thrust his chin out toward Reaghan. "Something is wrong."

Logan watched her a long moment before he shook his head. "Maybe she's just having a bad dream."

"Nay. It's more than that. It's as if she's in pain."

"They are all likely sore this morn. She didna hurt herself yesterday, did she?"

"No' that I saw," Galen answered.

"Go to her then."

Galen started to do just that when he recalled Mairi's visit the night before. "Mairi said Reaghan wasna meant for me, but she wouldn't tell me who Reaghan was meant for."

Logan snorted. "From what I've seen, Reaghan is like a daughter to Mairi. Mairi wants to protect her, just as any mother would. The fact that Mairi doesna trust us just pushes her to protect Reaghan more. If you want Reaghan, let her decide for herself."

"I suppose you're right."

"Of course I am," Logan said with a wide smile. "Now go see to her."

Galen didn't hesitate a second time. He walked softly,

his boots making nary a sound as he wound his way through the sleeping Druids.

The sun was rising, though its light had yet to break through the darkness. On the horizon Galen could see clouds reflecting yellow and deep orange from the sun. It was time to rouse the Druids, but first, Galen wanted to check on Reaghan.

He didn't go to her. Instead he made sure he was far enough away so he could see her face. She looked to be sleeping, but her eyes were squeezed shut and her hands were fisted tightly.

Was it a nightmare as Logan had speculated? Or was it something more?

Galen took a step toward her when something flew over him. He glanced up and saw a falcon. His gaze narrowed on the bird. It was odd to spot a peregrine similar to the ones at MacLeod Castle and Loch Awe.

Once the bird had disappeared over the trees, Galen lowered his gaze and found Logan staring after the falcon. In Galen's life of Druids and magic, he had learned there was no such thing as coincidence.

Logan turned back to him, his eyes hard and his jaw set. Galen gave him a nod to track the bird and see what he could find. Hopefully it was nothing, but they couldn't be too careful. Not with Druids in their care.

When Galen looked again at Reaghan she was leaning on her elbow and wiping her face with her other hand. Her hand shook, and she was pale as death.

She sat up and reached for a water skin from which she drank deeply before splashing some of the liquid on her face. The others were waking, leaving Galen no time to talk to Reaghan privately.

Oatcakes were soon passed around. Holding an oatcake between his teeth, Galen bent and covered the embers of their fire with dirt. As he stood, he took a bite of oatcake before turning when he heard Logan approach. "Anything?"

"Nothing. The bird went off to hunt."

"What do you think?"

Logan shrugged and took an offered oatcake. "This wasn't just a twist of fate. I still feel as if I'm being watched. Something is afoot here."

"I agree. We'll keep our eye to the skies."

Once the Druids had eaten, Logan got them on their feet and ready to begin the day's journey. Only Braden groaned aloud, but Galen could see the other's faces, and they weren't looking forward to it any more than wee Braden.

Logan once more took the lad and tossed him into the air. Braden laughed heartily, the sound brightening the mood in the camp. Only then did Logan lift Braden to his shoulders and set out.

Galen and Logan had both scouted ahead on their watches to look for places they could be ambushed or spots that were perfect for others to trap them.

Neither of them had slept, instead going over the safest routes they should take with the Druids. Some routes meant adding extra time, but they had little choice knowing Deirdre would be after them.

As Logan led the Druids off, Galen stayed to make sure no one left anything behind. He tried to catch Reaghan's gaze to ask her to stay to the back of the group so he could speak with her, but Mairi linked arms with Reaghan and they set off together.

Galen sighed, his worry settling like a stone in his gut.

The worst of the pain had faded, but Reaghan's body was shaky and weak. Mairi had known instantly what had occurred and gone to her. Reaghan wasn't about to push aside her offer of assistance, not when she could barely walk on her own.

"How bad is it?" Mairi whispered.

"The worst has passed."

"You are still in pain."

It wasn't a question. "Only a little."

Mairi's lips flattened in a tight line, her brow furrowed in concern. "You need to rest. Let me speak to the Warriors."

"Nay," Reaghan replied more forcefully than she intended. "Leave it, please. I will be all right."

"As you wish," Mairi said, but there was doubt in her tone.

Reaghan didn't care that the elder disagreed with her. She would get past the headache without Galen knowing. It was foolish, she knew, but Reaghan wanted him to see her as strong and capable. Not weak and sickly.

She had known Galen wanted to speak with her. It took all her control not to turn her head to him and drink in the sight of his muscular form in the glow of the morning sun.

He had worn his dark blond hair loose ever since the battle with the wyrran. It fell in waves around his face, accentuating his square jaw and bringing out the bronze color of his skin. She itched to run her fingers through the thick strands again as his arms held her tightly against his chest.

Reaghan took a deep breath and tried to quell the desire that awoke in her body with just a thought of Galen. It warmed her blood and made her heart race until it settled between her legs in a pulsing ache.

The pain that had clouded her vision and weakened her began to abate. Reaghan let her arms drop from around Mairi, no longer needing to lean on the elder.

"When did the pain begin?" Mairi asked.

Reaghan shrugged. "It woke me from my slumber. I didn't have any pain yesterday, so I thought it might be going away."

"Nay, my child," Mairi mumbled. "I'm afraid that isn't so."

Reaghan frowned and turned her head to Mairi. "How do you know this?"

"The headaches have been coming on for over a month now. I don't think they would just go away so easily."

Since Mairi had her head down Reaghan couldn't see into her eyes and discern if she was lying. Reaghan wanted to believe the elder, but she wasn't sure she could. Mairi's reasoning was plausible, but there had been something in her voice that told Reaghan the elder knew more than she said.

Reaghan decided a direct approach would be her best strategy. "You wouldn't keep anything from me about this, would you, Mairi?"

"All I want is for you to be safe from Deirdre. I would never endanger you."

Reaghan's heart fell. Mairi hadn't answered her question, and that in itself was all the response Reaghan needed. The higher the sun rose the more sadness crept over her. Because she realized that something about her past, something about the pain in her head, was being kept from her.

It made Reaghan begin to analyze everything Mairi had ever told her. She knew the elder cared for her, of that there was no doubt. But why did Mairi persist in keeping things about her past hidden?

Reaghan continued to keep her distance from Galen, since she wasn't yet ready to talk to him. She suspected he had seen she was in pain and would want to know why. Even if he hadn't seen her this morning, he would know something was wrong now. Though she longed to confide in someone, Galen had enough to worry about with getting all of them to MacLeod Castle.

After their first rest, Reaghan positioned herself near

Odara. The elder was having a difficult time of it, her small frame barely able to keep up. Reaghan gave her a drink from the water skin and wrapped an arm around her.

"You are good to me," Odara said.

Reaghan smiled. "Why wouldn't I be? You've always been kind to me."

"Mairi tells me you had another headache this morning."

"Aye." Reaghan looked into the kindly green eyes. "Why do I feel as though Mairi knows more about my past than she is telling me? Why do I feel as though she knows what is happening to me, but refuses to help?"

Odara sighed, her wrinkles becoming more pronounced as she frowned. "Mairi just wants what's best for you. We all do, sweetling."

"I want an honest answer. Why can't anyone tell me what I want to know?"

"Sometimes not knowing is for the best."

"Only those with that knowledge would dare to speak those words."

Odara narrowed her gaze at Reaghan. "You think I enjoy keeping secrets? It kills the soul slowly and surely every day those secrets are kept."

"Then tell me. Tell me why my past is such a secret," Reaghan pleaded.

"If only it were that simple." Odara released a pent-up breath. "Reaghan, all I will tell you is that your past is better left forgotten."

Her words made a thread of fear wind around Reaghan's spine. "And the headaches? You know what is causing them, don't you?"

"Not exactly. I would love to take the pain from you, but I haven't that kind of magic. The headaches will end soon."

*   *   *

Brenna pulled back her magic and dropped her head in her hands as the fatigue pulled at her. She sat surrounded by the Druids of her village, their hands linked, murmuring ancient words to give her magic added strength.

"Well, daughter?"

Brenna lifted her head and looked into her father's dark eyes. "The peregrine is still willing to allow me to use her vision and hearing. I've seen the Warriors once again. They are taking the Druids to MacLeod Castle."

Her father, Kerwyn, was head of their village. He walked around her slowly as if digesting her words. He always took his time formulating things in his mind. Her father was never hasty about anything.

Until it came to asking her to use her magic to connect with a falcon and spy for him. It had begun as a favor to fellow Druids to ensure that a man once considered their ally no longer leaked their whereabouts.

But once her father learned just how great her power was, and how long she could stay connected to the falcon, he had bid her use the bird to observe the goings-on at MacLeod Castle.

Brenna, like most in her village, wasn't sure if the rumors about the MacLeods being at their castle once more were true. One look, though, and she had not only seen the MacLeods but many other Warriors.

And Druids.

When the two Warriors had set out on a journey, Brenna had bid the peregrine follow them. Thankfully, the bird had done as she asked.

Brenna wasn't sure how much longer she would be able to use the falcon. Not only was the peregrine eager to return to her home, but the Warriors had noticed the bird and were becoming suspicious.

"When can you connect with the falcon again?" her father asked.

"Give the child time to recover," Daghda, one of the elders, stated.

Brenna met Daghda's eyes and gave the woman a nod of thanks. Brenna could have connected with the peregrine again, but with rest she could keep the connection far longer.

Kerwyn stared at Brenna for several moments before he turned and walked out of the circle. Brenna was glad to know that she had been given a respite, but she was certain her father would return soon.

His need to know about the Warriors was more than interesting. From all Brenna had seen of the Warriors they were protecting the Druids.

It hadn't taken the rumors long to reach the Isle of Skye about Warriors attacking Cairn Toul and Deirdre. Brenna hadn't believed a word of it. Until she had listened to a conversation between the Warriors Logan and Galen.

It appeared they had not only attacked, but had succeeded in killing Deirdre. Except Deirdre wasn't dead after all. She was just without a body.

"Brenna?" Daghda said as she knelt in front of her. Her gray hair was kept away from her face by intricate braids that joined together at the back of her neck to form one thick braid. "Are you well?"

Brenna smiled and patted the hand atop hers. "Aye. Just tired."

"Kerwyn asks too much of you."

"It is my obligation to help our village any way I can."

Daghda snorted. "Not at the price of your life, child. You should tell your father you need your rest. If not, he will continue to push you until you are drained of all your magic."

Brenna licked her lips as she rose to her feet. She helped Daghda to stand and together they walked out of the circle. "Why is my father so concerned with the MacLeods?"

"Ah," Daghda said with a frown, her intelligent green eyes seeing much. "He doesn't believe the MacLeods fight Deirdre. He fears they are there to draw Druids to them in a false plan to keep them from Deirdre, only to eventually turn all the Druids over to her."

"Do you believe that as well?"

Daghda let out a long breath. "Child, at my age, I've learned not to jump to conclusions. Of all of us, you've seen the MacLeods and the Warriors at their castle the most. What do you think?"

"I'm not sure," Gwynn murmured.

"Don't think to lie to me."

Brenna's head jerked to the elder. The tone had been sharp, and Daghda's eyes were soft as they stared at her. "I'm not sure anyone wants to hear my opinion."

"I do," Daghda said. "Now tell me."

Brenna swallowed and glanced around to make sure no one was near as she walked Daghda to her cottage. "I believe the Warriors are fighting Deirdre. I watched as the two Warriors at Loch Awe battled the wyrran. If they were working with Deirdre, why not just let the wyrran take the Druids?"

"Good question. One I think you should pose to your father."

But Brenna knew better than to question her father. On anything.

SIXTEEN

Galen was leading the group when he called a halt for the noon meal. It had taken all he and Logan could do to keep the Druids moving.

The only one not giving them problems was wee Braden. The lad had bonded with Logan, and it was obvious Logan had a soft spot for the boy. Braden seemed to sense when he could be with Logan and when he needed to stay with his mother and the other Druids.

"I fear we willna get them on their feet again," Logan grumbled from beside Galen.

Galen shrugged and twirled a long blade of grass in his fingers as he lowered himself to the ground. "I cannot blame them. They are weary."

"We've taken twice as many breaks today as we did yesterday."

"Aye, and yesterday the fear of wyrran tracking them was enough to spur them into action."

Logan rubbed his temple with his thumb. "Makes me almost wish to spot a wyrran."

"Does your god seek more blood already?"

"My god always wants more blood," Logan answered cynically. "I couldna help but notice Reaghan has kept her distance from you today. What did you do to her?"

Galen turned his head away before Logan could see the scowl. "Nothing. I fear it could be her magic brings on dreams that cause her to seek the comfort of her brethren."

"Hmm. That is certainly a possibility. In all my immortal years, and we know that is no' many compared to some, I've no' learned much regarding Druids."

"Just like you, I've gathered most of my knowledge from Cara, Sonya, and Marcail. If Isla stays at the castle, I think we will learn even more."

Logan squatted and rested his forearms on his knees. "Sonya said if a Druid holds enough magic, then the magic will give that Druid a certain gift. For Sonya it's healing."

"And for Marcail, it's taking away another's pain."

"It stands to reason Reaghan's could be anything."

Galen looked to where Reaghan stood talking to Braden, a smile on her lips. "I find I'm very curious to know what her magic is."

"Especially when she thinks she doesna have any."

That was one of many things which bothered Galen about these Druids. "Do they fear her, you think? Is that why they lie to her about her magic?"

"Maybe it was her magic that took her family and caused the supposed fever then memory loss. Maybe the Druids are just protecting her from herself."

Galen shrugged, but for some reason he just couldn't imagine that to be the truth. "It's a possibility, I suppose, but *mies* do not use magic to hurt or kill. Only *droughs*."

"Is she *drough*?"

Logan's softly spoken question made Galen think back to when he held Reaghan in his arms. She had been unsure but eager. There had been no Demon's Kiss around her neck, the small vial that held the first drops of a *drough's* blood after the ceremony. And there hadn't been any scars on her wrists from the ceremony.

As his mind recalled her subtle scent of rosemary and

her warm skin, Reaghan lifted her face and looked at him with her storm-colored eyes.

"Nay, she's no' *drough*," Galen finally answered. "There is more to her than we are being told, however."

The first fat raindrop landed on the back of Galen's hand. He tilted back his head and saw the clouds he had noticed the previous eve had grown thicker, heavier with rain. They blocked the sun as the wind began to pick up.

"Shite," Logan cursed as he stood. "Just what we need."

"We cannot stay out in the open with rain."

Logan nodded and grimaced. "I'll remain at the back and push them. Lead us to shelter."

"We need to get moving before the rains come," Galen called to the Druids. "Our meal must be cut short. Eat while you walk if you must."

As Galen headed to the front of the Druids, Mairi reached out a hand and grabbed his arm. The image of hope mixed with fear assaulted him. Galen opened his power and sought more. If they wouldn't willingly give him answers about Reaghan he would find them himself. But just as quickly as her hand had grabbed him, Mairi dropped it.

Galen's eyes cleared and he found Reaghan watching him, her brow creased as if she knew the pain that the simple touch from Mairi had caused.

"Is this necessary?" Mairi asked, jerking his attention to her.

He sighed and silently prayed for patience. "If you want to walk in the middle of a storm, then you may linger."

"I've seen these clouds many times before. They will pass us," she argued.

"You may know the weather at Loch Awe, but this isn't the loch, and the weather holds different. I'd rather no' chance any of you becoming sick or injured while we travel in the rain."

Mairi grimaced. "If we must then. Though I assure you, there won't be a storm."

He managed to refrain from responding and continued to the front. As soon as he reached the head of the group, the others fell into step behind him. He pushed them hard, harder than he should have, but he knew the look of those clouds. Whenever the rainstorm unleashed, it would most likely be a vicious one.

He wouldn't allow the Druids to be caught in it. In the distance before them he could see the lightning as it streaked violently across the sky into patterns he found thrilling. The thunder, when it did hit, shook the ground beneath them.

They were heading toward the tempest, and although Galen didn't like it, there was nothing to be done. The more he walked the more he felt the occasional raindrop. It wasn't long before it began to drizzle.

He stopped himself just in time from looking back at Mairi. If he wanted to gain her trust, telling her "I told you so" wasn't the best course.

Galen's wool kilt helped to propel away the rain, but the others would soon be soaked. He thought of Reaghan, as he always did, and had the insane notion of wrapping his plaid around her.

To his left, a bolt of lightning zigzagged from the heavens to the ground. In front of him, the lightning forked from the clouds and it landed on the ground like many fingers seeking the dirt.

The thunder boomed around them, but despite it, his enhanced hearing detected a cry. A cry that sounded suspiciously like it came from Reaghan.

Galen turned around to find Reaghan bent over at the waist, her hands clutching her head. Mairi and Odara were on either side of her, talking, but Reaghan didn't seem to hear them.

He saw Reaghan begin to sway and knew she was going to fall. Galen used his speed and rushed to her. His arms wrapped around her before she could topple sideways. He lifted her in his arms, cradling her head against his neck.

"What happened?" he demanded of the elders.

Odara wouldn't meet his gaze.

Mairi wrung her hands as her gaze stayed on Reaghan. "She suffers from headaches."

"The thunder must have brought it on," Odara said.

Galen held Reaghan tighter as she buried her head in his neck and her hand fisted in his saffron shirt. He felt the tremble that ran through her, and when he glimpsed the tear that fell down her cheek, it nearly broke him in two.

"Galen?" Logan called as he ran up. "What is it? Is she hurt?"

"Aye," he answered. "We will discuss this more. For now, I want to get Reaghan somewhere she can lie down."

"How far are we from the cottage?" Logan asked.

"Not very, but we willna make it before the sky splits open."

As if the clouds had been waiting for those exact words, it began to pour. The rain came in sheets of gray that hampered sight and deafened any sound.

"We must hurry then," Mairi said.

Galen grimaced and pulled Reaghan tighter against him. "Doona worry. I have you now. Let me take care of you, Reaghan."

As he set out once more, he glanced down to find Reaghan's eyes squeezed shut, just as they had been that morning. Was that what he'd seen when he thought she was having a bad dream?

If it was a headache, why had she ignored him as she had? Reaghan was more mysterious than any woman he knew, and he feared he might never learn the truth about her.

Maybe you doona want to.

He frowned at his conscience. Of course he wanted to learn about Reaghan's past and everything the Druids wanted kept from him.

Galen continued to trudge through the rain and soaked ground for nearly an hour until he crested a hill and finally spotted the old cottage. Many times he had used it on his travels, and he was surprised that no one had made it theirs yet.

It wasn't large, and with all the Druids inside they would be quite crowded. But they could build a fire and get dry.

He slowed his pace and whistled to Logan. Galen didn't want to get closer before he knew for certain no one lived there.

Logan ran past him. Galen watched as his friend scouted the cottage looking for tracks—of any kind. Only when he found none did he venture toward the cottage. A few moments later, Logan waved him forward.

Galen leaned down and kissed Reaghan's brow. "Soon you'll be dry," he promised.

The Druids were as eager as he to get to the cottage, and they didn't wait for him. They ran toward Logan, who had disappeared inside the cottage and was most likely already starting a fire.

Galen took his time, careful not to jar Reaghan too much and cause her more pain. Her hand still clutched him, her body taut with suffering.

By the time he reached the cottage, he could barely shoulder himself inside. He was disappointed not to find a fire, but when he saw the clean bed with a blanket waiting, he gave Logan a nod of thanks.

Galen tried to lay Reaghan down, but she refused to release him. He would have gladly held her the rest of the night, but she needed to get out of her wet clothes.

Mairi stepped forward and tried to pry Reaghan's

fingers open. "You need to rest, Reaghan. Release Galen so we can get you out of your wet gown and cover you."

There was nothing Mairi could do that would make Reaghan release her hold. Galen finally leaned down so his mouth was next to her ear and said, "Reaghan, I doona want you to become ill. Let them take care of you. I will be back."

Her fingers loosened and he laid her gently on the bed. Reaghan never opened her eyes, but he could feel her reluctance to let go of him.

Maybe it was because he knew how much pain she was in, maybe it was because she knew Mairi and Odara kept the truth of her past from her, but he was disinclined to leave Reaghan.

And strangely, he felt as if he should be holding her, as if he could do something for her pain.

SEVENTEEN

Reaghan felt the loss of Galen's heat instantly. She hadn't wanted to let go of him.

But now that he was gone, the throbbing consumed her. Her stomach pitched violently, and she feared she would become sick, spilling what little food she had consumed.

Hands began to tug at her dress and limp body. She wanted to yell at them to leave her alone, but all her strength was being used to stop her nausea.

The cool air on her wet skin made her shiver, which only increased the pain in her head. She rolled into a ball and prayed they would leave her alone. Finally, a blanket was placed on top of her. She snuggled beneath the warmth, wishing someone would warm her feet. They were so cold they ached nearly as much as her head.

"How is she?" she heard Galen ask.

Reaghan tried to open her eyes so she could see him, but she had her back to the room. The bed was up against a wall, and it would take too much of her waning strength to turn over.

She winced as wood popped from a fire. People were speaking, their voices low and their words unintelligible, but she knew they were packed close together.

Outside the sound of the rain was a constant roar punctuated by the thunder and flashes of lightning. The storm was ferocious and would delay them.

Reaghan hated her weakness and the pain that assaulted her. She had felt the headache coming before they halted for the noon meal. Two in one day. Two brutal ones at that.

It frightened her just as much as her unknown past did.

A wave of renewed pain washed over her. Reaghan gripped the blanket with all her might, wishing it was Galen and hoping she could stay out of the darkness that wanted to take her.

She didn't know how she knew the darkness wanted her. Maybe it was the way it came at her quicker, more forcefully, each time, but she was powerless to stay conscious when it swarmed over her.

Her lips parted and she whispered Galen's name. She tried to shout, but was too weak for more than the murmur she was able to form.

She needed Galen. His strength was the only thing that could keep the darkness away. While he had carried her, she'd been in pain, but the darkness hadn't dared to come.

Now it collected around her, and in one fell swoop took her under.

Galen watched as Reaghan's hand went slack on the covers. He had built the fire as quickly as he could, but then Mairi had wanted to talk about the storm and their journey.

He knew she was worried about Reaghan and was talking to quell her own fear. He listened to her as long as he could before he excused himself and weaved his way through the Druids to the bed, only to find Reaghan unconscious.

"It's all right," Odara said. "This is better for her. She can no longer feel the pain."

As her words penetrated his mind, he turned his head to look down at her. Odara's bent form hovered near the bed, her wrinkled face lined with worry. "What do you know of these headaches?"

"Only that they will get worse. And Mairi cannot stand to watch Reaghan in pain."

"Does this have something to do with Reaghan's magic?"

Odara's eyes snapped up to his. "What did you ask?"

"Her magic?" Galen repeated. "It was her magic we felt upon finding the loch. She has more magic than all of you combined."

"I know. Reaghan's magic is very strong."

"So why make her believe she has none? And does it have anything to do with her headaches?"

"In a way," Mairi grudgingly answered as she joined them.

Galen looked from Mairi to Odara. "And the other? Why make her believe she has no magic?"

Odara shrugged and smoothed a hand over her wet hair, which was pulled back in a tight braid. "We thought it would be best."

"She seeks answers. If you doona tell her, she will find someone who will. You are her family, the people she trusts. Whatever the answers are, however distasteful, they should come from you."

Galen bent and placed a hand on Reaghan's brow. Her skin was hot to the touch and a fine sheen of sweat covered her face. He wanted to lie beside her and gather her in his arms, but he needed to keep watch since Logan had left to hunt.

"When she wakes she will be better," Odara said. "I'll stay with her, Warrior, and let you know as soon as she opens her eyes."

Galen sighed and straightened. "Thank you."

He turned from the bed before he gave in and lay down beside her. Mairi's gaze met his before she turned and exited the cottage. Her intent was clear. She wanted to speak with him. Galen didn't waste a moment following her.

"You wanted to talk?" he asked as he closed the door behind him and stepped into the downpour.

"Thank you for helping us with Reaghan."

Galen walked closer to Mairi. "I would have helped anyone in need. Do you still fear me?"

"I cannot help what I've been raised to believe, Galen. I see you with Reaghan and I know there is something growing between the two of you."

"Maybe."

"She is important to me, to our people."

He narrowed his gaze and advanced on her. There was a sinking feeling in his gut, as he began to suspect just how important Reaghan was. "How?"

"I cannot tell you. I've taken a vow, Galen."

Despite the tremor in her voice and the misery in her gaze, Galen had to know. "I'm going to ask you once more, Mairi. Tell me how Reaghan is important."

"Reaghan is ours to protect. Leave it at that, I beg you."

It was fear and worry for Reaghan that made Galen take another step toward Mairi. He knew he shouldn't use his power, knew he would regret it later. But Reaghan's life could be in danger. Whatever it was Mairi and Odara kept secret must be terrible indeed to inflict such sorrow.

All Galen knew was that he had to have Reaghan in his life. Being with her allowed him to be normal, allowed him to forget the powers his god gave him.

He wouldn't let her be harmed. And if using his power made Mairi more afraid of him, he would shoulder that as long as he knew Reaghan was safe.

As much as Galen didn't want to, he grabbed Mairi's arms. Instantly images of her talking to Reaghan and watching over Reaghan flashed in his mind.

Galen pushed deeper, searching for more. There was

an image of Reaghan standing at the loch, but she was dressed in a gown from another era. Then he saw Reaghan with Mairi once more down at the loch. The two leaned over the water so their reflections were visible. Reaghan's was the same, but Mairi was just a young girl barely older than ten summers.

Galen dropped his hands, his lungs burning for air as he processed what he had seen. "What have you done to Reaghan?"

"I have done nothing," Mairi stated as she blinked from the rain that fell into her eyes.

"I saw her with you when you were just a young girl. You two were looking into the loch at your reflections."

Mairi's face paled and she raised a trembling hand to her mouth. "How did you . . . ?"

"My god gives me the power to read people's minds. Reaghan told me of a parchment she found regarding her and the Foinaven Mountain. She knows you are keeping things from her."

Mairi's hand shook as she wiped at her face. "We would never harm her. It is our duty to protect her."

"You keep saying that," Galen bellowed over the storm.

Lightning lit the sky as he paced in front of Mairi, unmindful that the rain was coming down even harder.

"Galen, there are things you don't know, things you cannot know."

He paused and leaned down so his face was near hers. There would be no more half-truths. He would know all of it. "I can find out. Shall I dig deeper into your mind?"

"You see images," Mairi said, though she shrank away. "But you do not hear what is going on."

"I can hear what a person is thinking. All I have to do is touch you."

For long, heart-thudding moments, Mairi stared into his eyes. She finally sighed and lowered her gaze. The rain ran down her weathered face, falling into her deep wrinkles. "You came for the artifact."

"I did, but how is this relevant to Reaghan?"

"Galen, Reaghan *is* the artifact."

Galen blinked and stepped back from the elder. He shook his head as her words sank in. He had known. Somehow, deep down, he had known, but he hadn't wanted to believe. "How?"

"What is happening to Reaghan she did to herself in an effort to keep hidden from Deirdre."

Galen couldn't breathe. His world was tilting around him, threatening to break apart at the seams. "Why? I need to understand, Mairi."

"Galen?" Logan said as he walked around the cottage. "Is everything all right?"

"Nay," Galen answered, his throat hoarse as he yelled. "Everything is not all right. Reaghan is the artifact, Logan. Reaghan."

Mairi took a step toward Galen. "You cannot let her know."

"Explain yourself," Logan commanded.

"Every ten years Reaghan loses her memories."

Galen took in a steadying breath. "Why every ten years? Why not just once?"

"How would you explain to everyone a woman who doesn't age? She is reborn, so to speak, every ten years. We use the same story each time so no one gets confused."

Galen closed his eyes. "The fever."

"Aye," Mairi answered. "There is a fever during that time, so we aren't lying to her. It begins with the headaches. They will grow more frequent and more severe until it is time and her magic takes hold, wiping away the last ten years of the life she's led."

"So she will remember nothing when she wakes

from this fever?" Though Galen knew the answer, he had to ask.

"Nothing." Mairi wrapped her arms around herself and shivered. "I've seen this occur many times. She will be all right."

He nodded and glanced at the cottage.

Logan snorted and crossed his arms over his chest. "You say it's to hide from Deirdre. Why?"

Mairi looked from Logan to Galen. "The spell to take her memories is so that if Reaghan were ever captured by Deirdre, Deirdre would never be able to sift through layer after layer of erased memories to find the one thing Reaghan is keeping hidden."

"And what is that?" Galen asked. "What is Reaghan hiding?"

"I'm not exactly sure."

Logan growled.

Mairi threw up her hands and hastily said, "I swear, Galen. I'm not lying. The reason was lost through the years."

"How long has she been in your village?" Galen asked.

"At least three hundred years."

Logan whistled long and low. Galen rubbed the back of his neck. "So your village has been hiding her for three hundred years?"

"I think you had best start from the beginning," Logan said.

Mairi shook her head slowly. "I swore never to tell anyone but another elder."

"Things have changed," Galen said. "We can protect Reaghan, but you must help us."

After taking a deep breath, Mairi began. "The story has been passed down so many times I'm not sure what is truth anymore."

"Just tell us what you know," Logan urged.

"The story is told that Reaghan came to our village all those years ago with a proposition. She would use her magic, as powerful as it was, to help shield the village from Deirdre and in exchange we would protect her. She explained the spell she would perform would erase her memories and continue to do so every ten years until such time as the spell would need to be broken and all her memories returned."

Galen frowned. "How do we break the spell?"

"I have no idea," Mairi answered. "The spell took a great amount of magic. In some stories it is said a man came with her to help with the spell, but the enchantment took such magic that he died."

Galen had thought he would get answers, and all he was getting was more questions. How much of Mairi's story was truth he had no idea, and that was what frustrated him the most. "Do you know what she's hiding from Deirdre?"

"Knowledge of some kind, I believe."

Logan scratched his neck and grimaced. "Just what kind of knowledge does Reaghan hold that would make her want to put that kind of spell on herself?"

"Knowledge that could either harm or kill Deirdre perhaps?" Galen said.

Logan smiled and rubbed his hands together. "Now, that is good news."

"Not if Deirdre gets her hands on Reaghan," Mairi said.

Galen nodded and put his hands on his hips. "Isla told us Deirdre planned to raid your village for the artifact. If Deirdre knew Reaghan was that object, she would have told Isla she was after a person."

"So Deirdre doesn't know," Logan said.

"Maybe no', but the man with the wyrran was certainly after Reaghan."

"Coincidence?" Mairi asked.

Galen thought back to the way the man had stared at Reaghan. There wasn't recognition as if he knew her, only intent. "I doona think so. I think the attack by the wyrran was merely a raid to look for Druids."

"But once Deirdre discovers where the attack took place she'll likely piece things together," Logan said.

"Let's hope no'."

Mairi walked to the cottage door and paused with her hand on the latch. "We must keep Reaghan safe. At all costs."

"Of course," Galen agreed.

"I will gather together what food we have left for our meal this evening," Mairi said before she entered the cottage.

Galen waited until she was inside before he bent over and placed his hands on his knees and gulped in air. "It never entered my mind what we sought was a person."

Logan moved to stand beside him. "This explains almost everything."

Almost, but not all. Galen straightened as another streak of lightning forked across the sky. Trails from the droplets of rain ran down his face, but he paid them no heed. "Reaghan is looking for answers to her past. I wonder if this occurs each time she's about to lose her memories."

"Maybe some part of her knows what is happening, and she's scared so she looks to find answers."

"Answers that could break the spell, perhaps?"

Logan shrugged. "Anything is possible. I wondered when you would use your power to gain your answers. I was watching the entire time."

Galen twisted his lips. "I gather you would no' have waited?"

"No' if I feared for the safety of my woman."

Galen was about to say Reaghan wasn't his woman, but he couldn't get the words past his lips. He knew she wasn't, but saints help him, he wanted her to be.

"We're battling Deirdre, Logan. I have no time for a woman."

Logan chuckled and leaned against the cottage. "Tell that to the MacLeods. They found their women among this mess Deirdre has created. If they could, why no' you?"

Why not him?

"At least now I know why I cannot read her mind." Galen chose to ignore Logan's question. He didn't want to think of Reaghan as his or why he wanted her so desperately.

"Her magic," Logan said. "The reason shouldn't matter, my friend, no' if you have found happiness with her."

They had shared a night of passionate lovemaking. Was that happiness? At the time Galen would have said aye. Now, he knew too much, and knowing just what Reaghan was, meant he couldn't have her.

Galen rubbed the back of his neck. "Reaghan's magic was strong enough to keep wiping away her memories every ten years. If it's that important that she would do this to herself, then Mairi was right when she said Reaghan wasn't meant for me."

"So Reaghan cannot have happiness?" Logan pushed off the cottage wall and scowled at Galen. "You of all people know everyone deserves some contentment in their lives. Whatever she is hiding can be kept secret at MacLeod Castle where she will be safer. I can also guarantee that with her exotic looks, one of the other Warriors will step forward to woo her."

The thought set Galen's blood to boiling. He took a

menacing step toward Logan and growled, only then noticing his god was loose as a fang sliced his tongue.

Logan grinned knowingly. "I thought that might get you riled. You want her. Claim her, Galen, before someone else does."

EIGHTEEN

Reaghan came awake gradually, carefully. The pain in her head was gone, but her body was sore from being so tense. She rolled onto her back and smoothed away the still wet hair from the side of her face she had been sleeping on.

Her eyes took in the small cottage. The only thing that broke the drone of the rain was the fire. She craned her neck to find the floor littered with sleeping bodies. Curled up at her feet was Braden, whose sweet face looked simply adorable in sleep.

The fire made the cottage cozy despite the rain. Her gaze snagged on something in the shadows near the hearth. She turned over to see who it was.

The scrape of the blanket on her skin reminded her she was naked beneath the covers, just as Galen walked from the shadows, his cobalt eyes holding hers.

His boots made nary a sound as he stepped over the bodies until he stood beside the bed. He squatted down, his back to the fire.

Reaghan didn't like that his face was hidden in shadows. She sensed something bothered him, something he wanted kept from her. And she feared she knew what it was. Her sickness, her weakness.

"How do you fare?" he whispered so as not to wake anyone.

Reaghan shrugged. "Better."

"Is the pain gone?"

"Aye. Thank you for carrying me. I could have walked."

Despite the shadows, she saw him frown. "There is nothing wrong with leaning on someone when you need them. I doona think it a failing that you were brought low by such agony, Reaghan."

She knew he meant every word, but he was a Warrior. Pain he might feel, but his god healed him of anything. Galen had long forgotten what real pain felt like.

He said the right words, words she had wanted to hear, but she couldn't help the kernel of doubt that had planted itself in her mind. She felt she was weak, too weak to be the woman Galen might want in his life.

"Are you hungry?" he asked. "Do you think you can eat?"

Reaghan nodded and held the blanket to her chest as she sat up.

"Stay here. I'll return in a moment."

Reaghan picked at the warn blanket and let her gaze wander the cottage. Was it just coincidence that Galen and Logan had stumbled upon the place? Or had one of them known of it?

It didn't look as though it had been used in a while, so it could be one of theirs. The thought of Galen using the cottage as his home didn't seem as farfetched as she might have thought.

Some bread, cheese, and cold meat from the night before were placed in front of her along with a skin of water. "Eat your fill," Galen told her.

She looked longingly at the food. "I should save some for the morrow."

"You should eat," he ordered her. After a moment he rose and returned with something in his hand. "Your gown is nearly dry. Here is your chemise."

Reaghan's hand brushed Galen's when she reached for
her chemise. Heat flared inside her at the touch. He was so
tall, so muscular, so warm, that all she wanted to do was
lay her head on his shoulder and sleep in the safety of his
arms.

His deep blue gaze seared her, made her recall his
soft, demanding lips as he kissed her, his gentle caresses,
and the feel of his hot, hard body as it glided over her,
inside her.

Her lips parted as her heart pounded in her chest. He
lifted an auburn ringlet to his nose. His eyes closed as he
inhaled deeply. Chills raced over her skin as she watched
him, mesmerized by his actions.

"Ah, Reaghan, how you tempt me."

She knew all about temptation, especially when it came
to Galen. Reaghan cleared her throat and looked away
before she pulled him down for a kiss. Instead, she tugged
on her chemise and began to eat.

"How long did I sleep?"

"A while," he answered as he sat and faced her on the
bed, careful not to disturb Braden.

"And the storm?"

Galen sighed and glanced at the closed shutters. "It
doesna appear to be lessening as of yet."

She tore off a piece of bread. "How did you know about
this cottage?"

"I've used it off and on since finding it some time ago.
Apparently so has someone else. It's been at least a score
of years since I've been here, yet the blankets were relatively new and the wood fresh."

"So someone lives here?"

"I wouldna go that far. Whoever it is, they haven't been
here in at least a week if no' longer."

They sat in silence until she finished her meal. The food

did make her feel stronger. Reaghan wiped her mouth with her fingers and took a drink of the water. "Will we leave in the morn regardless of the weather?"

"I doona know." Galen's brow furrowed and he shook his head. "We need no' tarry long anywhere, but I fear taking a group of Druids, all female, I might add, out in this kind of storm."

"You don't think we can weather it?" Reaghan teased.

Galen's smile was slow as it spread over his face. "I know you can. It's the older ones I fret about. It's summer, aye, but the wind coming off the mountains cuts right through a person, especially with wet clothing."

Reaghan thought of Odara and Mairi. Then her gaze snagged on wee Braden. "Maybe we should wait then. I'm eager to reach the castle, but not in exchange for lives."

His hand came up to cup her cheek. Reaghan let out a shaky breath and rubbed her face into his large palm. His eyes darkened, heat flaring in their depths. She burned for his touch, hungered for his mouth. With just one caress he scorched, he enthralled.

He captivated.

Galen's thumb glided over her bottom lip and a moan tore from his throat, filled with torment and desire and longing.

Reaghan placed her hand over his heart and felt it hammering as rapidly as her own. She didn't resist when his hand shifted to the back of her head and he pulled her against him. She was eager for his kiss, ready to taste him again, and excited to feel her blood sing with desire.

He whispered her name before his mouth slanted over hers, his beard scratching her face. His kiss was intoxicating, invigorating. Heat slammed into her as her hands glided over the soft material of his shirt and over the lean, hard sinew of his muscles.

The kiss was filled with potent desire and a hunger that made it urgent and soul-stealing. It left her gasping for breath and praying for more. She clung to Galen, her body his to do with as he wished, eager and wanting all he had to give.

He deepened the kiss, and she drowned in the desire that weighted down her body. It was too powerful to be denied, too commanding to try and control.

Her body throbbed, remembering his touch, his kisses. She knew any moment someone could wake and see them, but Reaghan didn't care about anything or anyone other than Galen. She threw caution to the wind and sank into his kiss.

Deeper and deeper, he pulled her under the tide of heady desire and desperate longing. But Reaghan had never been more ready and thrilled to follow Galen down that path.

"Reaghan," he murmured against her skin as he kissed across her jaw and then down her neck. "God's teeth, I want you."

She heard the desperation, the hunger, the yearning in his voice. It matched her own feelings, ones she was afraid to say aloud.

Reaghan opened her eyes and cupped Galen's face between her hands. She smiled into his eyes. "Not half as much as I want you. I feared I would never know what it was to experience passion, to know what it was to have a man hold me. You've given me all that and more."

The desire in Galen's eyes dimmed, but did not disappear.

"Did I say something wrong?" she asked.

He shook his head and kissed her forehead, her nose, and then her mouth. "Never, Reaghan. I just worry about getting all of you to the castle. I wish we were there now.

I'd take you to my chamber and make love to you for weeks."

"Weeks," she repeated with a laugh. "We'd have to eat sometime."

"I'd gather us food to last days at a time."

Her smile grew. "Won't the MacLeods need you?"

"They'll have to get by without me," he said and winked. "When it comes to you, nothing else matters."

She wanted to believe him. Desperately. But her blocked memories kept her from reaching out and grasping what Galen dangled before her. "I find it difficult to believe a handsome man such as yourself doesn't have a woman."

It had been said in jest, but the smile left his eyes and face. "Once, long ago, I dreamed of finding a wife, of having children and a simple life. I fought for my laird because he asked it of me, not for fame and fortune as others did. Had I known it would turn Deirdre's gaze on me I wouldn't have done it and then I'd never been cursed with a god."

"And I wouldn't have known you." Reaghan shifted to her knees and laid her head on his chest. She inhaled his aroma of pine, content to stay just as she was the rest of the night.

After a moment his arms wrapped around her and he rested his chin atop her head. "You're right. I wouldn't have met you. A tragedy, that would have been."

Galen meant every word. It would have been a misfortune. He had come to terms with what had happened to him, with what was inside him, but he found it almost worth it to have met Reaghan. Being unable to touch someone because of his power made him cherish each moment he was able to hold and kiss Reaghan.

She was special, and not just because of her powerful magic or because she was the artifact. She was special because of the way she touched his soul, the way she looked at him as if he could save the world.

He had known he was in trouble the first moment he laid eyes on her and felt the strong, undeniable attraction between them.

His body was still aroused, his cock still impatient to be inside her, from that frenzied kiss. Her kisses were like the sweetest nectar, her lips a beacon he had to taste.

She was responsive. Passionate. Fiery.

And he wanted to claim her as his own, to know she was his and his alone.

Galen didn't know how long he sat there before he realized Reaghan was asleep. He had watched over her most of the night. He couldn't let her go again, not when he needed the feel of her against him as desperately as he did.

It took some doing, but eventually he leaned against the headboard with her head on his chest and her arm slung over his abdomen.

He could imagine having her by his side every night as he climbed into bed. The more he thought of having her as his own, the more he worried about her memories being taken every ten years.

It was a small price to pay knowing she would be his. But for how long? He didn't imagine her spell would last forever, but even if it did, would it be so terrible to woo her over again every ten years?

The answer was a resounding nay. He couldn't lie and say part of it wasn't that he couldn't read her mind. It was only one of the things that made her so appealing, but there was so much more.

The way she held her head when she listened to someone. The way her eyes danced when she teased. The way her laugh hit him square in the chest. The way her hair cascaded around her in a tumble of curls. The way her eyes softened just before he kissed her. The way her body melted against his.

And there were a million other reasons. He didn't know Reaghan's past or her secrets, but he knew her as he'd never known another woman in all of his two hundred and fifty years.

NINETEEN

Logan shifted in his perch high in a nearby tree. He knew there was a possibility the frequent and ferocious lightning might strike the tree. But that's what made it so appealing.

He had decided to keep watch the entire night, not because Galen didn't want to take his turn, but because Logan had seen the restless and troubled look in his friend's eyes as Galen watched Reaghan.

Nay, it was better for all concerned if Galen stayed inside so he would be there when Reaghan woke. And in truth, Logan didn't mind keeping watch.

He thought back to the time at MacLeod Castle when he had volunteered to come with Galen on their search for the artifact. Hayden, the best friend a man could have, though he was more of a brother to Logan, had been taken aback when Logan volunteered.

Logan had done it partly because Hayden needed to stay and face Isla, but also because Logan had needed time away. It wasn't because of something anyone did to him. In fact, it was the opposite.

Everyone, especially the women, made the castle feel like a home. That's the way the MacLeods wanted it, but it reminded Logan too much of his own home.

The longer he stayed and shared his meals with everyone, the more difficult it became to bear. Hayden had enough troubles of his own, with his past hounding him as it always did, so Logan kept his anxiety to himself.

Maybe he should have shared his thoughts with Hayden, but although Hayden was moody and temperamental, he craved the home the MacLeods had offered them. Would Hayden have really understood the torment in Logan's soul?

Logan blinked away the water that fell onto his eyelashes and into his eyes. This journey with Galen had turned out far differently than Logan had expected.

The battle with the wyrran had been just what he needed. What he needed still. He knew it was only a matter of time before there was another skirmish. At the rate the Druids were moving, that time could come more quickly than any of them realized.

But Logan was ready.

He smiled and lifted his hand to see the silver skin and long, silver claws. Aye, he was more than ready to appease his god with more blood and battle and death.

When they set out at dawn the rain had thankfully ended, though the torrent had left the ground squishy and muddy.

Reaghan barely noticed the hem of her gown covered in mud as they sloshed through the sodden terrain. Her gaze was on Galen's back as he led them closer and closer to MacLeod Castle.

She had drifted off to sleep in his arms, cradled in his strength. The ever-present worry was in his gaze whenever he looked at her now, and she couldn't dispel the fear it was because she was sickly.

When she had awoken that morn Galen had been gone. It had felt good to sleep next to him, as if that were the way her life should be.

She didn't understand the trust she had for Galen, or the attraction that seemed to grow the more she was around him. She barely knew him, and yet she knew instinctively he would protect her at all costs.

It went against everything she had been taught by the Druids about Warriors.

Reaghan's thoughts were halted when a small hand slipped inside hers. She looked down to find Braden looking up at her with his big brown eyes.

"You scared me yesterday," he said.

"I'm sorry. I will try not to do it again." It was a promise she was likely not to keep, but for the lad, she would do anything to keep his innocence from the evil that was out in the world.

Braden nodded. "Galen wouldna let any of the others touch you."

"Is that so?"

"Aye," Braden said, the look not that of a boy, but of the man he would someday become. "He said he would keep you safe, and he did."

Reaghan smiled and squeezed Braden's hand. "You will make a fine Highlander, Braden."

He beamed, his smile wide and infectious. "Really? Do you think Galen or Logan will teach me how to wield a sword?"

"You need to ask your mother first, but I imagine they would be pleased to do so."

Braden spun on his heel and raced back to his mother. Reaghan watched him and couldn't help but laugh at the lad's enthusiasm. He spoke so fast Fiona couldn't understand him and had to get him to repeat it three times before she caught all of it.

When she nodded, Braden raced to the back of the group where Logan was. The Warrior held out his arms as Braden jumped to him. Logan easily caught him and swung him up on his shoulders, all while Braden talked nonstop.

When Reaghan turned back around it was to find Galen's gaze on her. He paused, his cobalt eyes boring into hers, heating her blood and making her heart thump against her chest.

She licked her lips and took in a shaky breath when he turned away. How she wished they were already at the castle so she could talk to Galen without Mairi always within earshot. Reaghan thought of his suggestion of locking them in his chamber for a week, making love to her throughout the day.

To have him all to herself. Alone, in his chamber, touching him, kissing him, learning more of his spectacular body. She remembered his kiss the night before. The passion. The need. The hunger.

The throbbing began between her legs, insistent and heated. She wondered if she could get him alone soon. To have his large hands on her, the hard length of his body over her, his delicious weight atop her. And his staff inside her, thrusting deep, hard, and fast until they both succumbed to a climax that left them breathless and sweating.

Of a sudden Galen whistled as he turned and paused. He motioned the group onward. Logan trotted to the front of the Druids, Braden squealing with every step Logan took.

Reaghan was just wondering what excuse she could find to speak to Galen when he snagged her hand as she walked past. She lifted her skirts with her free hand and let him pull her to the back, uncaring that others watched.

"What's wrong?" she asked when he finally halted.

He pulled her against him, molding her body to his. "I felt your eyes on me. God's blood, Reaghan, I cannot go another heartbeat without tasting you."

His mouth came down on hers, his tongue slipping past her lips. He devoured her, his arousal pressing into her stomach as his hands spanned her back.

She sighed and wrapped her arms around his neck. The kiss was slow, languid. It fueled her already heated passion. Her breasts swelled against his chest, eager for his touch.

Reaghan moaned when he cupped a breast and rolled a nipple between his fingers. She wanted to lift her skirts, to wrap her legs around his waist and have him fill her.

The urgency that swept through her to have him made her skin burn. As if he felt her need, he rocked his hips against her.

"Ah, Reaghan," he murmured, and kissed down her neck to the sensitive spot behind her ear. "I'd take you now if I could."

When he lifted his head, Reaghan clung to his strong shoulders and wished they were anywhere but traveling, wished she had the magic to bring them to the castle in the blink of an eye.

It was going to be a long journey to MacLeod Castle.

Dunmore kicked open the stone door to Cairn Toul and strode inside. He had ridden his horse nearly to death to get to the mountain as hastily as possible. As it was, his mount was useless to him now.

When he walked past Deirdre's chambers he felt a stir in the air. He paused and turned to find Deirdre standing in the doorway. Surprise ripped through him. Who had found her a Druid so she could regain her form?

That was supposed to have been his right. He had promised her he wouldn't fail, and yet somehow he had.

"Mistress," he said and bowed.

"Rise, Dunmore."

He straightened and blinked at the beauty before him. Deirdre had always taken his breath away. While others had found her startling white hair and eyes frightening to look upon, he found them stunning. He loved the high cheekbones in her heart-shaped face and her full lips.

"How?" he asked. "Did someone else bring you a Druid?"

"Nay. I had . . . other means. I will still need Druids."

"Of course."

Deirdre peered around him. "Where are my wyrran?"

"We were following the scent of strong magic when we encountered Warriors."

Her white eyes narrowed and her long, white hair that grazed the floor twitched. "Warriors? What color where they?"

"Green and silver."

"Galen and Logan," she murmured. "I don't suppose you captured them."

Dunmore slowly shook his head. "We were after the Druids, but the Warriors were protecting them."

"Interesting," Deirdre said, as she leaned against the stone doorway and traced her red lips with a long finger-nail. "Why were Galen and Logan away from MacLeod Castle? Did they stumble upon the Druids, or had then been searching for them?"

"I intend to discover all, mistress, just as soon as I get more wyrran."

She turned her attention back to Dunmore. "Do you think the Druids will stay where you found them? It's more likely the Warriors are taking them to MacLeod Castle."

"I suspected as much," Dunmore lied, not wanting Deirdre to know he hadn't thought of that.

Deirdre smiled, proving once more that he could never lie to her. "Where were these Druids you found?"

"Loch Awe."

Deirdre froze, her eyes burning with fury. "Loch Awe? Are you sure?"

"Aye, mistress."

She tipped back her head and let out a scream so full

of rage that Dunmore took a step away from her. Deirdre had always been easy to anger, but he had never seen her like this.

The scream finally ended and her chest rose and fell rapidly as she focused on him. "Forget finding the Druids before they reach MacLeod Castle, Dunmore. I have another task for you. I think a visit to the MacClures is in order."

"As you wish," he murmured. Dunmore knew Deirdre's mind. Whatever she had planned with the MacClures would mean battle. And death.

He smiled, eager to begin.

TWENTY

Galen stared up at the night sky, so different from the night before. Not a cloud marred the beautiful darkness, the moon just a sliver among the sparkling stars.

Even while Galen admired the beauty above him he knew where Reaghan was at all times. His senses were honed in on her, as if an invisible thread connected them.

He had kissed her in front of everyone, uncaring that others saw or what they might think. He hadn't asked Reaghan, hadn't thought of anything other than holding her against him. Of sealing her lips with his. He was powerless to do anything about the attraction, the passion that had him in its grip. What was worse, he didn't want to do anything.

Yet, he worried about Reaghan. She wanted answers to her past, a past the elders had kept from her because she had asked them to. The secret Mairi and Odara carried, one that Logan and Galen were now a part of, weighed heavily upon them, and Galen didn't know how much longer it could be kept from Reaghan.

A secret that the entire MacLeod Castle would be privy to soon.

Galen blew out a breath and circled the sleeping camp on silent feet. He had no doubt Reaghan would find a home at MacLeod Castle. The Druids there were friendly, loving. They would eagerly invite her into their group.

Even once the headaches and fever took her memories, Galen was sure nothing would change. But what about ten years later? Or ten years after that?

When would Reaghan begin to feel the need for answers again? He wanted to tell her everything.

"I know that look," Logan said.

Galen grunted, unsure if he wanted to talk. Or even if he could, his mind was so mired in thought.

"I doona need magic to know your thoughts are on Reaghan."

"They seem forever on her," Galen admitted.

They stood twenty paces from the Druids, but they kept their voices low, whispers not even the wind could hear. "If you're worried she doesn't care for you, ease your mind. She only has eyes for you, my friend."

"I wish that was all that troubled me." Galen scrubbed a hand down his face and shifted his feet. "After what Reaghan told me, I believe she will stop at nothing to find her answers. It's very important to her."

Logan nodded thoughtfully. "Mairi said with the increase in her headaches her memories would be gone soon."

"I doona know if I can keep this from her. It seems she deserves to know. What if she ends up alone?"

"You will be with her, Galen."

"And if Deirdre takes me captive again? Or I'm killed?"

"She will be looked after," Logan replied. "You should know that without having to ask."

Galen turned away, feeling more of a fool than he had since he was a young lad. "There is this worry in my gut, Logan, worry that I cannot rid myself of."

Logan stepped around to face Galen, his brow furrowed and his gaze intense. "Is it Deirdre?"

"I doona know what it is. Ever since I saw the man with the wyrran looking at Reaghan, I've felt doom was ever on the horizon."

Logan let the tension out of his body with a deep sigh. "I think what you are feeling is common. Any man who has a woman who could be in danger would feel the same anxiety. However, we should pick up our pace on the morrow."

"We covered more ground today than I had hoped," Galen said. "We may be able to reach MacLeod Castle day after next."

Logan wrinkled his face in a grimace. "A day too long. Now if we were surrounded by water, I could help with that."

Galen chuckled at the humor sparkling in Logan's hazel eyes. "You mean you would want to show off."

"Only a wee bit." Logan grinned brightly. "Besides, I like to keep these Druids on their toes."

Galen saw how Logan's gaze shifted to Braden, who slept curled on his side, the deep sleep of an innocent. "The lad does make things bearable, doesn't he?"

"Aye," Logan murmured. "Do you know, he asked me to teach him how to use a sword when we reach the castle?"

Galen's brows rose in surprise. "What did you tell him?"

"How could I say nay? Apparently his mother gave her permission, and he was so excited. I'll need help."

"You?" Galen shook his head and wrinkled his nose. "You'll do fine."

"I doona want to ruin his training."

The honesty and panic in his eyes hit Galen square in the chest. Gone was the teasing tone and laughter, and in their place was a Logan he had never seen before.

"You willna ruin anything, Logan. He has come to you because he trusts you, and he adores you. All of us will help with his training if that is your wish."

"I'd rather someone else train him," Logan said, and propped his hands on his hips as his chin fell to his chest.

"I doona want him depending on me. I'll disappoint him, and I couldn't stand to see the sorrow in his eyes when it happens."

Galen wanted to reach out, to clasp his friend's shoulder, but Galen knew he would see exactly what was causing the remorse coursing through Logan. And Galen wouldn't do that to his friend.

"I know you and Hayden have a tight bond, Logan. I know you have shared secrets with each other. I'm no' Hayden, but I will help if I can."

Logan lifted his face and grinned, but it didn't reach his eyes, which burned with misery. "There is much Hayden doesn't know. He is my brother in every way except by blood. You all are, yet I cannot share what I have buried inside me."

Galen knew only too well how Logan felt. "We all have pasts we'd like to forget. We've all done things we regret. Doona let whatever is in the past destroy you."

"I thought leaving the castle for a bit might help, but it hasn't," Logan said as he looked into the distance.

For a moment Galen thought Logan might run off into the night, but he knew the Warrior would never leave him to protect the Druids alone. "If you doona return to the castle, Hayden will skin me alive."

That brought a snort from Logan. "Hayden would, too."

"I know. I'm fond of my hide where it is. Besides, it would upset Reaghan, and I cannot have that."

Logan's gaze swung back to Galen. His eyes crinkled in the corners and a genuine smile appeared. "Did you just make a jest? Galen Shaw, you surprise me."

"I have to do something to save myself from Hayden."

This time Logan chuckled deep and low. He reached up and slapped Galen on the shoulder before he walked away.

Galen stood rooted to the spot, his face frozen as a brief image of a young boy calling after Logan, begging him to return home, sliced through Galen's mind. He sucked in a mouthful of air and looked at Logan's retreating back.

The terror and distress Galen had heard in the young boy's voice as he called after Logan was agonizing. Galen wondered who the boy was, but he couldn't—and wouldn't—ask Logan about the memory.

"Just what secrets do you hold, my friend? And will they tear you apart as I fear they might?" Galen whispered into the night.

Reaghan awoke with a start, the dream so vivid in her mind she could still feel the wind from the sea, still feel the spray of the waves on her face.

She swallowed and sat up, afraid to think about the images she had seen in her dream. She had worn a different style of gown, one that must have been from centuries earlier, with a girdle and a veil held in place on her head by a gold circlet. She had been staring at the opposing castle situated high on the edge of a cliff.

Though she had never seen the castle, she knew it. She also knew its name—MacLeod Castle.

Reaghan lifted a shaky hand to her face and swiped at a strand of hair caught in her eyelashes. How could she know that's what the castle looked like? Did she have magic, as Galen and Logan had said? If so, then was her gift seeing the future?

"Nay," she murmured to herself.

If she had seen into the future, and seen herself at MacLeod Castle, she wouldn't have been wearing a gown from long ago.

Reaghan got to her feet and tried to find Galen. When

she couldn't spot him, she went to Logan. "What does Deirdre look like?"

Logan's hazel eyes narrowed, his attention focused on her. "What?"

"Deirdre? What does she look like?" Reaghan asked a second time.

"She's not aligned with us if that's what you want to know."

Reaghan blew out a frustrated breath. "Does Deirdre have long white hair that touches the ground? Are her eyes as white as her hair?"

The stillness that came over Logan was answer enough. Reaghan fisted her hands and struggled to bring a breath into her lungs. "It's her, isn't it?"

"How did you know?" Logan demanded, his voice low, harsh.

Reaghan shrugged. "I've seen her before in my dreams. I've seen so many things I can't explain."

"Give me another example."

She licked her lips, knowing it was a bad idea to tell him more. "MacLeod Castle, it is on a cliff, the sea below it, wild and untamed?"

Logan smiled, but Reaghan could see it was forced. "You must have heard Galen describe it to one of the Druids."

"I wish that were the case, but I don't think it is. For the past year I've seen more and more things in my dreams."

"We told you there was magic inside you. I suppose that is your gift."

She forced her own smile, her stomach filling with dread. Logan didn't believe it was her magic any more than she did, but she saw the concern in his eyes and it terrified her. "I suppose it is."

"We'll be leaving soon. Go break your fast," he urged her.

She didn't hesitate, but turned on her heel and walked away. If it wasn't her magic, then what caused such strange images to come to her? How did she know what Deirdre looked like?

And not just her hair and eyes either. Reaghan could have told him Deirdre favored black, and her voice could command the wyrran with just a whisper.

Reaghan couldn't recall ever seeing wyrran before they attacked the village, but she knew instantly what they were when she caught sight of them, even when she had first heard their shrieks. Not because of the descriptions of her fellow Druids, but because she had seen them countless times in her dreams.

A warm, strong hand gently grasped her arm. "Reaghan?"

She melted at the sound of Galen's voice and turned toward him.

"Logan found me."

"It's not my magic," she said.

He glanced around the camp as the others ate, their gazes lifted to him. "Follow me."

Reaghan fell into step beside him. Galen gave a small nod to Logan as they walked past him. "Where are we going?"

"I would like some privacy, and I think you would as well. The others will catch up to us soon enough. Now, tell me what happened."

"I thought Logan already had."

Galen shrugged nonchalantly, but she saw the apprehension in his dark blue gaze. "He told me you described Deirdre and MacLeod Castle."

"I did. It's not my magic, Galen. So do not try to tell me it is."

"All right," he said, and lifted his hands in a conciliatory gesture. His gaze shifted to the ground before him as they walked. "Tell me what happened."

She wrapped her arms around her middle. "It began some moons ago. I see things, Galen. People and places I've never been, but yet I know these things and people."

"Like Deirdre?"

She nodded, unable to speak.

"Have any of the Druids ever described her?"

"Nay. They've only ever said her name. I kept seeing this woman with incredibly long, white hair. Her eyes would pierce me to my very soul, and I knew she was *drough*."

They walked in silence for a while before Galen said, "Tell me what else you have seen in these dreams."

She glanced at him. His expression was closed to her, and she had no way of knowing if he was thinking her as daft as Logan did, or if Galen believed her. "As I told Logan, I've seen MacLeod Castle."

"How? Where were you?"

"I was standing on one of the cliffs at a distance from the castle. What struck me as odd was that I was wearing a gown from centuries earlier. Why?"

He grunted in response. "What else have you seen?"

"I know that in the mountain range, Foinaven, which I seek, there is an entrance to the valley between the mountains. It is hidden from those who don't know of it. I know every section of those mountains as if I had lived there. As if it had been my home."

Galen heard the fear in her voice and it tore at his soul. He stopped and pulled her into his arms. "These dreams or visions cannot harm you."

"I know," she mumbled against his chest, her arms holding on to him tightly. "I know I've been out in the world before, but I don't know when or how."

"Does it matter?"

She leaned back to look at him. Her brow was furrowed and her gaze searched his. "I have a past that is blocked to me. Do you have any idea how it feels to know there are memories there, memories that could tell me about my family and what I did wrong?"

"What makes you think you did anything wrong?" he asked. "Maybe someone did this to you."

"If that were the case, why would Mairi and the others keep it from me? Why not tell me?"

Galen pulled her against him again and rested the palm of his hand on the back of her head. "I know they want to keep you safe, and if that means they have to keep your past from you, they will."

"It's my life, Galen, my past. I have the right to know."

He knew she did, and that's what was killing him. To hear her speak of Deirdre and MacLeod Castle had left him speechless, but it was when she described the mountains and the secret entrance that he realized she must have been referring to the place she had lived as a young girl.

What worried Galen most of all was if Reaghan somehow remembered who she was. Would she leave? Set out on her own?

A strange, hollow ache began in his chest just thinking of a world without Reaghan in it. Though he didn't want to think about why, he knew he needed Reaghan. He needed her, hungered for her, as he did the sun on his face and air in his lungs. He couldn't allow anything to happen to her no matter what.

"You know, don't you?" she said. "You know what happened to my memories."

Galen knew in the moment she looked at him with her somber gray eyes that he wouldn't be able to lie to her. "I do."

"Is it as terrible as I fear?"

He took her hand and began to walk. "I know the elders kept it from you because they care about you."

"Please. Tell me," she said, her voice breaking.

Galen laced his fingers with hers and took a deep breath. It was tearing her to pieces not knowing, and if she was going to lose her memories, he didn't see why the truth should be kept from her.

"Reaghan, you put a spell upon yourself in an effort to hide something from Deirdre. The headaches are caused because you are about to lose your memories, as you do every ten years."

She missed a step, but kept walking, her head held high. He was amazed at the strength he saw. Despite what she had learned, she didn't crumble to the ground, not that he would have thought less of her if she had. But it proved how strong she was that she could keep walking. Galen saw the tears swimming in her eyes, and it tore at him.

"That is why I see events from the past in my dreams?" she asked.

"I believe so."

"This has been happening for a very long time based on what I see in my dreams. How long do I have before my memories are gone?"

Galen squeezed her hand. "I'm no' sure."

She stopped and turned to him. "I don't want to forget you."

"You willna," he promised. "I'll make sure of it."

Galen wiped away a tear before he covered her lips with his own.

TWENTY-ONE

MacLeod Castle

Broc braced a shoulder against the stone wall and watched Sonya, his eyes feasting on her beauty. She had her face turned toward the forest as she leaned as far over the side of the battlements as she could without falling over.

After a moment she scowled and lowered her head. Broc had hidden in the shadows many times over the last weeks watching Sonya, always watching. He knew she had been trying to listen to the trees that spoke to her, but evidently she hadn't been able to hear them.

He pushed away from the wall and stepped from the shadows. By the way Sonya held herself rigid, he could tell something was wrong. "What is it?"

She whirled to face him, the skirts of her green gown tangling in her legs. Sonya braced her hands behind her on the stones. "Broc."

He held back the shiver that raced down his spine at the sound of his name on her lips. She whispered it, almost as if she didn't believe he was there.

Broc slowly walked to stand in front of her. "Sonya, what is it? Did the trees tell you something?"

"I don't know."

The pain in her gaze was like a punch to his gut. "Is it Galen and Logan?"

She lifted her hand to press it to her forehead, and he saw how it shook. "The trees are trying to talk to me. I'm too far away to hear what they are saying, but it's important."

Broc didn't need to hear any more. He looked down into the bailey of the castle where Lucan was continuing Cara's training with a sword. "Lucan," Broc called, to get his attention. "I'm taking Sonya to the trees."

Broc didn't wait for Lucan's reaction. He unleashed his god, his large, leathery wings sprouting from his back. He had carried Sonya before, but he hesitated to scoop her in his arms now.

Instead, Broc held out his hand. "I'll take you to the forest."

Her amber eyes watched him as she placed her hand in his. Broc closed his eyes and held back a sigh of pleasure when he pulled Sonya's lithe body next to his.

"Hold on," he whispered as he spread his wings.

Her arms wrapped around his neck as she pressed her face against his chest. The feel of her heat, her breasts crushed against him, made his heart pound faster and all his blood pool between his legs.

The desire that surged through him made his legs weak, leaving only one thought in his mind—kiss Sonya. Take her. Seize her.

"Broc?"

Her velvety smooth voice caused his eyes to open. He swallowed and launched himself into the air. For just a moment, her fingers clutched him, but as they glided through the sky, she relaxed against him.

Broc could feel her smile against his bare chest. All the tension that had radiated from her on the battlements faded to nothing. He took his time flying to the village outside MacLeod Castle so he could savor the delight of having Sonya's body so close.

All too soon they arrived. Broc didn't need to turn around to know the other Warriors watched him. Sonya's communication with the trees was vital to all of them.

He used his wings and slowly lowered them into the middle of the village, hidden from the Warriors' view. When Sonya's feet were once more on the ground Broc had no reason to hold her. He was unwilling to let her go though.

For an insane moment he thought about telling her how he desired her, how he had always yearned for her. But as he looked into her lovely amber eyes, he knew now wasn't the time.

There would never be a time for them. Broc had known it from the first moment he had seen her as a young girl playing in the loch with her sister. Sonya had been a beautiful child, and she had blossomed into a stunning woman.

"Thank you," she said, and stepped out of his arms.

Broc fisted his hands at his sides. The absence of her warmth against him hurt worse than a drop of *drough* blood in a wound. He ached for what he could not have.

He would never be able to hold Sonya as a lover, so the times he was able to touch her were burned into his skin and branded into his memory. He held those memories against his heart knowing they would be the only things to get him through the long darkness of eternity.

"I'll stay here while you go to the trees," he said.

Her tongue peeked out to lick her lips, and he nearly fell to his knees with the longing that cut through him.

Sonya glanced behind her. "I know Isla's magic keeps the wyrran from finding us, but I would feel better if you were near."

"Of course." He was always near her, always had been near her. He had kept her from harm more times than she knew. And he would always be there to make sure nothing happened to her.

They walked to the far end of the village. Isla's magic created a barrier around the castle and the village, preventing Deirdre or any wyrran from getting to the castle easily. Though Deirdre knew they were at MacLeod Castle, Isla's magic was strong and her barrier thick enough to keep out all but Deirdre herself.

Deirdre had penetrated Isla's shield not long ago as she tried to control Isla's mind, but Isla had managed to break Deirdre's hold once and for all. None of them knew if Deirdre had regained her form yet, but Broc surmised Deirdre had used a vast amount of her magic to try and claim Isla.

He didn't expect a visit from Deirdre for a little while. But he was always prepared, especially where Sonya was concerned.

Broc could feel Isla's magic vibrating around them, signaling they had reached the barrier. Just twenty paces away was the beginning of the forest that spread across the land.

He watched as Sonya reached out, using her ability to hear and speak to the trees. It had been the trees that had sent her to MacLeod Castle and for that Broc would be forever grateful.

Then he saw Sonya bend over, her arms wrapped around her middle. "I cannot."

Broc was at her side in an instant. He put his arms around her and pulled her against him so that he took most of her weight. The long, thick braid of red hair fell over her side to land at her breast.

"What do you need?" he asked.

"It's Isla's magic. It's keeping me from hearing the trees. I have to go outside the barrier."

He shook his head. "Nay."

She turned her face to his, the strain evident in the

lines around her eyes and bracketing her brow. "I have to know what the trees are trying to tell me. It's vital. I feel it."

Broc realized he could not dissuade her, but when she looked at him so trustingly, he'd been unable to even form an argument. "All right. We'll go through the shield, but the instant I say we leave, we leave."

Her small smile was enough to brighten his day. "Certainly."

Broc glanced at the clouds in the sky, silently praying he would be able to keep her safe. He followed her through Isla's shield, the magic enveloping him for a heartbeat until it fell away.

He had left the shield before. He knew if he turned around, the castle and village would be gone. Isla's magic made it appear as if nothing were there but rocks and grass; not even their words penetrated the shield to the world outside.

They hurried into the trees, Broc's Warrior senses alert to anything out of the ordinary. When Sonya walked into the trees he saw them begin to sway. And not in the direction from which the sea breeze came.

Sonya dropped her head back, and her eyes closed. Her arms lifted from her sides while she swayed with the trees. He had never seen her speak to the trees, never knew it could be so . . . arousing and sensual.

Her magic had always made his heart beat double time and his blood quicken. But now, as it surrounded him, shrouded him, consumed him, Broc had to sink his claws into a tree so as not to grab her and kiss her as he yearned to do.

The longer her magic encircled him, the more his hunger for her devoured him. He fought it, fought the tide of desire that threatened everything he was trying to build.

Sonya was a woman who deserved the best, and Broc was anything but that. The things he had done . . . he wasn't fit to even think of touching her. Yet the passion that grew in him, the desire for her that burned as bright as the sun, thought otherwise.

"Broc," Sonya said.

It sounded as though a thousand voices were added to hers. Broc walked.to her, afraid she was in pain, but the bright smile on her face let him know she was more than fine.

"I can hear them," she whispered, the other voices still accompanying hers. "It's been so long. How I've missed them."

Broc had no idea she had missed communicating with the trees so much. The sheer joy on her face made it clear though. He decided then and there he would bring her to the forest as often as she needed it. As long as there was no danger.

"What are they saying?" he asked.

She chuckled, the sound shooting straight to his groin then to his heart. "Touch me, Broc. Touch me and listen."

He was unsure if he could touch her in the aroused state he was in, but how could he not when she asked? It took just a heartbeat for him to make his decision.

He lifted his hand, ready to place it on her, but he paused. He didn't want to harm her, and he wasn't sure if her magic would conflict with his god.

"It's all right," she whispered with a smile. "Touch me."

How could he deny her? Broc took a deep breath and placed his hands on her arms. His eyes closed under the spell of Sonya's magic, and instantly the world altered around him.

His eyes flew open to find the forest as he had left it. He shut his eyes again, and with them closed he could feel the trees swaying, as if they bent and smoothed their limbs lovingly over him.

He could hear them murmuring, but couldn't make out the words. He might not understand what they said, but he knew they were just as happy to see Sonya as she was to be with them. It seemed they smiled down at her, as if touching her soothed them.

The cheerfulness ended, though, when a tree bent low, its branches cocooning them. The words came in a jumble, harsh and low, as if it were revealing a terrible secret.

Even with his eyes closed Broc could tell the news distressed Sonya. Her body began to shake, with fear or anger, he didn't know.

"Thank you," she told the trees. "Watch over them, please."

The pulsing magic was gone before Broc could prepare himself. He dropped his arms to his sides and staggered back a step. His head swam with what he had seen and experienced. But his body hummed with renewal, with the feel of Sonya's seductive magic.

He raised his gaze to hers and found her watching him. There was something in her eyes, something he couldn't quite name. "Why did you show me?"

"I wanted to share it with you."

No one had ever wanted to share something like that with him. He didn't know what to say, and was too afraid of saying something wrong to even try.

Sonya blew out a harsh breath. "We must get back to the castle immediately. Galen and Logan need our help."

Though Broc wanted to know the particulars, he didn't waste time trying to talk to Sonya about it. He took her up in his arms and jumped into the air as his wings spread wide.

There was a small crackle of magic as they once more passed through Isla's shield and the castle came into view. Broc flew low and fast. His friends were in trouble, and if they could do something about it, they would.

He landed gently in the bailey where the MacLeod brothers waited. Sonya stayed near him, and Broc had the urge to put his arm around her shoulders and tug her against him.

Fallon, the eldest, spoke first. "Did you hear the trees speak, Sonya?"

"Aye. Galen and Logan are on their way back to the castle. They have almost a score of Druids with them. It seems the wyrran found the Druids while Galen and Logan were there. They fought off the wyrran and saved the Druids."

"Do you know how far out Galen and the Druids are?" Quinn asked.

Sonya glanced at Broc. "Nearly two days' journey from here. All the Druids are female except for a young boy."

"I can find them," Broc said. His power of tracking anyone anywhere came in handy.

Fallon nodded. "Aye, but you cannot return them fast enough. Do you think you can carry me that distance?"

"Oh, aye," Broc said.

"We leave now then," Fallon said. He paused, and a smile pulled at his face as he turned toward the castle. "After I tell my wife."

Broc watched Fallon rush into the castle to find Larena. Love had found the MacLeods and given them good, strong women as their mates. Even Hayden, whom Broc had often doubted would be able to let go of his hatred, had found love.

Every time Broc thought of love, his gaze always sought out Sonya, and it did so now. She turned to him, her amber eyes bright with some unnamed emotion.

"Be careful," she told him. "The trees say there are no wyrran around Galen and Logan."

"But . . ." he urged when she paused.

Sonya lifted a slim shoulder. "The trees are frightened for us. Deirdre seems to have regained most of her magic."

Broc lifted his hand to stroke her cheek, but dropped it before he touched her. His gaze lowered to her mouth, her ripe lips just begging for his kiss.

It was torture being so near Sonya and unable to have her. Broc had suffered for so long at Deirdre's hands, and it seemed he would continue to suffer for years to come.

"Broc? Are you ready?"

He jerked at Fallon's call. Broc gave Sonya a small nod and turned to their leader.

"Which way, Sonya?" Fallon asked.

She pointed to the southeast. "Be safe."

Broc tore his eyes from her, then lifted him and Fallon high into the skies.

TWENTY-TWO

It didn't take Logan and the other Druids long to catch up to Galen and Reaghan. He'd have liked to have had more time with Reaghan, but that would have to wait until they reached the castle.

Reaghan had been lost in thought, and Galen had left her alone. She had much to digest after what she had learned. He knew the elders would not like it, but Reaghan had a right to know.

The long, low whistle that came from Logan at the back of the group caused Galen to turn around. Logan pointed to the sky. Galen spotted the falcon almost instantly.

"What is it?" Reaghan asked.

"That same peregrine was with us as we left MacLeod Castle and when we reached your village. It's also decided to make the return trip with us."

"You believe there is something to it?"

He smiled and resumed walking. "Oh, aye, Reaghan. For sure. I've learned when dealing with magic that there is no such thing as coincidence."

"What will you do about the falcon?"

"Nothing. For now. We'll see what happens when we reach the castle."

They walked in companionable silence the rest of the morning. When they stopped to rest for the noon meal

Galen left Reaghan to the Druids and sat beside Logan some ten paces away.

"What did you learn from Reaghan?" Logan asked.

Galen picked a stem of grass from the ground and sighed. "After what she had told me she saw in her dreams I knew she had to know the truth."

"You told her?"

"I did."

"And?" Logan asked. "How did she take it?"

Galen looked at Reaghan. "She was upset, but she is handling it well. It willna be an easy path for her, but keeping it from her seemed wrong."

Logan grunted as he swallowed his food. "I think you did the right thing."

While Galen had been listening he spotted something in the sky. A dark shape that was too big to be another bird of prey. "Logan," he said in warning.

Logan shot to his feet, a smile spreading over his face. "I think we might be reaching MacLeod Castle sooner than expected."

Galen climbed to his feet. There was only one Warrior who could fly, and thankfully, he was on their side. "It appears they are still some ways out."

"Is Broc carrying someone?"

"I pray it's Fallon." Galen glanced at the Druids, who were now staring at him and Logan.

Logan groaned. "God's teeth. Now they get to meet more Warriors."

"They would have eventually," Galen mumbled. He walked over to the Druids. "We will be reaching the castle very soon. Somehow the other Warriors at MacLeod Castle learned we were on our way. They've come for us."

Odara looked around before she turned and frowned at Galen. "Where are they? And how do you know?"

"Because Broc can fly," Logan said, and pointed to the sky.

The Druids as one looked in the direction he indicated. Several gasped.

"Do not be afraid," Galen said. "Broc is a friend."

Logan shook his head as the Druids huddled together, talking. "They willna ever stop being afraid, will they?"

"It's been ingrained in them. It will take time and patience on our part." Though Galen wasn't sure the Druids' fear could be eliminated completely.

"Time we doona have."

Galen didn't bother to respond since Broc now hovered just off the ground, allowing Fallon to jump down before landing beside him.

Galen hurried to greet them. For the first time since leaving Loch Awe, he felt everything would be all right. "It's good to see the two of you."

"How did you know where to find us?" Logan asked.

"The trees," Broc said.

Galen nodded, needing no other explanation. Somehow the trees had spoken to Sonya, and that was enough for him. "The Druids are frightened of all Warriors. We will need to be careful."

"Once we get them to the castle and they see Cara and the others they'll know they have nothing to fear," Fallon said.

Logan snorted, his lips twisted in a grimace. "Doona be so sure. It's the elders you need to win to your side. It hasn't worked for us, especially since Galen has taken a liking to one of the Druids."

"Good for you," Broc said with a grin.

Galen shook his head. "There is much neither of you know. We need to get Reaghan to the castle with all haste."

"Why?" Fallon asked as he let his gaze wander over the Druids.

Galen glanced at the group, his gaze lingering on Reaghan. "We found the artifact."

"As we knew you would," Broc said.

"The object isn't a thing. It's a person."

"Reaghan," Fallon whispered.

Galen nodded. "I told her just this morn. I'll explain everything at the castle. Just, please, get her to safety."

"I'll take her first."

Galen, Logan, and Broc followed Fallon to the Druids. Galen listened as Fallon explained who he was, and how they were going to arrive at the castle, and during that time Galen's eyes never left Reaghan.

Fallon called for Reaghan, Braden, and Fiona, along with Odara, to be taken first. Reaghan hesitated, but Galen nodded at her to go with Fallon as he jumped them to the castle.

As soon as they were gone Galen expected the tight knot of fear that had nestled in his gut to disappear. Instead it worsened.

"You'll be with her soon," Broc said.

Galen shook his head. "I always thought myself cursed to have the god inside me and to have been the unlucky one to have it unbound. Deirdre says we're blessed to have the god and our abilities."

"I think we're cursed and blessed. Blessed because we are able to stay alive and fight Deirdre as well as protect the ones we care about." Broc sighed softly. "But we're also cursed, because the thing that allows us to protect people is the same thing that prevents us from being with them."

"Yet the MacLeods have found a way to have their women."

"And Hayden as well."

Galen turned his head to Broc. "Hayden and Isla?"

"I knew there was a possibility," Logan said with a knowing smile.

"More than a possibility," Broc said with a grin. "I will let Hayden tell the story, though I'm sure he'll leave several things out."

Galen laughed, eager to return to the home and family he had found. "And I suppose you'll be happy to provide those details?"

"Of course," Broc said with a nod. "As will Ian, I'm sure."

"Much has happened while we've been away," Logan mumbled.

Broc caught Galen's eyes and jerked his chin to the Druids. "I could say the same thing, my friend."

Fallon soon returned, and in a blink he had taken four more Druids.

"I doona know how the trees knew, but I'm thankful they told Sonya," Logan said.

Broc growled. "Was it happenstance the wyrran found the village?"

"I'm no' sure," Galen answered. "Reaghan's magic is strong. None of the other Druids have very much, so despite the village's being protected, they might have sensed her magic."

Broc's mouth twisted into a scowl. "If that's the case, then it's a wonder they haven't found Reaghan before now."

"And why it was so important to get her to the castle. I suppose Isla's shield is still up?"

Broc nodded.

Logan waited until Fallon had left for a third trip before he said, "I expect there to be another attack."

"Of course," Broc agreed. "They've sensed Reaghan's magic."

"They'll know we're returning to the castle," Logan continued. "Whether Isla's shield is active or no', they will come."

Broc's smirk was lethal in its intensity. "And we'll be waiting for them."

Logan gave a single nod. "I cannot wait."

Fallon returned, and then left for a fourth time. Galen wondered how Reaghan fared at the castle. He knew Cara and the other Druids would see to her, but he wanted to be there with her.

"It willna be long now," Broc said as if sensing Galen's frustration. "Fallon has learned to use his power well."

It took Fallon one more trip before he stood in front of the Warriors. "Ready?" he asked.

Galen faltered. In order to return to the castle by Fallon's power, Galen would have to touch him.

"Galen?" Logan said.

He looked up to find Broc's hand on Fallon's shoulder and Logan's hand on Broc's arm.

"It'll be quick," Fallon said.

Logan sighed. "Think of nothing but the castle."

Galen took a deep breath and steeled himself as he placed his hand on Fallon's shoulder the same instant Logan grabbed hold of his arm.

The castle flashed in Galen's mind the moment a low, simmering anger filled his head. In the next instant, both were gone and he stood in the bailey of MacLeod Castle.

Galen turned and looked at Logan. That anger, the seething, festering fury, had come from Logan, and it was tearing his friend in two.

Logan's hazel eyes met his, seeming to dare Galen to say a word. When Galen said nothing Logan turned on his heel and walked into the castle.

"What was that about?" Broc asked as he stared after Logan.

Galen glanced to Broc and shrugged. "Things I shouldn't know."

"But you do," Fallon said. "Is there something we need to know about Logan?"

"Doona ask it of me, Fallon. What is inside Logan is his to bear and to share as he chooses," Galen said.

Fallon bowed his head. "I hope you will let us know when the time comes to help him, because it is coming. I doona need to read his mind to see that. It's in his eyes."

Galen forgot all about responding to Fallon when he caught sight of Reaghan with Marcail and Sonya. She stood on the castle steps, a smile on her face as she took in everything and everyone.

Her gaze moved over him. In a blink, she jerked her eyes back to him. Her smile widened and her gaze softened. All he could think about was getting her alone and kissing her.

And he was going to make sure that happened very soon.

TWENTY-THREE

Reaghan was overwhelmed, besieged. She hadn't wanted to depart for MacLeod Castle without Galen. He was her anchor in the storm that was now her life. Without him, she felt adrift.

Lost. Alone.

Fallon hadn't given her much time to think. One moment she was looking at Galen, and the next she was standing in the middle of a large bailey with people milling about.

Reaghan had seen a bailey before. She knew how they bustled with activity from men training, children playing, and women gossiping as they went about their daily chores.

She knew the sound of a blacksmith's hammer as it pounded iron. She knew the smell of horses and hay from the nearby stables. She knew the feel of the cool stones beneath her feet as she ran barefoot across the bailey.

She knew there was a door in the castle wall—a postern door—that led outside.

Her world began to spin viciously as her mind rocked from the knowledge. She knew MacLeod Castle because sometime in her life she had been there. The spell she had cast that erased her memories kept her from remembering when and why she had been at the castle.

The voices around her faded as her blood pounded in her ears. Her hands dampened and her stomach pitched to her feet as panic consumed her. Because she was the artifact.

How? Why? What did she know that Deirdre sought? What had been so important that Reaghan would do this to herself?

She stumbled trying to get away, trying to find Galen in the chaos.

"Deep breaths," said a soft, feminine voice Reaghan didn't recognize as gentle hands took hold of her arms. "It'll be all right."

Reaghan swallowed past the lump of dread in her throat. She focused her eyes on one stone in the bailey wall while she tried to make the world stop spinning. "Galen."

"He'll be here soon. I promise. Until then come and sit."

Reaghan allowed the woman to guide her to the castle steps. She was overcome with fear of what she was and what she had done to herself, but mercifully, the dizziness halted and the world righted itself. She took a few moments and let her gaze take in her surroundings.

The sight that greeted Reaghan was spectacular. She recalled the many times she had looked across Loch Awe at MacIntosh Castle and wanted to see the inside of it.

Now, she was within the walls of one of the most infamous castles in all of Scotland. There was so much to explore, so much to experience at MacLeod Castle.

Her terror still gripped her, but it was the knowledge of where she was and who surrounded her that allowed Reaghan to push the apprehension aside and take everything in.

Reaghan swiveled her head to find a woman with chestnut curls and mahogany eyes beside her. There was a low current of something . . . energizing. A memory crept up in her consciousness like a twisting funnel of smoke, a recollection of what surrounded, of what beat inside the heart of MacLeod Castle.

Magic.

Reaghan's skin prickled with excitement. She was with another Druid. And she could sense her magic.

"I'm Cara," the Druid said, "Lucan's wife. Are you better now?"

"Aye," Reaghan answered. "Much. Thank you."

Cara waved away her words. "Sometimes jumping with Fallon leaves people light-headed."

Reaghan remembered Galen had said they called Fallon's power "jumping." "I'm Reaghan."

"Reaghan," Cara said with a wide, friendly smile. "It is so nice to have more Druids here. I'll introduce you to the others as soon as you feel up to it."

Reaghan looked over to find Fallon had appeared in the bailey again, this time with Mairi and three others. Reaghan watched as the people of her village were welcomed into the castle.

"I'm eager to meet more Druids. We thought we were the last."

"Not the last, but close," Cara said as she waved a petite woman over. "This is Marcail, my sister by marriage. Marcail, this is Reaghan."

Marcail winked at Cara, their friendship obvious, as she lowered herself to the steps beside them. "Hello, Reaghan, I'm married to Quinn."

"Hello," Reaghan said. She couldn't stop staring at the numerous small braids which graced the crown of Marcail's dark head. "I apologize for staring. It's just that I've seen those kinds of braids before."

Marcail's brow furrowed as she shared a look with Cara. "Do you know where? In my village, only Druids with the most magic had such a custom."

Reaghan shrugged as she racked her mind to try and recall where she had seen the braids. To recognize things, but not be able to know why was frustrating. Maybe if she concentrated more she could break the walls of her spell. She smiled as she realized she did have magic. She had to have it in order to cast such a spell. "I can't remember, but I know I've seen such braids before."

"It's no matter," Cara said. "It will come to you later. There are so many people to introduce you to. We have twelve Warriors who live at the castle, well, thirteen if you count Larena."

"And Malcolm," Marcail interjected.

Cara nodded. "Malcolm is Larena's cousin, and the only mortal man."

"Galen told me." Reaghan had never met anyone who was so open and welcoming before. These Druids didn't know of her past, of who she was. She hoped she could become friends with these women. "He also said there were other Druids."

Marcail pointed to the middle of the bailey. "The woman with the thick braid of red hair is Sonya. She's our healer."

"Aye. Then there is also Isla." Cara looked around the bailey. "Isla is the tiny one with black hair standing next to the blond giant."

It was said with a smile, and Reaghan had no difficulty identifying Isla. "And you all have magic?"

"We do," Marcail answered. "Is it not the same in your village?"

Reaghan glanced away and shook her head. "Most have very little magic. I . . . I have some."

Marcail stood and smiled as a man bounded up the steps to her side. He had wavy, light brown hair and pale green eyes. She could see a resemblance between him and Fallon, and it didn't take long for Reaghan to realize the man was the youngest MacLeod.

"Quinn, this is Reaghan," Marcail said. "Reaghan, this is my husband, Quinn."

Reaghan rose to her feet and inclined her head. "Thank you for opening your home to us."

"All Druids are welcome here," Quinn replied with an easy, sincere smile.

"All Druids?" Cara asked with a smile.

Quinn rolled his eyes as Marcail began to laugh. Reaghan found herself smiling as she recognized they were speaking of Deirdre.

Warmth, like a lover's touch, spread over Reaghan of a sudden. She knew without looking that Galen had arrived. She turned, searching for him. It was his cobalt eyes that caught her attention as her gaze found him.

He stood with Fallon, Broc, and Logan in the middle of the bailey, surrounded by the Druids from her village. But all she saw was Galen.

All she cared about was Galen.

They lost themselves in each other's eyes as the rest of the world vanished to nothing. The castle and all others were forgotten as Galen started toward her. Reaghan never took her eyes off him. Her heart beat doubled in time and her hands itched to touch him, hold him.

He walked with purpose, commanding attention and respect. How could anyone think him nothing more than a mere man? The Warrior within was evident in the way he moved, the way his gaze devoured her.

A slow heat built in her belly, tightening with every step Galen took, until she was a smoldering mass of desire, desperate and frantic for his touch.

He stopped a step below her, putting them at eye level with each other. Her gaze dropped to his mouth, to his wide lips that she yearned to feel on her body once more.

"Reaghan," he whispered, his tone full of torment and ecstasy. "You must stop looking at me so before I carry you to my chamber."

She raised her gaze to his and grinned. "I wouldn't complain."

He groaned low in his throat. "You're going to be the death of me."

Reaghan lost herself in the depths of his blue eyes and their implicit promise of pleasure. His fingers grazed her cheek with the lightest of touches but left a trail of heat in its wake, heat that centered between her legs and left her throbbing for more. That was always the way with Galen. She could never get enough, and she feared she never would.

His hand dropped and he cleared his throat. "You're exhausted," he murmured, and took a step away from her.

Reaghan became aware that Cara and Marcail stood on either side of her. They had witnessed the exchange, but Reaghan didn't mind.

"We've prepared the chambers," Cara said. "I will show you to yours, Reaghan."

Reaghan didn't want to leave Galen's side again, but she knew he had things he needed to do. And the thought of a soft bed and warm food was too much to resist.

She eagerly followed Cara and Marcail into the castle. Reaghan drank in the sight of the great hall. There were two long tables that filled the space, and four chairs sat before a large hearth.

There was no time to look her fill before they started up the stairs. Cara led her up two flights of steps and down a lengthy corridor before Cara stopped before an open door.

Reaghan glanced inside to find a small chamber with a bed against the far wall and a window on the left side. She stepped within the chamber and spotted a small table beside the bed, four wooden pegs in the wall, and a chest. Above the bed was a shield that Reaghan somehow knew dated back four hundred years.

"This is more than I had imagined," Reaghan said as she turned to the door to find Cara and Marcail watching her.

"There is a village not far from here," Marcail said as her fingers grabbed one of the gold bands around her braids. "But Deirdre has destroyed it twice. It was decided all Druids should stay in the castle in case of another attack."

Reaghan glanced at the bed. "Is there room for everyone?"

Cara grinned and linked her hands in front of her. "Don't worry. There is a place for everyone."

"And the Warriors?" Reaghan couldn't help but ask.

"They will sleep in the village."

"Are you hungry? I could bring up some food," Marcail suggested.

Reaghan was starving, but she knew they had many others to see to. "I'll find my way to the kitchen."

"Nonsense," Cara said. "Rest, Reaghan. You've had a long journey, been attacked by wyrran, and you've had to leave your home. Let us see to you."

Now that she was at MacLeod Castle, Reaghan was too tired to resist. "Only for now."

Marcail smiled as she closed the door behind them, leaving Reaghan alone with her thoughts. She kicked off her shoes and climbed on to the bed.

Reaghan sighed as she fell back against the soft pillow. She had slept each night on the ground because she'd been so weary, but the feel of the supple bed beneath her made her realize just how hard the ground had been.

Reaghan rolled to her side and tucked her knees up to her chest. She knew she was filthy and needed a bath, but the other Druids from her village would also want to bathe. So she would wait.

Her stomach rumbled with hunger even though it hadn't

been long since their noon meal. She glanced through her open window to the sky beyond and realized the sun had begun to set.

She had been so caught up with MacLeod Castle and its people she hadn't realized it was nearing suppertime. Reaghan looked down at her soiled dress and frowned.

With a sigh she sat up and pulled off her gown and tossed it aside. She would wash it later. For now, she would do as Cara and Marcail suggested and rest.

The sounds from the bailey drifted through her window, reminding her of all that she knew of castles. She wondered how long her spell had been erasing her memories. The secrets Mairi and Odara had kept all made sense now, and though she was frightened to her very core of what she was, she was so very glad Galen had told her.

What information did she have that must be kept from Deirdre? That was the scariest of all. Something drastic and terrifying had to have happened to her in order for her to put such a spell on herself.

Would she ever know the reason? Was there a way to break the spell? And did she even want to try?

The thought of losing her memories of Galen and what she was, not to mention the last ten years of her life, made it difficult to breathe. She didn't want her memories erased again.

If somewhere in her memories there was a means to help Galen and the others defeat Deirdre, Reaghan would do all she could to make sure they had what they needed.

She didn't know how, but she would.

TWENTY-FOUR

The sun was casting its last rays of light into the darkening sky as Dunmore rode through the gatehouse of the seat of clan MacClure. The castle had been enlarged and expanded in the three hundred years since the MacLeod clan had fallen.

The MacClures were one of the clans who had gained coin and land with the death of the MacLeods. But Dunmore wasn't interested in the castle or the MacClure coin. He was only concerned about one thing, and that would soon come to pass.

"What is your business?" demanded one of the four guards who stood at the top of the steps that led into the castle.

Dunmore grinned and scratched his jaw with his thumbnail. "I was hoping you'd ask. I'm here to see your laird."

"What reason?"

Dunmore narrowed his gaze and leaned forward to stare at the insolent man. "That matter is for your laird only. Tell him I've been sent by Deirdre."

The guards paled, and the one who had spoken turned and hurried into the castle. Dunmore rested a hand on his thigh and let his gaze wander the bailey.

The children had stopped playing and huddled at the rear of a group of women who were whispering behind their hands. The men tried to appear less interested by pretending to continue with their work, but Dunmore wasn't fooled.

He knew his hulking appearance was menacing, but that was just how he liked it. He also had the favor of Deirdre, the most powerful Druid to ever walk the land. But he imagined it was his bloodred cloak that got the most attention.

The castle doors opened and a large, heavyset man stepped outside. Dunmore had seen the MacClure laird before, but it had been several years ago when the man hadn't had as much gray in his hair or wrinkles lining his face.

"Your name," the laird demanded in a deep, gravelly voice.

"Dunmore."

The laird sighed, resignation in the slump of his shoulders, and motioned him off his horse. "Come inside so we can speak. A stable lad will see to your horse."

Dunmore dismounted and tossed the reins to a lad who reluctantly came forward. Dunmore had been like the boy at one time, but that was before he'd found Deirdre and seen what her magic could do.

He followed the laird inside the castle to the dais where a meal was in progress. The great hall was filled with people, all of whom stared at him. Murmurs ran through the hall as they speculated on what had brought him to their castle. Dunmore hid a smile as servants hastened to prepare a space next to the laird.

"Tell me, Clennan, how do you know I come from Deirdre?" Dunmore asked as he sat.

Clennan turned bleak hazel eyes to him. "I was told someday I might get a visit from a man named Dunmore who wore a red cloak. I was to give him entrance and hear what he had to say."

"And who told you this?"

Clennan shifted uneasily in his chair as the conversation began to pick up again throughout the great hall. "Through the cold bitch, Isla."

Dunmore laughed. Clearly the laird didn't enjoy the pact his forefathers had made with Deirdre, but like them, he recognized when he was beaten and sided with her for his own interests. "You doona have to worry about Isla anymore."

"Why is that?"

"Because she has sided with the MacLeods," Dunmore said just before he lifted his goblet and drank heavily of the heady red wine.

Clennan's hand shook with fury. "Those that call themselves MacLeods," he said, spittle flying from his lips. "They took my land."

"It's theirs actually." Dunmore smiled when the old laird glared at him. "Well, you cannot deny that. Your ancestors stole what wasn't theirs, and the MacLeods took it back."

"What do you want with me?" Clennan challenged.

Dunmore bit into a piece of venison and chewed slowly, letting the laird wait. He swallowed and wiped his mouth with the back of his hand. "Deirdre requires you gather an army."

"For what?"

The hall grew deathly quiet as they awaited Dunmore's response.

With a smile, Dunmore rested his left elbow on the table as he took his dagger from its sheath at his waist. He spun the dagger in his hand and speared another portion of meat. "Do you really want to question Deirdre's orders?" he asked before he took a bite.

"Nay," Clennan murmured. "I would, however, like to tell my men why I have called them to me."

"This is really good," Dunmore said as he motioned to his trencher with his dagger. "You need to compliment your cook for me. And you can tell your men, they come to you because you are going to attack the MacLeods."

The entire hall gasped as one.

"They are Warriors," Clennan said. "We cannot battle them."

Dunmore sighed disdainfully and cleaned off his dagger with the laird's kilt. "Deirdre willna let you attack them alone. Her wyrran will be there."

"Will she no' spare some Warriors of her own?"

"Be glad she's granting you the wyrran. And myself. That is all you will need."

"So she has a plan?"

Dunmore sheathed his dagger and rose. "Do your part, laird, and you will survive this. Leave the planning to Deirdre. Have your men ready to ride out in three days."

"That's no' enough time," Clennan said as he jumped to his feet. "It takes that long just to reach the fringes of my land and back."

"Then you'd better hurry."

Clennan watched Dunmore stride from the castle, anger and more than a bit of trepidation settling in his gut. He had little time to think of Deirdre's messenger as his earlier visitor stepped from the shadows.

"Interesting," the man said.

Clennan's spine tingled at the delight he saw shining in the brown eyes of the man. "You knew he would come, Charon?"

Charon chuckled and raised a dark brow. "Of course. As I told you, I've been watching the coming and goings on Cairn Toul. Deirdre wants the MacLeods. It was only a matter of time before she needed you to take action."

"We doona stand a chance against those Warriors," Clennan said.

Charon shrugged. His uncaring attitude was evident in the way he regarded those around him. "It's no' as if you have a choice. You either do as Deirdre has requested. Or you die by her hand."

"Either way we die."

"Possibly."

Clennan stepped closer to Charon. He knew Charon was a Warrior, but Charon wasn't aligned with Deirdre. There might be a chance he could help them. "Ride with us."

"Against the MacLeods and the Warriors there?" Charon laughed and shook his head as he walked to the castle door. "I'm no' that foolish. Deirdre may manage to kill or capture one or two of the Warriors, but the Mac-Leods will continue to stand."

"You doona stand with Deirdre, but you doona stand against her. Who do you ally with?"

Charon paused as he pulled open the castle door. "I fight for myself. That's all that matters to me."

Galen forced himself not to ask Cara or Marcail about Reaghan. Most of the Druids brought to the castle had chosen to eat in their chambers, and Reaghan had been one of them.

Cara had been the one to inform him she had brought a tray to Reaghan, but Galen hadn't asked which chamber was Reaghan's. In truth, he didn't need to. He could feel her magic throughout the castle. All he would have to do was follow it to her.

"She's safe now," Logan said from across the table. "There's no need to fret."

"It's no' worry that's bothering me," Galen admitted.

Logan grinned. "Ah. I see. Then go to her."

Galen sat back and raked a hand through his hair. He had chosen to sit at the second table instead of his usual seat because he'd wanted time to gather his thoughts before the others heard his tale.

When the meal was finished and the women cleared

the table, Fallon's dark green eyes turned to Galen. "We would hear what transpired."

Galen put his elbows on the table and looked at his hands. "The Druids were exactly where Isla said they would be."

"Though the magic kept us from seeing the village. If it hadn't been for Reaghan, we might never have found them," Logan said.

Galen turned his head to look at the Warriors watching him. "They were reluctant to let us in. Their fear of Deirdre made them hide. They've also been told for countless generations that Warriors are evil and cannot be trusted."

Fallon's brow wrinkled in confusion. "So what did this magic of theirs do exactly?"

"It made the Druids very difficult to locate. We walked by their village countless times," Logan said. "The spell was centuries old, and with the Druids' magic fading, I'm no' sure how much longer it could have held."

"It seems strange that the wyrran located you so swiftly if you had such a difficult time finding the village," Quinn said.

Hayden shook his blond head. "No' really. Deirdre needed Druids, and if the wyrran had found Druids in one place before, it stands to reason they would return again."

Galen gave a nod to Hayden. "He's right. I'm fairly certain that's why the wyrran arrived. They didn't seem to be looking for the artifact. Instead, their objective was to grab as many Druids as they could."

"Had we no' been there, they could have gotten the entire village," Logan said.

Fallon clasped his fingers together and rested his chin atop them. "Thankfully you were there. Sonya was told by the trees that Dunmore was as well."

"Dunmore?" Galen repeated. "Is he the man I saw?"

Hayden gave a jerk of his head. "If he had a red cloak, then aye. He does Deirdre's bidding in every way. She rewards him with power and coin, and tempts him with immortality."

"Too bad I didna kill him." Galen rubbed his hands together, wishing Dunmore's neck were between them. "He tried to go after Reaghan. She escaped to the village, and I was about to pursue him when more wyrran attacked. There were too many for Logan to take by himself and keep the Druids safe."

"No' when the Druids stayed in the middle of their village," Logan said.

Quinn scratched his jaw and nodded slowly. "You made the right decision, Galen."

There hadn't been another choice. As long as Reaghan was in danger, Galen would choose protecting her over anything else—even killing Deirdre.

The women walked in from the kitchens then and took their seats at the table.

"We could hear some of what was being discussed," Cara said.

Isla looked from Cara to Galen. "But not all. Did you ask the Druids about the artifact?"

Logan snorted and shook his head, agitation pouring from him. "Oh, aye, we asked. They knew we weren't who we claimed to be, that we were somehow more. They didna trust us, and didna want us in the village. However, with just a word from Reaghan, they let us in."

"How?" Lucan asked.

Galen rubbed his nail in the groove of the table. "Her magic allows her to see into other's eyes and read the truth—or the lie—of their words."

Lucan whistled in response.

Galen met Logan's gaze. "It was no' until after the wyrran attacked and we convinced the Druids to return with us that we discovered the artifact wasn't an object. But a person."

"Reaghan," Isla said into the silence that followed.

Galen nodded. "One of the elders, Mairi, told me only because I forced her."

"I don't understand," Marcail said. "Reaghan is the artifact? How is that possible?"

Galen scrubbed a hand down his face and rose to his feet. Pent-up frustration and unquenched desire had him pacing the length of the tables.

"Galen, you can tell us," Sonya urged gently.

He stopped and looked around the table. All thirteen Warriors, including Larena, four Druids, and Malcolm stared at him, waiting. "It appears Reaghan put a spell on herself to lose her memories every ten years. The Loch Awe Druids were in charge of keeping her at the loch and away from Deirdre."

"Holy hell," Quinn murmured.

Isla stood and caught Galen's gaze. "When are her ten years completed?"

"From what Mairi told us, very soon."

TWENTY-FIVE

The hall had grown so deathly quiet that Galen's ears began to hurt. Each Warrior, Druid, and even Malcolm looked at him with a mixture of sympathy and understanding.

"What is it that occurs exactly?" Isla asked.

Galen began to pace again. "Headaches. An excruciating pain that consumes her." When Isla and Hayden exchanged a knowing look Galen halted beside Hayden. "What is it you know?"

"Maybe nothing," Hayden said. "While you were gone, we learned more about Deirdre's previous control over Isla."

Isla put her hand in Hayden's, their fingers linking together. "Each time before Deirdre took over, I would have such a pain in my mind."

"I doona think this is the same thing," Logan said. "What is happening to Reaghan happens every ten years, and only then."

Galen blew out a long breath. "The pain comes to Reaghan once a day, but we were told the episodes are lasting longer and striking harder every time."

"And the Druids can do nothing to stop the pain?" Sonya asked.

"It is part of the spell," Logan said.

The sound of quick running feet sounded moments before Braden rushed down the stairs and straight to Logan.

He launched his little body at Logan who easily grabbed him. Braden's face was white, and his arms shook as he wrapped them around Logan's neck.

"What is it, lad?" Logan asked as he held Braden against him. "You can tell me."

Braden swallowed nervously and looked at Galen. "Does your promise still hold?"

Galen's gut clenched in fear. "What promise?"

"To protect Reaghan."

"Aye," Galen said with a nod. "Has something happened to her?"

Braden's eyes filled with tears. "She's hurting, Galen. I heard her cry out."

It was all Galen needed to hear. He had never run so fast as he followed the feel of Reaghan's magic up the stairs and down a hallway. He threw open the door to Reaghan's chamber to find her curled on the bed while Mairi stood at the window.

"Why didna you tell me?" Galen demanded.

Mairi turned, her sad eyes locking on his. "There is nothing any of us can do but be here for her, Warrior."

"There you are wrong," Fallon said as he walked into the chamber to stand beside Galen. "You are in my castle now, under my protection. I will no' have someone suffer needlessly."

"We've tried everything to help her," Mairi said as she took hold of Reaghan's hand. "Nothing we have done has lessened the pain."

Galen's heart clenched when he saw the agony Reaghan was in. He went to the bed and took her other hand in his. It was ice-cold.

He didn't waste a moment in pulling the blanket around her and tucking it against her body. He rubbed his hands up and down her arms to help warm her as best he could.

"Galen, let me assist her," Sonya said as she walked into the chamber.

Mairi moved to block Sonya. "The spell Reaghan cast is very strong. To interfere might very well break that spell."

It was Broc who answered as he loomed behind Sonya. "We will no' stand by and do nothing if Sonya is able to help Reaghan."

"Galen, please!" Mairi yelled. "The spell must stay in place."

Sonya asked, "Why?"

Mairi shook her head, her hands trembling as she clasped them in front of her. "Every elder in our village has made a vow to protect Reaghan. As I told Galen, it has long been forgotten what it is she holds in the recesses of her mind, but whatever it is, it cannot fall into Deirdre's hands."

"And you think that by breaking the spell Deirdre will somehow know," Galen said.

Mairi nodded. "We do. I know you think us callous, but we are doing as Reaghan bid our ancestors. I've already broken one promise by taking her away from Loch Awe."

Fallon blew out a breath and laid a gentle hand on Mairi's shoulder. "Every Druid here is protected. Especially Reaghan. Whether the spell breaks or no', we cannot stand aside and do nothing if Sonya is able to help."

Reluctantly Mairi nodded and stepped aside. Sonya moved around the elder and lifted her hands over Reaghan as she closed her eyes. Galen held his breath as Sonya's magic filled the room to mix with Reaghan's.

"By the saints, her magic is strong," Sonya murmured.

A moment later and Isla stood next to Galen and joined her magic with Sonya's. Galen noticed how Hayden stood protectively behind Isla. In all the years

Galen had known Hayden, he had never seen the blond so happy or seen such love shining in his eyes before.

Galen walked to Mairi, whose frame seemed to bend and whither before his eyes.

"We've always guarded her," Mairi said.

"And you will continue to do so. Only we'll be here to help now."

Mairi lifted her gaze to him and patted his arm. "I hope I'm doing the right thing. We've always been taught that Warriors are evil."

"I willna lie, Mairi, there are evil Warriors out there. Please help your village to trust us."

"Our ways have been a part of us for many generations. I will do what I can to change my people's thinking."

"That's all we can ask."

As they reached the door Galen saw that all the Warriors were gathered there, waiting to offer their help if needed. "Can someone accompany Mairi to her chamber?"

It was Malcolm who stepped forward. "I will see her safely inside."

Galen turned on his heel and walked back to Reaghan. She looked so frail and weary that he wished he could do something to help, but he had no magic to contribute to speed the healing.

"Touch her, Galen," Sonya said. "You ease her pain."

Isla nodded. "Aye, I felt it increase after he was gone."

Galen didn't need to be told twice. He stroked Reaghan's brow and folded her hand against his chest.

Slowly, after what seemed like hours, Reaghan's hand began to warm in his and her muscles eased in relaxation. Galen took his first easy breath since he had heard Reaghan was hurting.

Isla slowly backed away from the bed. She looked long and hard at Reaghan and waited for Sonya to lower her arms. When she did, Isla said, "Have you ever felt such a spell before?"

Sonya shook her head. "I haven't. I would say her magic is as powerful as yours, Isla. It's something I never imagined I would say."

Galen didn't care how strong Reaghan's magic was if it couldn't halt the pain that continued to strike her. "Have you stopped the ache?"

"For now," Sonya said. "It will most likely return, if Mairi can be believed, but this should hold it at bay for a few days. If we knew more, we might be able to halt it for good."

"And possibly break the spell," Logan said from the doorway.

Galen squeezed Reaghan's hand before he tucked it beneath the covers and started for the door. "Mairi's concern about Reaghan does pose the question. What if we have somehow broken the spell by helping her?"

"Reaghan's magic is very powerful. I cannot see how easing her pain would break the spell."

Logan leaned a shoulder against the doorway. "Aye, but the markings stated she shouldn't be taken from Loch Awe. That could have alerted Deirdre."

Isla shook her head. "Deirdre could have easily captured her at any time. It has to be more than that. I didn't see the markings, but it could have just been a way of ensuring Reaghan stayed there. Whatever Reaghan is obscuring from Deirdre is veiled beneath Reaghan's spell and years of blocked memories."

"Does Deirdre have the means to procure those memories from her?" Hayden asked.

Isla glanced at the bed before she shrugged. "I don't know for certain. It would depend on the spell Reaghan used and just how deep the memory is she has suppressed."

Galen had heard enough and none of it good. He had

held out hope that somehow once they were at the castle Sonya and the others could help her. But without knowing what Reaghan had done, no one could break her spell.

He shouldered his way through his fellow Warriors, careful not to touch any of them, and walked down the hallway. He would take position as guard this night. He wanted to be alone, and keeping lookout would give him that.

Fallon motioned everyone out of Reaghan's chamber and shut the door behind him. "Logan, a moment," he called to the youngest of them.

Logan was with Hayden, and together they halted.

"Hayden, you might be of assistance as well," Fallon said. He reached them and sighed. "Logan, when I was jumping us back here today, Galen hesitated to touch me. I suspect it has to do with his power. Am I correct?"

Hayden leaned against the wall, his lips compressed in a tight line.

Logan crossed his arms over his chest. "When you first learned to use your power of moving from one place to the next in a blink, you had to have your god loose, aye?"

"Aye," Fallon agreed. "Everyone does."

"Until they master that power," Hayden said.

Fallon studied both Warriors and knew he wasn't going to like what he was told. "What is different with Galen?"

"He's had power from the moment his god was unleashed," Logan murmured. "Whether his god is loose or not, whenever Galen touches someone, he sees into their minds."

"God's blood," Fallon whispered. "He cannot control it?"

Hayden shook his head. "He's tried, still tries. But nothing he does can master the power so he has no control."

"Except with Reaghan," Logan said. "She's the only one he's ever touched whose mind he can't see into."

It all made sense to Fallon then. "He doesn't want us to know, does he?"

"Would you?" Hayden asked. "In truth, Fallon, we guessed as you did."

Logan dropped his arms and took a deep breath. "Galen admitted it to me while we were at Loch Awe. It is one of the reasons he's kept to himself so much during his life. People take for granted the casual touches that are shared. Inevitably someone will touch Galen, so he tries to keep to himself as much as possible."

"It explains so much. I will talk to him," Fallon said.

"Nay," Logan hurried to say. "He doesna want anyone to know. He fears they might shun him."

Hayden pushed away from the wall. "Galen is a good friend, a good man. He knows people want their thoughts kept to themselves."

"I understand what both of you are saying, but Galen is a part of this family," Fallon said. "Every Warrior and Druid here is. We have powers we didna ask for. We make the most of it and try our best to control them. Sometimes that isn't possible. It isn't a reason for anyone to reject Galen. And I willna allow it."

Logan nodded, his face solemn.

"If you doona want me to talk to Galen, I won't," Fallon continued. "But please let him know we need him."

"We will," Hayden said.

"Good." Fallon looked down the corridor and flattened his lips. "Now, let's talk about these Druids that arrived. It's obvious it's going to take some time before they trust us."

Logan snorted. "Patience isna a virtue I've acquired."

Hayden chuckled, his black eyes glinting. "Ah, but I think it will take more than kind words and easy tones to bring these Druids around."

"I think our best chance is the elders, Odara and Mairi," Logan said. "The others will listen to them."

Fallon considered their words as his mind thought over every possibility. "I think we need to leave this in the hands of our capable women. Cara has a knack for getting people to open up to her."

"Let's no' forget Larena and her ability to be invisible. She could spy on them if need be," Logan said.

Fallon smiled and slapped Hayden on the shoulder. "Along with Marcail, Isla, and Sonya, I think they can turn these Druids around."

"Meanwhile, we ready for battle," Hayden said with a smile.

TWENTY-SIX

Reaghan brushed her still damp hair. It felt good to be clean again, to get the dirt and grime from their journey out of her clothes and her hair. She had wanted to visit with the Druids from MacLeod Castle more last night, but she had been so weary she hadn't been able to keep her eyes open.

She recalled her head had begun to hurt. She had thought for sure she would experience another headache, or at least feel the remnants of it this morning, but, to her surprise, there had been nothing.

When she awoke, she'd been startled to find the tub of steaming water waiting for her. She hadn't questioned who had brought up the tub or filled it with the steaming water, just thoroughly enjoyed it.

The sun had already risen when she woke, so she was sure most of the castle inhabitants were about their day. She was glad to no longer be traveling, but she missed the time she had spent with Galen. Even if they had been running for their lives.

It had been the first adventure she'd had—that she could remember—and with Galen by her side, it had been truly wonderful.

She wished she could see herself in the new yellow gown. It was something else that had been waiting for her, draped over the foot of the bed. It had been so long since Reaghan had had anything new that she was anxious to thank whoever was responsible.

A soft knock on her door intruded on her thoughts. She hurried to it, hoping it might be Galen. When she opened it, she found Marcail instead.

"Good morn," the Druid said with a pleasant smile.

Reaghan returned the smile and opened the door wider. "Good morn to you as well."

"I thought I might escort you to the great hall if you're ready."

Reaghan's heart thumped wildly in her chest, her thoughts on Galen. "Aye."

As she followed Marcail out of the chamber and down to the great hall, Reaghan could only think of Galen. As she stepped off the stairs into the great hall, her gaze clashed with cobalt eyes that stole her breath. A slow sensual smile pulled at his lips while his gaze deepened with unmistakable desire.

"Sit anywhere you can find a place," Marcail said.

It was then Reaghan noticed that few of the Druids from her village were at the table. "Where are my people?"

"They fear the Warriors. I think it will take some time."

Reaghan waved at Braden who sat between Logan and his mother. "My fellow Druids need to be reminded it was Warriors who saved their lives. They are caught in their ways and refuse to bend or acknowledge that not everything is as it seems."

Marcail's unusual turquoise eyes widened a fraction. "I agree. These Warriors are good men fighting to keep our world safe from evil. However, enough of such talk. Please find a seat."

Once again Reaghan's gaze was caught in Galen's. He

nodded to her, and she was powerless to resist his call. She walked to the empty seat beside him.

He held out a hand to assist her as she climbed over the bench. "You look well."

"And smell better. A bath does wonders to restore me," she replied with a smile.

"How did you sleep?"

She filled her goblet with milk and reached for a piece of cheese and freshly baked bread. "Very well. Are you glad to be back?"

"It is home," he said, and pushed aside his empty trencher. "I'm always pleased to return. I thought I might show you around the castle today."

"The others don't need you?"

Galen grinned. "They can do without me for a little while. How would you like to see the sea?"

"Truly? I know it from the images I see in my dreams, but I would love to feel it for myself. When can we go?"

"As soon as you are ready."

Reaghan wasn't about to pass up an opportunity to be alone with Galen. "I can eat later."

"Nay," he said, and covered her hand with his. His thumb caressed the back of her hand. "The sea isna going anywhere, and neither am I. Eat, Reaghan."

As she lifted the bread to her mouth, she happened to notice how the others around the table stared at her. There were so many Warriors. If she hadn't gotten to know Galen and Logan, she could see how she might feel afraid of these men.

"Forgive our gawking," said a man with a vicious scar running down his face. "Galen is usually eating so much he has no time for speech."

Laughter filled the hall, and Reaghan glanced over to find Galen shaking his head as he smiled.

"Eating?" she asked.

"Doona pay Malcolm a bit of attention," Galen said, his gaze indifferent and his voice heavy with nonchalance. "He lies."

"Lies?" repeated a Warrior with honey-colored eyes and hair of the deepest brown. "Cara makes a special loaf of bread just for you so the rest of us can eat in peace."

Logan chuckled, an easiness about him Reaghan hadn't seen before. "Arran speaks the truth, I'm afraid, Reaghan. Galen's stomach is never full. He sneaks into the kitchens throughout the day to steal food."

Reaghan basked in the glow of companionship she found at the MacLeod table. Galen took their teasing with a smile and a shrug; clearly the jesting was done in love and friendship.

It was obvious everyone adored Galen, and he adored them. He hadn't been lying when he called this place home.

"Should I worry about my food?" she asked Galen with a teasing smile.

Laughter erupted again as Galen stole a piece of bread from her trencher and popped it into his mouth with a wink.

Fallon shook his head from his spot at the head of the table. "Reaghan, I believe you will fit in well with this brood."

She was pleased with Fallon's words, and hoped she would be able to find a place at MacLeod Castle. A place where, perhaps, her memories weren't taken from her every ten years. A place where she could stand beside Galen and fight Deirdre.

The more she thought about it, the more she wanted to be a part of the battle against Deirdre. Her power had grown too strong, and it was time more joined in to take a stand.

"As I said before, I doona take from ladies. Only rogues

like you lot." Galen replaced the bread he had taken from her trencher, his eyes shining with mirth.

Reaghan hurried to finish her meal as the conversation turned to rebuilding the destroyed cottages in the nearby village. She listened curiously, but her mind was on spending the day with Galen.

As soon as she swallowed her last bite of food, Galen took her hand. "Ready?"

"I should help clean," she said.

Isla shook her head and waved Reaghan to the door. "Go enjoy the day."

Reaghan waited until she and Galen were in the bailey before she said, "Everyone is so pleasant."

"They are good people."

"It's no wonder you call this home. It's not only beautiful, but there is so much magic that surrounds the castle. Despite the differences between all the Warriors, you are all a family."

"Every Warrior here had their families and their lives taken from them by Deirdre. Most of us spent years locked in her dungeons. We're the lucky ones who managed to escape, yet for all of that, we were alone. We were trying to survive in a world that doesna know of us, and canna know of us."

He paused as they passed through the newly built gate. The evidence of what had befallen the MacLeod clan still could be seen by the burn marks on the rocks of the castle.

"I cannot tell you how long I searched for the Mac-Leods," Galen continued. "All of us knew they were the key to destroying Deirdre, and when I finally found Lucan, they were hesitant to trust anyone. Yet they opened their castle to us, and offered all of us who had wandered the land a home."

"I'm glad the MacLeods are fighting Deirdre."

Galen nodded. "And we are lucky Fallon is leading us."

Reaghan forgot what she was going to say when she spotted the sea. She quickened her pace and reached the edge of the cliff just as a gust of wind hit her. She inhaled the sea wind full of salt and the beckoning call to explore.

"It's beautiful, isn't it?" Galen asked.

"Wildly so. What I've seen in my dreams does not compare."

"Nay, nothing could."

She felt Galen's gaze on her and turned her head to him. Her hair whipped in the wind and tangled around Galen. He chuckled deep and low in his chest as he pulled her against him.

"Reaghan," he whispered before his mouth descended on hers.

She sank into the kiss, losing herself in all that was Galen. He enticed, he teased, he captivated. She wound her arms around his neck and offered him everything she had—her heart and her soul.

She had feared his desire would wane, but his fiery kiss told her different. She tasted his yearning, felt his desire, and breathed in his unleashed passion.

Reaghan dove into the wanton desire that raged through her body. His hot, demanding kiss didn't allow her to think of anything but the hunger that built within her, the unrelenting passion that devoured them both.

He pressed her tightly against him, holding her prisoner to his kiss, as the heat of his body surrounded her. There was a promise in his kiss, a promise of much more to come. The desire they had tasted on the edge of Loch Awe was nothing compared to what had been building since.

She knew it.

Felt it.

And ached for it.

Galen's hard arousal pressed into her belly as he groaned deep in his throat. His hunger for Reaghan had spread faster, intensified quicker, than he had ever expected. It frightened him, this need he had to have her. Claim her. Own her.

He wanted her naked beneath him. He wanted to cup her breasts and watch her nipples harden. He wanted to spread her thighs and see the auburn curls that shielded her beautiful sex. He wanted to be inside her, deep and hard, to bring her to fulfillment and see her face as she peaked.

His body raged, demanding he take her, but somehow, Galen found the will to bring his body under control and end the kiss. With his hands on either side of her face, he smoothed her hair back. Her lips were swollen and wet with his kiss. She tempted him with her passion-filled gray eyes.

His cock jumped, eager to have her rub against it once more. He kept control of his body and the hunger that pleaded for more of Reaghan.

She rested her head on his chest as she looked out at the sea. "My body is not my own whenever you touch me."

"I shouldna have kissed you now. I want you too desperately."

"Do you regret it?"

"Never," he answered more harshly than intended.

She linked her hands behind his back and sighed. "I sense you are concerned about something. Is it my spell?"

"Nay. I worry over taking you away from Loch Awe. I worry over Deirdre attacking again. I worry over the headaches that pain you."

She put a finger over his lips. "You told me I would be safe here. As much as I loved Loch Awe and felt safe there, there is something different about this castle. Maybe it's the magic of the Druids who call it home, I'm not sure. But I think you're right. I am safe here. As for the rest." She shrugged. "What will be will be."

"You know I will help you in any way I can." He saw

the fear she tried to hide, and he wished he could ease it. But he knew nothing of spells.

"I'll hold you to that. Maybe you can help me break the spell."

Galen licked his lips and pressed her head against his chest. "Do you think I will abandon you when you lose your memories?"

"Nay. The thought of forgetting who everyone is and what I've done in the past frightens me more than I like to admit."

"Which is why you wish to break the spell?" Galen began to realize that was probably why no one had told Reaghan what she had done to herself before. Still, he didn't regret his decision.

"It's one of the reasons. I want to help you and the others against Deirdre. Whatever information I'm hiding could do that. I want to give it to you."

She leaned back to look at him, and as Galen gazed into her gray eyes, he knew he would move heaven and earth to do whatever she wanted. Reaghan had given him what no one else could. He was able to touch her and hold her.

Galen had forgotten how much he missed that contact until he'd had Reaghan. He was lost in Reaghan, in her beauty and the solace she gave him. Now that he had found her, he never wanted to let her go.

TWENTY-SEVEN

Reaghan followed Galen as he took her around the castle wall and down a vertical path to the sea. She had found herself awestruck by the castle. It was exactly as she had seen it in her dreams. Imposing. Majestic. Stunning.

The only difference between now and her dreams were the burn marks that scorched the stones and the evidence of repairs. The castle itself perched at the edge of the cliff, the towers stretching high in the sky, almost touching the clouds.

The gray stone looked as if it had been carved there by God Himself as it sat against the startling green of the grass and the many boulders and rocks that protruded from the ground. Even the backdrop of the dark blue waters of the sea only added to the mystical and magical elements of the castle.

The castle might have been built by, and for, mortals, but it had been destined for Warriors and Druids.

Now, as Reaghan navigated the path to the water with Galen, she no longer cared about the castle or how she knew so much about it. All she wanted was to feel the sea.

Rocks ranging in all sizes littered the ground, making it tricky to walk, but she refused to turn back. Galen never let go of her hand. Once he had her safely standing on one of the large boulders the sea crashed against, he remained by her side.

Laughter bubbled inside Reaghan the first time a wave splashed her. The water was cool, and the salt thick in the breeze and on her tongue. She watched as the waves rolled into shore, capped with white at the top, before moving back into the sea.

The cliffs stood like a sentry against the sea, much like the castle stood against Deirdre. The water might take bits and pieces of the cliffs each time it slammed into them, but in the end the cliffs survived, endured.

Just as the MacLeods and the Warriors who coexisted with them would.

"Is it everything you expected?" Galen asked.

Reaghan smiled and looked at the horizon where the bright blue sky met the indigo sea. She could see the reflection of the clouds on the water, and had to shield her eyes from the sparkle of the sun as it glinted off the sea. "Everything and more."

"You know the way down now. Come whenever you like. Just doona swim by yourself."

She swiveled her head to him and frowned. "Why?"

"There are currents that would suck you under and not let you go. Hayden swims daily. If you want to test the waters, talk to him so he can tell you where the safest places are."

Reaghan nodded.

"Come. I'll show you more," Galen offered as he held out his hand.

She took it, allowing his strong fingers to close around her hand and lead her back to the path. He steadied her as they climbed when her skirts got in the way. She had seen Larena wearing breeches, and though she had been shocked at first, Reaghan found herself wondering how it would feel not to have her heavy skirts in the way.

"This would be much easier if I wore breeches as Larena does."

Galen stumbled and jerked his head around to her. "I doona think that is a good idea."

"You don't think Larena should wear breeches?"

Galen continued onward, his face turned away from her. "I didn't say that. I doona think you should."

"Why?"

"Because I'd never get anything done seeing those long legs of yours encased in tight breeches."

Reaghan smiled as warmth spread through her. It made her giddy, excited. Just knowing Galen wouldn't be able to keep his hands off her made her want to turn him around and kiss him.

As they reached the top Reaghan spotted Cara in her garden and heard laughter coming from the kitchens. Galen paused as Cara rose to her feet.

"How did you like the sea?" Cara asked Reaghan.

Reaghan grinned. "It was stunning."

"Reaghan," Marcail called from the door of the kitchen. "Would you like to join us? I've been praying someone else who knows nothing about cooking arrives so I'm not sitting alone."

Cara laughed and shook her head as she walked toward the kitchen. "We've offered to teach you, Marcail."

"I've made a muck of it every time," Marcail answered with a conspiratorial wink to Reaghan.

Reaghan felt a pull toward these women, as if she needed to form a relationship with them. Something inside her told her it was important, and she was powerless to ignore the feeling.

"Go ahead," Galen urged. "I'll find you later."

She wanted to go with the women, but she wasn't ready to leave Galen. Her decision was made when Marcail took her hand and pulled her toward the kitchen.

"Hayden is looking for you," Marcail said to Galen. As

they turned to enter the kitchen, Marcail leaned close and grinned. "Don't worry. You'll get your time with Galen."

"Is it that obvious?"

Larena laughed while she stirred something. "Oh, aye, but there's nothing wrong with that."

"Not at all," Sonya said. "I quite like watching those Warriors fall for their women."

But Reaghan wasn't fool enough to think Galen would ever be hers. If she couldn't break the spell, she would lose her memories. She wouldn't remember anything, but Galen would. How would he manage to cope with such an event?

As if sensing her darkening mood, Isla said, "Sometimes the future is impossible to predict."

"But not Galen's stomach," Larena said.

Marcail sat between Isla and Sonya and rolled portions of dough into small balls. "I wasn't jesting when I said I couldn't cook. I come in here to be with them."

"She does help," Cara said.

Sonya snorted. "When she isn't becoming ill."

"Ill?" Reaghan said. "Is something wrong?"

Marcail's smile lit up her entire face. "I'm carrying Quinn's child."

"Congratulations," Reaghan said. She could feel the joy that surrounded Marcail, felt the excitement of the other women. "That's such wonderful news."

Cara bumped shoulders with Marcail. "We're all terribly thrilled, but what we'd really like to know is your version of when Galen and Logan found your village."

Reaghan stepped up to the large worktable and bit her lip as she recalled the first time her eyes met Galen's.

Galen spotted Hayden on the roof of a cottage in the village. Everywhere Galen looked the Warriors were hurrying to repair the cottages now that the Druids had taken over the castle.

"We wondered if we'd see you at all since Reaghan is here now," Ian, one of the twins, teased as Galen walked past him.

Galen rolled his eyes and continued on to the cottage where Hayden was patching the roof. "She's a sight better than you smelly brutes."

"True enough," Fallon replied with a smile.

Galen couldn't wipe the grin from his face. Just being with Reaghan made his day better. He leaped to the roof beside Hayden. "You wanted to see me."

Hayden finished tying off the straw and nodded. He sat back, his legs bent and his arms resting on his knees. "How was Logan while you were gone? He said he needed time away. Did it do him any good?"

"Some," Galen answered. He lowered himself beside Hayden and looked out over the village and the land surrounding the castle. "Something has changed in him."

"It's been going on for some time. I should have spoken to him sooner about it, but I thought he might get past it on his own."

"He's still a young immortal. We all go through a dark period."

Hayden nodded wearily. "Aye, I ken. This seems to be different. I sense a darkness in him that is growing, and I can sense it because that darkness was with me for many decades."

Galen fisted his hands as he tried to imagine Logan giving in to his god. "Aye. I saw it when Fallon jumped us to the castle and Logan put his hand on me. Do you think his god is about to take over?"

"I'm no' sure." Hayden blew out a breath and rubbed the back of his neck. "I knew Logan always hid his pain with his jesting and teasing."

"He hid it well then because I never knew."

"The demons of our past never go away," Hayden

murmured. "You can try to outrun them, but they always find you in the end."

Galen grimaced at the truth of Hayden's words. There was a part of his past he hadn't been able to outrun. And he had tried. Was still trying. "What is it in Logan's past that is rearing its ugly head?"

"That I doona know."

"I thought you two shared everything."

Hayden lifted his broad shoulders in a shrug. "I always knew Logan held something back. I think it's what he's been running from."

"Have you told any of the others?"

"Nay. I wanted to talk to you first. I'd hoped Logan would return more himself, but he seems to have sunk further into the darkness."

Galen fisted his hand as he thought of the image he'd seen in Logan's mind. "Has Logan ever mentioned a younger brother?"

"Logan doesna speak of his family. Why?"

"I saw a glimpse into his mind while traveling. There was a young boy who had similar features to Logan. He was calling for Logan, begging Logan to come back, but Logan walked away."

"God's blood," Hayden murmured.

Galen stood as he caught sight of Logan. "We all need to keep an eye on him. He may no' want us to interfere, but we are brothers in this."

"I willna allow Logan to fall to his god," Hayden vowed. "I doona care what he says, I will fight for him."

"Then we need to tell the others."

"Agreed. I'll see to it."

Logan halted in the middle of the village, his face to the sky. "Galen," he called and pointed upward.

Galen looked up and spotted the peregrine as it soared above them. "Shite."

"What is it?" Quinn asked from the ground below them.

Galen jumped off the roof to land next to Quinn as the other Warriors gathered near. "Logan and I spotted it as we left for Loch Awe."

"Then we saw it at the loch," Logan said. "And on our return journey here."

Galen met Logan's gaze. "We sensed magic in it."

"Deirdre, you think?" Lucan asked.

"Possibly," Logan answered. "And I aim to find out."

Fallon grabbed his arm to stop him. "No' yet. Deirdre will come regardless. We need to stay together now that we have more Druids to protect."

"And the artifact," Hayden added.

"And Reaghan," Fallon amended.

Galen met Quinn's gaze. "Want to try and communicate with the falcon? Maybe with your power you can learn something."

"Let's see then," Quinn said.

The next instant Quinn's skin had turned the black of his god. Black bled through the whites of his eyes and covered everything in onyx. Galen held his breath, hoping Quinn would discover who was controlling the bird.

"I cannot communicate with the falcon. The peregrine is being controlled with magic," Quinn said, his gaze locked on the bird. "However, she is allowing herself to be used thus."

"Meaning?" Fallon asked.

Quinn blinked, black fading from his skin and eyes. His gaze swept the Warriors around him. "Meaning, I doona believe it is Deirdre who is using the falcon."

"Then who?" Galen asked.

"That is the question," Quinn said thoughtfully.

Logan gave a quick nod before he turned on his heel and went back to the cottage he was repairing.

Beside Galen, Hayden sighed and said, "Logan willna be happy when he discovers we're all watching him."

"We watch each other," Galen said. "In this world Deirdre has forced on us, we doona have another choice."

Hayden grunted. "As Fallon says, we're family."

Galen glanced at the peregrine circling them. He couldn't shake the feeling that the falcon and Logan's need to uncover who was behind the magic controlling the bird just might be the tipping point that caused Logan to succumb to the darkness.

TWENTY-EIGHT

Reaghan couldn't believe how fast the day had gone. She had spent it with the women of MacLeod Castle. Cara, Marcail, Larena, Sonya, and Isla had opened their small group to her, and Reaghan had never been so happy.

The one thing that dampened her day was when she learned that many of the Druids from her village had still refused to leave their chambers, and they were even considering departing the castle.

All because of the Warriors.

Reaghan climbed the stairs to her chamber. It had been Larena who showed her around the castle, though Reaghan was sure she would get lost many times before she learned her way through the maze of corridors and stairways.

She didn't even question the fact that she knew she wouldn't leave. Part of it was the friends she had made, part of it was Galen, but another part was that for the first time she could remember, she felt as if she were where she needed to be.

She turned the corner to the hallway that led to her room and slowed when she spotted Galen standing outside her chamber.

His hair was damp from a recent bath. He smiled, the welcome in his eyes shining brightly. "Did you enjoy your day?"

"Aye," she said as she halted in front of him. "Have you been waiting for me?"

"I have. I didna want to disturb your time with the women."

She opened the door and stepped into her room. "How did you know which chamber was mine?"

"I know your magic, Reaghan. I could find you anywhere." He closed the door softly behind him.

Her heart hammered with anticipation as he barred the door, never taking his eyes from her. His sensual smile made her knees weak and her stomach flutter.

Desire had darkened his eyes. A shiver raced over her skin as she held her breath, anxiously awaiting the feel of his hands on her. She hadn't realized just how much she wanted—nay, needed—Galen until that moment.

Whatever the future held for her, whatever her dreams revealed, she wanted Galen by her side.

He walked until he stood in front of her, their bodies just breaths from touching. His fingers trailed across her cheek and down her neck to her shoulder. "I've thought of nothing but you all day."

"What did you think about?"

"This," he said as he jerked her to him and slanted his mouth over hers.

He kissed her deeply, passionately. Thoroughly. Reaghan melted against him, returning his kiss with fervor. Her hands roamed over the hard plains of his chest corded with muscles. He held her tight against his body so she felt every breath, every beat of his heart.

Reaghan yanked at his saffron shirt, eager to have it gone so she could feel the heat of his skin. He pulled the shirt over his head and took her mouth in another fiery kiss.

"God's blood, how I want you," he murmured against her lips.

Reaghan ended the kiss and stepped out of his arms. Her heart broke when she saw the doubt in his blue eyes. It wasn't until she began to undress that he realized she wasn't rejecting him.

"I've been thinking of you all day as well," she said. "I see you everywhere in this castle. I don't know what tomorrow brings, and I don't care. Not as long as I'm in your arms."

He stripped off his kilt and boots and backed her to the bed. "I took you that first night on the ground when you deserved better. Now, I'll have you on the bed."

"Ah, Galen. On the ground or a bed. It matters not to me as long as I'm with you."

Reaghan climbed onto the bed and held out her hand. She had little time to rejoice as he kissed her again, pressing her back onto the mattress.

He covered her with his body. The feel of him, the weight of him, left her dizzy and craving more. His hand trailed down her side and over her hip to her thigh. He palmed her thigh and bent her leg as he ground his arousal into her.

Reaghan moaned and tilted her head back as his lips left a trail of kisses down her neck to her chest. Her breasts ached, eager for his touch.

He cupped a breast and bent to take her nipple in his mouth. She slid her hands into his hair and sucked in a breath as his wicked tongue teased the tiny bud. Reaghan arched against him, each pull of his mouth on her nipple sending a wave of heat through her to her center.

She savored each delicious sensation that wound her tighter and tighter. Galen's hands caressed and teased, touching her soul as well as her body. Desire consumed her in its fiery, needful blaze. She was falling. Floating. Drowning.

And she wanted more.

Reaghan cried out when he slid a finger inside her, slowly pumping that finger in and out. Her hips moved with him, seeking more of the pleasure he offered.

Her hands skimmed his back to his taut bottom that flexed beneath her fingers each time he ground against her. She wanted him inside her, filling her, stretching her.

Suddenly, he rose above her and flipped her onto her stomach. Galen lifted her hips until she was balanced on her hands and knees. She looked over her shoulder at him and saw the longing, the craving in his eyes.

He guided himself into her, and Reaghan's head fell forward as he pushed deep, deeper into her. Her thoughts scattered when he began to thrust, leisurely at first then building faster, harder.

Her arms trembled from holding herself and from the desire that raced through her. Sweat glistened over their bodies, their labored breaths filling the quiet chamber.

He bent and kissed her shoulder. She cried out when he reached around her, his finger finding the small hidden nub nestled in her curls. His finger moved quickly back and forth over her clitoris, barely touching her as he brought her closer to her climax, closer to sharing another part of herself with him.

Galen hadn't tried to fight the desperation that had driven him to Reaghan's chamber. He had to touch her, kiss her. Claim her.

And God help him, with every arch of her back sending him deeper into her scalding wetness, he fell further under her spell.

Her sheath was tight as it drew him in, clamping around him firmly until his only thought was to see her peak, to hear her cry out, his name on her lips.

Galen's lids were heavy, his breathing rasping in his throat as he continued to thrust inside her, bringing them ever closer to the precipice of pleasure.

He was beyond control, but from the moans coming from her and the way her body bucked against him, so was she. He heard his name on her lips, knew she was about to peak.

Galen thumbed her clitoris, drinking in every sigh, every cry, until his blood boiled and his own climax threatened.

And then she came apart. Her body shuddered and her walls clamped down on his cock. The roar in his blood grew as the contractions of her sheath took him over the edge.

He plunged deep and let his release take him.

His body jerked with the force of the orgasm. He threw back his head and shouted with the power of it, the sheer intensity.

As the orgasm subsided, Galen wrapped his arms around Reaghan, and still inside her, he fell to his side, taking her with him. He buried his face in her neck and inhaled her rosemary scent while fulfillment and contentment wrapped them in its web.

He placed his hand over her heart and felt its rapid, erratic beating. Galen let his eyes drift close. Holding Reaghan against him, he felt as if everything were, right.

Perfect.

As if fate had aligned them together. But Galen knew how quickly life could be snatched away from him. It had happened before. It could happen again.

The thought of Deirdre getting her hands on Reaghan made his fury rise, but also his fear. Reaghan was precious to him. Not just because she held some secret from Deirdre, but because of who she was. His attraction to her might have begun because he couldn't read her mind, but it had gone far beyond that.

Galen didn't want to take a closer look at his feelings

for her. All he knew was that he wanted her, needed her. Yearned for her.

Reaghan's smile, her sweet laughter had brought a light into his life he hadn't known he was missing. He had seen how close Hayden had been to losing himself to his god, how close Logan now was.

Would he also find the darkness taking him if something should happen to Reaghan?

Galen knew the answer. He had come close once before when he had used his power to control another's mind. He didn't even want to think about it. But the coming days couldn't be ignored. Deirdre would see to that. If only they had managed to kill Deirdre the first time. Had they known her black magic was so powerful, maybe they could have been better prepared.

It wasn't just Deirdre's coming attack. There was also Reaghan's spell. He wished he knew exactly what she had done to herself. The why of it was obvious—she was hiding from Deirdre.

But was she just hiding herself or was she hiding something else, some secret? That was the question. And one that was likely never to be answered.

Galen had seen how Reaghan studied the castle that morning. He had wanted to ask her if what she saw was the same as her vision, but he hadn't wanted to speak of it. He'd been selfish and wanted Reaghan to only think of him and their time together.

Yet he knew they would both have to face her memories soon. How much she could recall without harming herself was what really worried Galen.

"What makes you fret so?" Reaghan asked.

Galen squeezed her. "I'm wondering if I should have someone stand guard in case Mairi tries to come through the door."

Reaghan's laughter shook her body. "I haven't seen Mairi since we arrived. The only Druid who has come down from her chamber is Fiona, and I think that's because of Braden."

"You haven't spoken to the others?"

"Nay. Cara says they overheard a few of them speak of leaving. The others won't come down because of you."

He frowned, wondering what he had done to the Druids other than save them. "Me?"

"Not you specifically, but 'you' meaning all the Warriors. They are fearful."

"I was afraid of that."

She frowned and softly caressed his arms. "I'm sorry, Galen. None of you deserve to be treated this way. I will speak with them."

"Doona worry about it. We want them to stay because they know we will protect them, and because Deirdre is searching for any and all Druids. There aren't many of you left."

"I know."

It was the acceptance in her voice that gave him pause. "Are you frightened here?"

"Nay." She turned in his arms until she faced him. "I don't know how to explain it, but it feels as if I'm supposed to be here."

"Your magic is telling you that, I suppose. Whatever the reason, I hope you stay. If Mairi wants to leave, she will try to talk you into going with her."

"I won't. As I told you, I want to help fight Deirdre."

Galen ran the back of his fingers down the side of her face, marveling at her satiny skin. "It is verra important to her that you stay with them."

She scooted closer to him and rested her head on his chest. "I wish I could remember the spell and why I did it.

I feel as though it's important, as if something hinges on my remembering."

"The past sometimes is better left buried."

"Is that what you wish you could do with your memories?"

Galen let his fingers glide over her back as he thought of the day the wyrran came for him, the day he lost his family. And of the day he had ruled another's mind. "Sometimes."

"And others?"

"Other times those memories of my family help keep me steady."

She inhaled deeply and fisted her hand on his chest. "I don't have those kinds of memories."

"Maybe no', but you're making new ones."

"I am, aren't I?"

He rolled her onto her back and kissed her. "I'll give you all the memories you could want."

TWENTY-NINE

Reaghan snaked her hands around Galen's neck. "Shouldn't we go down to supper?"

"Hm," Galen moaned as he kissed her throat. "I suppose if you're hungry. Or I could go down, get us some food, and bring it back here."

"Now that sounds heavenly."

Reagan was deep in Galen's kiss when the knock came. Galen sighed and put his forehead to hers. "I suppose you had better see who it is."

Reaghan would have preferred to stay in bed with Galen. She hurried to pull on her chemise and gown, forgetting her hose and shoes, and opened the door to find Braden. She smiled down at the boy. "What can I do for you?"

"Mairi has bade me find you," the lad said, as he kicked the toe of his boot against the floor in obvious displeasure.

Reaghan glanced over her shoulder at Galen. "I'll return shortly."

"I'll have food by the time you return."

Reaghan took Braden's hand and ushered him away from her chamber as she shut the door. "How did you know where I was?"

His small shoulders shrugged. "I asked Logan. He said I could most likely find you in your chamber. I like Galen. He makes you smile."

Reaghan squeezed his hand. "I'm pleased to hear you

like him. He and the other Warriors have been kind to bring us to their castle."

"Aye. Mum is glad to have their protection. She doesna like that the others are talking about leaving. Are you leaving?"

Reaghan shook her head as they stopped outside Mairi's chamber. "I've found my place. Tell your mother she doesn't have to leave."

"I will," Braden said with a smile, and ran off.

Reaghan took a deep breath and squared her shoulders before she knocked. The door swung open almost instantly. Reaghan stepped inside the spacious room and found Odara in the chamber as well.

"You wanted to see me," Reaghan said with a smile.

Mairi sat next to the window using the last of the fading light of the sun to mend a gown. She didn't raise her head in greeting, and Odara refused to meet her gaze as well.

A feeling of trepidation ran down Reaghan's spine.

"We have taken a vote," Mairi said. "We will be leaving this place."

Reaghan narrowed her eyes when she heard the elder speak with such disdain. Though Mairi hadn't trusted the Warriors, she had never shown such hatred. What had happened to cause such a change all of a sudden? "I didn't know there was a vote. I didn't get to cast mine."

"It doesn't matter. We didn't need your vote," Mairi said with a slight lift of a shoulder.

Something wasn't right. Mairi never acted so harshly, even with those she didn't care for. "I didn't hear you complaining about the Warriors when they were saving us from the wyrran."

"Those Warriors led the wyrran to us."

Reaghan looked at Odara to find the elder standing against the wall, her hands clasped before her and her chin to her chest. "There are other Druids here, Mairi. Why would you want to leave this place and chance having the wyrran catch you?"

Before Mairi could answer there was a soft rap and then the door opened. Reaghan stared in shock as Isla carried a tray into the chamber and set it on the table beside Mairi.

"That will be all," Mairi said, dismissing the Druid.

Reaghan saw the anger in Isla's blue eyes, and she couldn't blame her. Mairi and the others had no right to treat them as servants.

Reaghan stepped in front of Isla to halt her. "Why are you bringing Mairi food?"

"She refuses to come to the great hall and share our table," Isla said with a glance at Mairi. "None of us will see your fellow Druids starve, so we bring them their meals."

"And they treat you as servants," Reaghan finished. She fisted her hands and looked over Isla's head to meet Mairi's gaze. Why was Mairi acting this way? "You have no right."

Mairi set aside her sewing and stood. "I have every right. Those Warriors brought the wyrran to our home and put us in danger. They needed to take us from there. Now that we are safe, we will find our own way."

Isla chuckled and faced Mairi. "You are a fool if you think the wyrran won't find you. They know you are here, and they will make sure no one leaves. And if they see you, Deirdre will have you."

Mairi spat. "And you would know, wouldn't you, *drough*? You are worse than those animals that call themselves men."

"Mairi!" Reaghan yelled, so surprised at Mairi's attitude that it had taken her a moment to react. "Enough."

But the elder wasn't listening. She advanced on Isla, who held her ground. Mairi poked Isla in the shoulder with a knobby finger. "You deserve to rot in Hell with the other *droughs*."

"Talk to my wife that way again, and I'll deliver you to Deirdre myself," said a deep voice from behind them.

Reaghan turned to find Hayden's large form filling the doorway. She couldn't believe Mairi was saying such hateful things, nor could she believe Odara wasn't doing anything. They couldn't be acting so horribly just because they didn't trust the Warriors. Could they?

"It's all right, Hayden," Isla said as she walked to stand by her husband. "This . . . Druid . . . doesn't bother me. She is looking for someone to blame, and we take the brunt of it."

Hayden glared at Mairi. "Watch your tongue, old woman. No one is holding you here. If you want to leave, then go, but the castle is open to those who wish to stay."

"We'll all be leaving," Mairi said.

Reaghan had heard enough. She moved to stand beside Isla and Hayden. "Nay. I won't leave. Fiona and Braden also wish to stay. I don't know what has happened in the short time we've been here, but you must stop this, Mairi. These are good people."

"You don't know what you're saying," the elder shouted. "You will see, Reaghan, you will see that all I've told you is the truth about the Warriors."

"It is fear of the Warriors that has led you to mistrust them. Give these people a chance." Reaghan was embarrassed to her core to have her emotions get away from her like that. She shook her head and backed out of the chamber. "You need to rest. I'll return in the morning and we can talk."

Mairi laughed, the sound empty and filled with madness. "Ask your Warriors why they didn't tell you they healed the pain of your head last eve?"

"You need to stay here. You are protected from Deirdre as long as you remain," Reaghan said, ignoring Mairi.

She left before she crumpled into a heap of tears on the floor. Mairi's words echoed in her ears, driving a stake through Reaghan's heart.

"Reaghan, wait," Isla called behind her.

She didn't want to talk to the petite Druid, but Reaghan slowed her steps. "I cannot apologize enough for Mairi. I don't know what's come over her."

Isla grabbed her arm and turned Reaghan to face her. Hayden was ever near his wife, his black eyes watching Reaghan carefully.

"Never mind Mairi. I wanted to tell you that Sonya and I did use our magic last night. You were in great pain, and Sonya's healing magic is very powerful," Isla explained. "None of us will stand by and watch someone hurt if we can do anything about it."

Reaghan took a steadying breath. "Why didn't someone tell me?"

"Galen was worried," Hayden explained. "He had seen you experience such pain on your travels here, and he wanted to spare you."

Reaghan glanced at the floor, just noticing her bare toes peeking from beneath the hem of her gown. "Thank you for telling me. If the others won't eat with you, then let them get their own food. I don't want any of you serving them again."

Isla's smile was soft, her ice-blue eyes holding a wealth of kindness. "You've found a place here, Reaghan. I hope you can speak to the others and let them know they are welcome as well."

"I will try," she said.

Reaghan didn't move for several moments after Isla and Hayden walked away. She was still shaken from everything Mairi had said and done, and what Odara had *not* said and not done.

What had happened to the wise and tolerant elders she had known on Loch Awe? Had traveling away from their home done something to them?

Reaghan realized, now more than ever, that she had to know about her past and the memories her mind had blocked. She continued to her chamber, her feet as cold as the blood in her veins. When she entered her room she found Galen reclining on the bed with food surrounding him.

As soon as he saw her his smile faded. He rose from the bed and walked to her. "What happened?"

Reaghan shut and bolted the door. She walked to the window and stared out over the darkening sky and the clouds of deep red and the dark pink from the sun's descent.

"Reaghan, you're scaring me."

She chuckled at his words.

"You think that amusing?"

She shook her head and faced him. "I didn't mean to laugh, but the thought of an immortal Warrior with powers from a primeval god inside him being frightened struck me as humorous."

"We fear many things, especially since most of our families were murdered. Now, tell me what has happened."

"Did I suffer a headache last night?"

He searched her face for only a moment before he slowly nodded. "Aye. Braden rushed to the hall and told Logan. Sonya and Isla eased you."

"Something is wrong with Mairi and Odara." She swallowed, remembering the viciousness of Mairi's words. "Mairi was saying such hateful things, things she has never before uttered. And Odara isn't standing up to her as she usually does. They aren't the women I knew."

Galen shrugged and looked away. His dark blue eyes were troubled. "If you want, I can read her mind."

Tears sprang to Reaghan's eyes at his offer. As much as he hated to touch others, as much as it pained him to see and feel their thoughts and emotions, he was offering his power to help her.

"Nay," she whispered. "I would not put you through such a thing."

"For you, I would do it."

"Why me? Is it because you cannot read my thoughts?" She prayed he spoke the truth, because she couldn't handle another lie, not when she was so close to breaking down.

Galen gave her a half-smile. "The first time I saw you I was struck by your beauty. I've never been so tempted by a woman, and then when I gave in and kissed you and didn't see into your mind, I had to have you."

There was no lie in his eyes, of which she was grateful.

"So it was only because my memories are blocked," she said, not bothering to hide the sadness in her voice.

"In the beginning, I think that was part of it, and though I am thankful I can touch you and kiss you without worrying about my power, it's you, Reaghan, that I'm drawn to. Your smile, your kindness, your search for yourself."

She could see the truth of his words shining in his eyes. Reaghan let out a breath she hadn't known she was holding and walked into his arms. "Thank you for not lying. I am so tired of the lies."

His large hands rubbed up and down her back, offering her comfort and his strength for as long as she needed it. "Tell me what Mairi did."

"I'm so angry at her I could toss her out of the castle myself." She pulled out of the safe haven of Galen's arms and climbed onto the bed. She was starving, and the food smelled delicious.

Galen grunted as he joined her on the bed. "Sounds like it didn't go well at all."

Reaghan tore off a chunk of bread and gave the larger

portion to Galen. "She summoned me to say they had taken a vote and were leaving."

"What?" Galen's face was a mask of confusion and irritation. His lips were parted, the bread halfway to his mouth. "Are you jesting?"

"Unfortunately, I'm not. I don't know who was involved in the vote, but I wasn't. On the way to Mairi's, Braden said he and Fiona wished to stay, so I told Mairi. She wasn't happy, but it was when I told her I wasn't going that she really grew furious."

"I'm sorry."

She pulled apart some of the smoked fish and put it in her mouth. "The worst was when Isla brought Mairi a tray of food, and Mairi dismissed her as she would a servant. She was so hateful to Isla, telling her that she belonged in Hell with the other *droughs*."

Galen grimaced as he used a dagger to cut the venison into smaller portions. "She's lucky Hayden wasn't there."

"He was. He threatened to take Mairi to Deirdre himself if she continued. That's when Mairi told me about my headache. As if she wanted me to believe everyone was keeping it from me."

"I did want to keep it from you," Galen confessed. "I know how worried you are about them."

Reaghan placed her hand atop his forearm. "I appreciate it, but I'd much prefer the truth, as difficult as that truth may be to bear."

THIRTY

Galen didn't want to let Reaghan know how Mairi's change in behavior worried him. He knew Reaghan wanted the truth about anything that occurred, but he decided to keep his worries to himself for the time being.

"I told Isla not to bring any more food to them," Reaghan went on, unaware of Galen's turmoil. "If they're hungry, they can get their own meals."

He chuckled. "Good for you."

"Mairi called you and the other Warriors animals," she said softly.

"I've been called much worse. Doona let it trouble you."

Reaghan shook her head, her lovely auburn curls falling over her shoulders. "That's not like Mairi. Odara was in the chamber. She didn't say a word, Galen. That's not like her either. She's always spoken her mind."

"They've left the only place they've ever known. It can be more than some people can grasp."

"I may need your help in keeping Braden and Fiona here. I don't think Mairi intends to allow them to stay."

Galen snorted as he raised the goblet to his lips and drank the dark wine within. "Mairi cannot make them go with her. The others and I will ensure that."

"Thank you."

* * *

Charon stared at the remaining occupants of the tavern. He'd known better than to return to the village, but he'd been unable to help himself.

When he'd been here as a lad, the tavern had seemed a grand, forbidden place where all men gathered. Now, as he looked at it through a man's eyes, he saw it was nothing special. Just a rundown building in need of repair.

It had been well over two hundred years since Charon had seen the tavern and the village, but not much had changed. The village had grown to a large size at one time, but now many of the buildings and shops showed neglect from abandonment.

The people, however, hadn't changed at all. Oh, their clothes had altered, but they were still the poor, undignified, uneducated people they had been before.

There had only been one man who had stood out among this ragged lot, and that had been his father.

He'd been a great warrior, his father. His father would have handled the god inside him better than Charon. His father would have been able to stand against Deirdre. But more importantly, his father wouldn't have broken under Deirdre's torture.

"Ye want another ale?"

Charon looked up at the woman. She was pretty, if not a little haggard. She'd had a hard life, which showed in the lines about her face and the dark shadows under her eyes. She was still relatively young, which made him wonder why she was working in the tavern instead of tending to a husband.

"Aye," he answered. "What is your name?"

"Evanna. Why do ye care?"

Charon shrugged. "Just curious. Have you lived here your entire life?"

She looked away, but not before he saw the wistfulness

in her eyes. "Aye. I wanted to leave once, but life doesn't always go as planned."

"No truer words have been spoken. Bring me another ale."

As she sauntered off, a new swing to her hips, Charon leaned back in his chair. Their conversation had gained the interest of the two men nearest him.

"Ye passin' through?" one of the men asked.

Charon glanced at the man's kilt, the same red with green pattern he had worn with such pride. The same kilt Deirdre had taken from him in Cairn Toul. The colors he wore now were from a kilt he had stolen. It meant nothing to him. "Mayhap."

The second man smiled, showing several missing teeth. "Ye doona carry a blade."

"Looks can be deceiving."

"Where is it then?"

Charon was tempted to show them who he really was, but it wasn't time. Yet. "How fares your laird?"

The two men exchanged a glance, but it was the first man who answered. "He's gaining in years."

"Is that so?"

"Ye planning on trying to take over this clan, because there are many Highland warriors here?"

The second man nodded vigorously. "Many warriors. Ye wouldna stand a chance."

Charon laughed and winked at the barmaid as she set down his ale. "I've nay desire to rule this clan." He had another venture in mind, one the village would discover soon enough.

If Charon had his way, Deirdre and her threats would never bother him again.

He suddenly thought of the MacLeods and the Warriors who had joined them. Charon had helped them kill

Deirdre, but even then he had known she wouldn't die easily.

Maybe he should have returned to the castle with the MacLeods. It would have been nice to have so many Warriors he knew to guard his back. He'd watched Quinn, Arran, Ian, and Duncan do it for each other often enough while in Deirdre's Pit.

Charon had even tried to help them once, though they knew nothing about it. But he would never fit in at Mac-Leod Castle. There were too many deeds in his past that they could not accept.

He was better off alone. As he always had been.

Galen watched Reaghan soak in the steaming water. He longed to join her, but it wasn't big enough for the two of them. Maybe he should ask Lucan to build a tub that would accommodate two.

Her encounter with Mairi had upset Reaghan more than she told him, and so he thought a hot bath might help her relax. He never expected to be so aroused while watching her.

Galen swallowed as she tilted her head to the side, her glorious auburn curls pinned atop her head. Her skin glistened from the heat of the water and the candle glow. The flames cast a golden light about the chamber, making her hair appear darker.

"You're staring again."

Galen jerked his eyes to her face to find her smiling. "How can I no' when I've your beautiful body to feast my eyes upon?"

"Just your eyes?" she said with a sensual smile that made his balls tighten.

"If you want to finish your bath, you'd best keep your tongue silent lest I pull you from the water and show you what I'd like to do to you."

Her lids closed over her eyes for a heartbeat before she rose from the water. Galen's breath locked in his lungs as he stared at the magnificent woman who had come into his life so unexpectedly.

His gaze locked on small, pert breasts. Her rosy nipples were hard, wanting, begging for his mouth. A droplet of water beaded on a tip, tempting and teasing him.

"Reaghan, you have no idea what you to do me," he croaked through the desire that burned in him.

One long, lean leg lifted from the water and over the tub's edge to gingerly step onto the cool stone floor. The second leg followed.

Galen licked his lips, his cock hard and aching. The droplet on her nipple dangled for a moment before it plummeted down her body.

He followed a droplet as it crawled down her flat stomach to dip into her navel then continue downward into the auburn curls betwixt her legs.

Galen had never undressed so fast in his life. Every time he tasted Reaghan, he wanted more. Always more. He couldn't get enough, couldn't get close enough to her. Somehow, somewhere from Loch Awe to MacLeod Castle she had stolen a piece of his soul.

He felt as if he had known her for centuries instead of days. It was impossible, yet he didn't question it. He merely accepted.

"You're beautiful," he said as he came to stand in front of her.

He plunged his hands into her hair, scattering the pins that were barely holding her thick locks. He loved the feel of the heavy, silky mass.

Reaghan rose up on her tiptoes and gave him a quick kiss. "And you, my fierce Warrior, are magnificently handsome."

"Magnificent?" he repeated with a grin. "I like that. A lot."

"Hmm," she murmured against his neck. "I thought you might."

Galen sucked in a breath when she wrapped her slender fingers around his staff. She stroked his length and let a digit glide over the sensitive tip. He groaned, lost in the flames of desire, but he never loosened his hold.

"I think you enjoy this," she whispered seductively in his ear.

Shivers of delight, of anticipation, raced down Galen's spin. "You have no idea."

"Should I continue? Should I bring you to your knees with my hands? Maybe my mouth?"

Galen's cock jumped at the thought of her hot mouth on him. "Only if I can taste you as well."

Her breathing quickened, her eyelids heavy. "How is that possible?"

"I'll show you," he promised as he lifted her in his arms. "Just not yet."

She wrapped her slim legs around his waist as he brought her against the wall and kissed her. The passion that always simmered between them burst through in an instant.

Their kiss was frantic, their hands searching, caressing, learning. Holding. His hands held her thighs apart, spreading her, opening her. She cried out when the tip of his cock brushed against her moist sex.

The sight of her parted lips, her closed eyes, and the ecstasy that awaited pushed Galen to the brink. He shifted his hips, found her opening, and drove deep inside her.

Her wonderfully wet, deliciously hot sheath wrapped around him, holding him.

"Galen," she whispered, and sought his lips for another kiss.

Their tongues clashed and separated in time with each

thrust of his hips. Her fingers gripped his shoulders, her ankles dug into his buttocks as she urged him faster, harder.

Ruthlessly, he drove inside her again and again, letting the passion, the desire build until they were frenzied with it.

She gasped into his mouth, her body taut. And then she shattered in his arms.

Galen continued to thrust inside her, the urgency to give her more, to take her higher pressed him hard. He wanted to hold back, to take more of her in many different ways, but the sound of her cries as she continued to ride the wave of bliss was too much.

She whispered his name, beckoning him to join her. Galen thrust once more and let his orgasm take him.

Her hands caressed him, her whispered words mumbled in the fog of his climax. He stumbled to the bed and dropped them onto it. She pulled him into his arms, holding him in the shelter of her body as oblivion took hold.

THIRTY-ONE

Logan braced his hands on the cool stones of the battlements and watched the peregrine falcon soar through the air.

The gray and white striped feathers of the bird's underbelly made it easy to recognize. Which only confirmed to Logan that it was the same bird that had followed them from the castle and back again.

Logan found the falcon majestic to watch as it soared so effortlessly in the sky, its cry touching a chord deep inside him, but that didn't stop him from wanting to capture it.

There was magic with the bird. The only thing that kept Logan from killing the falcon right then was that he recalled Quinn saying it wasn't Deirdre's magic.

At least they knew this bird and what it was about. Better to have a known enemy than an unknown one, Logan's father had always told him.

The softest of sounds, which only his enhanced hearing discerned, alerted Logan he wasn't alone. He knew without turning it was Hayden. Logan had wondered how long it would take his friend to find him.

"Did your time away help?" Hayden asked.

Logan smiled. Hayden always got right to the point. It was one of the things that had bonded them so early on. Logan turned to face the man he considered his brother and shrugged. "I could say aye."

"But it would be a lie."

"Is it so obvious?"

Hayden sighed, his black eyes filled with concern. "To me it is, but then I know you better than most."

"That you do."

"Yet I doona know everything, do I?"

Logan looked away. "There are some secrets best kept locked inside."

Hayden walked until he stood beside Logan, his gaze now tracking the falcon. "So much happened during the few days you were gone. I tried to deny what I felt for Isla and what she meant to me. I hurt her badly, Logan, and in the end I nearly lost her."

"What happened?" Logan had known that if Hayden could accept Isla, then good things awaited both of them.

"My past. I couldn't stay away from her, yet I denied her with every breath I took because she was *drough*."

"And a *drough* murdered your family."

Hayden grew silent. "It was Isla."

Logan could only stare at his friend as his words sank in. "And yet you are with her. Hayden, you searched for *droughs* so you could challenge and kill them."

"I know," Hayden admitted. "When Isla told me it was her, it didna matter anymore. I had almost let my god take control of me. That was enough to make me realize I needed to take a hard look at my life. And then when Deirdre tried to take over Isla's mind, it all became clear to me. My life meant nothing without her."

Logan turned to the side and leaned his hip against the battlement wall. "I gather you told Isla all of that."

"Nay. I was too afraid of losing her still. So much had happened and been said between us, most of it my fault. I wanted to gain her trust so she would believe me when I told her how I felt."

"That you loved her," Logan said.

Hayden nodded. "That I loved her. I held her while Deirdre tried to take over her mind. I'd never felt so powerless. The Druids did all they could, but even Sonya's magic couldn't help."

"Because it was Deirdre?"

"Aye. Deirdre's hold on Isla was strong, but Isla fought it. Until I woke up and she was gone."

Logan's eyes widened. "Gone? She left you?"

"To save all of us. She was afraid Deirdre would gain control, so Isla planned to sacrifice herself. I went crazy when I found her gone."

Logan grimaced. He'd seen Hayden at his worst, and somehow he knew it had been so much more with Isla gone.

"Fallon managed to get through to me, and Broc found Isla. By the time I got to her, Deirdre had nearly killed her. Still, Isla found the strength to tell me she had slain my family, but I knew it wasn't her. Deirdre had taken over her mind and body and done the deed. Isla was blameless, as were all the *droughs* I executed over the years."

"I'm glad the others were here for you." Logan blew out a breath and knew he should have been there for his friend. But he would have been useless. Just as he was now.

Hayden chuckled. "And all I kept thinking was how I wished you were here to make a jest, to make me laugh."

"I wish I could have been."

They were silent for a moment, and then Hayden asked, "Are you leaving?"

Logan shook his head and tapped the stones. "Nay. Deirdre and her evil is a festering wound over our land. She needs to be destroyed, and it will take all of us."

"Tell me what sent you from here."

"The past and memories that willna loosen their hold."

Hayden's large hand came down on his shoulder in a

gesture of understanding, of brotherhood. "If you need me, you know I will be there for you."

"I know." Logan looked into his friend's eyes and forced a smile.

With a sigh, Hayden dropped his hand. "Now, what are we going to do about that bird?"

Logan saw the clarity in Hayden's eyes, eyes that had held the demons of his past for so long. Logan wondered if he'd ever be so content.

As soon as the thought went through his mind he knew it would never be possible. Some transgressions of the past refused to die, and soon one of them would rear its ugly head.

"Logan?"

He shook himself and shrugged. "So far the peregrine hasn't come too close to the castle. If it does, I'll be there waiting for it."

Brenna knew she shouldn't bring the peregrine so close to the castle, not with the Warrior watching so intently. Yet there was something about the Warriors that called to her.

Maybe it was the sadness she glimpsed occasionally in the Warrior's eyes. They were dangerous. She'd seen that in the way they battled the wyrran at Loch Awe.

The power of their gods, the savagery that had taken hold of them, should have scared her. But in the safety of her isle as she peered through the falcon's eyes, she was awestruck by them and the Druids who trusted them.

Brenna mentally asked the falcon to hunt and then return to the forest. With just a thought, Brenna severed the connection she had with the bird.

"Well?"

It was no surprise her father once more waited impatiently to hear what she had seen. "They do nothing."

"Nothing? I cannot believe that," Kerwyn said as he paced around her, using the walking stick carved out of an oak and inscribed with ancient Celtic writing.

Brenna glanced at Daghda before she rose and faced her father. "They do nothing. I believe they await an attack from Deirdre."

"Ah," he said with a knowing look. "They go to great lengths to make others think they go against Deirdre."

"And if they are going against Deirdre? Have you stopped to consider that?"

As soon as Kerwyn turned his dark eyes, cold and hard, to her, Brenna knew she shouldn't have spoken.

"Do not question my word," her father said between clenched teeth.

Brenna licked her dry lips and took a deep, steadying breath. "They could be taking a stand against Deirdre."

"They aren't. You know the tales of the Warriors after Rome was driven from our shores. You know the blood and death they delivered to our land. It is all a trick. No Warrior can be trusted."

Reaghan awoke with a sigh as Galen's fingers skimmed the sensitive skin of her back, leaving trails of chills in their wake.

"Morning," he whispered.

She smiled and cracked open her eyes. "Good morn. You're still here."

"And where else would I be?"

She shrugged and scraped her fingers on his whiskers.

He grabbed her hand and kissed it. "I'll rid my face of these whiskers so I doona scratch your face."

"They are getting a bit prickly."

His smile died as he let out a long breath. "Are you going to speak to the Druids today?"

"I have to. Most won't listen, I'm sure. Mairi is a good

leader, but her mind is clouded now. Whether by our travels or because of what we've always believed, I'm not sure."

"You've been taught the same things. Why don't you feel the same way about us?"

Reaghan rolled onto her back and looked at the ceiling. "Part of it is because you helped us against the wyrran and brought us here. You could have left us to face Deirdre alone."

"It could all have been a ruse to bring you to Deirdre."

"It could have been," she said, and turned her head so she looked at him. "But I looked into your eyes, Galen, and I knew I could trust you. I knew you spoke the truth."

He shifted to his side and propped up on his elbow. "You didna know me."

"It felt right to go with you and Logan, to give you my trust. If it hadn't, I wouldn't have gone."

"It could have been my kisses," he said with a lopsided grin.

Reaghan laughed and tapped his lips with her finger. "That could have had something to do with it."

"You might want to consider taking Cara, Marcail, or Sonya with you when you speak with Mairi. I would say leave Larena since she's a Warrior, and also doona include Isla because she was a *drough*."

"I like Isla, regardless of whether she was a *drough*," Reaghan said and frowned. "I don't want to exclude either Isla or Larena."

"I know, but your people need to trust us, and what better way to begin than with Cara, Marcail, and Sonya?"

Reaghan slowly nodded. "Now I understand how Deirdre came to be in power."

"How?"

"The *droughs* were too concerned with growing their own black magic, and the *mies* weren't able to realize that people change and sometimes you have to trust others to help. If the *mies* don't band together, then Deirdre cannot be defeated. And the *mies* from my village have little to no power to speak of. Who will stand against Deirdre now?"

"We will," Galen said. "And any Druid who wants to fight her."

"I will stand with you."

Something dark and possessive passed across his cobalt eyes. "Deirdre wants nothing more than to get her hands on any Druid she can."

Before she could respond there was yet another knock on her door. Galen jumped from the bed and began donning his kilt. Reaghan sat up and reached for her chemise.

"Who is it?" she asked.

"Marcail," came a soft voice.

Reaghan smiled and hurried to finish dressing. She glanced at Galen to make sure he was clothed, and unbolted the door. As soon as it opened she moved aside so Marcail could enter.

Marcail's gaze alighted on Galen sitting on the bed and a slow smile spread her lips. "Good morn, Galen."

He pulled on his boots and winked as he stood. "Marcail. Is there plenty of food this morn?"

"For you? Always."

"I'll see you both downstairs then."

Reaghan was surprised when he paused beside her on his way out the door to give her a quick kiss. Her gaze followed him until he walked through the door.

When she turned back, Marcail was staring at her. Reaghan licked her lips. "I suppose I should explain."

"Think nothing of it," Marcail said. "I came because Isla and Hayden told us what happened last night with Mairi."

"What Mairi said was unforgivable."

Marcail waved away her words. "Isla is a strong Druid. It will take more than hurtful words to bring her to her knees. Deirdre tried for five hundred years and never succeeded. I don't think your village elder will do it in one night."

"And Hayden? He was very angry."

"When it comes to protecting their women, all Warriors get irate. Mairi would do best to stay clear of Hayden for a while."

Reaghan glanced at the floor. "I told Isla not to serve my people again. None of you are servants, and you shouldn't be performing such duties."

"We were hoping that once a day or so went by, they would feel as if they could share a meal with us, but after what happened with Mairi, I don't know if that's possible."

"This is very unlike Mairi or Odara. I don't know what is wrong with either of them."

Marcail linked her fingers together over her stomach. "They do plan to leave still?"

"Mairi does, but I know Fiona and Braden wish to stay. I want to talk to the others and see if I can convince any of them to stay as well."

"I offer whatever help you need."

Reaghan smiled. "Thank you. Galen suggested I take you, Cara, or Sonya with me."

"Galen is often correct in his thinking. Ramsey said almost the same thing."

"Ramsey?" Reaghan said.

Marcail laughed and motioned Reaghan out the door. "I keep forgetting you haven't met many of the Warriors."

"I know very few, in fact."

"Then let's rectify that, shall we? I'll point out all of them while we break our fast."

She walked alongside Marcail to the great hall. As soon as she spotted Galen sitting at the table, she felt her lips curving into a smile.

"He watches you even when you don't realize it," Marcail whispered from beside her.

Reaghan jerked her gaze to the Druid. "He does?"

"Always," she said with a small nod and proceeded down the stairs.

THIRTY-TWO

Galen motioned Reaghan next to him. As soon as he'd seen her, he'd had to make himself stay seated and not go to her, not kiss her so that every male there knew she was his. Marcail whispered something before Reaghan walked over to him.

"What was that about?" he asked

"She was going to have the Warriors introduce themselves so I would know their names."

Galen set down his goblet. "Tell me who you know."

"You, Logan, and the MacLeods. I know Hayden, as well as Broc."

"All right," Galen said. "You know Cara is with Lucan, aye?"

"Aye. Marcail is married to Quinn, and Larena, the female Warrior, is married to Fallon."

Galen handed her an oatcake. "Correct. What do you know of Hayden?"

"Only that he is very protective of Isla. And very tall."

"True enough," Galen said with a chuckle. "So that only leaves six for you to know. The scoundrel across from me is Ramsey MacDonald."

Ramsey, with his cropped black hair and piercing silver eyes, regarded Reaghan for a moment. "Welcome to MacLeod Castle."

"He doesn't say much," Galen said. "But when he does, we tend to take notice."

Reaghan smiled at Ramsey. "I appreciate the welcome."

Galen then pointed down the table to the twins. "Those are the Kerrs. The one with the long hair is Duncan. The other is Ian. They are so similar, that without their hair being different, I fear none of us could tell them apart."

"Speak for yourself," said a man on the other side of Galen.

Galen leaned back so Reaghan could see Arran. "And this one is Arran MacCarrick."

"A pleasure," Arran said to Reaghan.

Reaghan inclined her head.

Galen motioned down the table with his chin. "The last Warrior is Camdyn MacKenna. He's the one toward the end of the table with the long black hair."

"And the man next to him with the scars is Malcolm?"

"That's right," Galen said.

"He seems . . . lonely and withdrawn."

Galen put his elbows on the table and grabbed a piece of cheese. "He doesn't feel as though he belongs. He spends a lot of time wandering the cliffs."

Fiona and Braden walked into the great hall then, and as usual Braden ran to Logan. Galen watched Logan with the boy for a moment before he felt Reaghan's gaze on him.

"Logan seems to enjoy Braden."

Galen nodded and turned back to Reaghan. "Logan's past is like a darkness growing inside him. If we doona maintain control, the god can take over, which is what Deirdre wants."

"So she can control you?"

"Aye. Logan, like many of us, keeps his past to himself, but for whatever reason Braden brings back the smile we've all expected from Logan."

Reaghan placed her hand on Galen's arm. "Then I'm glad Braden and Fiona are staying."

Galen gazed into her gray eyes. He wanted to take her back to her chamber and make love to her again. Galen was just about to suggest it when Mairi appeared at the top of the stairs.

"Reaghan," he said.

She frowned and turned her head. "This cannot be good."

"Let Fallon talk to her," he cautioned.

Just as Galen expected, Fallon rose from his seat. "Mairi. Would you join us?"

"I will not," the elder said, and let her harsh glare roam the hall. "I should never have allowed Galen to scare me into bringing my people here."

Reaghan's nails dug into his arm. Galen placed a hand over hers and tried to offer whatever comfort he could.

"Galen used his power to control minds to make us come here," Mairi continued. "He's turned Reaghan against her own people. He's taken her to his bed and turned her into an insatiable whore."

The anger inside Galen bubbled and rose as Mairi's viciousness turned on Reaghan. His fangs filled his mouth, and he knew if he looked down at his skin he'd find it the dark green of his god.

"Stop it," Reaghan said as she jerked to her feet. "Stop the lies, Mairi. I will hear no more of it."

The elder shook her head. "They aren't lies. Ask Galen what his power is. Every Warrior here has some kind of power."

"And every Druid has some kind of magic," Isla said, her voice hard and full of fury. "Why do you fear the Warriors so?"

"I've told you," Mairi screamed. "Galen forced us."

"Enough!" Fallon bellowed. "You are making outrageous claims, Mairi."

The elder raised her chin. "They are the truth."

Reaghan had never felt such rage in her life. To hear the woman she had considered a mother say such things about Galen was appalling. And Galen had yet to speak up for himself.

"You could have stayed at Loch Awe," Reaghan said. "You could have stayed and taken your own life as Nessa and the others did. No one forced you. Galen and Logan offered to bring us to safety. It was your choice. Yours alone."

Mairi snorted, her face a mask of hatred. Reaghan had never seen her like this before. The hall was deathly quiet, everyone waiting to hear what Mairi said next.

"No Warrior can be trusted, Reaghan. All but you and Fiona know that. I guess it feels good to have a man between your thighs. So good you will betray your own people."

Reaghan's knees gave out, and it was only Galen's strong arms that kept her on her feet.

"Arguing with her only makes it worse," Galen whispered.

Reaghan shook her head as tears stung her eyes. She was embarrassed, humiliated. The MacLeods had opened their home and given Reaghan and her people shelter. How had Mairi repaid their kindness? By treating the women as servants and degrading everyone at the castle.

"See?" Mairi screeched and pointed to Galen. "He whispers in her ear telling her what to do."

Reaghan tore out of Galen's arms and strode to the foot of the stairs. "Stop this now. Galen was giving me comfort. You've always been so kind and wise. Please stop saying such awful and untrue things."

The laugh that came from Mairi was filled with hysteria and cruelty. "He used his powers to get inside my head."

"He did it for Reaghan," Logan said. "I was there. He

threatened to do so because he wanted answers about Reaghan, answers you refused to give."

"And why would I tell you anything?" Mairi spat.

Galen finally stood. "We were worried about Reaghan."

"Tell me, Warrior, have you ever gotten into someone's mind and commanded them to do something?" Mairi asked.

Coldness swept over Reaghan when Galen didn't answer. She swiveled her head to find his gaze on the table, his skin flashing green. Reaghan's heart broke for him, for the position Mairi had put him in.

"It doesn't matter," she said.

At the same time Galen answered, "Aye."

"I knew it," Mairi said, and clapped her hands like an excited child. "I knew you were as evil as I suspected. I knew you got into my mind and forced me."

As one Cara, Marcail, Isla, Larena, and Sonya rose from the table and walked to stand beside Reaghan. Their show of support brought tears to Reaghan's eyes.

"I've heard enough." Fallon's voice, low and deep, carried throughout the hall. "If you doona wish to stay, then by all means, you are free to leave. You've never been a prisoner."

Lucan stood and leaned his hands upon the table. "We offered you sanctuary from the evil that is hounding you outside these walls. But we will not stand to hear such vile comments from you again about Galen, Reaghan, or anyone else in this castle."

"So leave," Quinn said as he gained his feet. "Leave and find yourself in Deirdre's hands. It matters no' to us anymore."

Mairi swung her gaze to Reaghan. "I'm not leaving without Reaghan."

"You doona have a choice in the matter," Galen said.

Reaghan started up the steps until she stood in front of

Mairi. "I'm only going to say this once more, so listen very carefully. I'm. Not. Leaving."

Mairi's smile was calculating and cold. "Oh, aye, you will. If you want the answers you've sought about your past and the memories that elude you, you will come with me."

"Why?" Reaghan was immediately suspicious. Why was it so important she leave with Mairi? "Why would you tell me now?"

"Why not?" Mairi asked. "If I leave you here, you will die. At least with me, you stand a chance."

There was an indignant gasp behind her. Then Cara said, "Deirdre knows you are here. They will be waiting for you. There is nothing you can do to get away from her except to stay here."

"With you?" Mairi asked, and sneered down at Cara. "I'd rather rot in Hell."

"That can be arranged," Lucan said with a deep, dangerous growl.

The color drained from Mairi's face, but she didn't back down. Reaghan wanted answers, but she didn't want to leave the castle. It was a choice she had never thought to have to make.

"You've always been like a mother to me. I don't understand why you're doing this."

"Reaghan," Mairi said. "I will tell you everything. Just come with me."

A shiver of dread raced down Reaghan's spine. The more Mairi talked the more Reaghan knew she lied. It was there in her eyes, in the bleakness and coldness of Mairi's brown gaze.

But Reaghan wanted to test her theory, wanted to back Mairi into a corner.

"Tell me now, and I will go with you."

Mairi rolled her eyes. "I'm no fool, lass. I'm not saying a word until you are away from this pit of wickedness."

"Tell me something now. In good faith."

Galen felt as if someone had ripped open his chest. He couldn't believe Reaghan thought of leaving with Mairi, but then again, Reaghan had yearned for answers for years. Why wouldn't she latch on to what Mairi offered?

He wanted to snatch Reaghan away from Mairi and keep her by his side forever, but he knew that wasn't possible. She was a piece of the puzzle to destroying Deirdre. But she was also so much more, more than he ever thought possible.

"Galen."

He started, and found Fallon beside him. "We cannot make Reaghan stay," Galen said.

"Talk to her," Fallon urged. "She will listen to you."

Galen had given her all the answers he knew. He had nothing else to tell her.

"Tell me!" Reaghan shouted to Mairi.

"You were born in our village. Your mother died in childbirth."

Galen held his breath, not knowing if what Mairi said was true or not because he wasn't touching her.

"You lie."

Reaghan's words, quietly spoken, reverberated around the hall. The relief that swept through Galen was so powerful it threatened to buckle his knees.

Reaghan was staying. He had never known how desperately he wanted her until that moment, how anxiously he feared her leaving him.

And right after that came the realization that she knew—everyone knew—one of his deepest secrets. The question was, how had Mairi known he had controlled another's mind before?

THIRTY-THREE

Galen didn't move. Couldn't.

Not when Mairi spun around and strode back to her chamber. Not when Reaghan slowly descended the stairs and walked out of the castle, the women following behind her.

He knew his fellow Warriors would have questions for him, questions he'd rather not answer. Questions he wasn't sure if he could answer.

For too long he had hidden the extent of his powers. It was only fair that everyone know the truth.

His blood pounded in his ears, his heart was in his throat. He had prayed Reaghan would turn and look at him, give him any indication she wasn't angry, before she left the castle.

But she hadn't.

Galen let loose the breath he'd been holding and returned to his seat at the table. No one spoke as Fiona and Braden quietly rose and left the great hall.

"How did Mairi know of your powers?" Quinn asked, finally breaking the overwhelming silence.

Galen shrugged, his gaze on the table. He couldn't look his fellow Warriors in the eye. Not now, not after betraying them. Possibly not ever. "I looked into her mind to try and find answers about Reaghan."

"I was there," Logan said. "We knew Mairi was hiding

something about Reaghan. He was worried what it could be. Galen did what any of us would have."

"True," Fallon answered. "Did the villagers treat Reaghan badly?"

Galen ran a hand down his face. How had things become so convoluted? All he had wanted to do was keep the Druids safe. It had never entered his mind that they would act so offensively to everyone, Reaghan included.

"Quite the opposite," Galen said, and forced himself to lift his eyes and look around the table. "Reaghan told me she found a parchment that mentioned her name and that of Foinaven Mountain. She wanted to find the answers to her past, to memories that were gone."

Logan nodded as Galen spoke. "Reaghan asked to come with us. It wasn't until Reaghan's pain came upon her that we saw firsthand the elders were keeping a secret."

Fallon's brow was furrowed, his jaw set. "Explain."

"They comforted her, but not once did they even try to offer herbs or something to dull the headache," Galen said.

Logan cocked his head to the side. The smile he gave was hard and full of cruelty. "That's when Galen confronted Mairi. He asked her to give him the answers he sought, and when she didn't, he looked into her mind."

"What did you see?" Lucan asked.

Galen met Lucan's sea-green eyes. "I saw glimpses of her with Reaghan. Reaghan never aged, but Mairi did."

"Like Logan, I'd have done the same in Galen's position," Hayden said. "Galen was protecting Reaghan."

Galen found Ramsey's eyes on him, but his friend didn't utter a word, just stared thoughtfully.

"Can you control someone's mind?" Ian asked.

Galen turned to the twin and gave a single nod of his head. "I've done it only once, and it nearly killed me."

"Tell us," Quinn urged.

Galen sighed and drudged up memories he wished he could forget. "I had just escaped Cairn Toul and was trying to find my way in a world that had changed so drastically. I came across a village on the border with England. There were English soldiers there who had killed a man and a woman, and one was about to rape a young girl."

He paused and swallowed. "I thought I could do anything with my powers. I didn't even touch him, just focused all of my god's power and stared at the soldier. I commanded him to leave the girl alone and attack his comrades. For several heartbeats he stood still as stone. And then he did exactly as I commanded."

"What happened to him?" Logan asked.

"I doona know. I fell unconscious. It took me days to recover. I never tried it again. I will admit, if Mairi had no' changed her mind on her own and come to the castle with us, I would have used my power on her."

Fallon dropped his head back on his chair. "We all have special powers. Some are stronger than others, and that we have no control over. We didna choose our gods. They chose us. We live with what we have and make the best of it."

Galen knew Fallon was telling him everything was all right, but to Galen it wasn't. It never would be. He stood and looked at each Warrior in turn. "I have no control over my power. If you brush up against me I will see into your mind, your thoughts, your feelings."

"Every person you touch?" Arran asked.

"Aye. Person, Druid, Warrior, or wyrran. Even animals. No matter how I try to master my power, it eludes me. There is only one whom I can touch and see nothing."

Logan murmured, "Reaghan."

Galen nodded. "Reaghan. Whether it's because of the spell she cast on herself, or something else, I doona know."

"You didna tell us before because you thought we would send you away, didn't you?" Lucan asked.

"Aye." Galen hated to admit his fears, but no one could begin to understand how much he dreaded being around so many people, knowing he would see into their minds whether he wanted to or not. Yet, to kill Deirdre, it had been worth the risk.

He had another family now, and he would fight to keep them.

Hayden rose and walked to Galen. "Every time you touch someone?"

"Every time." Before Galen realized what Hayden was about, Hayden clamped his hand on his shoulder.

"Now I know why you were always a step behind us," Hayden said.

Galen ground his teeth together, expecting to see the worst in Hayden's mind as he had in the past. Yet all he saw, all he felt, was friendship. A deep bond that bound them as Warriors and brothers.

Galen raised his eyes to stare into Hayden's black ones. "Why?"

"Because you would doubt words." Hayden dropped his hand and nodded to Galen.

Fallon rose to his feet then. "I think Hayden speaks for all of us. We need you, Galen. None of us believe you have forced those Druids, especially Reaghan, to do your bidding."

"Thank you," Galen said, and glanced at his uneaten food. His thoughts lingered on Reaghan. Without another word he left the hall and took the stairs to the battlements.

He scanned the land until he spotted Reaghan surrounded by the women. Galen wanted to go to Reaghan, to try and explain, but he wasn't sure she would listen to him at the moment.

It was enough that she wasn't leaving with Mairi. At least that's what he told himself.

"She's verra beautiful."

Galen glanced over his shoulder to find Ramsey leaning against the stones, relaxed and nonchalant. But Galen knew Ramsey well enough to know his friend had sought him out for a reason. "Reaghan is beautiful."

"Why don't you go to her?"

"She needs time," Galen said. "So much has changed for her."

Ramsey's boot heels hit the stones as he walked to stand beside Galen. "In all the decades I've known you, I've never seen you look at a woman as you do Reaghan. Why do you hesitate to go to her?"

"All of you take for granted touching another. I was not given that luxury with my god. I knew I would have to live my life alone. I had accepted my fate. Until I dared to kiss Reaghan. From the instant I realized her mind was blocked to me, I have no' been able to stay away."

"So you only want her because you cannot see into her mind?"

Galen inhaled deeply, his mind a jumble. "I cannot deny that is part of why I want her. But in the great hall when Mairi was asking her to leave, the thought of never seeing Reaghan again, of never holding her again, nearly broke me in two."

"So you do care for her."

"Enough that when she does lose her memories I will free her to find another."

Ramsey raised a black brow. "You would give her up even though you've found possibly the only woman you can touch without your power interfering?"

"I would."

"And that, Galen, is what makes you a good man. Forget Mairi and her spiteful words. Focus on Reaghan and what time you have left."

Ramsey's words echoed in Galen's mind long after his friend had walked away. Just how much time did he have left with Reaghan?

Mairi paced her chamber and seethed. Ever since coming to MacLeod Castle, since meeting Galen, Reaghan had changed. Gone was the girl so willing to please, and in her place was a woman who knew what she wanted and wouldn't be bent to another's will.

But Mairi had no choice but to ensure that Reaghan left with the rest of them. Mairi had vowed upon being named an elder that she would keep Reaghan with them.

"You were wrong to say those things," Odara said from the corner where she had sat since Mairi's return.

Mairi clucked her tongue. "It needed to be said. All of it."

"How did you know about Galen's power?"

"He told me he used his power for information about Reaghan."

"And the other," Odara pressed. "How did you know he had controlled another's mind before?"

Mairi paused and turned to Odara. In their youth, both of them had been the prettiest girls in the village, and since there were few men, they had become rivals instead of friends. Odara might have won the man Mairi had wanted, but Mairi's body had remained stronger, not bent and weak as Odara's now was.

"I guessed."

Odara's green eyes narrowed. "You've always been a terrible liar, Mairi. The truth, if you please."

"All right. I was told."

"By who?"

Mairi smiled. "It doesn't matter. Galen is a threat to us and Reaghan, and I need to see him dead."

Odara's hand went to her chest. "Dead? You plan to kill a Warrior?"

"Aye."

THIRTY-FOUR

The mist was everywhere, choking out the light and the air around Reaghan. It clung to her as if seeking to invade her skin.

In the mist she saw flashes of a mountain she knew instantly as Cairn Toul. There was another, one that brought peace to her heart and a smile to her face. Foinaven. Her home.

She took a step back when a face suddenly stared back at her. The white hair faded into the mist, but the pale skin and white eyes were visible. The lips were twisted in a snarl, hatred and malice pouring from the image.

Deirdre.

The drough's face faded, and in its place was one of remarkable beauty. Her blue eyes were clear and bright, her hair the color of gold. There were similarities between the woman and Deirdre, but whereas Deirdre was cold and evil, this woman was life and warmth.

No matter how hard Reaghan tried to think of the woman's name, it eluded her. The more she tried the more an ache in the back of her head throbbed.

And then the woman's face faded.

Reaghan reached out to touch it, to bring it back. She fell through the mist, falling endlessly. Spiraling downward into a chasm that swallowed her. She tried to scream, but no sound came from her mouth.

Her arms flailed, reaching for something, anything, to hold on to. There was nothing but the mist.

And a voice. Her voice.

You know how to break the spell.

Reaghan woke suddenly, her heart pounding in her chest. Her chamber was dark, quiet. Empty. There was no mist, no faces or memories.

Only the voice reverberating in her mind.

She sat up and threw off the covers. Her sleep had been scarce, and when she finally had fallen asleep, there had been the dream.

Galen had not come to her, but then again she knew he wouldn't. Maybe it was for the best. Though she knew Mairi's words were false, she wanted to prove to Mairi and everyone that she made her own decisions, not Galen.

Reaghan looked out her window and saw that dawn was not far off. She dressed and combed her hair before braiding it. Then she left her chamber and hurried to the kitchen.

Cara had told her they were all there in the mornings. Reaghan hoped the women hadn't chosen that morning to sleep in, not when she desperately needed to speak with them.

They had been her salvation the day before. Reaghan hadn't known what to do about Mairi, but they had. When she suggested she stay away from Galen to prove Galen hadn't been controlling her mind, they had all agreed, but they doubted Galen wouldn't come to her.

Reaghan knew what kind of man Galen was. He struggled with his powers and the god inside him just as every Warrior at MacLeod Castle did. Galen was a good man. She knew it in the depths of her soul.

When she entered the kitchen it was empty. Reaghan sighed and leaned against the wall. She went over her dream again in her mind. This one was so different from the previous ones. In the others she had seen places and people she knew, but it had been as if she were reliving events. Never before had there been a mist.

This new dream was different in so many ways. For one, the woman. Reaghan recognized her as she had so many others, but this time there wasn't a name. Only a feeling, as though this woman were very important.

Then there was her own voice telling her she knew how to break the spell.

Reaghan had always followed her instincts before. Yet, how could she when she didn't know what could break the spell? Anxiety, deep and immeasurable, had taken hold of her. As if she needed to hurry and end the spell.

But how?

"Reaghan?"

She spun around to find Sonya in the doorway.

"Is everything all right?"

Reaghan fisted her hands in her skirts, unable to explain the urgency inside her, an urgency that told her she was almost out of time. "I had a dream. In that dream I saw Deirdre and another woman. I don't know the other woman, but I sensed she was very important. Then . . ." Reaghan paused and took a deep breath. "Then I heard my own voice tell me I knew how to end the spell."

Sonya's amber eyes were troubled. "When a Druid has such a dream, it should not be ignored."

"I agree. The problem is, I really have no idea how to end the spell."

"It will come to you, I'm sure of it."

"I pray you're correct."

Sonya began to turn away when she suddenly stopped, her head cocked to the side and her eyes closed.

Reaghan remained beside her. She glanced around,

hoping to see Cara or Marcail or someone who might know what was wrong. "Sonya? Are you all right?"

The Druid didn't answer.

"You're scaring me, Sonya."

"I'm listening," Sonya whispered. "The trees are trying to tell me something."

Reaghan waited for Sonya to say more. She was intrigued. When Sonya opened her eyes, she blinked several times and then hurried off into the great hall.

Reaghan followed Sonya, but she paused once inside the hall when she saw Quinn with Marcail, his hand spanning her stomach. He stood behind her, whispering something into her ear that made Marcail smile.

"I need to hear the trees," Sonya said to them.

Quinn's head jerked up at the sound of her voice. "You know how dangerous it is, Sonya. To venture outside of Isla's shield would amount to capture and death at Deirdre's hand."

"The trees are calling for me," Sonya argued. "I must hear them."

Quinn kissed Marcail's cheek. "I'll talk to the others, but I doubt you will be allowed."

Once Quinn was gone Sonya paced the hall. Reaghan moved out of the way and watched as the others tried to comfort her. Sonya was distraught, her need to hear the trees outweighing reason.

It wasn't until Broc entered the hall that Sonya stopped her pacing. Reaghan saw the concern in Broc's eyes and the ease with which Sonya approached him, as if no one else were in the room.

As Sonya told Broc about the trees, Reaghan's gaze was caught by the man who stood next to the Warrior. Galen. Her heart leaped in her chest at the sight of him. His face was gaunt, as if he hadn't slept in days.

Reaghan wanted to go to him, to tell him about her dream. Galen would want to protect her as he always had. She took a step toward him when Broc's booming voice halted her.

"Nay, Sonya," Broc said, his voice rising above the redheaded Druid's. "It's too dangerous to leave the shield. We will no' put any Druids in danger, not when Deirdre is waiting for us to make a mistake."

"It's important, Broc."

A muscle moved in his jaw. "I know."

Sonya stormed out of the kitchen, but it was the yearning, the longing, Reaghan saw in Broc's eyes that made her breath catch.

Larena moved beside Reaghan. "It breaks the heart, doesn't it, the way he looks at her?"

"Why doesn't he tell her?"

Larena shrugged, her golden cascade of hair tied at the base of her neck. "I doubt he ever will. Nor will she tell him of her feelings."

Reaghan couldn't believe her ears. "Truly? I don't understand."

"None of us do," Larena whispered before she walked away.

Reaghan found her gaze once more on Galen. She had never expected a man like Galen in her life, but now that she had him, she never wanted to let him go.

He brought happiness and joy into her life where there had been none. He gave her the strength to make decisions, and the courage to see them through. She wanted to spend every night curled in the safety of his arms, to feel his heart beat and the rhythm of his breathing.

How had she gotten so used to having Galen near her in such a short time? Now Galen meant everything to her.

Her headaches and her blocked memories kept her

from giving him all of herself. There was something wrong with her, and the longer Reaghan stayed at MacLeod Castle, the more she wanted a real life. One without the spell.

A commotion pulled Galen's gaze from hers. They both turned to find Mairi and Fallon descending the stairs. Behind Mairi were the rest of the Druids from her village.

"You will be captured," Fallon said.

Mairi glanced at the Druids behind her. "It is a chance we are willing to take."

"Nay," Reaghan said as she hurried forward. She looked at the faces of Druids she had known for ten years, people she had shared her life with. "Please, listen to Fallon. He speaks the truth. The wyrran will be waiting to take you to Cairn Toul."

"We cannot stay here with Warriors!" someone shouted.

Reaghan licked her lips and tried again. "These men protected us from the wyrran. They brought us here to keep us from Deirdre. They are good men."

There was a loud snort. "They are evil! All of them!"

Mairi's fingers dug into Reaghan's arm. "You are coming with us."

"I'm not." Reaghan stared down into Mairi's eyes and saw a madness that hadn't been there before. "I'm not going anywhere."

"Oh, but you will."

Reaghan wrenched her arm out of the elder's grasp and stumbled backward when she saw the evil in Mairi's gaze. "You aren't Mairi."

"I am. My magic is stronger now. You can either come with me now, or you will regret it."

"Regret it how? You are an old woman with limited magic."

"Reaghan," Isla cautioned.

But Reaghan didn't care anymore. Mairi wasn't the elder she had known at Loch Awe. The vicious spite in Mairi made a tingle of apprehension race down Reaghan's spine. Though Reaghan didn't fear for herself. She feared for everyone else in the castle.

"I will kill Galen."

"What?" Reaghan couldn't have heard Mairi correctly. "What has Galen done to you other than save you from the wyrran?"

"He got into my head. He made me do things. He was the cause of Nessa's death. He told me to poison her." Mairi latched on to her arm again, and this time her broken nails cut into Reaghan's skin and drew blood.

Reaghan grimaced as she felt something push into her mind, something that was altogether malevolent. With each word from Mairi's mouth, the evil grew like a dark shadow, wanting to consume her.

She jerked out of Mairi's grip, and instantly the evil was gone. "What did you just do?" Reaghan demanded. "How did your magic become stronger?"

"Wouldn't you like to know?" Mairi asked, as she reached for Reaghan again.

"Stop this. Now." Reaghan felt something move and shift inside her, something that tingled along her bones and spiraled up inside her. Magic. It was her magic. Her fingertips hummed with it, ready to do whatever was necessary to protect Galen and the others.

Mairi smiled, a flash of white in her irises. "Galen dies now."

Reaghan reached for Mairi, but not before the elder had raised her hand and directed her magic at Galen. Galen was hurled backward and slammed into the stone wall so hard it shook the castle.

Magic flew from Reaghan's hands, but before it could do any damage to Mairi, the elder lifted her other hand to block Reaghan's magic.

Reaghan's eyes widened when she saw the malicious smile on Mairi's face.

"You weren't expecting that, were you?" Mairi said.

Before Reaghan could respond, Mairi threw another burst of magic at Galen. He was held against the wall several feet off the ground. The grimace on his face told Reaghan how much pain he was in.

Chaos erupted in the hall as the Warriors unleashed their gods and readied to attack Mairi. The Druids from the village stormed out the door with hysterical screams, but no one chased them. Everyone was focused on Mairi.

Reaghan tried to use her magic again. She could feel it inside her, but she couldn't use it. Somehow the spell was preventing it. She stepped in front of Mairi and the magic directed at Galen.

Someone grabbed her from behind and pulled her away. Reaghan struggled against the hold as she fought to get back to Mairi to stop her from harming Galen.

"Stay out of her way," Logan demanded.

Reaghan dodged his hands. "Help Galen."

"Galen is a Warrior. He can handle one old woman."

Reaghan shook her head. "Mairi isn't herself. Her strength, her speed, her magic aren't hers."

Logan paused, his gaze meeting hers. "Shite."

As soon as Logan released her, Reaghan started back to Mairi. The Warriors alternated attacking Mairi, but each time she threw them back with magic she had never had before. But the Warriors never stopped attacking her.

Reaghan glanced at Galen to see his god unbound and his lips peeled back to show his fangs. He fought Mairi's hold, straining against the magic that would bind him.

Galen let out a roar when a gash opened diagonally

across his chest. A moment later two more joined the first. Slice after slice scoured Galen's body, going deeper, running longer with each one. Reaghan knew Mairi was doing it, prolonging Galen's torture.

Something inside Reaghan snapped. Her magic filled her, and as she stepped toward Mairi, she saw the women of MacLeod Castle do the same.

As one they directed their magic at Mairi. Mairi couldn't withstand the onslaught. Her magic began to wane. There was a pause when Mairi's eyes widened as she looked at Reaghan.

For that one instant, Reaghan saw the elder as she had known her, the wise, patient woman.

And then the Warriors moved in. Reaghan could no longer see Mairi, and she didn't wish to.

Reaghan ran to Galen as he slumped onto the floor, blood coating his shirt and kilt. He met her gaze before he looked around her to the group of Warriors.

"Mairi?" he rasped.

Reaghan swallowed and glanced behind her. Through the crowd of Warriors she saw a body lying still upon the floor. "Dead."

Galen let out a breath and closed his eyes. Reaghan knew he was immortal, knew his wounds would heal, but the extent of his injuries left her worried.

Logan and Ramsey soon joined her and helped Galen to gain his feet.

"I'll be all right," Galen told her when he opened his eyes. "I didn't think Mairi had that kind of magic."

"She didn't. Something evil had taken over," Odara said from the top of the stairs.

THIRTY-FIVE

Deirdre screamed and threw the ewer beside her against the wall. The shattering did nothing to calm her. The long tendrils of her hair lifted around her, searching for something, anything, to grab onto and kill.

But she was alone.

The spell had been perfect. She had known the Druids would be in MacLeod Castle and knew there would be one who couldn't withstand her magic. It had surprised Deirdre that it had been the leader of the Druids. Deirdre hadn't expected the elder to have such a weak mind, and therefore be capable of being manipulated into allowing Deirdre to take over.

It had been a flawless plan. Get into Mairi's mind and have her convince the Druids to leave the castle. That had been the easy part.

But once Deirdre had realized there was something important about the Druid named Reaghan, she had dug deeper into Mairi's mind. Mairi didn't know much other than that Reaghan had cast a spell on herself to keep something hidden in her mind, something Reaghan and the others wanted kept from Deirdre.

Deirdre thought it would be simple to persuade Reaghan to leave with the others, but Deirdre hadn't taken into consideration the Warriors—and the bond that had grown between Reaghan and Galen.

Galen. Deirdre had known his powers were great. She had seen his potential when he'd been in her mountain, but he had fought against her and everything she threatened him with and offered him.

It hadn't been just his power that had been immense, it had been his mental strength as well. He stood against her as none but the MacLeods ever had.

Deirdre knew she had lost Reaghan when the Druid refused to leave, but Deirdre had added magic to the pathetic amount Mairi had. She had almost killed Galen. With a little more time she could have eliminated Galen and taken Reaghan.

Instead, Mairi had been killed when the Druids and Warriors worked together to overcome the elder.

The only reward was that the Druids of Loch Awe would now be hers. The brainless wretches had actually feared the Warriors at the castle. It had taken but a little push to send them running right into her wyrran's waiting claws.

It was only a matter of days before the wyrran would bring the Druids to her and their magic would be hers.

And one less Druid would roam her land.

Reaghan lifted her hand covering the wound from Galen's chest and saw the blood which coated her fingers. Her heart hammered from Mairi's attack and Odara's words, but it was enough that Galen was alive.

Galen had risen with the help of others and now sat at the table. Reaghan's mind was in a whirl with all that had happened and all she had seen.

She could still feel the magic within her, magic she hadn't thought existed. Reaghan could barely feel it now. It was almost as if it hid unless she was in a situation where she needed it. It was the only explanation she could think of.

"Odara, I think you had better explain yourself," Galen said, his voice carrying in the great hall.

Odara shrugged. "It's as I said. Someone was in Mairi's mind. Mairi might have been a wee bit concerned about so many Warriors in one place, but she trusted Reaghan's instincts. The things Mairi said . . . I've never heard her say such awful things before. And I've known her my entire life."

"It was evil," Reaghan said. "I felt it when she touched me."

"Aye," Odara said with a nod, as she descended the steps slowly. She walked to stand beside Mairi and sighed. " 'Evil' is the right word. As elders our first concern is always the safety of our people. Regardless of how Mairi felt about any of you, she should have known we were protected here."

Reaghan walked to stand near Mairi. "Who would want to penetrate Mairi's mind? And to what purpose?"

"Deirdre," Ramsey said.

Fallon nodded. "Without a doubt. But I'm as curious as Reaghan. Why Mairi?"

"And why would she want Galen dead?" Logan asked.

Reaghan raised her eyes to Galen. His brow was puckered and his jaw clenched. He looked at Mairi's body as if she could somehow tell him why she had tried to kill him.

Suddenly he rose and squatted beside her. "She's not dead yet," he murmured.

Reaghan took a step forward when she realized what he was going to do. "Galen, nay!"

But it was too late. He placed his hand on Mairi and closed his eyes.

Everyone in the hall waited with bated breath until his eyes snapped open and he stood. Reaghan started toward him when she saw how pale he was, how his eyes couldn't focus.

She reached him before anyone else and wrapped her arms around his back. "You need to sit."

He nodded and swallowed, his breathing ragged and harsh, as if it pained his body to inhale. The fact he leaned his weight onto her told Reaghan he was weaker than she had first thought.

Hayden reached his hands out to help Galen sit but Reaghan quickly said, "Nay. Let him recover before you touch him."

"I'm sorry." Hayden jerked his hands away and backed up a step. "How can we help?"

"Water. He needs water." Reaghan reached down and tore a strip off the hem of her chemise. She wiped the sweat from Galen's brow, her heart in her throat.

His eyes were closed, his hands fisted as they lay on the table. He shook, and his skin had taken on a waxy look. The more he sat without speaking the more apprehensive she became.

As soon as Larena handed her a goblet of water Reaghan lifted it to Galen's lips. "Drink for me," she urged him.

He parted his lips and let her pour some of the cool liquid into his mouth. Once he swallowed, she gave him more. Little by little he drained the goblet until nothing was left.

"Reaghan," he whispered.

She set aside the goblet and wiped at his brow again. "I'm here."

Ramsey sat opposite Galen and glared, though Reaghan saw the worry reflected in Ramsey's silver eyes. "Galen, you fool. Why did you take such a risk?"

"Had to," Galen murmured.

Reaghan laid his head on her shoulder. "Nay, you didn't."

"Can you talk?" Lucan asked.

Reaghan frowned. "It can wait. He needs to lie down."

"Nay," Galen said, and covered her hand with his large one. He lifted his head and took in a shuddering breath. "Lucan is right. I need to tell everyone what I saw."

Reaghan was pleased to see Galen's color was returning. But it was his eyes that caused her heart to plummet to her feet. He had seen something, felt something, that had wrenched out a piece of his soul.

"Galen."

He smiled, though it didn't reach his eyes. His hand lifted and he ran his fingers along her cheek. "It had to be done."

Her breath locked in her lungs at his touch. How she had missed his warmth, his strength. She had been such a fool to stay away from him.

Galen dropped his hand and slowly rose to his feet. If he continued to touch Reaghan he would pull her into his arms and kiss her. He barely had the strength to continue to hold himself up, and there were things he had to tell the others. "I did manage to see something in Mairi's mind."

"Why?" Ramsey asked. "Why would you try such a thing?"

Galen turned his gaze to his friend. "No one else could."

"That doesna mean you risk your life," Hayden said.

Arran shook his head, his arms crossed over his chest. "Foolish, just as Ramsey said, but it was also brave."

"Aye," Duncan and Ian replied in unison.

Galen wanted to laugh. Brave? Nay. His concern had been for Reaghan and his family at the castle.

"What did you see?" Quinn asked.

Galen forced his body to remain standing though his legs shook like a newborn colt's. He hadn't been this weak since he had controlled the soldier's mind decades ago. "Deirdre, just as we suspected. I'm willing to guess she managed to discover the Druids hid the artifact."

"And that the artifact is here," Fallon ground out. "Shite. That's why she wanted the Druids to leave."

Ian ran his hand back and forth over the top of his shorn hair. "That still doesna explain why she wanted Galen dead."

"It has to do with me, doesn't it?" Reaghan said.

Galen closed his eyes, wishing with all his heart the artifact were anyone but Reaghan.

"You were the only Druid who had made a connection with a Warrior. Couple that with the fact you are the artifact and it's no wonder she went after Galen," Odara said.

After a moment Reaghan swallowed and folded her hands in her lap. "This is just another reason for me to try and find a way to break the spell."

Galen wanted to fold Reaghan in his arms, to protect her forever.

"It nearly killed you, didn't it?" Broc asked him.

Galen leaned on the table as his strength waned. "I had to look deeper than I have before. That is all."

Logan let out a string of curses and slammed his hand on the table. "God's blood, Galen, you cannot lie to us. You nearly killed yourself gaining that bit of information, information we could have guessed."

"Maybe," Galen said, and lifted his head to look at Logan. "But we couldn't have guessed that Deirdre is sending the MacClures to attack us."

"By the saints," Cara whispered as she buried her head in Lucan's chest.

Camdyn leaned across the twins. "How do you know such a thing?"

Galen licked his lips, his mouth and throat parched. He reached for the ewer of water, but his arm shook so much he couldn't pour it.

Reaghan took it from him and filled the goblet. Galen

then lowered himself back onto the bench and drank. He wiped his mouth with the back of his hand when he finished.

Just thinking about what he had managed to do left him shaken, his soul scarred. It had taken more of his power than any of them could have guessed.

Delving into Mairi's mind hadn't been the problem. It had been letting go. Deirdre's hold on the elder had been complete. The wickedness which swarmed Mairi had tried to suck him in as well.

Being near such malevolence and willingly using his god to seek answers was not something he had ever done. Or something he ever wanted to repeat. Yet, he would do it all again if it meant Reaghan could be safe.

"I felt Deirdre in Mairi's mind. It was as if Deirdre had scraped Mairi's brain, leaving marks much like our claws would. The evil was everywhere. As soon as I sensed Deirdre I followed her, and somehow the next thing I knew, I saw a glimpse of her mind."

"Holy hell," Quinn murmured.

"I saw her plan for the MacClures to attack us," Galen said, suppressing the shudder that racked his body at touching Deirdre's mind. "They have already gathered their men."

Fallon linked his hand with Larena's. "Galen, I doona know how you did it, and I doona want you doing it again, but I'm grateful for your power. We can prepare and be ready."

"The MacClures won't get through my shield," Isla said. "They will do as anyone without magic and continue on."

Galen wished she were correct. "Wyrran are with them."

"It fooled the wyrran before," Ian said.

Isla grimaced. "That was before Deirdre knew I was here. Now that she does, my shield won't stop the wyrran. It will slow them, though."

"That's all we need," Camdyn ground out.

Galen wiped his hand down his face. His strength was returning, but more slowly than he would have liked. He needed to be ready for battle. As it was, he was useless.

Sonya pointed to the door as she said, "There are Druids out there who are in danger."

"That was their choice," Odara said. "They knew what awaited them, and they chose certain death over these walls."

"We aren't going after them?" Sonya asked, her eyes round with disbelief.

Fallon sighed and rubbed his eyes with his thumb and forefinger. "I vowed never to keep anyone prisoner, Sonya, and that's exactly what I would be doing if I brought those Druids back."

"They don't know what they're doing. It's wrong of us to leave them to Deirdre," she argued.

"I need everyone to stay inside the castle walls," Fallon said. He looked around the hall. "No one leaves. No one. We have no idea when the attack will come, but we will be ready."

Quinn rubbed his hands together. "Arran, Ian, Duncan, Hayden, and I will set up first watch."

"I can take a quick flight over the area to see how close the MacClures are," Broc offered.

Fallon nodded. "Good idea, Broc. Stay high enough so they cannot see you."

"Of course." Broc removed his tunic and started for the castle door, his skin already turning the dark, indigo blue of his god.

Galen watched as Broc's wings spouted from his back. "I can take watch."

"You will rest first," Lucan said.

Galen wanted to argue, but he knew Lucan was right.

He was no good to anyone in his current condition. "Just for a little while."

"I'll help him," Reaghan said.

As soon as her slender hands came in contact with him, all Galen could think about was taking her in his arms and holding her. He wanted to part her sweet thighs and bury himself to the hilt.

He was afraid to touch Reaghan, afraid he wouldn't be able to keep his hands from her. She had pulled away from him yesterday and created a chasm Galen was afraid he'd never be able to span.

Galen put his arm around her shoulders and allowed her to take some of his weight. He was thankful she was there so he didn't have to try to make the climb to his chamber by himself.

With the Druids now gone, Galen once more had his chamber, which was on the opposite side of the castle from Reaghan's. He guided her to the room and pushed open the door.

Galen lifted his arm from her shoulders and stumbled into the chamber to collapse on his bed. He fully expected Reaghan to leave, so when he sensed her beside him, his heart beat double time.

"You shouldn't have put your life in danger."

He shrugged. "These people are my family, and that includes you. I would do anything to protect you."

"You saw more in Mairi's mind than you told us, didn't you?"

"I did," he admitted. "I saw evil more deadly, more intent, than you could imagine. I fear for us, Reaghan. I fear nothing we can do will ever defeat Deirdre."

THIRTY-SIX

Reaghan's stomach fell to her feet like a stone. "There has to be a way to end what she has begun. I refuse to believe she will win."

Galen's head jerked in a nod as he looked at her. "I agree. I've always believed goodness would overcome the evil of this world."

She knew Galen was trying to calm her. She appreciated him telling her the truth, but it made her realize that she had to determine how to break the spell so that whatever information she held she could give to the Warriors.

She recalled her dream where she had told herself she knew how to break the spell. Why couldn't she remember? Why, when Galen needed to have the information she had hidden. And what was it, exactly, she had hidden in her mind? What could be so important, so vital, that she had given up her life to protect it?

Galen had said Deirdre would have come looking for her. Did she hide something that could hinder—or God forbid, *help*—Deirdre?

There was no way she would have helped Deirdre. Not willingly anyway. Regardless of her past and the memories hidden from her, Reaghan would wager her soul she had set herself against Deirdre.

Reaghan sighed and lifted her gaze to talk to Galen. She smiled when she found him asleep. Slowly, carefully, she joined him on the bed until she was snuggled against his healing body. Then, she wound a lock of his hair around her finger and let her gaze wander over him.

The lines that had bracketed his mouth and eyes had eased. It was peculiar seeing Galen look so vulnerable, so drained. She had gotten used to his invincibility, his immortality and immense strength, but what had happened in the great hall proved he wasn't as indestructible as she thought. He had taken a great risk for her and the others at MacLeod Castle.

A risk to his own life.

He hadn't hesitated either. His only thought had been to save his family. Family he now considered her to be a part of.

"Oh, Galen," she whispered.

She smiled when she traced her finger down his cleanly shaven jaw, remembering how he had teased her with his whiskers. Her finger smoothed over his wide lips. Those lips had brought her such wicked pleasures, such incredible kisses.

So much had happened since she had first caught sight of Galen. Her entire world had changed—for the better. She ached for the Druids who had been too afraid to see the Warriors were only protecting them.

Like Sonya, Reaghan had wanted to go after them. But Fallon's words, as awful as they were to hear, had been correct. To make someone stay was to imprison them, which would do more harm than good.

She prayed her fellow Druids managed to escape, even though Reaghan knew in her heart Deirdre would capture them.

And Mairi. Reaghan's eyes filled with tears as she thought of the elder. Had Mairi known Deirdre invaded her mind? Had Mairi fought against the evil?

Reaghan would probably never know the answers. Mairi

was gone, no longer to be used by Deirdre. But Reaghan worried about Odara. She had thought Mairi was the strongest of the elders, but now Reaghan began to wonder if it hadn't always been Odara.

Reaghan sighed and snuggled closer to Galen, seeking the warmth of his muscular body. She laid her hand atop his and linked their fingers.

Her thoughts of Mairi, Deirdre, and the coming attack began to fade as sleep lulled her. As she drifted off to sleep, she felt the dull ache that signaled a headache, but for the first time she wasn't scared.

She would face the pain and whatever the future held with Galen at her side.

Odara looked at the MacLeod brothers around the table. It was surreal seeing them in the flesh after hearing the tales spoken about them.

It would be so easy for the Warriors to lash out at everything and everyone after what had happened to the brothers and their clan. Yet they had opened their home, had vowed to stand against Deirdre, and had found love.

That had been the deciding factor for Odara upon arriving at the castle. She knew the others had feared Galen and Logan, but she had come to like and respect the Warriors.

Just knowing she would be surrounded by thirteen Warriors had made Odara more than a little frightened. Until she met the Druids who lived at the castle and saw how they interacted with the Warriors. That had been enough for her.

Odara waited for the questions to begin. She knew the Druids of the castle would want to talk to her, and she wasn't surprised to find the MacLeods with them.

"Why didn't you fight against Mairi and her talk of leaving?" Sonya asked.

Odara chuckled and shook her head. "I have known Mairi my entire life. She's stubborn, and once she decides something, she won't let it go. Had I not sensed the evil inside her, I would have said something. I tried to talk to a few of the women, but Mairi was very convincing in her lies. Or I should say, Deirdre was. I kept quiet so I could watch Mairi."

Marcail leaned forward and put her forearms on the table. The gold bands at the ends of her tiny braids clinked together each time she moved her head. "I want to know about Reaghan, if you know more than what Galen was able to learn from Mairi."

"Mairi and I were told of Reaghan together." Odara bit her lip and looked down at her hands, hands that now trembled with age, her once beautiful skin marked with dark spots. "We were told that under no circumstances should Reaghan ever leave the village."

"Why?" Lucan asked.

Odara shrugged in response. "We were never given a reason, just told that she should never leave."

"Do you know any part of the spell Reaghan used?" Cara asked.

"Nay."

Larena sighed loudly and glanced toward the stairs. "I was afraid of that."

"How long was the spell supposed to last?" Fallon asked.

Odara lifted her brows as she looked at the leader of the Warriors. "As far as we were told, forever."

Lucan drummed his fingers on the table, his forehead puckered in thought. "Do you know what Reaghan is attempting to hide from Deirdre?"

Odara hestitated, unsure if she should speak of what she knew little about. She wanted to give these people truths, not something she had no proof of.

"Please," Sonya said. "Tell us what you know."

Odara swallowed and leaned forward. "When my mother lay on her deathbed, she told me Reaghan kept within her knowledge of a place that held vast power."

"Hm. Vast power is something Deirdre would certainly want to obtain," Fallon said.

Lucan grunted. "How would it hold the power? And where?"

"I don't know," Odara said. "My mother died right after, so I was never able to ask her."

Isla dropped her chin into her hand. "We may never know. There are too many uncertainties. We cannot help Reaghan unless we know everything. I fear we will ultimately harm her, and I've no wish for that."

"Is Reaghan speaking of strange dreams?" Odara asked.

Sonya sat straighter, her mouth pinched. "Aye. Why?"

"It's the start of her spell regenerating. Usually by this time the headaches are almost constant and she falls into a deep sleep where a fever overtakes her. She wakes a day or so after, and then she remembers nothing."

"Sonya's healing may have slowed it," Quinn said.

Odara slowly nodded. "Or altered it somehow. I've not seen much of Reaghan lately. I know of her headache upon arriving, but nothing after."

"As far as we know, there have been no more," Cara answered. "Galen would have sent for Sonya if she had had another headache. When Reaghan isn't with him, she's with one of us."

Odara rose, her old knees creaking. "Then the spell has been altered, and mayhap for the better. I never liked seeing her in pain."

"Will you stay with us?" Marcail asked.

Odara smiled as she walked to the stairs. "I've sworn to guard Reaghan, wherever she may go. I will stay as long as she does."

* * *

Galen felt better as soon as he opened his eyes. The strength he had become accustomed to after two hundred and fifty years had returned once more. Now he could stand with the other Warriors and protect Reaghan.

A soft, feminine sigh caught his attention. He glanced to his side and found Reaghan curled beside him. She had one hand tucked beneath her cheek, her lips slightly parted as she slept.

Galen shifted onto his side to face her. He never grew tired of looking at Reaghan. To him, she was the most beautiful, stunning woman to ever walk the earth.

The night before had been horrid. Galen wondered how he could have survived it without Reaghan by his side. He had always thought himself a rational, tolerant man, but Reaghan gave him more clarity. She opened his eyes to new possibilities.

She lived each day to its fullest. She looked ahead, never to the past. Some could argue that was because she couldn't recall her memories, but Galen knew it was just how Reaghan had decided to live her life.

It was a lesson Galen wished he had learned a century earlier.

Reaghan's eyelids fluttered open. Her sleepy smile stirred his passions and caused the blood to rush to his cock. He fisted his hand so he wouldn't reach for her, wouldn't feel the warmth of her satiny skin, wouldn't taste the sweetness of her lips.

Her gray eyes were warm, soft as they met his gaze. "How do you feel?"

"I'm myself once more."

She licked her lips and frowned as her gaze dropped. "You scared me. You're supposed to be immortal."

"I would give up my life if it meant saving you." He

said the words from his soul, and he'd never spoken words so sincere.

Her gaze snapped to his. "Oh, Galen. I'm not worth it. I'm unimportant, while your quest to end Deirdre's tyranny is vital."

Galen couldn't hold back any longer. He drew Reaghan against him, their faces breaths apart. His body focused entirely on her long, very feminine form pressed against him. Of her lush curves and the promise of pleasure.

Her eyes widened a fraction before darkening with desire, desire he recognized and had come to crave with increasing regularity.

"You're important to me. Never forget that," he whispered.

He didn't give her time to argue. He took her mouth in a kiss, putting every ounce of his yearning, his longing . . . his need into it.

He wished he could give her pretty words to tell her how much she meant to him, how much he desperately needed her, but it wasn't his way. Instead, he would show her the only way he could—with his mouth and hands and body.

His heart hammered when she melted against him. She opened her mouth to him and plunged her hands into his hair. He pulled at her gown and heard a seam rip. Suddenly, her hands joined his as they tore at each other's clothes, tossing garments around the room until they were both blissfully naked, their limbs intertwined.

Need unlike Galen had ever experienced surged through him. Reaghan's scorching kiss, her hands, urgent and grasping, only spurred him onward.

He pulled his mouth from hers and fastened his lips over her nipple. Her nails dug into his back as she arched into him, seeking more.

Galen alternately tongued her nipple and suckled the

tiny bud. Her body shook, her soft cries filling the chamber. With a small nip, he moved to her other breast.

His fingers found her curls, stroked her hot, silken sex. He burned to be inside her, to have her pull him in deep and hold him tight.

Ruthlessly he teased her clitoris before plunging a finger inside her. Her hands were greedy as she caressed his shoulders, his back, his neck, feeding the uncontrollable, undeniable hunger he had for her.

Unable to hold back any longer, Galen moved to stand beside the bed. He grabbed Reaghan's hips and turned her so she lay lengthwise, her hips at the edge of the bed.

He smiled down at her, recognizing the flushed skin, the heavy-lidded eyes. Her breasts rose and fell with her rapid breathing. She watched him with her storm-colored eyes, wordlessly waiting, silently impatient. With her thighs spread wide, Galen filled her slowly, penetrating deeply into her snug channel.

Reaghan's lips parted, a small moan of pleasure spilling from her mouth. Her fingers dug into the blanket as her legs wrapped around his waist, tugging Galen deeper.

He cupped her breasts, teasing her nipples with his fingers. She arched her back, his name a whisper on her lips. Her body quivered and writhed beneath him, but Galen wasn't finished.

His mouth took over for his fingers as he continued to reduce her to a desperately pleading mass. He lifted his head and saw the silent need upon her face.

Galen straightened and unwrapped her legs from his waist. He placed first one leg, then the other, atop his shoulders before he gripped her hips and began to move. He held her steady as he penetrated her again and again, each time going deeper, harder, faster.

The more he pounded into her, the more her breaths

came in panting gasps. He felt her body tighten, felt her muscles locking.

He kept her still, immobile even as she came apart before his eyes. He'd never seen anything so profound, so glorious as Reaghan's face awash with bliss.

Her sheath clutched around his cock, urging him to follow her into oblivion.

Galen didn't hesitate.

His nerves were stretched taut and burning with pleasure as he continued to fill her. He released her legs and fell forward, his hands on either side of her head as he tipped into his orgasm.

Galen cried out Reaghan's name as he drove into her once, twice more, before he let go.

Her arms came around him and pulled him atop her. Galen drew in a broken breath. Everything he had ever wanted, would ever dream of was in his arms.

THIRTY-SEVEN

Reaghan lay in Galen's arms, sharing in the warm glow of their lovemaking. Somewhere between falling asleep beside Galen and now, she had come to realize how much she desperately needed him.

Because she loved him.

The depth of her feelings for Galen was crystal clear now. Why hadn't she realized it sooner? Her heart swelled, her soul sighed.

Nothing mattered but Galen. And ensuring that Deirdre could no longer harm him or anyone else ever again.

She hadn't begun to live until he had come into her life. He had given her a family, given her more than she had thought possible.

She wanted to tell him of her love, to shout it from the highest tower for all to hear. Even without her memories, Reaghan realized that Galen made her life complete.

He rose up on his elbows and kissed the tip of her nose. "Have I ever told you how much I love watching you as you peak?"

"Nay." She grinned, embarrassed, but also excited by his words. "You watch me?"

"Oh, aye. I enjoy the expressions that cross your face."

"I think I'll keep my eyes open next time and watch you."

Galen shook his head. "I wouldna advise it. All I'm doing is watching you."

Reaghan used her nails and tickled his sides. He grabbed her hands and rolled to his back laughing. Someone cleared their throat and Reagan turned her head to find Logan in the doorway.

"I didna realize," Logan mumbled as he turned his head away. "I just came to see if Galen had recovered. Obviously he has. I'll let Fallon and the others know."

Once Logan had shut the door behind him, Galen sighed. "Our time is up."

"Aye." Reaghan wasn't yet ready to leave the chamber and face the battle that was coming toward them.

She climbed off the bed and began to search through the scattered clothes for her own. Reaghan pulled her chemise over her head and was reaching for her gown when Galen took her hands in his.

"It will be all right," he told her.

Reaghan smiled and rose up on her toes to kiss him. "I know. I cannot help but worry though."

"I'm a Warrior, remember?"

"Galen, I . . ." Reaghan hesitated to tell him of her love. Even if he didn't feel the same for her, she knew he cared.

He frowned, his blue eyes searching hers. "What is it? Tell me, Reaghan."

"I lo—"

Galen's door burst open and Hayden poked his head in and said, "Broc is on his way. Fallon wants all of us in the great hall."

As soon as Hayden was gone Galen turned back to her. "What were you saying?"

"It can wait. Come, I know you want to be there when Broc arrives." Reaghan smiled and hurried to finish dressing.

Together, they walked from Galen's chamber. Her apprehension grew the closer she got to the great hall. She needed to talk to Isla or one of the others. They had to help her find some way to end the spell.

Yet as soon as she and Galen descended the stairs Broc arrived.

"The MacClures and their army will be here by first light," Broc announced.

Reaghan, like the rest of the occupants in the hall, stood silent, each lost in thought.

Logan was the first to speak. "Even with the wyrran they are no match for us."

"Not to mention that Isla's shield will slow them," Hayden added.

Reaghan swiveled her head to Galen. Shield or not, she knew that in just a matter of hours the castle would be under attack. She was confident of the Warrior's ability, having seen them firsthand, but she still feared for Galen.

"The Druids will hide below the castle in the old dungeons, just as before," Fallon said.

Lucan nodded and folded his arms over his chest. "I'll guard them."

"Nay," Ramsey said. "You three brothers need to fight together, just as your god intended you to do. You're unstoppable together, and that's exactly what we need."

Fallon blew out a breath and bent forward to lean his hands on the table. "Ramsey is right."

"I'll guard the Druids," Larena said. "I'll use my power and stay invisible so that if anyone or anything does get inside the castle they'll think the Druids aren't guarded."

"Good idea," Fallon said, and winked at his wife.

Quinn said, "Everyone else knows their place."

Sonya cleared her throat. "Fallon, a word."

"Go on," he told Sonya.

"The trees are trying to tell me something. They are most urgent," the Druid said.

Before she was even finished talking Fallon was shaking his head. "I doona want anyone to leave the castle."

"Then let Isla remove the shield," Sonya argued. "The trees wouldn't be this insistent if it wasn't important. They've proven that in the past."

Lucan moved to stand beside Fallon. "We cannot chance having the shield removed for even a heartbeat."

"I know," Fallon said with a sigh.

Sonya strode to stand in front of Fallon. "Get me to the trees, or I go myself."

Reaghan watched, fascinated by how Sonya dared to stand against Warrior, much less their leader. If the Druids of Reaghan's village had seen this, they might have realized these Warriors would never harm them.

"I can fly her over the trees," Broc said. "I'll stay high enough so no one sees us."

"All right," Fallon relented with a sigh.

Broc gave a quick nod. He held out his hand to Sonya, and together they walked from the castle.

"Come," Marcail murmured next to Reaghan. "We need to gather food. Once we are down in the dungeon, we won't be able to return until the battle is over and the MacClures are gone."

With one last look at Galen, Reaghan followed the women into the kitchen.

Galen waited until Reaghan was gone before he turned to his fellow Warriors. "My strength is restored."

"And we're glad of that," Hayden said.

Galen glanced at the kitchen doorway. "Did you question Odara?"

Lucan gave a small nod. "She thinks Reaghan might be hiding the location of a large mass of magic."

Galen cursed and raked a hand through his hair. "I feared it might be something like that."

"We doona know for sure," Ian cautioned.

Arran grunted. "Whether it is a hidden source of magic or something else, we all know it must be important."

Galen inhaled deeply. "We can focus on this later. For now, let's prepare for battle."

Duncan slapped his hands together and rubbed them. "I've been itching for another battle. Though it hardly seems fair to fight mortal men and wee wyrran."

"Maybe so, but I'm more than ready," Camdyn said, deadly intent in his gaze.

Galen caught sight of Malcolm, who stood at the back of the hall in the shadows, silent and always watching. The mortal couldn't return to his own lands, and he wasn't a Warrior, so he didn't quite fit in at the castle.

When Malcolm realized Galen watched him, he pushed from the wall and walked away.

"What do I say to him?" Fallon asked.

Galen turned his gaze to Fallon. "He cannot fight with us nor can we send him with the women."

"Nay. He was a fine warrior for his clan before he was attacked. But with his one arm useless, I fear he will only get himself killed."

"That may be exactly what he wants."

Fallon scratched his chin and cursed. "For my wife's sake, I hope that's no' true. Larena will be devastated if Malcolm died."

"And yet Malcolm wants to be set free. He's only existing, no' living," Galen said.

Galen stretched his arms over his head and studied the sky as he stood on the battlements, waiting for any sign of Broc and Sonya. The hours had passed at a steady rate. It was well into the afternoon, and it wouldn't be long before the sun disappeared from view altogether. Broc and Sonya had been gone longer than anyone expected. The women were nervous for their return, the men determined to find them.

"You think something happened, don't you?" Reaghan asked from beside him.

Galen took comfort in her nearness. He had a bad feeling about the coming attack, and an even worse feeling about Broc and Sonya. "It shouldn't have taken so long."

"Broc will protect Sonya."

"That's what I fear." Galen gripped the stones and silently willed Broc to appear. Suddenly, amid the heavy clouds, Galen spotted the large, dark blue wings. "Here they come!"

Behind him, Galen could hear the others rushing into the bailey as Broc flew over them.

No sooner had Broc landed and set Sonya on her feet than Ramsey asked, "What took so long?"

Broc looked at Ramsey, his face grim. "I had to land in a tree. Sonya needed to touch one of them as they spoke to her."

But it was Sonya's words that gave everyone pause. "There is a group of Druids heading toward us. My sister is among them."

Galen's stomach clenched. Druids arriving at the same time they were being attacked? It couldn't be coincidence.

He listened with half an ear as Sonya spoke about her sister and the Druids she had been raised with. Galen took Reaghan's hand and brought her attention to him. "I wish I could take you somewhere safe."

"I am safe. I'm with you."

Galen could see the truth of her statement shining in Reaghan's gray eyes. "I doona like the feeling I get about the upcoming battle."

"It'll be all right. We'll have more Druids here to protect as well."

"If they get here before the battle."

* * *

Supper was a somber affair. Ever since Galen had told her he had a dreadful feeling about the battle, Reaghan couldn't shake the worry that assaulted her. The perfect time to tell Galen of her feelings had been when they were alone on the battlements, but now his concentration was on the upcoming battle. She didn't want to interfere with that.

Reaghan nudged her trencher away from her. She couldn't eat with the heavy atmosphere in the castle. Before the meal was half finished, Fallon and Larena rose and left the hall.

A few moments later Quinn and Marcail followed. Just a heartbeat after that, Lucan and Cara were the next to leave. Hayden and Isla stood as one and made their way to the stairs.

Reaghan wasn't surprised to see Fiona lift Braden in her arms and make her way to their chamber. The remaining Warriors spoke in low tones, both eager for battle and uneasy about protecting the Druids.

"Come with me," Galen said as he took her hand.

Reaghan let him pull her to her feet and then up the stairs to the battlements. As soon as the cool night air touched her face, Reaghan took in a deep breath.

Galen sat against the wall and pulled her down between his legs, her back leaning against his chest. No words were spoken, though there was so much Reaghan wanted to say.

She looked up at the sky and smiled. She had always thought it a beautiful sight to see the clouds, darkened by the night, moving over the moon.

"It's beautiful, isn't it?" Galen asked.

Reaghan nodded. "Sometimes when the moon is large and hangs low in the sky, it makes you feel as if you could just reach up and touch it."

Galen chuckled, his chest rumbling with the sound. "As a lad, I used to climb up the trees and try to reach for it."

"Did you ever touch it?"

"Nay, but there were times I thought if I were a wee bit taller I could have."

His arms tightened around her. It felt so good to be enveloped in his warmth, his strength. She could believe for just a moment that they were the only two people in the world.

"I'm glad you came to Loch Awe," she said. "For as long as I can remember I've wanted an adventure."

"You certainly got it."

She could hear the smile in his voice. "Aye. I also found you."

"Nay, I found you."

"We found each other."

He bent and kissed the side of her neck. "Aye, Reaghan. We did find each other."

"Cara told me Deirdre has attacked the castle before."

"Three different times."

Some of Reaghan's apprehension waned at the news. "What happens tomorrow?"

"We wait for the attack. If the Druids arrive at the same time, we're hoping Isla's magic shielding us will give all of us the time we need to bring the Druids inside before the wyrran break through."

"How do you know the MacClures and the wyrran won't see the Druids?"

"We doona."

Reaghan understood then the extent of everyone's nervousness. "I worry for your safety."

"No need," he said, and tugged at one of her curls. "I'm immortal, remember. Besides, Deirdre willna kill us. She will imprison us again."

"To torture and to try to turn you to her evil ways."

"Aye. I survived in her mountain once. I can do it again."

Reaghan lifted his hand and put her palm against his before linking their fingers. The thought of him once more enslaved by Deirdre sent a cold chill down her spine. "Don't get captured."

"I ask the same of you."

It was the way he said it, the words forced, as if he couldn't put enough emphasis on them. She snuggled against him and watched the moon and clouds. "I'll make sure to keep away from any danger."

"Good, because you mean too much to me."

Reaghan smiled, the warmth from his words spreading over her body. It was the right time to speak, the right time to tell him of her feelings. "I love you."

He sucked in a breath, and though no words passed his lips, his arms tightened around her. It was enough for Reaghan.

Whatever tomorrow brought, she had this moment.

And Galen.

THIRTY-EIGHT

The first streaks of light broke through the gray of the morning. The sky was clear, the sunrise vibrant with colors of deep orange and royal purple.

Galen had seen many such mornings in his years as a Warrior, but it was the first since his god was unbound that he had felt such fear claw at his belly.

"A beautiful morning," Logan said as he walked up.

Galen nodded.

"Is Reaghan with the other Druids?"

Galen cracked his knuckles and faced Logan, Reaghan's words of love echoing in Galen's head. "Aye. I made her promise she would stay in the dungeon until I came for her."

"You think Deirdre will try to take her?"

"I think Deirdre will take all of us if she's able."

Logan rubbed his jaw, his gaze moving across the sky, following the flight of the peregrine. "I've seen the bird every day, Galen. It has to be connected to Deirdre regardless of what Quinn said."

"One battle at a time. We send the MacClures and wyrran back to Deirdre, and then we can capture the falcon."

"Speaking of the MacClures, Broc just returned from his shadowing of our attackers. Look."

Galen raised his gaze to see a dark mass plummet

from the clouds. Broc's large, dark wings were folded against his body for more speed.

Broc flew over the bailey and yelled, "They've come!"

Galen unleashed his god in the next heartbeat. He flexed his hand, his claws scraping the stones. After a shared glance with Logan, they jumped from the battlement to the ground outside the castle wall.

Galen wanted to be the first to encounter their attackers. Several of the Warriors were spread over the land, with the remaining Warriors on the battlement waiting to stop anyone or anything from getting inside the castle.

The MacLeods stood sentry at the castle. They were the last defense for the Druids, and Galen knew the brothers wouldn't allow anyone to pass.

The only Druid who wasn't hidden with the others was Isla. She stood with Hayden at the top of the south tower in case the shield needed to be lowered to allow the Druids inside.

Now, with the MacClures nearly upon them, Galen was surprised Hayden hadn't carried Isla to the dungeons himself. He was very protective of his woman, as was evidenced in the way he stood in front of her, blocking her from potential attacks.

Broc continued his flight, alerting them to the MacClures' movements and how quickly they approached. "They come on the right. Be prepared!"

"Let the battle begin," Logan murmured.

Galen followed Logan's gaze and spotted the MacClures as they guided their horses toward the edge of the shield. They rode on the right-hand side of the village just as Broc had said they would. Galen took a step toward the MacClures, only to halt at Broc's shout.

"The Druids!"

Galen paused. On the other side of the village was a group of Druids running toward them. They were screaming, calling out for Sonya. And just as they had all feared, the wyrran took notice and started toward them.

"Shite," Galen said, and looked back at the castle. "Lower the shield!"

Fallon gave a nod to Isla. A breath later, magic passed over Galen as Isla removed the shield.

"Get the Druids to the castle," Galen told Logan as the MacClures gave a battle cry and charged.

Galen was ready. His god rose up inside him, bellowed his rage, and demanded blood, demanded casualties. Galen had no doubt all their gods would be appeased this day.

He dodged a sword from his first attacker and knocked the MacClure off his mount. Galen had no desire to kill the horses in an attempt to unseat their attackers, but he would if necessary.

Before the MacClure could roll to his knees, Galen had jumped on his back and jerked his head to the side, breaking the man's neck.

More MacClures raced toward Galen. The ground shook with the thunder of hoofbeats. The horses shied away from the wyrran who ran among them, causing the MacClures to spend vast amounts of energy and time bringing their mounts under control.

Galen used it to his advantage, leaping from horse to horse and killing the men before they even knew what was happening.

For the first time Galen embraced his god. He let the thoughts and feelings that rushed through him each time he touched a MacClure or their horses feed his god. Galen's only thought was to decimate the MacClures so they would leave. The wyrran could easily be taken care of once the mortals were gone.

And to his surprise, he began to stop experiencing the emotions of others. Soon, he was touching them and feeling nothing. But with just a thought, he could be in their minds.

Finally—finally!—after two hundred and fifty years he was learning to control his god. All he had needed to do was embrace his power.

Galen threw back his head and roared after killing another MacClure. When he looked up it was to find Hayden shooting fire from his hands not far from Galen.

It caused the horses to rear in fear, sending their riders tumbling to the ground where Ramsey waited to kill them.

Reaghan wrapped her arms around her middle and tried to act calm for Braden's benefit. Even though they all tried to laugh and talk about mundane things, the boy could sense their apprehension.

"We need to help them," Braden said.

Cara knelt in front of him and smiled. "Braden, the Warriors don't need us. We would only be in the way."

"Nay," he said. "They could be injured. They need us."

"Braden, please," Fiona said, and pulled him into her lap.

Odara helped Fiona to soothe Braden and after a moment he relaxed in his mother's arms.

Reaghan took a deep breath and tried not to think about Galen. He had brought her to the dungeons hours before dawn. The others had already been here, and as soon as she was inside, the door was shut and Larena stood guard.

No matter how hard she strained her ears, Reaghan could hear nothing. They sat in silence, the two candles giving off limited light as they waited and hoped for Braden to fall asleep.

Reaghan wasn't sure how much time passed before Cara let out a small sigh and whispered, "Both Fiona and Braden are asleep."

Marcail moved to the door and pressed her ear against it. "I can hear nothing yet."

"You will," Cara said.

The longer Reaghan waited, the more frayed her nerves became. And then, they heard the roar of the Warriors.

Reaghan's heart tumbled to her feet and her skin grew clammy. They could hear the pounding of horse's hooves, the shouts of the MacClures. And the shrieks of the wyrran.

Marcail sat with her hand on her stomach and her eyes closed. Cara had an arm around Marcail's shoulders, offering what little comfort she could.

Sonya was on the floor, her knees drawn up to her chest and her forehead resting on them. She hadn't spoken a word since Reaghan had entered the dungeon.

"Sonya," she said.

The red-haired Druid lifted her head, her amber eyes red from her tears.

"Your sister will be safe. I know Broc and the others will see that it's so."

A single tear fell from Sonya's eye. "I pray you are right."

Suddenly, Odara let out a strangled cry, her hand over her heart. Reaghan rushed to the elder. "What is it? Odara, tell me what's wrong."

"Let me," Sonya said, and laid a gentle hand on Reaghan's shoulder.

Reaghan hurried to move out of the way and allow Sonya room. Odara's face began to turn red as she struggled to take in a breath.

"It's her heart," Sonya said.

Reaghan saw uncertainty in Sonya's amber gaze and that gave her pause. It was almost as if the Druid were afraid. Reaghan didn't understand. From what she had been told, Sonya's healing magic was very powerful. Surely she could help Odara.

"What is it, Sonya?" Cara asked as she and Marcail came near.

After a moment Sonya shook her head. "We must hurry. Odara's heart is giving out."

"Nay," Reaghan whispered as she met Odara's frightened green gaze.

The three Druids held their hands, palms down and fingers outstretched, over Odara. After a heartbeat, Reaghan joined her hands with theirs. She prayed her magic would join in and help Odara. Reaghan felt the magic rush from her to mix with that of the others. It moved around the small chamber and into the elder. It didn't take long for Odara's raspy breaths to even out, and her eyes closed as if she rested.

Reaghan thought everything was going to be fine until Marcail winced and said, "Reaghan. We need more of your magic. We're losing Odara."

She didn't argue, just focused on more of the magic inside her. Reaghan called to her magic, begging it to rise stronger within her.

Her breath locked in her chest when her magic answered. Its commanding strength surged through her and then out of her hands and into Odara.

Reaghan's body began to hum as the magic filled every pore. Time slowed, held no meaning, as she heard a soft chanting in her head. The words were ancient. They were words she knew and recognized.

There was so much magic filling Reaghan that it felt as if her skin would burst from it. She wanted to bask in it, to revel in the pure joy it brought her.

And somewhere in the soothing chant of voices in her mind she heard her name. She concentrated, seeking the source. It took what felt like hours before the sound of her name grew stronger as her mind latched on to it.

It was a deep voice, a male voice. Tears filled her eyes as she realized it was her father's voice. His words were like a blur as they penetrated her mind. She didn't understand what he was saying. The more she tried to slow his words to understand them, the faster he spoke.

Until he—and the chanting—was gone.

Reaghan opened her eyes and looked at the elder. Odara took a deep breath and everyone relaxed, her face once more peaceful. Reaghan waited until Sonya dropped her hands before she did the same.

"Thank you," Reaghan said.

Sonya smiled, but the sadness in her eyes stunned Reaghan. "Nay, thank you. Without your magic, I fear she would be gone."

"Rest, Reaghan," Cara said. "I will watch over Odara."

Marcail tucked a blanket around Odara and looked at Sonya. "Is everything all right?"

"Aye. I'm just worried for my sister," Sonya said.

But Sonya had been looking at Reaghan when she spoke. Reaghan sensed the lie for what it was. She kept it to herself as she resumed her seat against the wall. Her mind was filled with the knowledge that she did have magic, great magic.

It had felt good to have it flow through her. As joyous as it was, she wanted to sort through the jumble of words her father had somehow sent her.

Reaghan buried her face in her hands as the sounds of the battle filled the dungeon. Her ears rang with the shouts from the men and the roars of the Warriors. She thought of Galen and prayed he would survive and stay out of Deirdre's reach.

To help turn her mind from thoughts of Galen being captured, Reaghan closed her eyes. Moment by moment the sounds around her faded as she delved deeper into her mind, searching for the message from her father. She sensed it was important, sensed she needed to decipher it quickly.

His message seemed to be in some kind of code, one in which Reaghan didn't know how to break. But she wasn't going to give up. All the answers she needed were in her mind. If anyone could break through the spell, it had to be her.

She nearly screamed with jubilation when a few of her father's words became clear to her. Other words were still jumbled, almost as if they weren't meant to be understood.

Her stomach fell to her feet when her mind translated words which spoke of the spell. But what about it? Was he giving her a clue to breaking it?

Reaghan didn't know how long she had sat, lost in her thoughts, when she heard a soft creak. It brought her out of her musing. She opened her eyes and saw Odara still asleep, and Cara and Marcail resting beside her. Sonya had her legs to her chest once more with her forehead resting on her knees. But it wasn't until Reaghan looked at Fiona's sleeping form that she realized Braden wasn't in the chamber.

Reaghan rose and walked to the entry. The door was open only a crack, not wide enough for any of them to get through.

But wide enough for a wyrran. Or a small boy.

Reaghan didn't hesitate. She threw open the door and yelled for Braden as she raced down the long corridor.

Only a few torches were lit, casting dark shadows everywhere, but Reaghan never stopped. She raced up the stairs to the great hall and skidded to a halt in front of Larena.

Larena stood with her feet braced apart, her hands on her hips. "What are you doing?"

"Braden," Reaghan said as she tried to breathe. "He's gone. I think he went to help the Warriors."

"By the saints," Larena cursed, her face going white. "I'll go look for him."

Reaghan grabbed Larena's arm. "Nay. You must guard the others. I'll look for Braden."

Larena's lips thinned in displeasure. "Hurry back."

"I will."

Reaghan hoped it was a promise she could keep. Already she had broken her pledge to Galen to stay in the dungeon, but she couldn't let Braden get caught in the fighting. He was but a lad who knew nothing of battle or weapons.

She ran into the bailey and looked to the battlements, but she didn't see Braden amid the Warriors battling wyrran. Her ears throbbed with the deafening roars and piercing shrieks.

The MacLeods stood as one, fighting side by side and slaughtering wyrran who climbed the castle wall. Among the Warriors she glimpsed, there was no green-skinned one.

Reaghan was about to return to the castle when she saw the postern door unbolted.

"Nay, Braden," she whispered in torment.

But even as she prayed the boy wouldn't leave the castle, she knew he had. The sounds of the battle were thunderous, more terrifying now that she was in the thick of it.

Reaghan took a deep breath and stepped through the postern door. She came to an immediate stop as she saw the sheer mass of MacClures and wyrran. Among them were Druids who were trying desperately to reach the castle.

Broc swooped down from the sky and lifted two of the Druids to fly to the castle. The wyrran had cornered a small group of Druids, most likely for Deirdre, but the MacClures were killing any Druid they saw.

And then she saw the red cloak.

Reaghan's heart pounded so loudly she feared it would jump from her chest. Dunmore, the man from the loch, the man who wanted to take her. Reaghan couldn't allow him to see her.

She framed her back against the castle wall and slowly sidestepped so she could look for Braden and not bring notice to herself. He would be difficult to see amid the battle, but she had to find him.

Reaghan drew in a ragged, broken breath when she caught sight of Galen. He was fighting without his shirt, his dark green skin splotched with blood. But it was the violence in which he fought, the utter strength and power he wrought with his body, that held her entranced.

Just as when he had battled the wyrran in her village, Reaghan couldn't take her eyes off him. Galen moved effortlessly, dominating and annihilating any and all who came near him.

His roars were booming, the strikes of his claws ferocious. He was a Warrior.

And he was magnificent.

Some feared the Warriors, but Reaghan had known from the beginning Galen was different. Her love for him had only grown each day she had been with him and had seen the man, the Warrior he truly was.

It was that love which gave her the strength to search for Braden. Galen would stop at nothing to protect those he cared about, and Reaghan could do no less.

She tore her gaze from Galen and focused on finding other Warriors. Braden had wanted to help them. Reaghan guessed he would stay near a Warrior to render whatever aid the lad thought he could.

It didn't take her long to find Braden standing not far from Logan. She tried calling out to him, but the boy couldn't hear her over the battle. Reaghan could go back into the castle and get the attention of a Warrior on the battlements, but they were busy fighting wyrran.

She was on her own.

Reaghan squared her shoulders and lifted her skirts as she raced toward Logan and Braden. The lad had found a sword lying on the ground and was trying to lift it as a MacClure came at him.

A scream lodged in her throat when the MacClure struck Braden with a sword. His small body fell to the ground without a sound as the sword dropped from his hands.

Reaghan rushed to Braden's side. She stood over him, the sword he had attempted to lift in her hands, as a wyrran came at her.

She had never been so petrified in her life. The wyrran smiled at her, its lips unable to cover the mouthful of teeth. Its long claws clicked together just before it swiped a hand at her.

Reaghan leaned back to avoid being scratched. She tried to swing the sword, but she was more effective in using it to keep the wyrran's claws at bay than to harm the ugly creature.

Suddenly, Broc fell from the sky behind the wyrran and severed its head from its body. "Reaghan, what in the name of all that's holy are you doing?" Broc demanded.

Reaghan set the end of the sword on the ground and leaned on it. "Braden. He's hurt. Take him to Sonya."

"I'll take both of you."

"Nay," Reaghan said. "I'll make my way to the castle. Just take Braden before he dies."

Broc frowned but lifted the boy in his arms and jumped into the air, his wings spread wide. "Get as close to the castle as you can. I'll come for you."

Reaghan kept the sword in her hands as she started toward the castle. She smiled when she saw Broc reach the castle with Braden. She had saved him.

An icy chill overtook Reaghan, one of menace and evil. She glanced over her shoulder and saw that Dunmore had spotted her. He spurred his horse toward her, his gaze intent on her and her alone.

Reaghan lifted her skirts as she began to run. Behind her she heard a man yell the MacClure name.

A sharp, ferocious pain slammed into her. Reaghan

stopped, her feet refusing to move. The sword dropped from her fingers as her vision swam and the world tilted. Her legs gave out and she fell to her knees.

The pain was cruel and brutal as it stole her breath and her ability to move. Something had struck her in the back. But she had promised Galen she would stay safe. She wouldn't give up now. She would crawl to the castle if she had to.

But no matter how many times her brain told her body to move, nothing happened.

It grew more difficult to breathe. Each time her lungs emptied, her body struggled to fill them up again. She felt something warm and heavy slide down her back.

Reaghan toppled to the side and cried out from the unbearable agony. All she could do was watch from where she lay as Galen and the other Warriors battled back the MacClures and the wyrran.

Reaghan, however, knew her time was at an end.

THIRTY-NINE

Sonya rushed from the dungeons into the great hall when she heard Broc bellow her name. It had taken all of them to keep Fiona inside the dungeon as Reaghan searched for Braden. Fiona's grief-stricken cries had broken Sonya's heart.

Exhaustion and weariness weighed heavily on Sonya. She had slept little. Not even Broc's promise to fly the Druids into the castle had helped ease her worry. Nor would it until her sister was beside her.

Then it had taken all she had to save Odara. At one point, Sonya hadn't thought she would be able to help the old woman. She worried that the fear she had long had of losing her magic was coming to pass.

And it couldn't have come at a worse time, when others would need her so desperately.

"Sonya, hurry," Broc yelled as he carefully laid something on the floor.

Her steps wavered when she caught sight of Braden. Tears gathered when she saw the boy's chest and the deep slash that cut him diagonally from hip to shoulder. Sonya knelt beside him and held her hands over the wound.

It took a moment for her magic to come to her, once more bringing to mind her unease that she might one day lose her healing magic when it was needed most.

Braden's wound was severe, but his little body was

strong and he fought for life, which helped Sonya's magic. Still, it took everything she had, pouring all of her magic into Braden, before the wound began to close.

The fact that the wound was large and gaping meant she had to use her magic even longer. She couldn't rest, couldn't rebuild her strength, for fear Braden's body might give out.

When the last of the wound had come together, Sonya lowered her hands and nearly fell over.

Broc's strong arm came around her. "It's over now."

She wanted to do nothing more than sleep for a sennight.

Then they heard the anguished, heartbroken roar.

Galen swiped his claws across the chest of a MacClure and watched as the mortal fell backward, his lifeless eyes staring at the sky.

He glanced around for his next victim, only to discover that the few remaining MacClures were running away. Galen looked around at the carnage. So many lives had been taken, and all in Deirdre's bid for dominance.

Galen started toward the castle to help the others with the wyrran when auburn locks lying amid the grass caught his eye. He paused, his heart suddenly unable to beat.

"Nay," he whispered, refusing to believe what he saw.

Reaghan was in the castle. Safe from harm. It wasn't her. It couldn't be her.

It's one of the other Druids who just arrived.

It didn't matter how many times Galen told himself that, he had to know for sure.

With heavy feet and a sinking heart, he started toward the woman. He saw the spear sticking from her back. She lay at such an angle that Galen couldn't see her face.

He took a few more steps then halted. All his breath left his body when he glimpsed Reaghan's face. Galen ran the remaining steps to her, the roar which tore from his throat stripping him of his soul.

Galen dropped to his knees and smoothed Reaghan's hair from her face. His hands shook, his god having ducked away at the grief that assaulted Galen.

Carefully, he put his hand under Reaghan's shoulders and brought her against his chest. He buried his face in her hair, unable to believe she was gone, that he hadn't known she needed him.

"Galen?"

He opened his eyes to see Duncan behind Reaghan, his hand on the spear. Galen nodded. A scant heartbeat later Duncan yanked the spear from Reagan's back.

She cried out, her hands clutching him. Galen stroked her hair and her back. "You'll be all right."

"I'm going to get Sonya," Duncan said.

Galen barely heard him as he lowered Reaghan so he could look into her eyes. Her skin was deathly pale, her breathing weak.

"Galen," she whispered with a slight smile on her lips. "I had to save Braden."

"It's all right. Doona talk. Sonya is going to help you."

Reaghan swallowed and slowly licked her lips. "I cannot feel my legs. I know . . . now I know how to break the spell."

"Shh. You're going to be all right," Galen whispered. Blood poured from her wound, soaking his hand. He pushed against the wound to try and stanch the flow, but it continued to seep between his fingers to coat the grass.

She touched his cheek as she smiled, her eyes drifting closed.

"Please," Galen said, choking. He felt the tears roll down his face, felt his heart shatter into a million pieces. "Reaghan, please doona leave me."

Her eyes closed and her hand dropped. Galen cried out

and pulled her to him, rocking her. He willed her to stay alive until Sonya could reach them, silently praying that God not take Reaghan away from him, not when he needed her.

Loved her.

Galen could feel the life draining from Reaghan's body. He called to her, saying her name over and over again.

"Sonya's here," he dimly heard Logan say.

Galen lifted his face and found himself surrounded by Warriors and Druids. "Help her," he begged Sonya.

Sonya closed her eyes and tears began to fall from them. The healer knelt beside Reaghan and lifted her hands. Galen waited for the blood flow to slow, for the wound to begin to heal.

But nothing happened.

Sonya's tears increased. "I'm trying."

"Please, Sonya. I need her. She's dying, and you're the only one who can save her."

"Bring Isla!" Fallon bellowed.

But Galen knew it was too late. A shudder ran through Reaghan as her last breath passed her lips.

Grief. Agony. Rage.

They all ripped through Galen like lightning. He could do nothing but hold Reaghan. He had possessed the most important thing in his life, and he'd let her die.

"I'm so sorry," Sonya whispered, and stumbled to her feet.

For a few short days Galen had held Reaghan, loved her . . . been loved by her. He'd been able to enjoy the simple pleasure of touching her, and being touched by her. Something he would never experience again.

How could he continue without her?

How would he even try?

Suddenly, Reaghan's skin began to glow. She grew

brighter and brighter, the light so brilliant Galen had to shield his eyes.

A white light burst from Reaghan's eyes and mouth and shot from her fingertips. Galen never loosened his hold. He buried his face in her neck while he heard Fallon shout his name.

Galen paid no attention. Wherever Reaghan was going, he wanted to be with her.

Wind rushed around Galen, pushing him against Reaghan, against the ground. It grew stronger and stronger until it paused of a sudden. A heartbeat later there was a loud boom and the wind picked up again, swirling up from the ground as if it came from Reaghan.

The magic Galen had come to recognize and crave as Reaghan's grew more solid. It filled the air and his very body, touching every fiber of his being.

Galen took a breath, the magic filling his lungs and burning him with its intensity at the same instant it soothed him with its purity.

He raised his head to find the white light was gone. As he gazed at Reaghan, he thought he saw her chest move. And then she took a gasping breath. Her body went rigid as she reached for him.

"I'm here," he said. His heart was bursting with joy, his world once more complete. As long as he had Reaghan, he could do anything.

Reaghan took a deep breath and let it out slowly. The pain that had devastated her body had vanished. She could still feel the remnants of it, but it was fading as if it had never been.

What was stranger was the beautiful, awesome magic which now filled her. It was many times stronger than what she had felt in the dungeons.

And with the return of her magic came all of her

memories. They raced through her mind, images of people and places and events she had experienced from the day she was born until that moment.

She grew dizzy and gripped Galen tighter. The words her father had given her were now as clear as water. He had given her the means to break the spell when she had tried to find her magic to heal Odara.

"Reaghan?"

She lifted her eyes to Galen's and smiled. "It's me."

He frowned, confusion filling his cobalt eyes. "I felt you die."

"Aye, you did, but I am back. Along with all of my memories. The spell is broken."

Odara stepped forward, supported by Marcail and Cara. "You mean you had to die?"

"Nay," Reaghan said, and slowly sat up so she could see everyone. "Thankfully, the magic used to break the spell was strong enough to pull me back."

Galen stroked her face with his fingers. The tears on his cheeks made her heart catch. He kissed her gently, reverently, as if he feared she might break. "You're back. That's all that matters."

"I am."

"I didna know how I was going to live without you."

Reaghan placed her hand on his heart. "You would have. You're a Warrior."

"Without you, I am nothing."

His declaration made her throat close up with tears. "I've been under my own spell for almost five hundred years. There were people who were kind, some who weren't. There were those who needed me, and those who didn't. Of all the people I've met and known, you, Galen Shaw, have been the only one who stirred my soul."

"I love you," he said. "I never thought I would know such joy."

She placed her hand on his cheek, her heart bursting with happiness. "I think I've loved you from the first moment I saw you."

Galen smiled brightly and gave a shout of delight. His dark blue eyes twinkled as he lowered his head to hers. "I'm never letting you get away from me."

"I don't ever want to," Reaghan answered.

His sensuous smile caused her stomach to flutter with desire. His languid kiss sealed their love and their future.

EPILOGUE

Sonya walked away from Reaghan and Galen and their joy. Reaghan had returned to life, but only because of her own spell. Had Reaghan not lived, Sonya wasn't sure what Galen would have done to her.

Just as Sonya had feared for months, when she had needed her magic most, it had deserted her. Sonya stared at her hands. Her magic was part of her. Without it, who was she?

With Reaghan and Galen headed back to the castle, the others searched for anyone left alive. Sonya was sick to her stomach to see the number of Druids from her home who had been killed. If only she had known sooner, Broc and Fallon could have brought them safely to the castle as they had done with Reaghan and her village.

She wondered what could have prompted them to leave their home. The Druids Broc had saved were in the castle, and Sonya couldn't wait to look for Anice. Her sister would have the answers to the questions that plagued her.

But it would have to wait. Sonya needed to gather her magic, and push aside her fear. There were those who would need to be healed, and everyone would expect her to use her magic.

Sonya had to make sure she was able to heal them. She wouldn't be able to look anyone in the eye if she couldn't.

A tremor of foreboding raced down her spine, but she refused to listen to it.

She stepped over decapitated wyrran and dead Mac-Clures as she checked a Druid for life. "Another gone," she murmured.

As she stood, Sonya caught sight of Broc slowly falling to his knees beside a Druid. He raised his haunted gaze to Sonya. The hurt, the grief she saw reflected in his depths propelled her forward.

Sonya lifted her skirts and hurried toward him. When she neared him, she paused at the torment etched on his face. The way he held the Druid, as if she were the most precious thing in the world, caused a flare of envy.

"Sonya, she needs you," Broc pleaded, his voice breaking with emotion.

Sonya pushed aside her jealousy. And then she saw the face of her sister. All the hope, all the joy she had been holding inside to share with Anice shattered in an instant.

It was all Sonya could do to suck in a breath to her starved lungs. Sonya covered her mouth with her hand, unable to believe it was her sister.

"Sonya!" Broc bellowed. "Use your healing."

Sonya knelt beside her sister and put her hand on Anice's chest. No breath moved in Anice's body. "I cannot help her, Broc. My magic does not work on those already gone."

"She's no'," Broc stated. "Heal her."

Sonya rose, her knees threatening to buckle for a second time that day, and took a step back. Anice had spoken of a Broc, but Sonya had believed her sister had invented him. How wrong she had been?

"How do you know my sister?" Sonya asked.

"Heal her," Broc said, his voice low and menacing. "You cannot allow Anice to die when you have the magic to help her."

"She's beyond my magic. She's gone."

Broc hugged Anice to him. "You failed her, Sonya!"

His words were like flails on a whip, striking at the most tender places inside Sonya. What was worse was that Broc was right. She had failed. She could have saved her sister if she had not been hiding in the dungeon.

Sonya looked up at the imposing structure of MacLeod Castle. She didn't belong there anymore.

She backed away step by step from Broc, but he paid her no heed. His attention was on Anice. The gentle way he smoothed away her sister's hair from her face was like a dagger to Sonya's heart. Broc had known her sister.

And he had kept it a secret from Sonya.

What a fool she had been, to have any feelings for the Warrior. She had thought him brave to spy on Deirdre and risk his own life. She had been deceived. In the most heinous of ways.

At the village Sonya turned her back on the castle, on the life she had hoped to build there, and dashed into the forest.

Galen rubbed his temples as he sat beside Reaghan in the great hall. It was difficult for him to see her up and moving about as if she hadn't had a spear in her spine just a few hours earlier.

While he and the other Warriors had cleaned their land of dead wyrran and MacClures, Reaghan and the Druids had seen to the wounded.

Now, they all gathered in the hall to hear what Reaghan had to say.

"You remember everything? Through all the years?" Galen asked, still unable to believe it.

"Aye," Reaghan said. "Each ten years when the spell would work, it was like a wall went up in my mind, blocking everything. With my spell shattered, those walls are gone."

Marcail shook her head in wonder. "How did you survive dying?"

"When we were in the dungeon using our magic to heal Odara I heard chanting."

"Ah," Marcail said with a smile. "It's beautiful, is it not?"

Reaghan inhaled deeply as she thought of the soothing cadence of the chant. "While I heard the chant, I also heard my father. He poured words into my mind, words I couldn't understand. It took so long to unlock a few, but I knew he was trying to tell me how to break the spell. Then I found Braden gone."

"And you left the castle," Galen said.

"I did," Reaghan admitted. "I think the spell began to break as soon as we left Loch Awe. It broke a little more when I used magic against Mairi, and then again when I used the magic for Odara. It was while I lay dying, my mind drifting to a realm I otherwise probably couldn't reach, that I realized how to end the spell."

Camdyn asked, "Death?"

"Nay. It was magic. I called forth my magic, all of it. I must have done it right before my last breath left me."

Isla smiled and folded her hands atop the table. "Very potent magic for sure."

"And the spell?" Cara asked. "It had to have been a very powerful spell."

Reaghan sighed and leaned against Galen. She was so glad he was near. She was glad the spell was broken, but it brought back memories that would pain her for a lifetime.

Fallon shifted in his chair. "Maybe you should start from the beginning, Reaghan."

Reaghan looked to Galen and then around the table at the Druids and Warriors who waited to hear what she had to say. "Long ago Druids were as common to Scotland as heather. There were large groups as well as smaller groups. The larger the gathering of Druids, the more magic."

"Aye," Isla agreed.

"My village consisted of over four hundred Druids," Reaghan explained. "We were the largest. And the ones most hidden. Our home was in the valley of Foinaven Mountain and shielded many times over by magic. If you didn't know the way or the magic needed to gain entrance, you could never find it."

Duncan whistled. "Are there still Druids there?"

Reaghan reached below the table and locked hands with Galen. "For centuries we lived in quiet seclusion. Every so often a Druid would come to us for protection."

"Protection from what?" Quinn asked.

"Deirdre. Her power was growing faster than any of us could have guessed. We thought we had time to combat her."

Ramsey crossed his arms over his chest and grinned. "You had something to use against her."

It wasn't a question. "We did. Every one of our Druids knew. It was a secret shared because everyone had used their magic. Somehow Deirdre was able to sway one of the Druids to her side. Deirdre learned we had a secret, but what, she didn't know. Though the spy had been swayed, at the last moment, he must have realized what he had done. He took his own life before he could give Deirdre more information."

"But the worst had already been done," Arran said.

Reaghan licked her lips. "Deirdre had learned of our location. She came with her wyrran. So many were killed. Deirdre didn't realize that any one of the Druids could have told her what she wanted. She and her wyrran murdered so many. Others, afraid of what Deirdre would do to them, took their own lives."

Galen's hand squeezed hers, giving her comfort with such a small gesture.

"What happened next?" Fallon urged.

"There were only a handful of us left. My father and I along with two very young girls and their parents. The girls were too young to know of our secret, but it didn't stop Deirdre from taking them. The parents . . ." She paused to clear her throat. "The father died fighting the wyrran, and the mother threw herself from the mountain."

"Which left you and your father," Galen said.

Reaghan nodded. "We ran as fast as we could. We kept away from other Druids. I fought against the plan my father had, but it soon became clear it was the only way."

Cara's brow furrowed as she asked, "What was the plan?"

"My father convinced me to use a spell that would erase my memories and continue doing so every ten years so that I could fit in with the Druids of Loch Awe. They agreed to take us in, and lent their magic to my father's plan."

She paused, unsure if she could go on. The pain and loss threatened to swallow her whole.

"It can wait," Lucan said.

"Nay, I need to finish." Reaghan glanced at Galen before she continued. "I didn't know the spell was so powerful there would be a price for using it. My father knew if he had told me I would refuse. He used all of his considerable magic to push the spell, but in granting me immortality it took his life."

Galen pulled her against him and kissed the top of her head.

"What was so important that your father would give his own life, as well as put such a spell on you?" Odara asked.

Reaghan straightened and looked around the table again. "There are a few reasons. One, because of the strength of my magic. If Deirdre got a hold of it, it would increase hers tenfold."

"Which we doona need," Ian murmured.

Lucan ran a hand across his jaw. "And the other?"

"I alone know the location of Deirdre's sister, Laria."

The silence was deafening.

"Her sister?" Quinn repeated, disbelief in every syllable.

Reaghan nodded. "Her twin, to be exact. Deirdre thought she was the one who received all the magic. They were raised in a small community of *droughs* made up mostly of family members. When Deirdre killed her aunt then caused the rest of the members to turn on each other, Laria walked away."

"I cannot imagine Deirdre allowing anyone to go free," Isla said.

"It was thought Laria had no magic, so she never underwent the ceremony to become *drough*," Reaghan explained. "Laria sought my village when she saw how quickly Deirdre was coming into the black magic. The Druids granted her request to join them, and she lived there for almost five years before Deirdre began to look for her. We had a seer who told Laria she was the one who could stop Deirdre."

Camdyn shook his head in confusion. "How? Deirdre has used black magic to become immortal. Did Laria do the same?"

"Nay. The *mies* of my village had exceptionally strong magic. Together they devised a plan. They would put Laria under a spell. She is essentially frozen in time, hidden in the mountains. Members of my family are the only ones who can unlock a portion of the tomb and since I'm the last, I'm the artifact."

"A portion?" Ian asked.

"Aye. From what my father told me, Laria is entombed in a maze."

Cara asked, "Why not just have Laria battle Deirdre right then if the seer knew Laria could defeat her?"

"It is Laria who will defeat Deirdre, but Laria is supposed to have help in the form of a rather powerful male Druid who comes from the Torrachilty Forest."

Arran frowned. "What if this male Druid was already born and dead?"

"I don't believe it will matter. The Druids there, especially the males, were supposed to be some of the most powerful."

Galen blew out a long breath. "And the dreams you were having?"

"My memories of places and people I had known."

"So you saw Deirdre?" Broc asked.

Reaghan shuddered just thinking about it. "I had to go near Cairn Toul as I left my home. It was the safest, easiest way. I stayed far enough away, but I did see her when she came out of the mountain."

Galen folded his hand over hers. "It's over now."

"Actually, it's just beginning." Reaghan looked at Fallon. "You sent Galen and Logan to find the artifact, to find me. Now that I have my memories back along with my magic, we need to awaken Laria to end Deirdre."

Duncan stood. "Then let's go."

Reaghan cringed and bit her lip. "It's not quite so simple, I'm afraid. There are other objects we will need to obtain to work our way through the maze to Laria."

"Do you know what the objects are?" Galen asked.

"We need to begin on the Isle of Eigg."

As the hall erupted in conversation, Reaghan turned to Galen. "With my spell broken, I'm no longer immortal."

"You being mortal doesna stop me loving you. I'm no' saying we'll have an easy go of it, but I'm no' about to give you up because you aren't immortal."

She smiled and gave him a quick kiss. "I also suppose this means you will worry about me?"

"Endlessly," he vowed, a twinkle in his blue eyes. "As long as I'm able to worry about you."

"I have something to tell you," Galen said.

She raised a brow. "And what might that be?"

"I finally have control over my power."

Reaghan threw her arms around his neck and hugged him. She leaned back and asked, "How?"

"I gave in to my god and the power during the battle. I didna try to back away from it. Somewhere amid all the killing, I discovered I could touch anyone and feel none of their thoughts or emotions. I still have the ability to feel thoughts, but to do so I have to put more effort into it."

"I would never have thought giving in to your power would help you control it."

He shook his head. "Me either. I'm just glad I can live a normal life now. Or as normal as a Warrior can."

"Want to read my mind to see what I'm thinking about?"

"Nay. Tell me," he urged as he nuzzled her neck.

"You, our future, and our love."

Two days after the battle, Broc still felt the loss of Anice as if it had just occurred. He had looked for her among the Druids, searching for her so he could bring her to the castle. How had he missed her?

He regretted his words to Sonya even more. He needed to find her and apologize. It wasn't her fault Anice had died. If it was anyone's burden to carry, it was his. He should have looked for Anice first, but he had assumed he would spot her in the pandemonium of battle.

How wrong he had been.

Broc left his chamber and descended the stairs to the great hall. The women were smiling, laughing, as they brought out the morning meal. One more Warrior had found his woman, adding to the love and laughter that was MacLeod Castle.

Broc was happy for Galen, but his own self-recriminations stopped him from celebrating with the others.

He waited for Sonya to exit the kitchens, hoping to catch her for a moment of privacy. Broc had been to her chamber many times over the last few days, but not once had she been there to hear his apology.

One by one the women exited the kitchens. When they sat and began to pass the food, a cold numbness began in Broc's stomach.

"Where is Sonya?" he asked, loud enough for everyone to hear.

Cara shrugged. "I went to her chamber yesterday, but she wasn't there. I thought she needed some time alone after Anice's death."

"I haven't seen her since the attack," Reaghan said.

Marcail nodded. "Me either."

One by one, everyone in the hall said the same thing. The last time Sonya had been seen was the day of the attack. The day Broc had blamed her for Anice's death.

The food was forgotten as the castle and surrounding area were searched. Broc had held out hope someone would find her, but it wasn't until he used his power that he realized she wasn't in the castle or village.

"We need to look for her," Fallon said.

Broc walked on unsteady legs across the great hall. The words he had said to Sonya replayed over and over in his head. "I will search for her. I will find her. And I will bring her back."

He didn't wait for a response. He strode from the castle and let his god loose. As soon as his wings spread he flew toward the sky, opening his power to find the one woman who had the ability to tear his heart to pieces.

* * *

Malcolm refused to look back at MacLeod Castle as he began his new journey. He had walked the land night after night, day after day, seeking a reason to go on.

Seeking a reason to remain.

He was of no use to anyone with just one arm. He couldn't fight beside the Warriors, and he refused to hide with the women. He was a Highlander. A warrior. He would not cower.

Malcolm knew he should have left a note for Larena, but he hadn't. She had a life and a good man in Fallon MacLeod. Malcolm owed Fallon and the other Warriors a great debt for giving him a home.

He had observed the battle from the forest, wishing he could help the Warriors, yearning to have a sword in his hand. But he knew if he stepped into the fight, a Warrior would drag him away. It would be done to help, yet the gesture would disgrace Malcolm even more.

So he kept to his hideaway and watched. Once the Warriors had defeated the MacClures and the few remaining wyrran had run off, Malcolm decided it was time to leave the castle.

Strapped to his waist was a sword he'd found in the castle armory. He'd learned to swing a weapon with either arm, but Malcolm was determined to either gain the use of his right arm again, or die. Either would do.

He no longer cared.

Read on for an excerpt from

DARKEST
HIGHLANDER

—the next exciting Dark Sword Romance
from Donna Grant and St. Martin's Paperbacks!

It was the growl, the low, menacing rumble that implied
doom for her.

Sonya sucked in a ragged breath and lifted her head
from the damp ground of the forest floor. Her spirit was
broken, her body failing rapidly.

She raged with fever, a fever she couldn't heal. Just as
she couldn't heal the cut which sliced open her palm. At
one time, the barest of thoughts would have propelled her
magic to take care of such injuries.

But that magic had failed her.

Nay, you failed.

Sonya squeezed her eyes close to shut out the loud, and
persistent, voice in her head. She was nothing without her
magic. How could she help the others at MacLeod Castle?
How could she look each of them in the eye day after day
knowing her magic was gone?

Vanished. Disappeared. Lost.

Everything she was, everything she had been was no
longer there. Her life had been defined as a Druid. Without magic she could no longer call herself a Druid.

And that distressed her far more than her sliced palm.

Another growl, this one closer, more looming. She
tried to gain her feet, but she was weak from lack of food.

Sonya had been dodging the wolf for days. Or was it
weeks? She had lost track of time after her flight from

MacLeod Castle. She no longer knew where she was, and even if she wanted to return to the castle, she couldn't get there.

If you want to live, get up. Run!

Sonya wasn't ready to die. She didn't give up easily.

Liar. You never try for the things you want. Like Broc.

A tear slipped down Sonya's cheek at the thought of Broc. Each time she closed her eyes she could see the Warrior kneeling in the midst of the bloody battle at the castle holding Anice in his arms as he bellowed for Sonya to heal her sister.

A sister who had known him. Broc, the one man Sonya had wanted for herself. The one thing she hadn't had the courage to make known her feelings.

Sonya shoved aside thoughts of Broc as she grabbed hold of the nearest tree with her good hand and pulled herself to her feet. She leaned against the trunk and glanced around the forest for the wolf.

Nowhere did she see the creature, but she knew he was near. The black beast was large and ravenous. It would take just one swipe of his huge paw to end her life.

Sonya cradled her wounded hand against her chest and wondered how much longer she could evade the wolf. It was a cunning animal.

The trees swayed above Sonya, reminding her of the magic that used to allow her to commune with them. How she missed their knowledge, their words. Their magic. Being among the trees had always soothed her, but no longer. Not since her magic had abandoned her.

Sonya knew she had to move if she wanted a chance at survival. Remaining meant certain death. After a deep breath, she stepped away from the tree and turned, only to freeze in place as the wolf stood in front of her.

He growled again, lifting its lips to show large fangs which dripped with saliva. The animal crouched with its ears back against its head, its muscles tensed, ready to spring at her.

Time slowed to a standstill. With her heart pounding slow and hard, Sonya knew she had only once chance to get away. She lifted her skirts and ran to her left.

Her feet slipped on the dried leaves and pine needles coating the forest floor, but she kept moving. Behind her, she could hear the wolf as it crashed through the trees chasing her.

And rapidly gaining ground.

With hair tangling about her sweat-soaked face, Sonya glanced back and saw the wolf almost upon her. A scream lodged in her throat, but before the sound could release, the ground fell from beneath her.

Suddenly, the earth rose up to meet her face. Sonya grunted as her head slammed into the ground and she began to roll. She tried without success to grab a hold of anything that would slow her descent. The sky mixed with the ground to become a whirl of colors which spun around her as she continued her brutal tumble.

When she finally came to a grinding halt, it was with her body wrapped around the trunk of a young elm. The breath left her lungs in a whoosh, her body wracked with blinding pain. She tried to stay calm and suck in air, but the more she tried to breathe, the more her body refused to take in the air.

When breath finally filled her lungs, Sonya took it in deep and winced at the agony that exploded through her. She opened her eyes, but her world had yet to stop spinning.

And then she heard familiar growl. Much closer than ever before.

Broc fisted his hands, urgency and fear filling his stomach as he flew across the sky in his search for Sonya. Not even concern of discovery by mortals could keep him to the thick rain clouds above him.

He knew in his gut Sonya was in trouble. Her leaving the castle was so unlike anything she would do, but then again, he had yelled at her, blamed her for Anice's death.

Broc regretted his words more than Sonya could possibly know. He'd been angry at himself—still was outraged—for failing to keep Anice safe as he had promised the girls when he had found them as babies.

It proved to him yet again that anyone who got close to him died. His grandmother had called it a curse. And it had followed him into his immortality.

For awhile he had thought the curse was gone, but then Anice died. But he wouldn't allow anything to happen to Sonya. Even if it took him leaving her life forever, he'd do it just to keep her safe. And alive.

He flew faster, his wings beating loudly in his ears. As a Warrior, a Highlander with a primeval god bound inside him, he had special abilities. Each god had a power, and his was the capability to find anyone, anywhere.

It was just one of the reasons he had gone in search of Sonya. Even if his god hadn't given him the power to find her, he'd still have looked for her. Because he had been connected to her since the moment he lifted her in his arms so many years ago.

Broc was close to her. He could feel it.

A smile pulled at his lips, but it died almost immediately as lightning lit the sky and it began to rain.

"Shite," he murmured and tucked his wings to fly above the canopy of trees.

Broc's claws scraped the leaves atop an ancient oak as the rain dripped down his face and into his eyes. He adjusted the satchel strap that lay on his back between his wings and over one shoulder.

The strap rubbed his wings, but inside he carried food,

coin, and clothing for both him and Sonya. The pain was a minor inconvenience as long as he found Sonya.

Inside Broc, Poraxus, the god of manipulation, roared with anticipation. It was a signal they were very close to Sonya. Every time Broc hunted someone he could feel them when he neared. Their heartbeat, the flow of blood in their veins. Their life essence.

It was no different now. Except this was Sonya. He had saved her as an infant, watched over her as she grew. He would not fail her now.

Broc clutched his chest as he felt fear spike through Sonya. The closer he came to his target, the more he felt them. If the terror now coursing him was any indication, he was he too late.

Just thinking she might be in danger sent rage flowing through his veins. His god roared again—this time for blood. And vengeance.

Broc reigned in his god. Sonya might need him, and he couldn't allow himself to reach the edge and his god to gain any control. The more he fought against Poraxus, the more his god struggled to take over.

It was because his god knew how much Sonya meant to him. Even if Broc refused to admit it to himself.

Broc peered through the dense canopy of trees to try and see her, but it was near impossible, even with his superior sight. Broc then maneuvered between two trees. He hated flying in forests. He wasn't able to spread his wings as he needed to in order to fly or glide.

So he rode the air currents with his wings as outstretched as he could get them. Several times the wings scraped against a tree and its branches, tearing the leather-like wings. Thanks to his immortality, he began to heal almost immediately.

And then he saw her.

Not even the rain could hamper his enhanced vision.

Broc tucked his wings and dove for Sonya who lay unmoving on the ground, curled around a tree.

Dread spurred Broc to her side. He knew she wasn't dead. He could still feel Sonya's heartbeat, though now that he had found her, it was fading from his senses.

His gaze scanned the area for whatever caused her fear and spotted the lone wolf approaching. Broc spread his wings and landed on his feet between Sonya and the wolf.

The wolf snarled, his anger palpable. Broc peeled back his lips to show his own set of fangs and growled. He didn't want to kill the wolf, but he would if it continued to threaten Sonya.

After several terse moments, the wolf sensed it was beaten and reluctantly backed away. Broc stayed as he was, listening long after the wolf was out of sight to make sure the creature didn't circle around to attack again.

Once Broc was certain the wolf had departed, he turned to Sonya. He was so unprepared for what he saw that, for a moment, he couldn't move. For one heartbeat, then two he could only stare at the woman who was the one thing he wanted above all else.

Sonya's vibrant red hair which was always secured in a single, thick plait was now wild and free in a tangle of curls about her. Her dark green gown was coated in dirt and drenched from the rain. One sleeve was torn at the shoulder, and she had another tear at her hem.

But what made Broc's stomach plummet to his feet was the wound he saw on her palm. She had wrapped a portion of her chemise around it, but the thin material had already fallen away leaving the ragged injury exposed.

Broc fell to his knees beside her. He was afraid to touch her, but he needed to feel her at the same time. He spread a wing to shield her from the rain and leaned close. Only then did he realize she was unconscious.

Careful his claws didn't cut her delicate skin, he gently caressed a finger from her temple down her cheek to her jaw. He longed to have her open her eyes so he could look into her amber depths.

Her skin was smooth and luminous. She had a high forehead where finely arched eyebrows, the same vivid red of her hair, curved above her eyes. Her was nose aristocratic and her chin stubborn. Her lips, however, were those of a siren—wide and full. And tempting as sin.

Tenderly, Broc lifted her hand in his to inspect the wound. The cut went from her index finger across her palm to end at her wrist. The slice was deep, and the skin around the wound blackening.

The dark yellow puss that oozed from the gash propelled Broc. He gathered Sonya in his arms and spread his wings, ready to jump into the air and fly to MacLeod Castle.

It was the lightning bolts which forked across the sky in a vivid and dramatic display of power that halted him. If he flew, there was a chance he could be hit by the lightning. Though it would pain him, he would survive.

Sonya wouldn't be so lucky.

He couldn't put her in that kind of danger. Reluctantly, Broc set her down long enough to remove the satchel and search through it for a cloak.

Once it was secured around Sonya, Broc tamped down his god. He watched the indigo skin of his Warrior form, along with his claws, fade from sight. Nothing showed of his wings or his fangs. When he wasn't in his Warrior form, no one could tell him apart from a mortal man.

It was a small blessing for having an ancient god inside him. And it had all begun with the invasion of Rome on Britain's shores. The Celts had battled the Romans for years before going to the Druids for help.

The *mies*, Druids with pure magic, could only offer guidance. However, the *droughs*, with their black magic had an answer—call up primeval gods from Hell to inhabit the strongest warriors.

And it worked. The men became Warriors and soon drove Rome from Britain. Yet their need for blood and death didn't end, and soon they were killing any who crossed their paths.

It took both the *mies* and the *droughs* combining their magic to end the Warriors. No matter how hard they tried, they couldn't make the gods return to Hell. Instead, they bound them inside the men.

But the gods took their revenge by passing through the bloodline to the next strongest warrior of that family. They were unable to get free until a *drough* found an ancient scroll which told her how to unbind the gods.

Ever since, Deirdre has been relentless in finding the gods and unbinding them. Broc was one of several at Mac-Leod Castle intent on putting an end to Deirdre for good.

Broc jerked on a tunic before he slung the strap of the satchel over his head. He once more took Sonya into his arms and stood. There was a village several leagues away. There he could get Sonya out of the weather and help her tend her hand.

Then he would beg her forgiveness for driving her away, and hopefully convince her to return to MacLeod Castle. Everyone needed her there. No one more so than him.

He cradled her gently, but securely, against his chest, shielding her face from as much of the rain as he could. He rested his chin on her forehead and felt her skin blazing with fever.

Broc looked down into her oval face, a face that had haunted his dreams and every waking moment of his life since she had come into womanhood and he had been tempted beyond his control.

"Live, Sonya. I refuse to let you die."

Why hadn't she healed herself as he knew she could? She was a Druid with powerful healing magic. The Druids at MacLeod Castle had put an incredible amount of strain on Sonya for her healing, but as a *mie* nothing should have halted that magic.

Even Quinn MacLeod, another Warrior, once had need of Sonya's healing because of Deirdre's magic.

Broc growled just thinking about his enemy. All *droughs* gave their blood and their lives to the devil in exchange for black magic, but Deirdre had gone beyond that. She worked in league with the devil. Deirdre had lived nearly a thousand years, and during that time she had destroyed many lives.

Broc cursed Deirdre with every step he took, but he cursed himself even more. From the day he had delivered Sonya and Anice to the Druids, he had sworn to protect them.

He had failed Anice, and if he didn't get Sonya to cover quickly, he would fail her as well.

The thunder had become almost a constant boom, each clap so close to the next. The storm was right over them as was evident by the lightning striking closer and the wind howling around them.

One lightning bolt landed on a tree just in front of them and caused the pine to burst into flames and split in half. Broc paused to avoid being crushed as part of the tree fell and landed in front of him.

He lifted his face to the sky and roared his anger. His rage fed his god, and it was all Broc could do to keep him tamped down. It had taken too many of his two hundred and seventy-five years learning to restrain Poraxus for Broc to lose control now.

But when it came to Sonya, his emotions always ran high.

Broc had to get out of the storm. He took a deep breath and leapt the burning tree. He held Sonya tight and ran, using the incredible speed his god gave him.

He didn't slow until he spotted the village.